SAVAGE

THE VIGILANTES
BOOK THREE

STONI ALEXANDER

SILVERSTONE PUBLISHING

This book is a work of fiction. All names, characters, locations, brands, media and incidents are either products of the author's imagination, or have been used fictitiously. Any resemblance to actual persons living or dead, locales, or events is entirely coincidental. The author acknowledges the trademarked status and trademark owners of various products referenced in this work of fiction, which have been used without permission. The publication/use of these trademarks is not authorized, associated with, or sponsored by the trademark owners.

Copyright © 2022 Stoni Alexander LLC
Cover Design by Better Together and Elayne Mayes
Cover Photo © Wander Aguiar

All rights reserved.

In accordance with the U.S. Copyright Act of 1976, the scanning, uploading, and electronic sharing of any part of this book without the permission of the publisher is unlawful piracy and theft of the author's intellectual property. Without limiting the rights under copyright reserved above, no part of this publication may be reproduced, stored in or reproduced into a retrieval system, or transmitted, in any form, or by any means (electronic, mechanical, photocopying, recording or otherwise) without the prior written permission of the above copyright owner of this book.

Criminal copyright infringement, including infringement without monetary gain, is investigated by the FBI and is punishable by up to five years in federal prison and a fine of $250,000.

Published in the U.S. by SilverStone Publishing, 2022
ISBN 978-1-946534-22-4 (Print Paperback)
ISBN 978-1-946534-23-1 (Kindle eBook)

Respect the author's work. Don't steal it.

ABOUT SAVAGE

FROM BESTSELLING AUTHOR STONI ALEXANDER

REVENGE SERVED HARD

My friends call me Jericho. My enemies know me as Reaper.

Ain't nothin' more important than family. So, when my baby bro is gunned down in front of me, I go on the hunt to settle the score. Fury drives me forward. Sleep becomes my enemy. I'm out for blood.

I work alone. No spotter. No backup. I get you in my sniperscope, you're already dead.

But someone hidin' in the shadows sees what I'm up to. Not good. Then, she inserts herself into my life. Even worse. She's the last person I want up in my business.

The. Last. Person.

I send her away. Not interested. Wouldn'cha know, she's got a stubborn streak that's worse than mine.

Way. Worse.

She makes me a deal I can't refuse, so I got a partner I never asked for and can't escape from. We're together twenty-four seven, takin' out the scum who shredded my family. Doesn't help that she's smokin' hot, brilliant, and all grown up with a body that does not quit.

I. Am. So. F*cked.

There's no way this'll end well... for either one of us. Turns out, I'd rather die with her than live without her.

"My Life My Rules"
— Jericho Savage

1

GOING IT ALONE

Jericho Savage's phone buzzed with in incoming message.
"Tonight's a go," Cooper Grant texted.
"Copy," Jericho replied.
"Who's your spotter?" Cooper texted.

Ignoring that, Jericho slipped his phone into his pants pocket before glancing around the kitchen table.

Sup-time was the one meal Jericho's grandmother insisted they eat as a family. It never happened before eight and, if everyone *was* there, it was mayhem. Jericho shared his six-bedroom McLean estate with his grandmother and three of his five siblings. As much as he adored his family, there were times when he just wanted to be alone. In a couple of hours, he would have that chance.

And he could not fucking wait.

"Hey, I thought Vincent was coming over," his sister, Georgia, said.

Vincent, their oldest sibling, was recently back in the area after moving away years earlier.

"That's what he said," Jericho replied before devouring the last bite of his burger. He'd already eaten one, but he could finish off that last burger on the platter, no problem.

Pausing, he eyed his family. Gram hadn't finished hers. To be fair, he did grill some massive quarter pounders. His brother, Mark, had just loaded up his second helping of everything. His baby brother, Bryan, met his gaze with a smile.

"I see you checking out that last burger," Bryan said. "I'll split it with you."

Jericho tossed his brother a nod. "It's all you, bro."

That burger, along with a bun, was on Bryan's plate in seconds. Gram slid over the sides and Bryan snatched another corncob. "Thanks, Gram. What's for dessert?"

"I made your favorite," Gram replied.

Bryan grinned. "Chocolate chip cookies."

Their grandmother pushed away from the table and made her way to the center island. After removing the foil, she returned with a platter of cookies stacked four deep.

"Whoa, that's a lot," Georgia exclaimed.

"They'll be gone by the end of the weekend," Gram said. "I baked more, so don't fight over these."

Like bees to honey, hands descended on the platter, scooping up the chocolatey treats.

"Soooo good," Georgia said between bites.

Rather than sit, Gram stood smiling down at each of them. If there was anything she loved, it was watching them eat. Jericho wolfed down two, pushed out of his chair, and kissed Gram's cheek.

"Delicious," Jericho said before stacking up the dirty dinner dishes. "What's everyone doin' tonight?"

"I'm on call," Mark replied. As a resident doctor, Mark pretty-much lived at the hospital. He collected the glasses and set them next to the dishwasher. "I feel like I haven't seen you guys in forever."

"That's cause you're hardly ever here," Bryan commented.

"Thanks for making the burgers, Jericho. Love you guys." Mark grabbed his backpack and took off toward the front door.

"I'm off tonight," Georgia said. "Bryan, come with me to Jericho Road."

"Gotta study for my *final* final," Bryan replied as he started loading up the dishwasher.

Jericho slapped him on the back "You did it, bro! College is in the bag. Watch out law school."

Shorter than Jericho and built like a string bean, Bryan grinned up at him. "Not gonna lie, I'm pretty excited about law school."

"You're gonna kill it," Georgia said. "Jericho, I'll grab a ride with you."

Jericho was swinging by his restaurant, but he wasn't staying. He had a job to do and wouldn't be back for a few hours.

"Are you taking off now?" Georgia asked.

"I'm makin' the rounds, starting with Kaleidoscope." Jericho hated lying, but he had to shut his sister down. When she decided to do something, it was impossible to change her mind. She had the Savage streak of bullheadedness.

"I'll see what my friends are doing or I'll wait for you at The Road," Georgia said.

Jericho did not want his sister going to his popular western-themed bar and restaurant by herself.

He glanced at the time. Ten after nine. His ALPHA hit was happening between ten-thirty and ten-forty. If things went according to plan, he'd be back at The Road by eleven-fifteen and on the floor by eleven-thirty.

"I'm gettin' there after eleven," Jericho explained. "I'll swing by here and pick you up on my way."

Georgia fisted her hands on her hips. "Jericho, I'm twenty-four years old. I don't need my brother as my wingman *or* my guard. I'll just see you there." She carried the leftover sides to the center island and began transferring everything to storage containers.

"I just want you safe," Jericho said.

She smiled at him. "I know, but you can't baby me forever."

"Sure, he can," Gram interjected.

The next few minutes were a flurry of kitchen activity. Everyone helped clean up while Gram sat at the table and worked her daily crossword puzzle. Once finished, Jericho made his way upstairs to his bedroom, at the end of the hallway. Behind his closed double doors, he unearthed his phone.

Cooper had sent another text. "Could you follow protocol, for once?"

Jericho texted back, "No."

He changed into a black T-shirt and black jeans, pulled on black boots and returned to the kitchen. The room was quiet. His grandmother was watching TV in the family room.

"Gram, I'll be home after closing."

She slid her gaze from the television. "What's with the all black? Why so drab?"

"Drab suits me." He smiled. "Love you."

"I love you. See you tomorrow."

Jericho left through the door leading into his six-car garage, slid into his truck, and headed out. The May evening had him rolling down his windows, but rather than jumping on the phone or pulling up a playlist, he drove in silence. He needed to clear his thoughts. Tonight's mission was important and he had one shot to get it done… and get it done right.

Twenty-five minutes later, he pulled into the parking lot of Jericho Road. His phone rang. It was Cooper… again.

Dammit.

While he didn't want to take the call, he couldn't ignore it. That would send the mission into a tailspin.

"Yo," Jericho answered.

"You don't have a spotter, do you?"

Cooper Grant was one of Jericho's closest friends. He was also his boss at ALPHA, the top-secret, quasi-government group that blurred the lines when it came to taking out the bad guys.

"You know I work alone."

"Dammit," Cooper bit out. "I uploaded pics to the portal. Al-Mazir's clean-shaven, and he's gained some weight."

"Copy."

"Are you at The Road?"

"I've got a damn tracker in my neck, for fuck's sake. You know exactly where I am."

Cooper chuckled. "Be safe."

"Always am." Jericho hung up and exited his truck. As he made his way through the parking lot, he pocketed his device, yanked open the front door, and walked inside.

Thursday night and Jericho Road—nicknamed The Road—was packed, the volume so loud, Jericho cringed. But packed restaurants were great for business. If there was anything Jericho was good at, it was running a successful eatery.

While he could have gone inside through his secret door out back, he walked through his restaurant on purpose. Although his kills were clean and he left no tracks, it was always good to be seen. Unlike Hansel and Gretel, Jericho Savage left no breadcrumbs on his way into, or out of, the forest.

He passed the massive bar that stretched all the way to the kitchen. His four bartenders were working the crowd, three-customers deep.

One of them caught his eye. "This is insane," he called. "Are you here to help out?"

"Be there shortly," Jericho boomed.

Another bold-faced lie.

Time took on a different dimension at The Road. Every night, his team worked nonstop until last call. By the time they'd realize he wasn't there, he'd be serving booze and chattin' up the customers alongside them.

Several customers turned in his direction.

"Hey, Jericho!" one woman called out.

"How's it goin, man?" asked a guy.

"How's everyone doin?" Jericho hollered over the chatter.

Before anyone had a chance to answer, he'd already made his way through the packed bar and into the main dining room. He called this area "managed chaos". He continued down the hallway, passing two smaller dining rooms, but slowed as he passed the room that housed the mechanical bull, nicknamed the Beast. A guy was being tossed onto the matted flooring while the crowd cheered.

"Idiot," Jericho mumbled.

A woman sidled over. "I was thinking of riding the Beast, but I'd much rather ride you." She tilted her head up, her wide smile filling her face.

"Hey, there darlin'. Havin' fun?"

"I would be having a lot more fun if we got to know each other better." She'd pushed up on her toes and stared at his mouth.

There was a time when Jericho had taken these women up on their offers and invited them into his office, but a few had turned out to be more trouble than it was worth. One had a boyfriend. Another had been married. Then, there were two women who had stalked him for weeks. He was all for having a good time, but he'd stopped screwing the customers years ago.

"You should stay away from me," he replied. "I'm nothin' but trouble."

She craned her head toward him while stroking his shoulder. "Yes, please."

"Gotta go."

He couldn't help but crack a smile as he made his way down the hallway toward his office. The large room at the back of the building was reserved for line dancing. On occasion, a local band would play, but most nights, a DJ managed the tunes from a booth.

The country song was so loud, the bass pounded through him

as he paused in front of the scanner on the wall next to his office. The light turned green, he opened the door and stepped inside. As he was closing the door, the woman he'd just rejected hurried over.

"I've had my eye on you for months," she said. "Seriously, no strings. I'm just super horny for you. You are so freakin' sexy. C'mom, just say yes. It'll be fun, I swear."

Jericho gave her props for being persistent, but he wasn't interested. "Not happenin'."

"Wait, *what*? You're rejecting me?"

"I am, darlin'."

He shut and locked his office door. Rather than ease into his worn chair and jump on his computer, he stood in front of another retina scanner mounted on the doorframe outside his walk-in supply closet.

The light turned green, he entered. In it, he stored a few reams of paper, stacks of plastic cups and paper plates. A pair of tattered jeans sat folded on a shelf, a few western shirts hung on the rack. On the floor stood two pairs of scuffed cowboy boots.

All these items were staged.

"Computer, open the door," he said.

"Hello, Jericho," replied the computerized voice.

A hidden door on the back wall slid open and he ducked into his *real* office. Nothing more than a standing desk with a computer, a leather love seat, and a heavy, metal safe on the floor.

Standing in front of his computer, he typed in his sixteen-digit code, the screen unlocked and he jumped onto the ALPHA portal to view the pictures Cooper had left him.

The leader of a small terrorist group, Abdul Al-Mazir, had entered the States posing as a visiting professor. He'd been plotting to assassinate the Secretary of Defense when the FBI had been tipped off. Al-Mazir was wanted for assassinating several top-ranking international government leaders. Interpol had issued a Red Notice for the fugitive who'd eluded law enforcement for decades. That had led to a decision to remove the threat, ALPHA style. Because Al-Mazir traveled with a security detail, Cooper and team decided a sniper hit would be the cleanest, least visible way to go.

Enter Jericho.

After studying the pictures of Al-Mazir and committing them to memory, Jericho reviewed the mission specs. When finished, he dropped his wallet, ring, and leather bracelets on the desk, then opened a second closet. There, he pulled on his Kevlar vest and chest harness for his Glock. His go-bag waited on a shelf. He unzipped it and unearthed the knife, still in its sheath, which he attached to his belt, then slid one of his Glocks into the chest holster.

With helmet in hand, he pressed a button on the underside of a shelf. A hidden panel on the back wall slid open. He scooped up the go-bag, ducked through the doorframe and stepped outside.

In the back of his parking lot, the black SUV waited at the curb. Dumpsters and NO PARKING signs kept customers from driving around back. He set the bag in the back seat, slid behind the wheel, and drove around the building toward the street.

Within seconds, he was outta that parking lot.

This SUV, one of several in ALPHA's fleet, stayed at Jericho Road. On more than one occasion, he'd needed to assist with a mission at the last minute. These vehicles came with license plate deflectors and an untraceable VIN. In the off-chance he got pulled over, the SUV couldn't be traced back to ALPHA. Even in the world of law enforcement, ALPHA did not exist.

Flying well below the radar was Jericho's jam.

On the drive, he didn't listen to music, didn't talk on the phone. He didn't run through his strategy, didn't plan for mission fallout. He simply cleared his mind of clutter.

Jericho parked in the urban Crystal City neighborhood, home to luxury condos that blended seamlessly with offices and retail establishments. It was here that the terrorist owned a penthouse condo with round-the-clock security.

With his bag slung over his shoulder and his helmet in hand, Jericho walked the quiet sidewalk bathed in the soft glow of the street lamps. Because of his height, massive size, and long hair, he stood out. Some found him sexy while others were easily intimidated.

If anyone saw him walking down the sidewalk at this late hour, chances were good they'd cross the street. That would work in his favor. Fortunately, the street was void of foot traffic.

Rather than enter Al-Mazir's building, he crossed the street and strode behind the building directly across from the terrorist's. If ALPHA had done their job, the surveillance cameras in the area had been deactivated. If not, the team would have to do major fucking cleanup.

Not my problem.

Using his pick set, he jimmied open the lock, and entered the building. After what ate up three minutes of his time and a shit-ton of patience, he found the service elevator and rode to the top floor. From there, he hoofed it to the roof.

He cleared the rooftop, which included checking around the air-conditioning units. Years ago, he'd learned that lesson the hard way when he'd arrived at his sniper spot to find someone waiting to ambush him.

Tonight, he was alone.

Moving into position, Jericho pulled on his helmet, then pulled out his goggles and homed in on his target's condo. Helped that the place was well lit. What *didn't* help were the three guards chillin' in the living room.

Al-Mazir's penthouse looked like a damn museum. Paintings and murals covered the walls, a life-size sculpture stood in the foyer.

"Too much fuckin' shit." Jericho pulled out the rifle and tripod, then attached the weapon.

According to Al-Mazir's schedule, he'd be arriving home in the next fifteen minutes. Jericho checked his phone. There were several texts and a few missed calls. Nothing that couldn't wait. He turned it off and repositioned the rifle toward the street.

Sixteen minutes passed before one of the guards got a call. Seconds later, all three guards stood.

Al-Mazir is pulling up.

One of them left the condo unit, one waited in the foyer, and the third checked every room.

Two black sedans pulled to the curb outside his building. Doors opened and two men exited the front car. *More guards.* One opened the rear door of the second vehicle. Al-Mazir exited. Jericho's pulse didn't jump, his breathing didn't shift.

Using the scope attached to the rifle, he zeroed in on his target. Rather than head inside, Al-Mazir waited as a woman emerged from the sedan.

Fuck.

Jericho removed his finger from the trigger. He couldn't take the shot with her there.

A few minutes after Al-Mazir and the woman vanished into the building, they entered his penthouse. He poured them drinks. She sat on one of the window-facing sofas.

Jericho repositioned to keep circulation flowing. Another lesson he'd learned the hard way. He couldn't make a slick getaway if he was dragging a foot that had fallen asleep.

Al-Mazir joined her. She'd barely taken a sip before he was on her. Jericho grunted. *It's bad enough I haven't gotten any in too damn long. Now I gotta watch him screw her.*

The security detail had left them alone, but one of them emerged from a back room. After a brief conversation Al-Mazir spoke to the woman before leaving with one of his guards.

Here we go.

Jericho eased back into position on the hard rooftop surface.

With his rifle aimed at the building's front door, he waited.

Both vehicles remained parked out front. Jericho had two seconds to take his shot.

That was one second more than he needed. Out of habit, Jericho inhaled a slow, deep breath and let it out.

The front door opened, Jericho found his mark.

POP!

He hit Al-Mazir between the eyes. The subject dropped. One of the guards rushed to his side while the other jerked his head in Jericho's direction. The guards would be swarming the building in seconds.

Get out.

Jericho wanted to bolt, but he acted with military precision. He'd done dozens of sniper hits over the years and muscle memory kicked into high gear. He removed the rifle from the tripod, shoved both into the bag, and pulled a second Glock. After slinging the bag across his back, he took off toward the rooftop door. Down the steps he flew, the tapping of his combat boots against the metal stairs echoing off the cinder-block walls.

A security detail would be waiting at the stairs' exit. He had no choice but to take the service elevator. He pressed the down button and stood to the side. The doors slid open. Like a statue, he silently counted to three.

Nothing.

He glanced into the empty cab, then entered. As the elevator descended, he pulled the Glock from his chest holster. Now, armed with two guns, he stood with his back against the side of the cab. The elevator stopped, the doors slid open. It was silent.

He listened for breathing, thought he heard something. The second he stepped off, a man opened fire.

BANG! BANG! BANG! BANG!

Despite the bullets pounding his Kevlar jacket, Jericho lit into the man.

POP! POP! POP! POP! POP! POP!

The man dropped.

Without slowing down, Jericho strode through the exit door and onto the street. With his helmet still on, he looked like a one-man SWAT Team. At the corner, he did a slow three-sixty.

I'm alone.

He crossed the street and walked the two blocks toward his SUV. As he got closer, he spied his close friend and fellow ALPHA Operative, Nicholas Hawk, leaning against his SUV, a lit cigarette dangling from his mouth. The only indication he was there on ALPHA business was the Kevlar vest he wore over his T-shirt. Hawk's laid-back stance was a sharp contrast to the shit Jericho had just encountered.

"I coulda used your help back there," Jericho bit out.

An alarm on Hawk's watch started beeping and he silenced it. "Time to bail your sorry ass out."

Jericho just shook his head. "You had me on a timer?"

"What's *your* damn rule? It's, 'I work alone'. I don't like it, but I respect it. On tonight's mission, I woulda brought every last one of you with me. The more, the fuckin' merrier." Hawk took a deep drag on the cigarette, then exhaled. As the smoke circled around him, his lips curved into a smile. "You had this." Eyeing the protective vest, Hawk asked, "How many bullets did it take?"

"Too many." Jericho opened the back door and set down his bag and helmet, but he didn't remove the vest. His ribs were fuckin' killing him, but he'd deal with that later… or never. Just part of the job. "Where'd you park?"

"Cooper dropped me." Hawk held out his hand. "I'll drive."

Pain fueled Jericho. It always had. "I got this," he said before opening the driver's side door. "Where you headed?"

"I'll hang with you." Hawk pushed off the vehicle, heading around the front of the SUV.

"I don't need any damn company." Jericho climbed in and winced.

Hawk slid in as Jericho started the engine.

"Put the damn cigarette out." Jericho pulled onto the street.

Instead, Hawk opened the window. "Did you hit the target?"

Silence.

Jericho didn't need to answer that.

"I thought so. Were you made?"

"Only by the dead guy," Jericho answered. "Last I checked, dead men don't talk."

"Some of 'em do. Let's hope this one didn't have a body cam."

From his pocket, Hawk's phone buzzed. He pulled it out, set the call on speaker. "Yo, baby."

"Hey, can you swing by the club?" Addison Skye asked.

"What's wrong?"

"That amazing—your word, not mine—security system you installed isn't working," Addison said.

"Be there in ten." Hawk hung up. "You get your wish," he said to Jericho.

"I'm gettin' laid," Jericho replied.

"Been awhile?" Hawk inhaled, then blew smoke out the window.

"No comment."

"You get to be alone," Hawk replied. "Drop me at Addison's club."

"Where?"

"Alexandria. Five minutes north of The Road. You gotta come with me tomorrow. It's opening night."

"What kinda club?" Jericho asked.

"Cosplay."

Jericho stopped at a light and fixed his gaze on his friend. "Seriously? Addison?"

Hawk laughed. "She's into playing dress up. Always has been, but she's throwing in some kink."

"I'll pass," Jericho said before driving through the intersection.

"C'mon, you like dressing up."

"On Halloween."

"You work every fucking night," Hawk protested. "Take one hour and meet me there. You might meet someone."

"Yeah, right. I'm gonna find myself a woman at a cosplay club." Jericho shook his head.

Five minutes later, Jericho stopped in front of a nondescript two-story building and parked. The neon sign out front was dark.

Lost Souls

"Who named the club?" Jericho asked.

"Her business partner. I'll pick you up tomorrow at ten. Wear a costume. You wanna come in now and say hey?" Hawk opened the SUV door.

"I'm in SWAT gear, idiot."

"She'll think you're ready to party." Hawk got out and leaned into the car. "Stay outta trouble, will ya?"

"Thanks for having my back."

"Yup." Hawk shut the door and Jericho drove way.

The last thing he wanted to do was play dress up, but he did plenty of shit he didn't want to do. He'd go, say hey to Addison, then get the hell outta there. Playing dress up, then screwin', sounded absurd.

Livingston Blackstone should never have suggested that she and her cousin, Addison, go into business together. *What was I thinking? I wasn't thinking. I definitely wasn't.*

She refreshed the screen, but the security system still wouldn't come online. After grunting out her frustration, she redirected her attention to the online membership form.

The office door flew open.

"We've tried for over an hour, but it's dead," Addison blurted. "Can you *please* help us?"

Addison was alone.

"Who are you talking to?" Liv asked.

Her cousin spun around. "Hawk was right behind me."

Hawk moseyed into the office, a smirk on his face. "Hey, Doc, how you doin'?"

Liv appreciated Hawk's easygoing nature. More like envied it. Just because she wasn't pounding her fist on the desk didn't mean she didn't want to. That, and scream obscenities at the computer. She pushed out of the chair.

"You drive, baby," Hawk replied. "You learn better when *you* grab the stick."

If Nicholas Hawk had been her type, Liv would have blushed. But he wasn't, so she didn't. Instead she sat back down and fixed her gaze on him as he rolled a chair next to her.

Hawk had short, dark brown hair that always looked like he'd just rolled out of bed. Intense blue eyes that drew her in, coupled with an exasperated expression that screamed "fuck off". That lit cigarette dangling from his mouth wasn't a selling point, but his rugged good looks paired with that perfect nose, angled jaw, and movie-star smile were a definite chick magnet. But Liv was never one to follow the crowd. What everyone thought was gorgeous, she found boring.

"I'm gonna talk to the staff," Addison said. "Livy, you got this?"

"I'm good," Liv replied.

Several clicks later, Hawk had walked her though activating the club's security system, which Hawk had personally installed. The best part? His twenty-thousand-dollar club-warming gift had saved them from having to take out a second loan.

"Thank you," she said. "How is it so easy when you do it?"

She wanted to take back those words the second she'd finished uttering them.

"Because I know which buttons to push, baby." He winked. "Seriously, you wanna run through it again?"

"I got it." She swiveled toward him. "Are you bringing all your friends tomorrow night?"

"Yup. You expecting a big crowd?"

She shrugged a shoulder. "There's some buzz on social media. We're hoping the half-price membership sale will help bring in some business."

"I'll sign up and you can charge me full price. Don't give my friends the discount. They're all rich as fuck."

"Everyone gets the discount, Hawk." She pushed out of the chair. "I should get out there."

"I thought you were a behind-the-scenes partner."

"I'm Addison's silent partner, but I'll be tending bar the first night. Please don't tell anyone who I am, 'kay?"

"Why so secretive?"

"Just being private, that's all."

As he rose, he took a drag on the cigarette. "If you're pouring, I'll take that drink."

They left the office and made their way down the short hall to the main room where Addison was finishing up her pre-opening-night meeting with their small staff.

After the employees filtered out, Hawk slid onto a barstool and Addison sat beside him. Liv walked behind the bar, set three lowball glasses on the shiny counter. "What's it gonna be?"

"Whiskey, neat," Hawk replied.

"Nothing for me," Addison said. "My stomach's in knots. I think we made a huge mistake."

Liv stared at her, then laughed. "Good one." She poured two whiskeys.

"Not joking." Addison pulled a hair scrunchie off her wrist and tied her long, dark hair into a ponytail sitting high on her head. "I already had to fire someone and we haven't even opened."

"I love it," Hawk said. "You're a badass."

"What happened?" Liv asked.

"The bartender asked for the weekend off," Addison huffed.

"Opening weekend and he's going to a wedding. I canned him. I'm sorry to do that to you."

"I can work the bar alone," Liv said.

"When'd you learn to tend bar?" Hawk said.

"How do you think I paid my way through grad school?" Liv sipped the whiskey.

"What costume did you decide on?" Addison asked.

"The latex cat suit," Liv answered.

"You gonna call yourself Pussy?" Hawk tossed back the top-shelf alcohol.

Addison swatted his arm. "Soooo not helping."

"I'll use Catwoman," Liv replied.

"I won't be able to sleep I'm so nervous and excited for tomorrow night," Addison said. "Are we crazy for doing this?"

Liv glanced around. Besides the bar area, there were several booths and tables and a dance floor. The far corner of the room had been set aside for picture taking. A cell-phone tripod stand had been cemented into the floor so costumed members could pose for group shots. The backdrop was a green screen that could be changed to a variety of scenes.

Lost Souls was the first cosplay club in the DMV—the District, Maryland, and Virginia—that catered to people who liked dressing in costume. Months earlier, Addison had told Liv she was going to a man's house for a private cosplay party. When Liv pressed her for deets about the host, Addison knew nothing. That concerned Liv, who'd blurted, "Instead of going to some stranger's house, let's open a cosplay club."

"Hey, Livy," Addison said, snapping her from her thoughts. "Where'd you go?"

"I was just thinking about when I first got back into town and you told me you were going by yourself to some stranger's house for a cosplay party."

Addison sighed. "That might not have been my best idea, but this—" she gestured to the club— "I think we're in over our heads.

We've both taken out loans, we don't even know if anyone is coming."

"Relax," Hawk said. "You're gonna kill it."

"Are you going to accept an invitation to play?" Addison asked.

"When have I ever said no?" Hawk replied.

Addison laughed. "No surprise there. I was talking to Livy."

The first floor of Lost Souls was all about the costumed fun, but the second floor… that was open to interpretation. While Addison was into the cosplay lifestyle, Liv was all about creating safe spaces to explore role play and no-strings sex.

She'd been in a sexless relationship for way too long. Then, after moving back to the area, she'd been all about her career. She wasn't into dressing up, but she was definitely ready for a late-night escape with a sexy stranger.

"An invitation to play…" Liv echoed. "Maybe."

"Promise me you won't hide behind the bar," Addison said.

"When I put on the cat suit, I'm going to turn into a completely different person." Liv waggled her eyebrows. "You'll see."

2

LOST SOULS

Jericho fucking hated debriefings, but he'd never win against strict ALPHA protocol. While he loved being an Operative, reporting in to HQ was a total time suck. Even worse, he was expected to wear a damn suit. Since that wasn't happening, he'd thrown on a white shirt and black pants. But there was no freakin' way he was putting on a jacket and tie. Those were for weddings and funerals, and neither of those weren't happening anytime soon.

At eight o'clock sharp, he pulled into the parking lot of ALPHA MEAT PACKING in Tysons, drove around back, and parked. The one-story, warehouse-looking structure, had reflective glass on the windows and a retina scanner at the employee entrance.

He exited his truck, strode to the back door, and paused in front of the scanner. That damn light stayed red. He stepped away, moved back. Still red.

"Motherfucker." He made a call.

"Hey," Cooper answered. "Locked out again?"

"This is the universe telling me I shouldn't be here," Jericho said.

Cooper chuckled. "No, this is *you* telling me you shouldn't be here."

A moment later, Cooper pushed open the back door and Jericho stepped inside. Cooper Grant was temporary co-lead of ALPHA, along with Providence Luck.

As the men made their way toward Cooper's office, Cooper asked if he wanted coffee.

"I was at The Road until three this morning," Jericho growled. "I'm gonna need the entire pot."

After stopping in the break room, they continued on with mugs in hand until they reached Cooper's office. Cooper slid behind his desk and opened his laptop while Jericho eased into a guest chair.

"Nice work last night," Cooper began. "Eyes on the ground said you hit your target."

"Since those weren't my eyes, I gotta assume you had Operatives there."

"You work alone, but ALPHA doesn't, not on a sniper hit."

"Well, I was alone in that building," Jericho bit out.

"What happened to Hawk?"

"He had me on a timer."

Cooper's eyebrows shot up. "I gotta hire better Ops." After a second, he said, "We think you were made, so you gotta lay low until we know you're safe."

Frustration slithered down his spine. "You know I hate that."

"Pissed off is better than dead."

"No one's gonna kill me." Jericho sipped the coffee. It wasn't nearly strong enough.

Knock-knock.

"Come on in," Cooper said.

ALPHA Operatives Stryker Truman and Emerson Easton entered. Stryker was one of his closest friends and Emerson was Stryker's fiancée.

"Were these your spies?" Jericho asked Cooper.

"Guilty," Stryker said. "You had a clean shot."

"It's what I do," Jericho replied.

"There were two men who went after you," Emerson explained. "You took down one, but we're concerned that the second tracked you after you left the building."

"Tell me you didn't lose him," Jericho said.

Stryker nodded. "Sorry, bro."

"Nice," Jericho said, his tone thick with sarcasm.

"I've got eyes on Al-Mazir's team," Cooper explained. "I emailed you a profile on his most trusted member, plus the one we think made you."

"I'm personally leading this mission," Stryker said.

"Is that supposed to make me feel better?" After a split second, Jericho smiled. "I know you got my back, dawg." He regarded Cooper. "If you're not giving me another mission, what about recon work? I've got one next week in Atlanta."

"You gotta chill until we get word on what these guys are planning."

I do not wanna be sidelined.

"They might not be planning *anything*," Jericho bit out as the frustration morphed into anger. "They were his *security* detail."

"We've got informants overseas who are tracking the terror cell's movements to see if any of them are making travel plans to the U.S," Cooper explained.

"Is Hawk in danger?" Jericho asked.

"We've got a team on him, too," Cooper replied.

"What a cluster," Jericho bit out, before pushing out of his chair. "Thanks for the heads up."

"I'm sorry," Stryker said.

"Don't sweat it." Jericho patted his back. "I'm not worried about some punk following me around. I'd take him down before he even saw me comin'."

"Will we see you at Addison's club opening tonight?" Emerson asked him.

"Hawk making you go, too?" Jericho replied.

"We'll all be there," Cooper said.

"Wearing costumes and ready to party," Emerson added.

"I can't effin' wait." Jericho left with a major chip on his shoulder. In the five years he'd been with ALPHA, he'd never once been sidelined.

Never.

"Welcome to a new fuckin' era," he said as he pushed open the back door and headed toward his truck.

Despite the beautiful May morning, Jericho's mood had soured. If need be, he'd do his own damn recon on the guys who were after him. It was *always* better to play offense than defense.

Liv entered the Alexandria Police Department and stopped to sign in.

"How you doing, Dr. Blackstone?" asked the duty officer.

"It's Friday, so I'm good," she replied. "You?"

"Same. I haven't seen you in a coupla weeks. Teaching a workshop today?"

She nodded. "To the rookies."

As Liv made her way to the conference room, she stopped by Sergeant Hayes' office to say hello. He was on the phone, but his face split into a smile, and he waved her in. "I gotta go," he said to the caller. "My favorite psychologist and gang expert just walked into my office." He hung up and rose.

Andre Hayes, a career law enforcement officer loved to serve his community. A strong advocate for mentor programs, he'd started a school program where first responders shared the value of education with children of all ages. As a former detective, he now ran the precinct's gang unit. He kept his Afro short, had a full beard and mustache, and always dressed for success in a suit and vibrant tie.

After a handshake, he gestured for her to sit. "Your training is really paying off," he began. "One of my detectives recently arrested several gang members because of you."

Liv tucked her long, wavy hair behind her ear. "Glad I could help."

As a gang expert, Liv consulted with police departments throughout the region helping them better understand gang behavior, gang recruiting tactics, and gang violence. Though unrelated, she also taught workshops to help first responders better handle mental-health-crisis calls.

When she returned to the area, six months ago, Andre had seen real value in her services and went to bat for her. As soon as one PD hired her, several more followed.

"What brings you by?" Andre asked.

"Teaching the rookies how to respond to mental health calls."

"Have you done a ride-along?"

"I've been on two," she replied. "The first was easy, but the second was intense. The man had a gun to his head, but the officer and I encouraged him to give up his weapon." She shifted in the chair. "Did you get a chance to look at my write-up on the Thriller Killers gang?"

Andre broke eye contact for a second. "Sorry, Doc, not yet. I've been swamped."

"No rush."

"What'd you learn?"

"The short version is that while they're new to the area, they're the fastest growing gang in Northern Virginia."

"Thriller Killers." Andrea hopped on his computer. After a few clicks, he said, "We haven't run into this gang."

"I'm surprised." Liv checked the time, pushed out of the chair. "My class is about to start and I'm not in it. Always good to see you, Andre."

"Same, Dr. Blackstone."

"When are you going to start calling me Liv?"

With a smile, Andre said, "Next time, alright?"

Liv hurried down the hallway and into the conference room. The table was full and there were several law enforcement personnel sitting against the back wall.

"Good morning, everyone," she said walking to the front of the room. "I'm Liv Blackstone. This workshop is about how to respond to an emergency call when someone is having a mental health crisis. Anyone here for a different class?"

No one's hand went up and no one left.

"Here's my twenty second elevator pitch. I've got a Ph.D. in psychology with a focus on gang behavior. I'm an expert on paper, but you're the pros on the streets. I've also got extensive training in first-responder and crisis management, but you're boots on the ground. And we're all here to—"

"Get a jump on the CECs," blurted a male rookie.

As the laughter died down, Liv smiled at the group. "This *is* three easy continuing education credits, but if you ever respond to a crisis call and you don't know how to walk the person back, learning some of these skills might make all the difference."

"True, true," said the same rookie.

Her gaze drifted over her audience. "Has anyone responded to one of these calls?"

A few hands went up.

"Who wants to share what they walked in on?" she continued.

"A man had barricaded his children in the bedroom because his wife had threatened to leave him and take their kids with her," answered a female cop. "He was threatening to kill his family before he killed himself."

Liv nodded. "How'd the responding officer handle it?"

"She stayed calm and encouraged him to put down the weapon. When he wouldn't do that, she asked him if they could bring the children out of the home to their mom, who was waiting outside."

"Good," Liv said.

"The victim ended up wounding the officer, then killing himself," the rookie explained.

"What worked and what didn't?" Liv asked.

"He let his kids leave and the officer lived, but he refused help and took his own life."

"The reason I'm here is to offer my assistance on how we can change the bad outcomes and ensure everyone gets the help they need." Liv slid out her laptop and plugged it in.

After a few clicks, her presentation appeared on the screen. "These are boring as hell," she said, and everyone laughed. "You can have a copy, but I'm all about the dialogue. What can we do to make a difference when responding to an emergency? How can you protect yourself, each other, and the victims?"

The morning rolled into the afternoon. When they broke for lunch, she checked her phone. Several texts had come in from Addison.

"Caterer has a prob. We are so screwed."

An hour after the initial text, Addison had sent a second. "Prob solved. Hawk's friend is donating a ton of finger foods. Whew!"

A few minutes ago, Addison had fired off a third text. "I'll be at the club by five. Can you make it by seven?"

Liv replied, "Good job on the food emergency. Yes, I'll be there by seven. I hope you're excited. This is a big night for us! Can't wait to celebrate with you!" She sent the text, left the building, and grabbed a salad at a nearby take-out place. Rather than return, she ate outside. The weather was spectacular, and she checked work emails while she ate.

Back inside, the afternoon session flew by. The students were attentive and did a good job participating. As was typically the case, twenty percent of the attendants contributed eighty percent of the time. She was there to offer her expertise. It was up to each individual to find value, or not, in what she offered.

When the workshop ended and she was packing up to leave,

the sole female detective in the gang unit popped her head into the room. "I was hoping you hadn't left yet."

Mirabel Morales walked in, her shoulder-length light brown hair tucked behind her ear. "The Sarge just showed me your report on the Thriller Killers gang. Nice work."

"Thanks. How's it going?"

"Slow," Detective Morales replied. "My informants tell me the TK gang is growing superfast. The violence between this gang and two established ones is out of control. If I worked every day twenty-four seven, I wouldn't be able to keep up."

Liv's shoulders fell. This type of news was hard to digest. No matter how much of a difference she and the detectives tried to make, the bad guys were one step ahead. "I'm sorry to hear that. How can I help?"

Mirabel moved closer. "Just between you and me, I think there's a—"

Sergeant Hayes entered the conference room. "There you are, Detective. We got a call that someone found two bodies behind a nightclub that's a hangout for one of the gangs."

Mirabel nodded. "I'm on my way." At the doorway, she turned back to Liv. "We'll talk soon."

Liv finished packing up, then hurried out. A rain shower had her trying to avoid puddles as she walked to her car. She slogged through heavy traffic to her upscale condo in Arlington overlooking the Potomac River and the nation's capital. Her Uncle Z owned it, but he'd moved to DC years ago. She'd lucked out. He was renting it to her for next to nothing.

By the time she got home, she had just enough time to shower and get ready. While she should have been a bundle of nerves, she wasn't. Despite the fact that she'd never owned a brick and mortar business before, she had every confidence she and Addison could do it. Addison had friends who were willing to step up and help them out. Hawk had been one, and the generous man who'd comped their food, another.

Liv opened her closet and pulled out the most conservative black latex cat costume. While she expected that most of the clubbers wouldn't wear masks unless their costume called for one, her simple black eye mask would further conceal her identity beyond the cat mask and attached cowl that came with the costume.

She was Addison's silent partner for a reason and she had no intention of telling anyone her real name. The less the members knew about her, the better.

At just after seven, she let herself into the club, and stopped short. String lights had been draped from one side of the room to the other, bathing the club in a soft, romantic glow. Addison had pushed four tables against the wall for the caterer. Some of the food had already been delivered and Liv lifted one of the metal lids. This one was filled with triangles of deliciously gooey cheese quesadillas topped with hot peppers.

"Hey!" Addison said as she hurried into the room from their shared office down the hall. "You look fantastic!"

"You did a phenomenal job with everything!" Liv exclaimed.

Addison beamed. "The lights were a last-minute add. They're so pretty. Speaking of pretty, what do you think of my costume?"

Liv eyed her cousin. Her breasts spilled from her white peasant top, her short skirt showed off her toned thighs while black boots covered her calves. This was an Addison Liv had never seen before. Her cosplay side.

"Very sexy," Liv said. "Are you a… bar wench?"

"A *renaissance* bar wench. Yup, I'm showing off the girls. It's their big night out."

Liv chuckled. "You look great. I'm sure you're going to get a lot of invitations to…" Liv paused. "Get kinky, role play. What are we calling the private hookups?"

"Invitations to Escape."

"That'll work. I'm gonna drop my bag in the office."

"Hawk installed a retina scanner so we don't need a key and we don't have to remember a code."

Together, they made their way to their shared office. Addison stood in front of the scanner. The light turned from red to green and they entered. Nothing but a used desk, an old chair, and a computer. Liv set her bag on the desk.

After logging in, Addison hopped over to the security system. She clicked on New User, then directed Liv to stand in front of the doorway scanner.

"Which eye?" Liv asked from the hallway.

"I don't think it matters."

Once Liv did, Addison called out, "You can't blink."

"Well, now I'm blinking like crazy." Liv relaxed her gaze and stared at the green light. Though her eyes started to water, she didn't let herself blink.

"Got it!" Addison said. "Okay, you're good. Pull the door closed and we'll test it."

Liv shut the door and stared at the scanner. The light stayed red.

"Still red," Liv said through the door.

They tried twice more, but the scanner didn't work.

"Ask Hawk to help you when he gets here," Addison said. "He's bringing all his friends. I can't believe you haven't met any of them. Well, you will, tonight. Two have fiancées who are super nice." Addison pulled the door closed behind her.

On the way back to the main room, Addison said, "The cowl on your costume has an eye mask. Why are you wearing a second one?"

"I don't want people to recognize me."

"Because you're concerned they'll corner you for psychological advice?"

Liv laughed. *Not exactly.*

BAM! BAM! BAM!

Someone was pounding on the front door and Addison rushed to open it.

Hawk walked in, carrying four oversized duffles. "I've been standing out there forever."

"Why didn't you call me?" Addison said as she took two of the bags from him. "Thanks for all the extra food."

"Hey, Liv, you look hot," Hawk said.

"Ahem," Addison said as she slowly spun around.

"Look at you," Hawk said giving her the once-over. "Wow, that is some costume."

"Where's your costume?"

Hawk was wearing a black shirt and torn jeans. "It was either pick up the food and get my ass over here, or throw on a costume."

Addison smiled. "Good call."

Hawk set down the bags. "Whad'ya need?"

"Help setting out food, then a reboot of the scanner," Addison replied. "It's not working for Livy."

After they transferred the food to the empty warmers, Hawk showed them how to fix the scanner. The next hour was a blur, but at nine o'clock, Liv and Addison opened the front door.

"Oh, wow," Addison murmured.

"Welcome," Liv said to the short line of waiting customers. "C'mon in!"

Liv went behind the bar and got busy serving drinks. Twelve guests turned into eighteen, then twenty-five. Her opening-night jitters faded as costumed customers continued filing in.

By ten fifteen, the place was packed. Wall-to-wall clubbers danced on their shiny new floor while a short line formed in the corner for group pics. Addison was working the room, signing people up for the half-price membership, while Liv chatted up customers from behind the bar.

Hawk pushed his way through and flagged her down. "You need a break?" he asked.

"I'm doing great," Liv replied. "What can I get you?"

"Another beer." Hawk turned and spoke to the group beside him. Liv eyed his friend. She recognized the tall blond. Cooper Grant. Acting head of ALPHA. She knew him because she'd spent four weeks tailing him. When she'd been assigned that top-secret job, he wasn't seeing anyone. Looked like things had changed for him. A pretty blonde stood close beside him.

Her gaze jumped to the Adonis towering behind them, dressed as Thor. Tall, broad shouldered, and a hard-muscled chest. But it was his rugged face, dark brown hair with sun-kissed highlights, and scruffy beard and mustache that hijacked her complete attention. Her heart leapt into her throat as she gobbled up all that male hotness.

Oh. My. God.

Didn't matter that years had passed.

That gorgeous beast of a man was Jericho Savage.

Jericho was *not* in the mood to party. He needed to hunt down the terrorist's guards and take them out, one by one. But, here he was, at some damn club opening playing dress up and pretending to have fun.

As he laid eyes on the bartender, curiosity had him taking a second look. Her face was framed in a black mask, her hair hidden beneath a cowl with cat ears, and her body covered in black latex. Nothing like a skin-tight cat suit to grab his full attention. Needing to check her out, he shouldered his way next to Hawk.

"Hey," Hawk said. "Whad'ya want?"

A closer look at that woman.

She stood there, frozen, her unblinking stare drilling into his. He tossed her a nod. "How ya doin'?" he asked.

She hesitated for a split second. "What can I get you?"

"Surprise me."

Hawk whipped his head in Jericho's direction. "What the hell?"

Jericho couldn't tear his gaze from her. "What's your name?"

"Catwoman. Where's your hammer, Thor?"

"I draw the line at props."

Her lips curved, but she didn't give him a smile.

Damn, that woulda been nice.

When she reached up and pulled two bottles from the top shelf, he checked out her backside. Tall with meat on her bones. She had a curvy ass and womanly hips. Her muscular thighs would look pretty damn fine wrapped around him while he sank inside her. From what he could tell, she was definitely his type. A growl escaped from the back of his throat. He hadn't had this intense of a reaction to anyone in for-fucking-ever.

Maybe the evening hasn't been a total waste of time.

She turned back. When their gazes locked, a hit of adrenaline powered through his chest.

"Okay, Thor, you look like a straight-up whiskey man, but maybe you live on the edge." She held up a top-shelf bottle of whiskey in one hand and a luxury tequila brand in the other.

He smiled. She had a sense of humor. "Tequila," he replied.

"Hawk?" she asked.

"Fill her up," Hawk said.

Liv jumped her gaze to the blond couple behind them. "And your friends?"

Cooper's woman held up two fingers. "Tequila for us, too."

Liv pulled down four lowball glasses. Jericho liked that she knew her booze. The top-shelf alcohol should be sipped, not downed. After pouring, she slid the glasses over. "Enjoy and thanks for being here."

Jericho wanted to park his ass on a stool and chat her up, but she moved on to serve someone else.

Damn.

Hawk gathered the drinks and passed them out, but Jericho

couldn't break his gaze. She was shaking a Manhattan and he'd never been so damn mesmerized in his life.

"Yo, Jericho!" A booming voice forced him to turn.

His close friend, Maverick Hott, stood there grinning. With drink in hand, Jericho left his coveted spot. After hugging it out, the two men spent time catching up. Maverick ran ThunderStrike, a paramilitary security firm. Over the years, Jericho had partnered with Maverick on some of his international missions.

Over the next thirty minutes, Jericho never lost sight of the bartender. She was churning out the drinks fast enough, but it was a lot to handle by herself. When the waiting customers grew to three-people deep, he had to do something. Towering over pretty much everyone, he searched for Addison. She was nearby, tablet in hand, talking to three customers. Jericho bulled his way over to her.

"Hey, darlin'," he said.

Addison tilted her chin to meet his gaze. "Hey, Jericho—I mean —Thor. Love the costume. Are you having fun?"

Addison was one of Hawk's closest friends. She was super pretty with a bubbly personality. If petite and energetic had been his thing, he would have asked her out years ago. But she wasn't, so he hadn't.

"Are you joining?" Addison asked.

"Joining what?"

She laughed. "Our cosplay club. First floor is open to the public, but you have to get on our list every night. Second floor is members only."

His curiosity piqued. "What are the member perks?"

She rose up on her toes and he lowered his head. "We've got a completely different set-up upstairs. Private rooms where you can role-play scenes from your character's movie or create your own."

Jericho stared at her. "Seriously?"

"Hawk didn't tell you?" She shook her head. "Of course, he

didn't. We've got ten suites where you can live out your cosplay fantasies. Intimacy level is up to the people playing. If you sign up tonight, we're offering half off the membership fee."

His flicked his gaze over to the sexy woman in the cat suit. "I'm in."

Two short minutes later, he'd signed up. She held the tablet up to his face, snapped a pic, then captured an image of his retina. Next, she set up his membership page.

"Once you download the app, you can complete your profile," she explained.

"How's the food working out?" Jericho asked.

"I'm so sorry, I completely forgot. Thank you so much. You saved us."

"Wish I'd known." Jericho peered over at the bar to check out the bartender for the zillionth time. "I would have donated all the food."

"I appreciate the last-minute rescue."

"Who's the bartender?"

"Catwoman," Addison replied.

"What's her name?"

"Cat. Woman," she said with a smirk.

"You're not helping me, Addison. Does she work here full time?"

"We're only open Wednesdays through Saturdays, so I'm guessing she'll be here."

"Didn't you set up a schedule?"

"Well, she's my—" Someone snagged Addison, and she got busy chatting him up for membership.

She's your what? Frustration coursed through him. He searched the crowd for Hawk.

Someone has got to know something about her.

When he spotted Hawk posing for pictures with, what looked like, an entire cheerleading squad, Jericho's patience had run out.

Go fucking talk to her.

He made his way through the crowded room and over to the bar. Catwoman couldn't clear out the customers quick enough. *Help her out.*

He lifted the bar door and stepped behind the counter.

She slinked over. "Can I get you something?" Her silky voice caught his ear.

"I'm Hawk's friend—"

"Thor, right?"

"I'm the guy who helped Addison when her caterer fucked up. Good news… the place is packed, but you need help. I got you."

She laid her hand on her chest like she was having trouble breathing.

"You okay?" he asked.

"Um, so… I really don't—"

"Customers are waitin' too damn long. Addison is sellin' memberships and the hold-up here ain't helpin'." Without waiting for permission, he turned toward the patrons. Hated that he had to stop talking to her, but he couldn't get to know her until he cleared everyone out.

"Yo," he boomed to a group of guys. "Whatcha drinkin'?" While drawing their draft beers, he asked, "You guys into the cosplay scene?"

"We're into chicks," said one of them.

He eyeballed them. "Three musketeers?"

"Yeah, man."

Jericho lined up the glasses. "There are five of you, but who's countin', right? You gotta become members."

"What's that about?" asked another.

Jericho whistled loudly. Half the people in the club whipped their heads in his direction. Except Addison. "Yo, Addison!" he belted out.

She turned toward him.

He waved her over. "Sign these guys up."

Jericho worked the crowd like he did every damn night at The

Road. He made 'em feel welcome, commented on their costumes, and told them they *needed* to sign up.

Boom. Done.

Now, Addison was the one with the line. He wanted to grab a tablet and help her out, but no way in hell was he leaving the bar. He'd worked his ass off so he could talk to the sexy bartender who was all curves, no words, and completely disguised from head to foot.

He was all for a little mystery, but c'mon.

Despite the lull, Catwoman was at the other end of the bar, talking to customers. Jericho was never one to *wait* for something to happen. He went after what he wanted.

My life my rules.

As he made his way toward her, her body stiffened and she hadn't even looked his way.

"You wanna take a break?" he asked her.

Fuck. What a bonehead question.

She turned toward him and another bolt of energy powered through him.

What the hell is it about this woman?

"I'm good," she replied, her gaze locked on his. "Thanks for your help. You're great talking to people."

"I own a bunch of restaurants, so I gotta lotta practice. Name's Jericho. What's yours?"

"Catwoman," she replied.

He hitched an eyebrow. "Not gonna tell me your real name."

"It's not important." A couple sidled over and she hurried away to serve them.

Is she shy? Not interested?

The bar filled up and he got busy again. When he finished, he glanced in her direction. Some dude was chattin' her up pretty good. Scraggly brown hair, amber beard and stache, reflective sunglasses. Tall and thin, he wore a T-shirt and jeans, sleeves of tats covered both his arms. The tat on his neck continued below his shirt.

A growl rolled out of Jericho.

He trusted his gut because his gut was never wrong. Dude needed to move on. And Jericho was gonna see to it that he did. Feeling territorial, he moseyed over.

"Are you a member?" the guy asked Catwoman.

"I work here," she replied.

"What's your name?"

"Catwoman."

The customer pulled out his phone. After a few taps, he shot her a smile. "You got yourself a membership, Catwoman. My friends call me Guapo."

Jericho bit back a laugh. That was Spanish for handsome. Dude needed some damn humility.

"I'm gonna send you an invite to meet up, you know, upstairs," Guapo continued. "You got a fave scene you wanna play out from a Batman movie? I can help with that."

The lights brightened and Addison hurried behind the bar. "Last call," she announced.

"Dang, girl," Guapo said. "I'm just making some convo with your bartender, here."

The two women exchanged glances.

"Can we get you something to drink?" Addison asked, her brusque tone catching Jericho's ear.

Why is she so protective of this woman?

"Nah." Dude pushed away from the bar. "I'll catch up with you later, doll." Using his hand as a gun, Guapo fired off a shot at Catwoman before he moseyed toward the door.

Addison poured herself a glass of water and chugged it down. "Whew, that was insane. We got so many new members. How'd you do working the bar alone?"

This time, Catwoman shifted toward him. The air turned electric, the energy buzzing through him. Their chemistry was crazy intense. Drawn to her, he stalked one step closer. His fingers twitched to touch her. He wanted to take off her mask, remove the cowl from her head. What did she look like and why was he so damn attracted to her?

I gotta get to know her.

"Your friend, Jericho, was a huge help," Catwoman said. This time, her gaze stayed rooted on his. Heat pounded his chest. He couldn't tear himself away from her.

"Oh, yeah," Addison echoed. "So many people joined, thanks to you. And thank you again for the food. You're a total life saver."

Jericho tossed them a nod. "Congrats on your club. If you need anything, lemme give you my number."

Addison lifted her phone from her pocket and Jericho pulled out his. After she rattled hers off, he shot her a text.

"Got it," Addison replied. "You taking off?"

Jericho shifted his gaze to Catwoman. Damn, he did not want to leave her. She had a sexy mouth. Full lips, but not too full. *Fuckin' perfect.*

I gotta kiss her.

The desire to touch her had him biting back another growl.

What he didn't like was that she hadn't smiled at him, not even once. *She's not interested. Move on.* But something in him refused his own direction.

"I'll see ya," he said to her.

Her lips tugged upward. "Thanks for the help."

The timbre of her voice was too damn sexy. He could wrap himself in her and escape... for a long while.

"Where's Hawk?" Jericho asked.

"I'm guessing he's upstairs trying out one of the rooms with a cheerleader," Addison replied. "Or the entire squad." She laughed.

"We've gotta clear the suites before we leave," Catwoman said.

Jericho's gaze drilled into her. "I'll do it with you."

Her barely audible moan caught his ear.

Normally chill around women, he had one speed with this one, and it was full throttle.

"Technically, the rooms aren't even open," Addison explained. "But Hawk set up the security, so he's got access to the entire club."

Jericho called his friend.

"Hey, bro," Hawk answered. "Whaz up, baby?"

"Are you upstairs with the cheerleaders?"

Hawk laughed. "I'm outside, talking to the guys."

Jericho hung up. "He's outside. When you scanned my retina, did I get access to the suites?" he asked Addison.

"Uh-huh," she replied.

"There could be people playing up there." He swung his gaze to Catwoman. "Let's go clear 'em."

Her breathing hitched.

Now, we're getting' somewhere.

Rather than take the elevator, she opened the fire door. He held it while she walked through.

Damn, she smells good.

He didn't want to make small talk with her. He just wanted to be by her side, so he caught up with her on the stairs. Being around her was easy. No idea why. He wasn't gonna analyze the situation. He was a face-value kinda man.

At the top of the stairs, she stood in front of the retina scanner. The light turned green and she murmured, "Progress."

The quiet hallway was bathed in amber sconces. Definitely sexy. All the doors to the private suites were open. The air was buzzling with so much electricity, his breathing quickened. He wanted to pull her into his arms and taste her cherry lips.

Together, they walked into the first room on the right. She flipped on the light.

Red bulbs illuminated the space. More than seeing her shadowy figure, he could feel her next to him. She was standing so damn close a growl shot out of him before he could check himself.

Fuck. Fuck me.

For a man who was all about control, he had none around her.

She fixed her gaze on his. The air ignited with frenzied energy. Her breath hitched again. He glanced at her mouth. She glanced at his and her moan landed between his legs. His junk moved in the tight space of his black leather pants.

Jesus, I wanna kiss her. Real bad.

She sashayed into the bathroom, flipped on the light. "We're good in here."

We sure as hell are.

With her gaze cemented on his, she sauntered past him and into the hall.

One by one, they checked every suite. Each time they entered one, he eyed the futon or the bed or the mattress on the floor. All the rooms were designed a little differently, but the basics were the same. A place to play, a table with condom packets, a chair or a bench, and a handful of BDSM toys hanging on the wall. The only variation were the different colored light bulbs.

When they entered the tenth room with the purple lights, she brushed past him on her way to the bathroom. His body came alive, the desire to touch her no longer an option. It was an absolute, like breathing. He ached to press her up against the wall, trap her with his body, and kiss her hard, deep, and long.

They'd barely said a word to each other. No small talk, no flirty banter. But Jericho didn't want to talk to her. He wanted to fuck her. Normally a chill guy around women, he was thrumming with a carnal greed that had hijacked all logical thought.

He stood in the doorway, his fingers curled around the top of the frame. If he stepped in, he'd full-on maul her. Heaving in a lungful of air, he waited. A cold shower wouldn't even help. But this mystery woman… she could relieve him.

Upon exiting the bathroom, her gaze roamed freely down his long physique, then back up. She walked right up to him, tilted her face toward his. "No one's here."

"We're here," he murmured.

"Looks that way." She ran her tongue over her lower lip while she studied his mouth.

His eyes never strayed from hers, but his fingers twitched. He wanted to rip that mask off her, take her face in his hands, and kiss the hell out of her. Kiss her until she stripped him naked and climbed him like a damn tree.

He'd grown hard and the tight fit was killing him. He needed to adjust himself, but that wasn't gonna happen. Instead, he dropped his hand and cupped her chin. "I got plans tomorrow night, but I'm gonna break 'em," the deep timbre of his voice rumbling out of him.

She leaned up, but even in her black boots, she wasn't eye to eye with him. "What's that got to do with me?"

He hitched a brow while they stared into each other's eyes. "Everything."

Her mouth was on his, the intensity of her kiss sending a rush of energy whipping through him. He clutched her in his arms, drew her flush against him, and welcomed her eager tongue. She groaned into his mouth while she slipped her hand into his hair, gathered it in her fingers and tugged.

Mewling like a feral cat, she thrust her tongue against his. He couldn't slow down, couldn't stop growling. Then, she bit his lower lip before abruptly ending their embrace.

"Ohgod." She sucked down several jagged breaths.

"Here, tomorrow night." He walked out, leaving her alone in the purple room.

3

INVITATION TO ESCAPE

Stunned, Liv stood there trying to get her breathing under control. She'd been on fire from the moment she'd laid eyes on him. Seeing Jericho brought back the best of memories… and the worst. He vowed he'd destroy her if they ever crossed paths again.

And she couldn't blame him. She deserved his vengeance.

But… he had no idea who she was and she'd keep it that way.

Back on the first floor, she found Addison cleaning up. With her heart pounding out of her chest, she swept her gaze across the room. Jericho was gone.

The tension running down her shoulders released.

Addison rushed over. "We did it! We did it." She threw her arms around Liv, her elated expression a joy to see.

"Congratulations!" Liv exclaimed.

"You, too. After we clean up, we've got to have a drink."

No argument from Liv, though she'd be drinking for a completely different reason.

Thirty minutes later, the place looked like it did before the event began. After the bouncer left, Liv locked the front door and pulled up a stool at the bar.

"What can I get you?" Addison asked.

"I'll take some of that expensive tequila." Liv removed her mask and pulled off the cowl, then finger-combed through her long, wavy hair.

Addison poured a finger's worth in each glass, then sat beside her cousin. "This is so huge. I'm so proud of us."

"Me, too, honey," Liv said. "We've got some kinks to iron out, but Hawk and his friend really came through for us."

"I can't believe you've never met Jericho before tonight," Addison said. "He seemed pretty pissed when he left. Did something happen upstairs?"

"We kissed."

Addison's glass froze in midair. "No way. Well, I wouldn't have expected that. You two are so different."

"He's very sexy with all that raw, animal magnetism. And, mygod, so hot. I kinda mauled him."

Addison eyes grew large before she took a mouthful of tequila. "That's not like you, but I love that he's pushing your buttons. Jericho's like a grizzly bear… or a mountain man." She paused. "He's a grizzly mountain man, that's what he is."

"I love that about him. He's a beast. Like someone who would tear off my clothes to get at me."

Addison laughed. "Wow. I have never, *ever*, heard you talk like this."

"He wants to meet here, tomorrow. But I won't play until we close."

"You're one of the owners. You can do whatever you want."

"I'm not gonna abandon you."

"Liv, I got this, plus we've got a few employees. I'm already looking for a bartender, so don't sweat it. Seriously. Have some fun. You haven't done that since you've been back. All you do is work. Work, work, work."

Liv sipped the tequila. "Do you remember that summer at the lake when we told each other all our secrets?"

"Not sure those secrets were that big of a deal."

"Well, I was a freshman and I had that huge crush on that senior." Pausing, Liv sipped the liquor. "It's funny. I can't even remember his name."

"I was in middle school and had that secret high school boyfriend."

"How did your dad not know about him?"

"Because I was good at being sneaky." Addison swallowed down another mouthful. "I'm even better at it—" She pursed her lips.

"What secrets do you have, now?" Liv asked. "I mean, besides our club?"

Addison stared into her glass before downing the remains. With a sweet smile, she said, "All the kinky things I want to do when I'm here."

Both women laughed.

"And you get to start tomorrow night," Addison said. "Lucky girl!"

Liv finished her drink. "We'll see."

"What made you bring up secrets?" Addison asked.

Liv hesitated. "No reason."

Addison peered over at her for an extra beat. "Yeah, not buying that."

Liv poured more tequila into their glasses. "You can't say—"

"Don't even—"

"You and Hawk are best buds."

"You're my ride or die friend *and* my favorite family member." Addison beckoned with her fingers, gesturing for her to talk. "Give it up, babe."

"Okay, so I know Jericho. Well, I *used* to know him."

"No way."

"We were best friends in high school."

"With benefits?" Addison asked.

"Uh, no." Liv tucked her hair behind her ear. "I was living

under Bernard's roof. You know, my dad ruled with an iron fist. I didn't even kiss a guy until college."

Sipping the tequila, Addison waited.

"I ruined our friendship," Liv continued. "Killed it, obliterated it. He hates me and I deserve it."

"What happened?"

"I've never talked about this to anyone." Anxiety had her heart pounding faster.

Addison took her hand.

"You know how my dad never let any of us go to parties."

"But didn't Shelby sneak out all the time?"

"All the time. I never did, except for this one time, junior year. There was a party on the next street, so I snuck out and went. I was drinking and having the best time. It felt amazing to be out with my friends." Liv sipped the tequila. "I'd been sticking close to Jericho, but at some point, I broke away to talk to some friends, then go to the bathroom. There was this guy, Perry. He was a senior and super cool. He found me standing in the bathroom line and told me there were bathrooms upstairs." Liv's heart kicked up in her chest. "I was naïve and gullible, so I went with him. Instead of taking me to the hall bathroom, he brought me to the one in the parent's bedroom. After I used it, he cornered me as I tried to leave." A shudder slid down her spine and she trembled.

Addison gave her hand an encouraging squeeze. "Take your time."

He'd pinned me against a wall and was kissing me—or trying to—I was fighting him pretty hard, but he was strong. He'd unzipped his pants and pulled out his penis when Jericho burst in. He pulled him off me and told me to run home." Liv was full-on shaking and she pulled her hand from Addison's to hug herself. "Sorry, I've never talked about this before." Her chest tightened and tears pricked her eyes.

Addison pushed off the stool and hugged her. "You're lucky

Jericho went looking for you. I don't understand why he was angry."

"He beat up Perry really badly. Perry told his parents and his dad pressed charges against Jericho. Jericho told the police the truth about what happened." Shame and guilt swept through Liv. "When the police came over to verify his story, my dad told them Jericho was lying."

"Ohgod, no," Addison whispered.

"I was so scared of what my dad would do to me, I didn't corroborate Jericho's story. He got charged as a juvi and it messed his life up for a while. He never spoke to me again."

"I'm so sorry. Why didn't you ever tell me?"

Liv broke eye contact. "I wasn't okay, not for a while. I was ashamed, scared, confused. Losing Jericho broke my heart, but I didn't have the courage to tell the truth." She sighed. "He hates me and I don't blame him. If he finds out I'm Catwoman, he'll want nothing to do with me."

"Maybe he will."

"Not Jericho. He can hold a grudge forever. Thing is, I'm super attracted to him, plus seeing him again made me so happy. Please don't tell him it's me."

"I would never."

Liv hugged her. "Thank you for listening."

"Oh, Livy, you're shaking." Addison rubbed her cousin's back.

Liv heaved in a breath. "I'm okay."

Once outside, they locked the front door, then walked to their cars. Her heart felt heavy. The emotions she'd buried long ago had risen to the surface. She needed to confront her past and make things right between her and Jericho.

She drove home thinking about him. Would she accept his club invitation and how would she keep him from finding out who she was? Once at home, she stripped out of her costume and stepped into the shower. As she crawled into bed, she checked her phone.

One message waited in the Lost Souls app. Excitement coursed through her as she clicked on it, but disappointment filled her when she saw that Guapo had sent her an Invitation to Escape.

She wasn't interested, so she declined his invitation and didn't leave him a private note. After setting her phone down and turning out her light, she stared out the picture window at the city across the river.

So pretty.

Her phone buzzed with a message. She tapped on the Lost Souls app and her heart dipped.

"I promise you'll have a good time," Guapo wrote.

Liv wasn't interested, so she didn't reply.

Relaxing against her propped pillows, she fixed her gaze out the window and thought about kissing Jericho. It was two in the morning, she was too wired to sleep, but she had a meeting with the Fairfax County Chief of Police at ten.

As she closed her eyes, her phone buzzed again.

This Guapo guy needs to be told no. That's the only way he'll get off my back. When she tapped into the app, her heart skipped a beat.

Jericho had invited her to escape with him in the Purple Room at ten o'clock that evening, and he sent her a private note. "One kiss was not enough."

Liv accepted his invitation and sent him a reply. "Gotta say, it was a great start."

If he knew the truth, he'd never hook up with her. She would make sure he had a good time, then never see him again. It would be her apology for what she did to him.

Yeah, like that's gonna even the score.

If he learned who she really was, he'd want nothing to do with her. Absolutely nothing.

Or he'll do everything in his power to shred my life, just like I did his.

Jericho got to Lost Souls fifteen minutes before his scheduled Invitation to Escape so he could appreciate Catwoman slinking around the bar. But she wasn't there. Addison and some guy were slinging drinks.

She'd hijacked his thoughts the entire day and he was more than ready to spend the evening with her.

More. Than. Ready.

But he knew how to take care of a woman, so tonight wouldn't be about him. It was going to be about her, starting with that damn costume. He couldn't wait to strip it off her. What did she look like? Did she have long hair or shorter hair? Blonde, brunette, redhead or something in between? After thinking about her all day, he couldn't wait to find out.

Once Addison had served him a top-shelf whiskey, he headed to a corner booth. Sitting alone, he nursed his drink while surveying the crowd. Compared to last night, things were running smooth.

It had been years since he'd opened his first restaurant, but the first-night jitters were still fresh in his mind. His plan, after high school, was to enlist in the Navy, looking to earn a coveted spot as a SEAL. When his life went sideways, he tended bar until he could figure out next steps. It was his beloved Gram who gave him the money to open his own restaurant. It was a huge first step, but she had so much confidence in him, he wasn't gonna let her down. At nineteen, he didn't know the first thing about running a business. Now, fourteen years later, he owned a dozen restaurants and clubs in Northern Virginia. Some he owned alone, but his band of brothers—Stryker, Cooper, Hawk, and Prescott—had chipped in as silent partners. Pooling their monies had been a smart decision for all of them.

A server swung by. "How you doing with that drink?"

He eyed the almost empty glass. "I'm good, thanks."

She glanced at his arms. He'd worn a different Thor costume.

Last night, he'd worn one with sleeves, but this costume was a breast plate that left his arms exposed.

"You've got some amazing guns," she said. "Wow, just wow. You could lift me with one hand and toss me like a ball."

His gaze did not drop to her body. That would be him checking her out. He wasn't interested.

A costumed customer loomed into view wearing a smile and a two-piece outfit that showed more skin than he needed to see. Since he knew nothing about popular cosplay costumes, he had no idea who she was.

"Hello, Thor." She slid into the booth across from him. "You look lonely."

"Can I get you a drink?" asked the server.

"What are you drinking?" she asked him.

"Whiskey, neat," Jericho replied.

The woman scrunched her nose. "I'll have a wine spritzer."

On a nod, the server left.

"I'm with my friends," said the stranger. "Who are you with?"

"I'm waitin' on someone."

"Can I borrow you while you wait? I've got a room reserved and I'd love to see how you wield your hammer."

His attention got hijacked when Catwoman moseyed in. Adrenaline and frustration spiked through him. Still covered from head to foot, she'd swapped out her boots for sandal stilettos, but she hadn't ditched the cowl or that damn mask.

Dammit.

She stopped to talk to Addison who tugged down on the suit's center zipper, exposing more of her breasts. When Catwoman started to zip it back up, Addison slapped her hand.

Thank you, Addison.

Addison pointed his way. She turned toward him. Their eyes met. Even across the room, the attraction was palpable. He couldn't look away, couldn't stop checking her out. Couldn't stop the desire pounding through him.

One controlled step at a time, she sauntered over.

He pushed out of the booth.

Even in her heels, she had to tilt her head. His heart pounded hard and fast as he stared into her whiskey-colored eyes.

She placed her hand on his shoulder, pushed onto her toes, and kissed him. One simple peck on his lips that jump-started his libido. "Hi."

"How ya doin?"

She curled her fingers around his triceps sending electricity coursing through him. To his surprise, she was trembling. That, he wasn't expecting.

"You look great." He ran his hand down her arm, hoping to calm her.

Maybe the cosplay scene wasn't her thing. Maybe she'd changed her mind about hooking up. While he'd wanted to ask Hawk about her, he hadn't. He wanted to get to know her firsthand and *not* filtered by Hawk. As much as he loved his friend, Hawk wasn't the best person to ask about women.

She glanced behind him. "Who's your friend?"

"You're hot," the woman said to Catwoman. "I've been into cosplay for years, but the kink scene is new. I'm open to anything."

Catwoman flicked her gaze to him. "Is she… did you—"

"Just us," he murmured before kissing her, this time letting his lips linger on hers. That simple, innocent gesture revved his engine, but it was the way she smelled that had the strangest effect on him. She smelled… familiar. He stared into her eyes, searching for a clue, but he had no idea who she was.

"Hello?" The woman had slid out of the booth and stood beside them. "Is this party for three?"

"No," Catwoman replied. "It's not."

Ignoring her, the woman smiled at Jericho. "I'll look you up." She stroked his arm. "See ya, Thor." She slithered toward the dance floor.

Jericho shifted his attention. She was studying him so freakin' hard. "You okay?"

Blinking softened her gaze. "Just thinking."

He gestured to the booth. "You wanna sit, get to know each other?"

Surprised flashed across her face. "So, about that... I'm more about no-strings sex. I'm super attracted to you and I like that we *don't* know each other. If that's not what you want—"

"Works for me."

The tightness around her mouth relaxed. She didn't smile, but maybe she was too damn nervous about the hookup. In a matter of minutes, he'd have her splayed on her back and loving every single thing he was doing to her.

He dropped cash on the table and extended his hand.

When she folded her fingers around his, he pulled her close and kissed her. "Why are you shaking?" he asked. "I gotta know you're okay before we go upstairs."

"This is gonna make me sound like a prude, but I've never hooked up with anyone. Even though we don't know each other, we know the same people, so..."

"You can hunt me down—"

"I feel safe with you."

His heart swelled in his chest. Those words meant everything to him, yet the guilt still crept into his soul. He was a cold-blooded assassin. He took out bad guys without remorse. But when it came to a woman, he wanted her to feel safe around him... always.

She peered into his eyes. "Did I say something wrong?"

"All good. What about tonight? You wanna role play?" He didn't know the first thing about it, but he could fake his way through. How difficult could it be?

"Are you into that?"

"Never done it."

"Let's keep this simple." She peered into his eyes while the electricity crackled around them. "I want to fuck you and I want you to fuck me back." she said, her voice gritty with lust.

A growl shot out of him. That, he could do.

With his hand on the small of her contoured back, he led her to the elevator, pushed the button. Need thrummed through him. When the doors slid open, she entered. He followed. Before the doors closed, they came together in a whoosh of energy, their mouths crashing into each other's while she pressed her curvy body against his hard one.

But it was the intensity of her kiss that turned him hard as steel. Tongues against tongues, bodies sandwiched together. The harder she ground into him, the more he needed to bury himself inside her heat.

The doors opened to the dimly-lit second floor. Panting, she broke away. He clasped her hand and took off down the quiet hallway until he got to the last suite on the right. The door was closed, so he stood in front of the scanner. The light turned green, he opened the door and gestured for her to enter. When she did, he shut the door behind them.

Nothing but sweet, sweet ecstasy awaited them.

The purple light bathed the room in a sexy glow, but his full attention was fixated on her. Her breathing had shifted, her shoulders rising and falling as she sucked down air.

"I need you naked," she murmured. Confident hands helped him out of his costume. Relieved she'd stopped shaking, he stood in the center of the room while she removed his breast plate, then undid his black, leather pants and freed his trapped cock.

He'd gone commando.

He stood there comfortable in his nakedness, his hard-on shooting to the moon, his gaze cemented on hers.

She wrapped her fingers around his long, thick shaft. "One size does *not* fit all."

He chuffed out a laugh. He loved a woman with a sense of humor. "Too small? Too large?"

"Just right."

He was ready for anything and everything… and he couldn't fucking wait.

Liv had opened the club to explore sex with strangers. But when it came to Jericho, she just wanted Jericho.

At the moment, she was clinging to what little self-control she had left. Unable to stop moaning or running her fingers over his sculpted body, she needed him on her, in her. She wanted to appreciate everything he'd grown into, every sexy thing he'd become.

Jericho Savage was total male perfection. So much to explore, so much undeserving pleasure. She loved the granite curves of his biceps and triceps, his sinewy shoulders and strong neck. His pecs were hard muscles under soft, tanned skin.

And those thick, toned thighs were like Sequoia tree trunks. Her insides were pulsing so hard, she had to force herself to focus on him. If she didn't, she'd rip off her costume, roll a condom over him, and fuck him hard and fast. Their moment would be just that… and she wanted—*no, she needed*—to make their evening last as long as possible.

This should have been about hooking up and moving on, yet they stood, unmoving, staring into each other's eyes while their hands explored. His on her ass, hers on his sublime back. Strength beneath silky-soft skin. When she grabbed his tight ass and squeezed, her panties turned to liquid.

"You are so fucking sexy," she murmured. "I need you deep inside me."

A half groan, half growl rumbled from the depths of his chest. "I'm gonna fuck you good." His deep timbre vibrated through her while his piercing gaze turned her inside out.

Kneeling at his feet, she stroked his cock while its moist head glistened in the purplish light. She lifted her face toward his. "Are you clean? Should I cover you in a condom first?"

"I'm clean. Taste me."

With her gaze still on his, she licked his shaft, then ran her tongue over its head.

"Fuck, yeah."

She did it again and again before taking him into her mouth. His excitement oozed and she moaned, the pulsing between her legs impossible to ignore. With her fingers around his massive shaft, she guided him into her mouth. He was too big to take in all of him, but she appreciated what she could handle.

Strong hands gripped her shoulders while she ran her teeth lightly over his shaft before circling the head with her tongue.

His husky groans matched her own, the pleasure forcing her to close her eyes. As she found her rhythm, she was able to take more of him in her mouth. All she wanted to do was pleasure him, make him feel good until the eruption of ecstasy exploded out of him in a torrent of need.

The more she sucked, the deeper his groans. "I'm gonna come. You can pull—"

She didn't want to pull off. She wanted to be a dirty girl. She wanted to suck him dry. She wanted him for that one night in every way that made her a woman and him a man. Her insides pulsed so hard, and her throbbing clit was about to explode from the overwhelming desire.

She relaxed her jaw and stroked his shaft, now soaked from his own lubrication along with her saliva.

"I'm gonna come so fucking hard."

His orgasm shot out of him and down her throat, drenching her with his ecstasy. She couldn't swallow all of it, so some dribbled down her chin. Never before had she let herself go with such wild abandon.

The freedom felt exhilarating.

When he finished, she slowly pulled off. Then, she disappeared into the bathroom to clean off. Seconds later, she found him standing in the middle of the room, his eyes lidded, his face relaxed. She stood tall and kissed him. He held her tightly and returned the embrace with strong, ardent strokes of his tongue that made her weak in the knees.

When the kiss ended, they stared into each other's eyes. More guilt crept in. She could have been honest and told him who she was, but he never would have agreed to this.

Never.

"Fuck, you're good at that." His baritone voice rumbled through her.

Even that had changed over the years. Deeper and more masculine than she remembered.

"I need you naked," he said. "We gotta get you out of that damn mask."

"Naked, yes, but I'm not taking off the cowl or the mask."

His eyebrows jutted into his forehead for a brief second before he shrugged it off. "I don't even know your real name."

"That's not what this club is about, for me. Let's not make this complicated—"

"Fuck, you're married." She couldn't miss the bite in his tone.

"I'm not, and I'm not in a relationship either." It hadn't occurred to her that he was with someone, but how could he not be? That woman from earlier was interested. "I'm not into men who are with other women, but for tonight, I don't want to know—"

"I'm single." He clasped her zipper. "Love the costume. Gonna love it more when it's on the floor." While staring into her eyes, he tugged down on the zipper until it bumped against the belt. Then, he unfastened the belt and continued to unzip until it reached the end. At her crotch.

The spandex gave way, letting her breasts spill out. His gaze dropped to her chest. "Jesus, your breasts are phenomenal. You got some full-sized girls, there."

The throbbing between her legs had spread to... everywhere. Like a geyser, she was about to burst.

"Please," she begged. "I'm on fire. I can't—"

"I got you." He kissed her while he fondled her breast with one hand and massaged her ass with the other. After teasing her hard nipple with his thumb, he lowered his head and sucked.

"Ohgod, yessss," she hissed.

She sunk her fingers into his long hair and choked out a sound while his talented tongue flicked over her sensitive skin.

The harder he sucked or licked or pinched, the more ardent her mewling. He was evoking sounds out of her she'd never made before. Then, he broke away, leaving her desperate for his touch. He stripped her out of the costume, leaving her naked, save for the cowl over her head and her mask.

She wanted to pull off the cowl so he could run his hands through her hair, so she could feel his fingers on the back of her neck. She needed the damn mask gone, too, but that wasn't happening either.

"Time to take that damn cowl off." He slipped his fingers under the material.

She covered his hands with hers and pulled them away. "No."

He let go, backing away without protest. Her heart warmed with appreciation.

He pulled her close, pressing his hard chest to her soft one, and slipped his hand around the back of her neck, over the cowl. His mouth found hers and his tongue pressed inside. She raked her fingers through his hair, tugging on the thick strands. When the kiss turned incendiary, he broke away, panting. Then, he brought her to the bed, threw back the sheet.

"I gotta taste your pussy."

She trembled, the excitement coursing through her. Jericho's face between her legs was the ultimate turn on. She loved that he wanted to eat her, loved that she could spread her legs wide for him.

As soon as she lay down, he placed a pillow beneath her head. "Watch me eat you."

"Ohmygod," she bleated.

Planking over her, he stared into her eyes, as if searching her masked face for a clue. Another tremble skirted through her. *Please don't recognize me.*

"You're so fuckin' hot," he murmured.

She melted from his panty-searing kiss. He nibbled her neck, kissed her chest, then her breasts and nipples. His moans made her shudder, the intensity of his mouth on her body exhilarating. Being with him was so surreal. By the time he kissed his way past her tummy to her pussy, she was shaking with desire, her body primed, soaked, and desperate for a release.

With his face between her legs, he stared into her eyes. "You've got the body of a goddess. I can't wait to make you come."

He stroked her dripping pussy, then lowered his face. Jericho licked her clit and ran his talented tongue over the entire length of her opening. She cried out, every nerve in that small, sensitive area poised to explode.

He took his time, licking and stroking, but when he sucked the hood of her clit, she started writhing beneath him.

"Ohmygod, ohmygod," she moaned. "So good. More than I deserve."

Her brain shorted. She held her breath, but he didn't stop. Relief flooded her and she inhaled. With his face buried in her pussy, he stroked her inner thighs. Back and forth while his tongue worked its magic on her. Then, he fingered her while sliding one hand under her ass and pulling her closer.

The euphoria sent her soaring higher and higher. *This* Jericho was beyond her wildest imagination. He was in complete control of her body, slowing down right before she'd climax, then building her up all over again.

She couldn't breathe, couldn't think, couldn't stop writhing or crying out. The power in his touch, his hot breath on her sex, his husky groans that reverberated through her, all propelled her toward a dizzying climax.

The release started deep inside, exploding out of her in a violent wave of ecstasy, tearing through her like a tornado. She cried out, then groaned as she bucked and convulsed from the onslaught of pleasure.

The ecstasy was exhilarating and draining. The aftershocks pulsated through her even after he withdrew his fingers and mouth. But he didn't wipe his face on the sheet or leave her for the bathroom. He hovered over her and dropped his mouth on one nipple, then the other, while he massaged and fondled her womanly mounds. Her nipples were gloriously tender from his mouth and teeth and she loved every carnal second with him.

Then, he stared down at her, a wildness emanating from his eyes, made black by the purple light.

"We're just getting started." He took her hand and placed it on his shaft. He was ready to go, no wait-time needed.

She needed to keep their hook-up as impersonal as possible. "Fuck me from behind."

"Not the first time," he pushed back. "Not with tits like that or a mouth made for kissing. No fucking way."

Jericho had changed in a lot of ways, but his absolute desire for control had not.

"No offense to Addison," he said, "but I got my own condoms. Latex and no-latex."

"Either work. What's wrong with the condoms?" Liv had blurted that stupid question before realizing it only mattered to business-owner Liv, not fuck-partner Liv.

"I need extra-large." He extracted a few from his pants pocket, then walked into the bathroom, flicked on the light. "Too fucking bright." A few seconds later, he returned. He tossed two down and tore open the third packet. "Tell her to lower the damn wattage in the bathroom."

She stifled a laugh.

"That's funny? I'm still seeing those bulbs like a shit-ton of blinding, yellow suns."

He rolled on a condom as she rolled onto her stomach and raised her ass off the bed.

After crawling on, he kissed both butt cheeks, then caressed her skin. "You got a sexy, sexy ass. Who are you? Seriously? I thought I knew everyone in this town. How did I not meet you?"

She craned around. "Too many questions."

"I'll fuck you from behind, but I'm not gonna come this way."

"Why not?"

"I gotta kiss you."

She lowered her head so he couldn't see her, and she smiled. She liked kissing him too.

"Drop down for me."

When she did, he positioned his cock at her opening. Slowly, he entered her and moaned. "Jesus, you feel good. Nice and tight."

Taking his time, he worked his massive shaft into her expanding space. "I'm a big boy. You doing okay?"

"Mhm. You feel amazing." She lowered down onto her elbows and he thrust the rest of the way.

"You are so wet for me." With both hands on her hips, he started thrusting. The more he thrust, the more she wanted him to thrust.

"Harder," she commanded.

"We gotta work up to that, darlin'."

She loved how he fucked her. Slow, deep, and so damn good. More than that, she loved that it was *him* doing the fucking.

He thrust to her end and withdrew, their moans falling in line with each other. She loved having him inside her, loved knowing that she could bring him the ultimate pleasure.

She owed him that, at the very least.

She started moving against his thrusts, faster and faster.

"Jesus, you feel too fucking good," he growled.

"Take me. Fuck me hard. Fuck me for your own pleasure. Punish me, Thor. I've been a bad, bad girl."

He took her hard and fast, tunneling into her with speed and intent. He released a long growl, then a series of garbled words, ending with, "coming so hard."

She massaged her clit, pushing herself over the edge. Wave after wave of orgasm had her shaking while her insides clamped down on him.

"Whoa, you're milking me dry," he ground out. "Fuuuuuuck."

Liv couldn't have had sex while staring into his eyes. It would have been too personal. It would have been more than she could handle. Sex with Jericho had never happened before. And if she could control herself around him, it would never, ever happen again.

But she knew the truth. Her truth.

She was just getting started.

That man was as good as it gets.

4

MAYHEM

The following afternoon, Jericho walked into Henninger Security. Hawk stood by the check-in counter talking to owner, Tucker Henninger. The state-of-the-art facility offered gun enthusiasts, and law enforcement personnel, shooting ranges plus an array of classes that included gun safety and personal defense.

When Hawk saw Jericho, he waved, like Jericho wouldn't have been able to find him otherwise. After Jericho tossed a nod to Tucker, Hawk and Tucker continued their conversation.

"So, these ghost guns are a real problem," Tucker said. "When someone joins here, I include the weapon's serial number."

"Got it," Hawk said, as his phone rang in his pocket.

"Since ghost guns don't have serial numbers, it makes it hard as hell for me to register them," Tucker explained.

"Why do you register weapons?" Jericho asked.

"Keep the crazies from joining. They might not be so willing to register their weapon if they're about to go shoot someone."

The conversation continued, but Jericho was distracted by thoughts of Catwoman. After sex, she'd dressed in the bathroom, then took off. It wasn't like he wanted to snuggle, but he coulda taken a brief break and gone another round with her. That's how much she did it for him.

Didn't matter that she'd bolted. He was confident they weren't finished. Last night was too damn fun.

After Hawk finished up with Tucker, he and Jericho took off toward the firing range. Once inside, they found two lanes next to each other and started prepping. For them, it meant ear protection, goggles, vests. It was one thing to get hit during a mission, but he'd seen people get shot by accident at target practice.

Today, he'd brought two guns. His ALPHA-assigned Glock and assault rifle. After they finished firing multiple rounds with their handguns, they packed up and made their way toward the back exit.

Tucker's outside range was available to a select group of law enforcement clients. Years ago, he and Hawk had flashed their ALPHA-assigned FBI badges, told Tucker they were undercover, and left it at that. As ALPHA Operatives, they'd been given badges to most three-letter agencies, which included FBI, DEA, ATF, CIA plus the State Department. Smoke and mirrors to cloak their top-secret organization.

Jericho swiped his membership card at the back exit. The lock clicked and out they went.

"Why haven't you installed scanners here?" Jericho asked as they made their way to the firing area.

"Tucker doesn't want to spend the money," Hawk replied.

The outside shooting range was like a small village with four abandoned buildings. Local law enforcement departments used the facility when training their rookies. Today, the two men had the place to themselves.

After ascending the stairs in the five-story building, they walked onto the roof. The bright sunlight had them slipping on their shades.

Jericho set up the tripod and attached his rifle. Next, he lay on the hot rooftop and aimed at the closest dummy. This was an easy hit, but he always started with that one, then went for the long-range targets.

Jericho set his position, inhaled and held, then fired.

BANG!

He hit the target in the abdomen.

BANG!

This time he missed the target altogether.

"What's going on with you?" Hawk asked.

"I can't concentrate."

"I got you."

"I don't need a spotter."

"You sure about that? Get over yourself and take my damn help."

"Fuck you," Jericho blurted.

"Ah, fuck you back," Hawk replied.

Both men laughed.

"The breeze is affecting the trajectory of the bullet," Hawk said. "Slide four inches to your left and angle the gun up five degrees."

Even though Jericho didn't like being told what to do, he repositioned himself and the rifle per Hawk's instruction.

"That's it," Hawk said. "And let out some of your breath before you fire. You're holding too much air and that's causing your shoulders to raise higher than they should be."

Jericho inhaled, then released some air, held, and fired.

BANG!

The bullet pierced the dummy between the eyes.

"You're welcome," Hawk said.

Jericho shot him a smile. "Thanks."

When Jericho set up for the next hit on a farther target, he missed. Again, he needed coaching from Hawk. Like the first time, he repositioned himself and his weapon, then fired. Worked again, but he was fighting the image of Catwoman. Her curvy body kept popping into his thoughts. Never before had anything or anyone gotten in the way of his ability to concentrate, especially at long-range practice.

Pushing to his feet, he raked his hands through his hair, then went in search of a hair tie. He found one in his duffle and pulled his hair into a half-bun. Then, he extracted a towel and wiped his face.

"I didn't have this problem the other night," Jericho said. "I think I'm gonna call it. I can't stay focused."

"Talk to me, babe." Hawk lit up a cigarette, took a long draw, and blew out the smoke.

"I hooked up with Catwoman last night."

"Nice. You should be *more* laid back, not less. No good?"

"It was great. She's cool. Super sexy."

"She doesn't seem like your type."

"What's that mean? It was a hookup."

"She's an intellectual. Lotsa degrees. I gotta say… she's hot, so I get why you're into her."

Jericho's chest tightened. "How do you know what she looks like? Did *you* fuck her?" His hands curled into fists.

"Hell, no. Relax, baby. You're a mess over this woman."

"What *does* she look like?"

"How the hell would I know?" Hawk puffed on the cigarette, then stomped it out. "You wanna shoot or what?"

"You're lying. You know her."

"I keep your secrets, bro, *and* I keep everyone else's." Hawk flashed a grin. "That's why everyone confides in me. Look, she doesn't want anyone to know who she is. Don't sweat it. You had fun. Did she?"

"I took good care of her."

"Then, do it again," Hawk replied.

"Maybe I will."

Jericho packed up, they trotted downstairs, signed out at the front desk, and left.

"Thanks for having my back today," Jericho said in the parking lot.

"You got it," Hawk replied.

"Me and Bryan are meeting my oldest brother for dinner."

"I thought *you* were the oldest," Hawk said.

"I got an older brother, Vincent. When my dad left us, Vincent went with him, but he's back. Come with us."

"You sure?"

"Absolutely," Jericho replied. "We're going to Raphael's."

Jericho's phone rang. It was his youngest brother, Bryan. Jericho answered. "What's up?"

"Are we meeting Vincent tonight?" Bryan asked.

"Yeah."

"If you come home, I'll grab a ride with you."

"Be there in twenty. You okay if Hawk comes with us?"

"Of course." Bryan hung up and Jericho shoved his phone in his pocket.

"Is your dad back too?" Hawk asked, picking up the conversation.

"No idea. I haven't heard from him since he walked out. Who abandons their wife and six kids? What a loser."

Jericho set his bag in his truck. "You wanna follow me?"

"Follow you? I'll be back at your place before you pull outta the parking lot." On a chuckle, Hawk jogged to his Mercedes convertible.

Jericho drove home with the windows open and the country music pulsing through his speakers. He hadn't thought of his dad in years, wasn't about to start now.

He parked in front of the house, next to Hawk's sports car, and found his friend chatting with Gram in the kitchen. She adored his friends, especially Hawk. She said he reminded her of her late husband.

Gram was ladling her homemade pasta sauce over a bowl of pasta.

"Thanks, Gram," Hawk said taking it from her. After a bite, he said, "Mmm, this has gotta be your best batch ever."

She beamed at him. "Thank you, sweetheart. Are you staying for dinner?"

"Not tonight. I'm going to Raphael's with the Savage bros."

"Come with us, Gram," Jericho offered.

"Thank you, honey, but that restaurant is too loud for me."

"We're eating in my private dining room."

Gram shook her head. "My book club friends are coming for dinner." She patted his back. "You have fun."

Hawk finished the bowl and dropped it in the dishwasher. "Perfection. If you have any left, I'll be back tomorrow."

Gram's eyes lit up. "I'll save some for you."

"Okay, I gotta get cleaned up," Hawk said to Jericho. "I need a shirt and where can I shower?"

"The guest suite in the basement is empty. Lemme grab you somethin'."

"Give him a shirt *after* he showers," Gram said with a laugh.

Jericho vanished upstairs and into his bedroom. He grabbed a button-down and returned to the kitchen where Hawk was showing his grandmother something on his phone.

He tossed the shirt at Hawk. "We're outta here in thirty," Jericho called out as he headed back upstairs.

Liv pulled up to her parents' home in Potomac and eyed the string of cars parked out front.

Dammit, they're having a dinner party.

When her mom had invited her over, she *assumed* it was going to be a simple evening, just the three of them. Her first mistake was assuming anything.

Once inside, as she made her way toward the kitchen, the conversations grew louder. Her mom and dad were on the porch surrounded by their usual group of friends, plus several people she didn't recognize.

Liv froze.

I can't do this, tonight.

As she slowly backed out of the room, her mom spotted her, broke from the group, and beelined inside.

"Livy! I'm so glad you could make it. We decided to throw a last-minute dinner party. Stanley's here. You remember Stanley, don't you?"

How could Liv forget? Stanley was the first and *last* time she let her mom fix her up. The weekend after she returned to the area, her parents threw a dinner party. Enter Stanley. He was pleasant looking, he had a good job with a big-four accounting firm, and he seemed nice enough, so she agreed to have coffee with him.

At the end of an hour, no sparks. Rather than ignore her gut, like she did with her former boyfriend, she didn't agree to see him again.

Clearly, her lack of interest in this man hadn't stopped her mom from inviting him over.

Her dad entered the kitchen. Judge Blackstone had a commanding presence that usually scared the hell out of any man she brought home for them to meet. If that wasn't bad enough, he never liked any of them anyway.

"Hi, Dad."

"You're staying for dinner, aren't you?"

Never any small talk. He always got right to the point.

"I can't."

"Your mom put this dinner party together with you in mind."

Guilt-trip time.

Liv laughed. "I don't think she invited *your* close personal friends for my benefit."

"How's the consulting going?" he asked.

When the conversation wasn't going his way, he'd change the subject.

"Fine."

"Livingston, when are you going to open your own practice? Hang your shingle… make a name for yourself. You're a brilliant psychologist. Hire several therapists and take a percentage of their fees. You could be *the* therapist in the mid-Atlantic region."

Ugh.

"Thanks for the advice, Dad. I'm good."

"Good is never—"

"Good enough," Liv said, finishing his sentence and forcing herself *not* to roll her eyes. That would only incite one of his long-winded lectures. He'd pace, point his finger at her, and pontificate. She'd rather swallow tacks.

Even without the lecture, her dad pointed his finger at her, in his attempt to drive his point home. "That's right. Good is never good enough. Gotta go for greatness. Open that practice."

Stanley sauntered in. "Hey, Liv."

"Livingston," her dad corrected.

Now, she really wanted to roll her eyes.

"Right, sorry, Judge Blackstone. Livingston. How are you doing, *Livingston?*" Stanley was staring at her dad.

Liv hated when men kowtowed to him. "Hi, Stanley," Liv replied.

With an over-the-top smile, her mom looped her arm through her dad's. "We'll let you catch up."

"If you two want to take off, have dinner elsewhere, we'll understand," her dad said before stepping onto the porch.

Why? Why are they doing this to me?

"So, Livingston, how've you been?" Stanley asked. "All settled in?"

"It's Liv," she replied, though she didn't care what Stanley called her. She was still doing battle with her father and he wasn't even in the damn room.

"But your dad said—"

"I've been busy," she replied, cutting him off. "How 'bout you?"

"I sent you a few texts about getting together. Have things slowed down for you?"

Stanley was attractive, but he wasn't *interesting* looking. He didn't make her tremble, and she had no interest in touching him or kissing him. There was no spark, zero connection, and absolutely no chemistry.

Jericho crashed into her thoughts. He was all those things, and she hadn't stopped thinking about him all day. She desperately wanted to see him, kiss him, touch him, and be touched by him. Heat spread up her chest, past her neck to her cheeks.

Ohgod, I'm dying for him.

She chugged down a jagged breath.

"So, anyhoo," Stanley continued. "I'd love to take you, if you're free."

She had no idea what he'd been talking about. "I'm sorry, Stanley. I don't think we're a good match."

"Is that you talking, or Dr. Blackstone, the psychologist?"

She laughed. "What's the difference?"

"Well, for one, our parents think we'd be great together. I do, too. We're both working professionals, both educated. I assume you want children. I do, too."

This man didn't know the first thing about her.

I'm outta here.

Liv smiled, not so much at him, but because she was very clear about what she liked, what she didn't. As a therapist, she was great at helping others. Not so much for herself. This time, however, there was no doubt in her mind.

"Sorry, but this isn't going to work." She headed toward the front door. "Goodbye, Stanley."

As she pulled the front door shut behind her, a sense of satisfaction had her throwing her shoulders back.

In her car, she pulled up her playlist, toggled to Queen, turned up the volume, and opened the sunroof. A gust of wind snagged the back of her hair and pulled it out the top.

For once, her father had actually helped her. She didn't want to work in a private practice. She was an independent, thirty-two-year-old woman who loved *both* her jobs. The consulting gig that everyone knew about... and the other one. The top-secret one no one knew existed.

And when it came to men, she knew exactly what she wanted and *who* she wanted. She wanted to explore her sexuality with Jericho. In costumes, out of costumes. She wanted it all, and she wanted it with him.

And *only* him.

Jericho, Hawk, and Bryan sailed into Raphael's, another popular eatery owned by Jericho. Vincent hadn't arrived, so the hostess seated them in Jericho's glass-enclosed, private dining room in the rear of the large restaurant. As she set the menus down, she smiled at Bryan.

"How do you guys know the boss man?" she asked, her gaze glued on Bryan.

"Brother," Bryan replied.

"Like a brother," Hawk replied.

"What do you do?" she asked Bryan.

"GW law school in the fall."

"Nice." One more smile. "Enjoy your meal. Your server will be right in."

"We got someone else coming," Jericho told her.

She nodded before leaving.

"You gotta follow up with that," Hawk said as he flipped open the menu.

"Maybe," Bryan said, "She was cute, but I'm super busy."

"You can never be too busy for a woman," Hawk said. "Never."

A few moments later, the hostess returned, this time with a man Jericho didn't recognize. As the guys pushed out of their chairs, she handed Bryan a folded napkin, set down the extra menu and scooted out.

Vincent Savage swept his gaze from Jericho to Hawk to Bryan, then threw out his arms. "Hey, brothers! Good to see you guys! It's been a while. Help me out. Who's who?"

"I'm Jericho."

Vincent extended his hand. Shaking hands with his brother felt alien to Jericho.

When their dad and Vincent first left, Jericho and Vincent had stayed in touch. But over time, they'd drifted apart. Now, nineteen years later, Jericho would have walked by his own brother on the street. As hard-muscled as Jericho was, Vincent was soft and pudgy. He was average height with short, light brown hair, and clean-shaven. He'd dressed in a pair of dark pants and a T-shirt.

"Dude, you got like a foot taller and you look like a mountain man," Vincent said. "I'm sure the ladies love you, huh?" He snorted. "Are you married? Jeez, I don't know anything about any of yous."

"This is Bryan," Jericho said introducing his youngest brother.

"Great to see ya," Vincent said shaking his hand. "How old were you when I left?"

"I was like—" Bryan looked at Jericho.

"Two," Jericho replied.

When Jericho was a freshman in high school, his dad had called all six Savage kids into the family room. When their mom came in, her eyes were swollen and red from crying, Roger Savage told his family that he was moving to Oklahoma, without them. When Vincent asked if he could go, their father told him he had fifteen minutes to pack his bags.

At fourteen, Jericho stepped up to help his mom with his four younger siblings. At first, his mom fell apart, but after a while, they found their way.

"Sorry, bro, which one are you?" Vincent asked Hawk.

"I'm Hawk, Jericho's friend." After shaking hands, the men sat.

The server had entered the private room, but waited by the door. He hurried over and offered a friendly smile. "Mr. Savage, good to see you again." He acknowledged the other three. "Can I tell you about tonight's specials?"

Once he did, he took their drink orders and left.

"So, Jericho, why the royal treatment?" Vincent asked.

"Jericho owns the restaurant," Bryan explained. "He owns several."

Vincent nodded. "Me likey. Whatcha got? Any strip bars?" He threw his head back and laughed. "I'm always up for a good time."

"No strip bars," Jericho replied. "Why'd you move back?"

"I manage a casket company."

"That's not morbid or anything," Hawk mumbled.

"Dad owns a midsize casket company in Oklahoma," Vincent explained. "We moved back here, oh, about a month ago, to break into the East Coast market. We got a small distribution center in Chantilly."

"Well, we do have a lot of dead people in this part of the country," Hawk added, "and they need a home, too."

Bryan laughed.

"You married?" Jericho asked.

"Divorced twice, no kids. I'm a kid myself, so I got the snip-snip years ago. Don't want to find myself playing daddy when all I wanna do is play myself." He elbowed Hawk. "You get me, don'tcha?"

Hawk regarded him. "On so many levels," he said, the sarcasm oozing from him.

As Jericho and Hawk exchanged glances, Jericho bit back a smile.

"What's Dad up to?" Bryan asked. "I was hoping he'd be here."

Vincent shook his head. "No, you don't. Trust me on this. He's a mess. He's got a gambling problem that ain't purty. Do yourself a favor, don't call him. He'll ask you for money, then piss it away."

Bryan's shoulders dropped and Jericho's heart broke for his brother. Bryan was too young to remember their dad. Roger Savage wasn't the best, but he hadn't been the worst either… until he abandoned his family. Family was everything to Jericho and he resented his dad for leaving them.

While Jericho had no interest in spending any time with his father, he could understand why Bryan did. Jericho regarded his youngest brother. "You can always give him a call, you know."

The server returned with their entrées and the guys dug in. After a few minutes, the conversation resumed.

"Whad'ya do for fun around here?" Vincent asked.

"I own Jericho Road. It's a western-themed bar with line dancing and a mechanical bull. Place is always packed. You know your way around the area?"

"Hell, no," Vincent replied. "I just let the phone tell me where to go. Dang thing's smarter than me."

"You don't say," Hawk exclaimed, and Bryan snort-laughed.

"We can head over there after dinner, if you want," Jericho said. What he *really* wanted was to see Catwoman again, without the mask or the cowl. Her naked form popped into his head and a rumbly growl shot out of him.

"Got myself a girl, but I'm always up for meeting more purty ladies," Vincent said. "So, who's hitched, who's not?"

"None of us are married," Jericho replied.

"I like the *purty* ladies too much, myself, to pick just one," Hawk added.

Vincent threw his arm around Hawk. "You and me's gonna become real good buds. I can tell."

Hitching an eyebrow, Hawk said, "I can't fuckin' wait."

This time, both Jericho and Bryan laughed.

"I'd feel right at home with some line dancin'," Vincent continued. "What's the name of your place again?"

"Jericho Road."

"Need me to help with the spelling of Jericho?" Hawk asked, his tone still dripping with sarcasm.

"Nah, I think I remember," Vincent replied. "J-e-r-i-c-k-o."

"C-h-o," Bryan corrected him.

"What's Cho?" Vincent asked. "The club's nickname?"

"We call it *The Road*," Hawk piped in.

Vincent flicked his gaze from Hawk to Bryan. "Yous guys are confusin' me." He handed Hawk his phone. "Can you plug in Cho on my map app?"

With a smirk, Hawk got busy on Vincent's phone. The server came by to say goodbye. Since the meal was comped, Jericho handed him a cash tip.

"Thank you, Mr. Savage. I hope everything was to your liking."

"It was great."

After the server left, Vincent said, "If the meal was free, why'd you give him money?"

Hawk shook his head. "For fuck's sake, you do know servers work on tips?"

"Well, duh." Vincent pushed out of his seat. "I gotta use the little boys' room. Where's it at?"

Jericho pointed.

Once he'd left, Hawk blurted, "Hard to believe you three are related. Is it me, or is he as dumb as a bucket of fucking hair?"

Bryan laughed. "He's okay."

Jericho checked his phone for messages. "I don't remember him being this—"

"Stupid?" Hawk offered.

The brothers laughed.

Hawk gestured to the folded napkin left by the hostess. "Did she give you her number?"

Bryan read it out loud. "'You're so cute! Call me sometime.'" He grinned. "This never happens to me."

"Nice," Hawk added.

When Vincent walked past the private dining room, the three of them pushed out of their chairs.

"Where the hell's he going?" Hawk asked.

"Looks like he's headed toward the exit," Bryan added.

They found Vincent in the crowded waiting area looking lost. "Where'd you guys go?"

"Ohmygod," Hawk mumbled.

Ignoring him, Jericho glanced around for the hostess, hoping he could encourage Bryan to talk to her. She wasn't at the hostess stand.

"You wanna wait?" Jericho asked Bryan.

"Nah, I can text her," Bryan replied.

Jericho pushed open the door and walked outside. Darkness had settled in on the evening. No breeze, low humidity. He inhaled a deep breath. He'd take the guys over to The Road, check on things, then swing by Lost Souls, hoping to strike up a convo with the sexy, mysterious bartender.

The front door could be accessed by a long ramp or three steps. Both led to a large parking lot. As the guys headed toward the steps, a car drove slowly past. Everything happened in slow motion and, yet, it was over in an instant.

The passenger's arm stretched out the window, gun in hand.

"GET DOWN!" Jericho hollered.

BANG! BANG! BANG!

The car sped away as Jericho reached behind for his Glock. *Fuck, fuck me.* He'd left his weapon at home.

"Aiiiieeeee!" Bryan screamed.

"Jesus, I'm shot," Vincent blurted.

"Jericho, talk to me!" Hawk yelled.

Jericho rushed to Bryan's side. "Not hit! You?"

"No!" Hawk called out. "I got Vincent."

Blood gushed from Bryan's abdomen. Jericho yanked off his shirt and applied pressure to the wound. His brother was breathing, but he was unconscious. With his other hand, Jericho whipped out his phone, dialed 9-1-1.

The hostess ran outside, panic strewn across her face.

"Keep everyone inside!" Jericho yelled to the terrified young woman.

"What's your emergency?" asked the operator.

"There's been a shooting at Raphael's restaurant," Jericho explained. "My brothers were shot. One in the stomach. Don't know about the other." He gave her the address. While she wanted him to stay on the phone, he needed full attention on his brother.

"Hawk, update me," Jericho said.

"Vincent took one in the arm," Hawk said. "What's going on with Bryan?"

"A bullet in the gut." Without removing Bryan's shirt, he searched for another wound. "Not sure if he took a second."

Patrons walking in, stopped to stare in horror. A server came running out. "Use this." She thrust out a handful of towels.

"I don't want to stop applying pressure," he said. "Get everyone away from here."

She ushered everyone inside.

Jericho glanced over at Vincent. He was on the ground while Hawk applied pressure with a towel. He stared down at his brother, then leaned close. "I got you, bro. You're gonna be okay. You're doing great, Bryan. Hang in there with me, bud."

Jericho flicked his gaze into the parking lot, but the shooter was long gone.

First responders arrived. As a police cruiser pulled in, Jericho hollered for Hawk.

"I'm staying with Bryan," Jericho said. "Handle this for me."

"Got it," Hawk replied. "I'll get to the hospital as soon as I can."

Jericho tossed Hawk the keys to his truck.

A police officer asked what happened and Hawk stepped in.

Paramedics started Bryan on an IV, attached an oxygen mask around him, and secured his neck in a brace before carefully lifting his still body onto the gurney, then loading him into the ambulance.

"Are you coming with me?" Vincent asked Jericho.

"No," Jericho replied before jumping inside with Bryan.

On the ride over, he ran through the events. They were heading for the steps. The car—*I don't even remember the fucking color*—rolled by. Jericho saw the gun before the shots were fired, but not fast enough to protect Bryan. He regretted not bringing his weapon, but he wouldn't have opened fire. There had been too many civilians in the parking lot.

Minutes later, the ambulance pulled up to the hospital. Jericho jumped out and waited while they lowered the gurney. He stayed with Bryan as they rushed him inside. Bryan was taken to triage while Jericho stood there as the swinging silver doors shut him out.

He called Hawk.

"I'm still at the restaurant," Hawk answered. "Police are waiting for the crime techs to arrive. Customers aren't being allowed in and the manager is routing everyone out the back door. How's Bryan?"

"In triage. I gotta call my family. Can you swing by and pick up Gram?"

"As soon as I'm done here," Hawk said. "Hang in there. He's gonna be okay."

Jericho hung up and called Gram. A shiver skirted down his spine. After too many damn rings, she picked up.

"Hey, Gram, Hawk is coming by to get you."

"Hi, dear. What for?"

"There was a shooting." He swallowed, hard. "Bryan was hit."

"No, no, no, Jericho." The pain in Gram's voice shattered him.

He told Gram to be ready for Hawk and hung up. One by one, he called his siblings. Each time he told them, the knot in his chest grew tighter. When he hung up, a man waiting in the ER approached him.

The good Samaritan held out a sweatshirt. "You can have this."

"Thanks." He pulled it over his bare chest. It was tight, but it worked. "You wanna text me your address so I can get it back to you."

"It's okay. I hope everything works out." With a kind smile, the man returned to his seat.

Jericho stared at his hands. They were covered with Bryan's blood. He strode to the bathroom to wash off. He had blood on his face, too.

Is this the universe getting back at me for being an assassin? Don't take Bryan. Take your anger out on me.

Emotion tightened his throat and he threw water on his face, hoping to wash away the pain. Didn't help, not one fucking bit.

He returned to the waiting room, but he couldn't sit. The anger coursing through him made him want to punch his fist through a brick wall. Was that a random drive-by shooting? Doubtful.

Who'd I piss off—Ah, fuck. It was Al-Mazir's men.

They'd come after him, but missed. Or they wanted to get him back by taking out his guys.

Jericho would wage a full-blown assault against those motherfuckers if Bryan didn't make it.

The registration clerk hurried over. "The doctor wants to talk to you." She pointed toward the swinging double doors. "Go to the nurse's station."

He entered the triage area. Private rooms lined all four walls while a large nurse's station filled the center of the oversized space. He hurried over. "I'm Jericho Savage and my brothers were shot."

A doctor walked over. "Mr. Savage?"

"Yeah."

She clicked on a tablet. "Vincent Savage was hit in the arm. He's in surgery having the bullet removed. I expect him to make a full recovery."

"What about my younger brother, Bryan Savage?"

The doctor's expression fell and a pain shot through Jericho. "He's in surgery. There was a second bullet lodged between his ribs. The damage to his internal organs is more extensive. We've got a great surgical team working on him, but it's gonna be a while. If you give us your number, we'll call you once they're out of surgery."

Jericho rambled off his number and returned to the waiting room where he stood by the windows, staring out at nothing. His thoughts were locked on finding the motherfuckers who attacked his family.

His phone rang with a call from his brother, Tim. Thirty-year-old Tim Savage lived in Fairfax with his wife and two children. "I just got your message."

After Jericho updated him, Tim told him that both Annie and Owen were sick and his wife was at a different hospital with her sister, who was in labor. "I'm sorry I can't be there. How you holding up?"

"I'm okay," he lied.

From the moment his dad left, all he ever fucking said was "'I'm okay.'" But he wasn't okay then, and he wasn't okay when Gram had to move in because their mom got sick. He sure as fuck wasn't okay when she died. And he wasn't okay now.

But he'd always been their rock. They'd spent their lives leaning on him. Kinda hard to switch roles now.

"What's wrong with the kids?" Jericho asked.

At this point, he was on auto-pilot.

"Annie has strep and Owen's battling a cold, but we're watching him for strep."

"I hope they feel better." Jericho's phone buzzed with an incoming call. "Gotta go." He hung up and answered. It was his other brother, Mark.

"I'm trying to find someone to cover for me," Mark said. "What's happening?"

"They're both in surgery. Vincent's got a flesh wound. Bryan's not doin' so good."

"I'll be there as soon as I can."

As Jericho hung up, Hawk pulled up to the curb. Jericho strode outside, opened the passenger door and helped his grandmother out.

Normally stoic, fear sprang from her eyes. That took him right back to when his mom had died. He'd seen that same look, mixed with grief. Now, here they were, all these years later, staring into each other's eyes again.

"Are you okay?" she asked. "Of course, you aren't. How's Bryan?"

Hawk strode over.

After Jericho updated them, Hawk left to park. He ushered Gram inside and found a vacant chair in the busy ER waiting room.

A few moments later, Hawk joined them. Jericho was too pent-up to sit, so Hawk did, and held Gram's hand.

Jericho hated that his grandmother was a wreck. Nothing he could do to calm her. He couldn't tell her everything was gonna be okay. He didn't fucking know.

Thirty minutes later, his phone rang. The surgeon would meet them in the ER lobby. The three of them made their way over. A moment later, the doctor walked over. "Are you the Savage family?"

"Yes," Jericho replied.

"Vincent is out of surgery. He did well, and has been moved upstairs to a room. He's still groggy, so please don't stay long."

"What about Bryan Savage?" Jericho asked.

"Still in surgery," said the doctor. "You'll be called as soon as he's out."

After thanking the doctor, they made their way to the elevator bank. On the walk to Vincent's room, Gram asked, "How long has Vincent been back?"

"He said about a month," Jericho answered.

"And my good-for-nothing son-in-law? Is he back?"

"Yeah," Jericho replied. "They opened a casket company in Oklahoma and a second one in Chantilly."

"I'd like to order one of their caskets," Gram said. "If I so much as see that son of a bitch, I'm going to put him in it, for good."

Hawk put his arm around her. "My kinda woman. Take no shit, take no prisoners."

They walked into Vincent's room. The overhead light was out, but the sink light illuminated the room. He was sleeping on his back, his arm in a sling.

Gram cleared her throat. Vincent's eyes fluttered open. His face was pasty white. "Hey, I'm all patched up."

"You're in town for a month and you don't call your grandmother. Shame on you Vincent Savage."

Jericho and Hawk exchanged glances.

"I'm sorry, Gram."

She leaned over, kissed his cheek. "How are you feeling?"

"My arm is sore as hell," Vincent said before shooting a glance in Jericho's direction. "I'll take a raincheck for a night at Cho."

Jericho tossed him a nod.

Knock-knock-knock.

A uniformed officer stood in the doorway. After introducing himself, he asked if he could come in.

"Sure," Vincent said.

"Mr. Savage," the officer said to Vincent, "I was wondering if you know of anyone who would want to hurt you."

"Nope. I just moved here from Oklahoma and was meeting my brothers for dinner."

"It's my restaurant," Jericho offered. "We can talk in the hallway."

Both men retreated into the corridor.

"Any reason to think this was a targeted hit?" asked the officer.

I just took out Al-Mazir, so, hell yeah, it was a revenge hit.

Jericho shook his head. "No. I haven't fired anyone recently. I also own Jericho Road—"

The officer smiled. "I love that place. It's a good time."

"Fights break out and I've kicked a few people out, but nothing major." Jericho shrugged, trying to play things chill. "I think it was wrong place, wrong time."

The officer jotted something down.

"I've got another brother in bad shape."

The officer checked his notes. "Is that Bryan Savage?"

"Yeah. He's in surgery."

"Can I get a copy of the surveillance video?"

"My manager will get it over to you." As Jericho finished texting his MOD, Gram and Hawk joined him in the hallway.

The officer handed Jericho his card. "Thanks for talking. I hope your other brother pulls through." He took off toward the elevator.

Jericho's head was buzzing. He needed to talk to Hawk about the Al-Mazir hit, but not until they were alone.

When they returned to the first floor, his sister Georgia was there, her eyes brimming with fear. She rushed over and hugged Jericho. "I got here as soon as I got your message."

After updating her, he suggested that she and Gram head to the cafeteria. Gram shook her head. "I'm waiting right here until the doctor comes out of surgery."

Jericho situated Gram and Georgia nearby, then pulled Hawk aside. "Do you think this was a deliberate hit?"

Hawk's eyebrows slashed down. "On who?"

"Me, 'cause of Al-Mazir."

Hawk broke eye contact and fished a cigarette out of the pack. He raked his hand through his hair and down his scruffy cheeks. A long moment passed before he regarded Jericho. "They would have taken you out, not your brothers."

"Maybe the motherfucker was a terrible shot," Jericho murmured.

"A hit by Al-Mazir's terror cell would be targeted. That felt random. You and I weren't hit, but your brothers were. If anyone was gonna get pumped with bullets, it would be us."

"If they made you with me, then I agree. Unless they were trying to make me suffer by hurting my brothers."

"Doesn't really matter. Whoever did this is a dead man."

"Damn straight," Jericho replied. "I just gotta finish the job."

5

LIV'S SECRET ASSIGNMENT

The surgeon called Jericho with an update on Bryan. The medical team had found extensive organ damage and internal bleeding. She was able to remove the bullets, without causing further damage, and stop the bleeding. Now, it was up to Bryan. She wished him the best and hung up.

Jericho pushed down another massive wave of emotion as he tried softening the blow for his family before they made their way to Bryan's recovery room.

Georgia started crying when she saw Bryan hooked to tubes. At least he looked peaceful. An image of a young Bryan flashed in Jericho's mind. He was only six when their mom had died and too young to totally grasp the full extent of what had happened.

Night after night, Jericho had slept on Bryan's floor until he fell asleep. Because of Bryan, Jericho had hired a lawyer and become his four younger siblings' legal guardian. What choice did he have? They had no father and no mother. One of life's hardest curveballs.

As he stared down at his baby brother, he silently willed him to wake up.

C'mon, Bryan. Open your eyes. You can do it, bro. I know you can. Fight, Bryan. Fight like hell. You gotta live. You just gotta.

Georgia had pulled chairs on either side of the bed. Gram sat in one and took his hand. Georgia slumped in the other and clasped his other hand. Gram hadn't shed a tear, but one slipped down her cheek as she closed her eyes, bowed her head, and prayed.

Tears welled in Jericho's eyes. The weight on his chest felt like a herd of elephants were camping out on him. He needed to get out of there, needed to avenge his helpless brother. But he swallowed down the agony and stood guard over his family.

His brother Mark texted that he'd be there as soon as his shift at the hospital ended. Jericho replied with an update and told his brother to stay where he was. There had been no change.

Jericho couldn't stop the anger coursing through him. He paced in the hallway, he stood in the doorway, he stared down at Bryan from the foot of the bed. No change.

It was after three in the morning when Jericho asked Hawk if he'd drive Gram and Georgia home.

"I don't want to leave him," Gram replied.

"Why don't you and Georgia sit together on the sofa?" Jericho suggested. "Then I can have a coupla minutes with Bryan."

Gram looked like a shell of herself when Jericho helped her to the sofa. Normally, she was up by five and didn't slow down until the news ended at eleven thirty. At seventy-eight, she was a force to be reckoned with. Now, she looked like her heart had been ripped from her chest all over again.

The two settled on the sofa, holding hands.

"You can take off," Jericho said to Hawk.

From the nearby recliner, Hawk shook his head. "Not leaving you."

Jericho eased down beside his brother. He patted his hand, then held it. Then, he leaned forward and whispered what he always used to tell him when Bryan had trouble falling asleep. "I'm right here and I'm not going anywhere. I promise."

No response from his brother, so he gave his hand a gentle squeeze. After a while, Gram and Georgia fell asleep. Hawk pushed out of his chair.

"I'm gonna give you two some time together." Hawk squeezed Jericho's shoulder and left the room.

Jericho stared at the machine monitoring Bryan. His vitals hadn't changed much. Maybe a spike in his heart rate, then it would settle back down.

Jericho leaned close again. "You can't leave. You gotta fight, Bryan. Savages are tough. We can get through anything, as long as we've got each other. And we've always had each other's backs. I'm not leaving until you open your eyes."

Minutes ticked by.

Jericho whispered, "We got the closest because you needed me the most. Turns out, I was the one who needed you. I promise you, I will get to the truth, and when I do, I will annihilate the people who did this to you."

BEEP-BEEP-BEEP-BEEP-BEEP-BEEP-BEEP-BEEEEEEEEEEEEEEEEEE.

Jericho jerked his head toward the monitor. Bryan's heart rate had flatlined. "Oh, Jesus, we're losing him."

Hawk burst into the room, a coffee cup in hand. "I'll get the doc."

Georgia rushed over, her eyes wild with fear. "What's happening?"

"Come," Gram said. "Georgia, let's step out." Gram locked eyes with Jericho. Never before had he seen such anguish and helplessness emanating from them.

The medical team rushed in, ushered Jericho out, and closed the door behind him. Jericho had been with Bryan when he left this earth. Hell, maybe he'd even helped him let go and begin the long journey home.

Jericho couldn't breathe, and he couldn't control the stream of tears sliding down his cheeks. His heart had been shredded into a million pieces and left on the floor.

The medical team stayed in the room longer than Jericho would have expected. When they exited, they murmured their condolences.

The physician stopped. "I'm very sorry. His injuries were extensive. You're welcome to spend time with him. If you need help making arrangements—"

Jericho nodded. He had no words. No fucking words at all.

When they returned to Bryan's side, pain squeezed every muscle in Jericho's body. But he didn't give a fuck about how he was feeling. He only cared that his brother had been murdered and his family was in another free fall.

The tubes and wires had been removed. Bryan looked like he was sleeping, at peace. Jericho was grateful for that.

One by one, they said their goodbyes. Georgia was sobbing hard, and Gram was doing her best to console her. Emotion constricted around Jericho's throat like a boa, squeezing the breath out of him. One by one, they filed out, leaving Jericho alone with his brother.

As he peered down at Bryan's lifeless body, full-blown rage enveloped his soul. He would kill the motherfucker who did this. Rip out his heart and watch the light leave his eyes. Revenge burned a white-hot trail through him. Now, he was a man on fire.

"I won't fail you, brother," Jericho murmured. "You have my word."

Like zombies, they walked to the elevator. Leaving Bryan there was the hardest thing Jericho had ever done.

"If you need help with the funeral, say the word," Hawk said on the short ride to the first floor.

"You're a good friend," Gram said.

"Thanks, bro," Jericho uttered.

The drive home was filled with heart-wrenching emptiness.

Once there, Hawk told Jericho he'd check in with him later. He slid into his convertible and rolled out.

The family went inside, made their way to the kitchen. No one knew what to do, what to say. They looked catatonic, standing in the kitchen staring at one another.

"I'll make coffee," Gram said, going through the motions.

"I'm so sad." Georgia choked back another gut-wrenching sob as she made her way to the sofa in the large family room, flopped down, and cried.

In the quiet kitchen, Gram wrapped a firm hand around Jericho's arm. Grief poured from her eyes.

"I keep anger and hatred from my heart," Gram began. "I work hard to forgive, you know that. I've even tried to forgive your dad. Still working on that one. You've got close friends in powerful positions. For a restaurant owner, you're gone a lot. I never ask questions, never pry, but I'm not as naïve as I pretend to be. I haven't lived seventy-eight years with my head in the sand. You make calls, you do what you gotta do. You've got to make this right. You know that, don't you?"

"Yeah, Gram, I do," he said, peering into her eyes. "I sure as hell do."

Liv entered the Department of Justice building in Northwest DC, flashed her employee badge, and made her way through security. On her way down the hall, she checked her watch. It was ten in the morning.

Sixty minutes earlier, while parking at a police station in Herndon, her phone had buzzed with a text. "DOJ."

Those three letters meant she needed to get her ass downtown. She needed to change her plans and rearrange her schedule. She didn't respond. After deleting the text, she drove out of the parking lot. On the way, she called the police captain, explained that she had a personal emergency, apologized for the last-minute change, and said she'd call back to reschedule her training class.

Reaching the end of the hallway, she stopped in front of an unmarked door and ran her government-issued ID through the scanner on the doorframe. The door clicked and she pushed it open. This hallway was devoid of traffic. She continued until she reached an exit sign halfway down. That door led to a set of stairs that took her to the basement of Justice.

At the bottom, she swiped her card again. The light turned green and she opened one more door, then continued on to a small office. The hairs on the back of her neck prickled and she looked over her shoulder. There was something creepy about being in the basement of the government building.

She arrived at her destination.

Knock-knock.

"Enter," said the familiar male voice.

She opened the door and smiled. The slight man sitting behind his desk was working away on his computer. Four screens, mounted on the side wall, went dark. He rose, walked around his desk, and gave her a quick hug.

His tight smile was gone before he sat back down behind his desk.

"Hello, Uncle Z." She sat in the tired-looking chair across from his desk.

"Hello, Livy. How are you doing?"

"Fine, a little frazzled." She dropped her bag on the floor, then remembered the time she saw a roach scurry across the floor. She snatched it up and shoved it next to her on the chair.

Nothing in the office was warm and inviting. That's because Z didn't like company. He was all business at work. There was little room for chit chat. He reserved the conversations for family events. Large, dysfunctional, gatherings where everyone pretended they got along with everyone else. It was a small sacrifice to keep the peace.

Knock-knock-knock.

"Enter."

The door opened. Sinclair Develin walked in and glanced over at Liv. "Twice in a few months." He flashed a smile. "Must be another ALPHA emergency."

She offered a warm smile. "Good to see you, Sin."

Known as DC's Fixer, Sin ran Develin and Associates, but the power he wielded in the nation's capital dwarfed every three-letter agency, every PAC group, every lobbyist. If a bigshot ran into trouble, Sin was their best way out.

"How are you?" Z asked.

Sin arched an eyebrow. "What's going on?"

He was less into chit-chat than her uncle.

"ALPHA Operative, Jericho Savage, took out terrorist Abdul Al-Mazir," Z began.

Liv's brain screeched to an abrupt halt.

What the hell?

"I heard that went according to plan," Sin replied.

"I'm sorry," Liv interrupted, "did you say Jericho Savage?"

"I did," Z deadpanned. "We think someone in Al-Mazir's security detail made him, along with ALPHA Operative, Nicholas Hawk. Last night, Jericho Savage, Nicholas Hawk, and two of Jericho's brothers were having dinner at Raphael's in McLean. As they exited the restaurant, the brothers were gunned down."

Liv's heart plummeted. "Oh, no."

"The oldest one, Vincent Savage, just moved back after being gone for nineteen years. He's being released from the hospital today. The youngest brother, Bryan Savage, just graduated from college and would have started law school in the fall. He didn't make it."

Ohgod, no. Pain slashed Liv's heart. Family was everything to Jericho.

She'd gone to Lost Souls last night, hoping to run into him.

When he didn't show, she served drinks hoping to distract herself from missing him. It hadn't worked.

"Jericho's gotta be wrecked," Sin said, plucking her from her thoughts.

"While sources claim the terrorist group is *not* responsible for the shooting, we don't have confirmation," Z continued. "What I do know is that Jericho is going to hunt down the shooter and probably get himself killed in the process."

"This is bad," Liv murmured.

"It is," Sin agreed.

"Sin, I need you to go to ALPHA and bring Cooper Grant up to speed," Z said. "Jericho is too important to the group to lose him."

"Got it." Sin rose. "Liv, if we ever run into each other outside this office—"

"It'll be nice to meet you," she said with a wry smile.

He tossed her a nod and left, shutting the door behind him.

Z shifted to her. "I need Jericho monitored. When he goes rogue, you need to let me know."

"Uncle Z," Liv began, "I can't accept this job."

Up went Z's eyebrows. The man showed zero emotion at work, so those jutting brows were a sure sign of displeasure.

"You don't have a choice, Livy. His brother's death will send him off the rails. I need a full work-up in seventy-two hours. If he needs to be sidelined, I need to know ASAP. In addition to being ALPHA's best sniper, Jericho does a lot of their out-of-town recon work. He's one of the best Operatives ALPHA has. While I don't want to pull him, if his head isn't in the game, he'll do something reckless and get himself killed."

"Uh-huh." Liv had done her best to catch most of what Z had just told her, but she was still shocked to learn Jericho was a sniper.

"What questions do you have?" her Uncle asked.

"Seriously? That's it?"

His phone rang. He answered. "Two minutes." He hung up, fixed his gaze on her. "It's a straightforward assignment. Email your write-up using the secure portal."

"It's *not* a straightforward assignment, not when it comes to him."

"Your history with Jericho is irrelevant. Your job is to watch the watcher, in this case, an ALPHA sniper. You don't need to engage him or reconnect. I know things ended badly between you two, but that was a long time ago. If you treat this job like all the others, he won't even see you."

She shook her head.

Strangely, that elicited a smile. "Stubborn, just like your dad. You owe me." He paused. "Your words, not mine. So, consider this job me calling in that favor."

Backed against a wall, she accepted the assignment with a simple nod.

"And it goes without saying, do not discuss this with anyone."

"If you're referring to your daughter, Addison has no idea I do this," Liv said. "And she's more like a sister to me than my real one. No worries, our little secret is safe." She pushed out of her chair, slung her bag over her shoulder.

"Liv, you have to separate your personal feelings when dealing with Jericho. What's past is past and you made a choice. Can't change that. If he's not fit to work, I need to know."

On a sigh, she left his office and started the long trek back up to planet earth from the depths of hell.

The good news, if she could call it that, was that Jericho had no idea what she looked like. Her crazy cat disguise was working in her favor. Since they hadn't seen each other since high school, he would walk right by her. She'd always been taller than average, but it wasn't until college that she started filling out. Back in high school, she'd kept her hair super short because she hated that she couldn't control the waves. Then, during college, she'd let it grow long. Now, she loved her wild, untamed hair, and she loved her curves. She accepted herself, and she was good in her skin.

As she exited the building, she breathed deep. The day was clear and sunny, but her heart was heavy. She hated that she had to spy on Jericho, but she hated more that he was hurting and she couldn't go to him.

When his mom had died, he had leaned on her pretty hard. While she'd been sad, she'd been strong for him, and for his siblings. Georgia and Bryan had both been so young.

This time, however, she couldn't break protocol.

Back at her condo, she entered the spare bedroom she used as her office. There, she booted up the computer Z had bought her. After rescheduling the Herndon PD training course, she logged in to ALPHA and typed in Jericho's full name.

Jericho David Savage

She had no idea who the Operatives in ALPHA were, until she was assigned to watch one of them. If she typed in Sinclair Develin, she wouldn't get a hit. That didn't mean Sin wasn't in ALPHA, it just meant she didn't have the authority to view his profile.

While she waited for Jericho's file to complete running, she boiled water for tea. Moments later, she was at her desk, reading his entire work history. That included the restaurants he'd opened, the business deals he'd done alone, and the ones he'd done with four men.

Stryker Truman
Cooper Grant
Nicholas Hawk
Prescott Armstrong

She'd spent an entire month watching Cooper Grant. He'd

been ALPHA's top choice as co-lead of the top-secret organization, temporarily replacing Dakota Luck who had to step away to run his real estate company. Out of the two men and one woman she'd been was tasked with watching, Cooper had been the obvious best choice.

She didn't have a month to watch Jericho. She had three measly days.

She read every sniper and recon mission assigned to Jericho. There were dozens. He averaged seven jobs a month, in addition to making sure his stable of restaurants were running smoothly. Looked like he spent the most time at Jericho Road.

As the afternoon rolled on, she finished learning about his missions before moving on to his personal life. He'd had two long-term relationships in his twenties, but never made it to the alter.

"Whoa." He lived in a ten-million-dollar, 21,000 square foot estate in a posh McLean neighborhood. Six bedrooms and nine bathrooms. The white-brick exterior reminded her of a European chateau.

While three days wasn't enough time to complete a full work-up on him, she would stay as close to him as possible without actually engaging him.

Unless Catwoman gets involved.

Her insides warmed, but she shut that down.

He's grieving the loss of his brother. I need to watch him, not screw him.

Her stomach growled and she glanced at the time. It was close to five. She'd worked through lunch but would make herself something to eat once she located his whereabouts.

To help her get started, she tapped on the tracking device assigned to him. Every Operative had a chip inserted into the back of their necks. From what Z had told her, they all hated it—and she couldn't blame them. Recently, their newest Operative, Danielle Fox, had been able to track down Cooper Grant when things had gone sideways. After that, according to her uncle, the Operatives stopped complaining about the chip in their necks.

She clicked on Jericho's location. He was at home. After opening an ALPHA app on her phone called XYZ, she paired it with his tracking number. Jericho's location appeared on her screen. Going forward, finding him would be simple.

Never before had she watched a watcher who posed a risk to others and to himself. Every other assignment had been new-hire related. She'd tailed agents from the Bureau or the CIA, along with military or law enforcement who were being considered for ALPHA, or a top-secret or high-risk position with a different three-letter agency. She loved the job. It was so different from anything she'd ever done. It was exciting, but from a safe distance.

Prior to moving back, she'd been one of several psychologists working in a private practice. One of those therapists had been her long-time boyfriend. Despite her ability to help her patients, she couldn't help herself. That four-year relationship had really ended after the second year, but it had taken her another two years to acknowledge it and leave.

The rancid memory had her pushing away from her desk. After a quick dinner, she dressed in all black. With her long hair pulled into a tight twist, she was ready to get to work.

Before leaving, she checked Jericho's location. He was on the move, heading east on the GW Parkway. She grabbed her phone and was gone. Rather than jump in her car, she walked to the back of the parking lot and climbed into a black SUV that Z gave her to use for work.

As she drove out of her neighborhood, she wondered if he was headed to Jericho Road.

Her gut told her no.

Jericho had to get out of the house. The grief and guilt were killing him. He'd been running on pure adrenaline and he wasn't about to slow down any time soon.

That morning, he'd jumped into action with a call to a funeral home. When that one didn't meet his needs, he moved on. After a number of calls, he found one that worked. Then, he started calling Bryan's friends. As many as he could. Each time he told them what happened, his heart broke.

Mid-afternoon, his brother Tim came over to help with funeral plans. His wife's sister had had her baby, so Patty was back at home with their two young kids. When his brother had walked in, both men lost it. It was an ugly scene with gut-wrenching sobs.

Gram had been cooking all day. It was her therapy. Normally solid in the kitchen, she'd sliced three different fingers, two of them twice. Her hands were covered in Band-Aids. Though Georgia hadn't stopped crying, she'd called Bryan's college, then talked to someone in the pre-law office.

Everyone had their own way of coping with grief. Whatever got them from one minute to the next.

Earlier in the day, he'd called the hospital to check on Vincent. The doctor had been in the room and Vincent said he'd call him back. He never did.

On his way out, Jericho found Gram, Georgia, and Tim in the kitchen, huddled around Tim's laptop. All three of them peered at him with the saddest eyes.

"I'm making a list of everything we have to do," Tim said.

Jericho hated that it sounded like one of Tim's project management gigs, but his brother was great at his job.

"I'm heading out," Jericho said.

"Now?" his sister blurted.

When Jericho slid his gaze to Gram, a knowing look flashed in her eyes.

"My Georgia peach," Gram began. "Everyone handles grief in

their own way. Jericho is headed somewhere where he can clear his head."

Georgia stood. "Sorry, I'm a mess. I'll walk you out."

They went outside to the large, circular driveway.

"I've got someone covering for me tonight," Georgia began.

Three years ago, when his sister had graduated college with a degree in restaurant management, Jericho had jumped at the chance to hire her. Rather than give her a cushy job, he started her at Jericho Road. If she could handle that insanity, she'd shine at any of his other restaurants. She paid her dues for six months and did a stand-up job.

Next, he offered her Manager on Duty at Kaleidoscope. That restaurant was tanking big time. Constant staff turnover and a sub-par cook were killing his bottom line. Georgia loved her job *and* the challenges that came with it. Several months later, she'd turned the place around and asked for more responsibility. Jericho promoted her to General Manager of both Raphael's and Carole Jean's allowing her to split her time between the two.

He was grateful she'd been at Carole Jean's when Bryan had been gunned down. Had she been at Raphael's, and seen everything go down—

"Take as much time off as you need," Jericho told her, shutting down the tragic memory.

"Work is good, it keeps me from crawling into a ball and dying."

Jericho pulled her in for a hug. "Doesn't get any worse than this, sis. We've been through this before and we found our way. One fucking minute at a time."

"We're Savages," she whispered. "We'll get each other through this, right?"

"Right."

He kissed her forehead, jumped into his truck, and drove up the long driveway and through the neighborhood. After hopping onto the GW Parkway, he called Vincent.

"Hello?" Vincent answered.

"It's Jericho, how you doin'?"

"I'm home."

"I woulda driven you."

"Nah, I knew you'd be busy. I heard about Bryan. I'm sorry, man. That sucks."

"Yeah, it does. I know you didn't know him—"

"I know he didn't deserve to die, for sure."

Bryan was the one who wanted to get to know his brother, not Jericho. Jericho put the dinner together because Bryan wanted to reconnect with family. Now, Bryan wouldn't have that chance.

"When's the funeral?" Vincent asked.

"Next week."

"Once things get back to normal, I'll meet you at Cho."

Jericho didn't have the energy to tell him there was no Cho. "Not gonna feel like partying for a while, but I'll text you about the funeral."

Hawk was calling so Jericho ended the call.

"Hey," Jericho answered.

"How you holding up?" Hawk asked.

"Fakin' it."

"Stryker emailed you a link for his IDware," Hawk explained. "I called the house to check on everyone. Gram said the funeral is next week. Headed to The Road?"

"Yeah, I'm gonna check the surveillance from Raphael's."

"Need another set of eyes?"

"I'll let you know."

"I know you, babe, and you're gonna go after the shooter."

"What would you do?"

"Same," Hawk replied. "I'm here if you need help."

Jericho pulled into the parking lot of Jericho Road. "There is one thing you can do for me."

"Name it."

"If anyone asks if I'm going after the killer... lie."

"No one lies better than me, baby."

Jericho could hear the smile in Hawk's voice. "Thanks for being there for me, for all of us." He hung up and went inside. The restaurant was busy, but not over the top. The insanity didn't start until around nine.

Pausing at the hostess stand, he asked if Jamal was working.

"Oh, yeah, I saw him a little while ago," the hostess answered.

Jericho normally stopped at the bar to wait on a few customers and chat with the regulars. Instead, he headed toward his office, pausing outside his GM's office. Jamal was on his computer. When he glanced up, sadness flashed in his eyes.

Jamal made his way over and offered a hug. "I'm so sorry, man. What are you doing here?"

"I needed a few minutes alone," Jericho said. "I've been up for twenty-four, but I'm too wired to sleep."

"What can I do?" Jamal asked.

"Run The Road for a few days."

"You got it."

Jericho walked to his office, shut the door, and locked it. He strode to the scanner, the light turned green, and he entered his ALPHA office. After logging in to his computer, he opened the surveillance system videos. A few clicks and he was reviewing the footage at Raphael's the night of the drive-by.

He felt like his heart would explode out of his chest when one of the cameras picked up the car as it rolled by.

BANG! BANG! BANG!

Anger and pain slashed through him as both brothers fell to the ground.

"Ohgod."

Jericho pulled up the front-facing camera and found the spot on the video where the shooting happened.

The triggerman wore a black ski mask, but the driver didn't. Jericho clicked on Stryker's email and downloaded Stryker's propriety IDware. If the driver could be ID'd, and he had a criminal record, the software would give Jericho everything he needed to know.

He needed a clearer picture of the men, so he rewound the video to when the car drove into the parking lot. The shooter kept his head down as they searched for a parking spot. When one opened up on the side, the driver backed in. By then, the triggerman had already pulled on the ski mask.

Dammit.

Jericho replayed the video of the car pulling out of the spot, a nearby pole lamp lighting him up. Every millisecond made a difference. Finally, Jericho stopped the video at the exact spot where the driver's face was clear enough to upload.

Gotcha.

Jericho glanced at the time. He'd been working for two hours, but he'd stay on this for fucking ever. He didn't recognize the driver from the Al-Mazir hit. Al-Mazir's security detail were large men. These two guys were small.

Within minutes, the software returned three results with a 73% match.

That's a start.

He plugged in the first name. Deceased. The second was a twenty-five-year-old man who lived in Falls Church. The third was twenty-eight and lived an hour north of Baltimore.

Using ALPHA's software, he learned both men had criminal records. The first had served a year and gotten paroled. The second was awaiting trial. He pulled a burner from his safe and called the one living in nearby Falls Church.

"Hello?" answered the stranger.

"I got a job for ya," Jericho said.

"Who the hell is this?"

"Name's Reaper. I got your number from a friend. He says you're reliable. I got five grand if you're the right guy."

"Right guy for what?"

"I need a driver for a job I got."

"For what?"

"Not over the phone." Jericho was staring at the clock on his computer. He needed the guy to stay on the phone another minute. "Lemme show you I'm serious." Jericho opened his safe and grabbed ten bundles of twenties. He set them on the floor and snapped a pic, then texted it to the guy.

"You ain't shittin' me," said the man.

"You got forty minutes to meet me at Springfield Industrial Park. There's an empty warehouse on Graybill. You come alone, you take the job, you get the money."

"I'll be there."

Jericho hung up. A few keystrokes and he had the man's location. Falls Church. Using his personal phone, Jericho made another call.

"Hold on," Hawk answered, breathing hard. Seconds later, "Whatcha need, babe?"

"I think I found the driver. Can you get eyes on him, make sure he's meeting me alone?"

"I'm in the middle of… doesn't matter. I got you."

"I'll text you his address," Jericho said. "I told him to meet me at the abandoned warehouse on Graybill at Springfield Industrial Park."

"Give me five to… um… finish up here."

Despite the anger coursing through him, Jericho's lips twitched. Hawk was like a damn rabbit. The women were lining up for him, and he was more than happy to help them… and himself.

Jericho didn't give a damn about Hawk's sex life. He was a man on a mission and he would stop at nothing to avenge his brother's murder.

6

KILL #1

Thirty minutes later, Jericho stood inside the entrance of the abandoned warehouse. The place wreaked of piss and stale booze, but he didn't give a fuck. He had a loose plan and a clear goal. He thought of his brothers, lying on the ground. He thought of how Bryan's life had been cut short. He wanted answers and he'd do whatever it took to pry them from this motherfucker.

His burner buzzed with a text from Hawk. "He's alone."

A car pulled into the parking lot and the engine went quiet. Jericho's heart rate didn't increase, his blood pressure didn't jump. If this was the driver, he would get revenge, and get it fast.

The warehouse door creaked open. "Hello?"

"Yup," Jericho replied. "You alone?"

"You got the money?"

Jericho flipped on a million-candle-power flashlight and shone it in the guy's eyes. "Don't fuck with me," Jericho boomed.

"Holy hell! You're blinding me."

"You alone?"

"Yeah."

After clicking down the brightness, Jericho shone the light on the open bag of cash. The man was short and slender, but he was packin' heat, so Jericho's guard was up.

"If I hire you, down payment is yours," Jericho said.

"How much we talkin'?"

"Five now, five after," Jericho replied.

"Whad'ya need?"

"You got a name?"

"Lucky."

"A coupla guys owe me half a mil," Jericho lied. "They *say* they don't have it. I got word they're plannin' on skippin' town. I need someone to take care of 'em, but it's gotta look smooth, you know, a random thing."

"Like a drive-by," Lucky replied.

Jericho forced a smile through gritted teeth. "I hear you're the man, Lucky."

Lucky puffed out his chest. "I've done a few."

Jericho shoved down the anger. "Nice. You drivin' or you the one doin' the poppin'?"

"I drive."

"You got a good partner? He's gotta have a clean shot. You know, one and done."

Lucky snickered. "Hey, man, I like that. I've done some jobs with my cousin. Dude's a great shot. Never misses."

"Your cousin got a name?"

"Don't matter."

"My associate said your last job *wasn't* clean, so I'm not sure your cousin's the right guy."

"Why not?"

Jericho pulled out his burner and showed Lucky a few seconds of the video from Raphael's parking lot. "This you?"

"Whoa, dude, how'd you get that? You a cop?"

"Not a cop. This video is eyes on you. If I hire you, you gotta make sure there're no cams."

"Right, gotcha. I can do that."

"I'll text you his address, but you gotta follow him. Make it look like an accident."

"No problem."

Jericho showed Lucky the paused video on his phone. "I gotta know... this you?"

"Yeah, drivin'."

"Who was your cousin's target?"

"I dunno. He said it was a scare job."

"Who you scarin'?"

Lucky shrugged his shoulders.

"Did Al-Mazir's guys send you?"

"I don't know nobody named Al."

"Who ordered the hit?"

"No idea."

"You're a dumb ass. I can't hire you."

"Look, man, I don't need this job."

"You must be rich if you're walkin' from ten grand."

"I'm a TK. I got big plans. Money, power, respect. We're gonna have it all."

"What the hell's a TK?"

Lucky's eyebrows shot up. "You don't know? Now, who's the dumb ass? I'm a TK for life and I'm gonna die a TK."

Jericho grabbed the Glock tucked in the back of his pants. "Fine by me."

POP!

Jericho hit him between the eyes and the guy dropped.

"See you in hell, asshole."

He searched the guy's pockets, found his phone and turned it off. After stashing it in his pocket, he collected the bag of money, turned off the flashlight, and bolted.

Seconds later, he was on his way back to The Road. He knew he should slow down, take a deep breath, mourn his brother, but he couldn't. Not until the triggerman was dead.

I'm comin' for you motherfucker and I'm not stoppin' until every last one of you is dead.

Liv crouched behind the dead man's car, shaking. The chirping of crickets and frogs sounded like trumpets in the quiet night. Her heart, beating triple-time in her chest, roared in her ears.

She'd just witnessed Jericho murder a man, execution style.

The moment felt like one of those nightmares where she was stuck in place, unable to make her legs work. She wanted to run screaming to the safety of her vehicle and *unsee* what had just happened. But her feet wouldn't move.

C'mon, c'mon, get the hell outtta here.

She pushed up and ran across the street, then over to the SUV parked behind an overgrowth of bushes in an empty parking lot. Once inside, she put her hand on her chest. Not only could she feel her heart racing, it was thumping wildly in her ears.

Calm down.

She could not stop trembling.

She knew, firsthand, how angry Jericho could get. He'd turned a guy's face into mincemeat when he'd pulled him off her all those years ago.

But he didn't kill the guy.

When she'd gotten to the warehouse, she'd parked across the street and hurried over to the building. The windows were dirty, so she'd hidden by Jericho's truck. A car pulled in, a slender man got out, and walked into the building.

Though risky, she moved near the open door. With her back pressed against the building, she peeked inside. From her vantage point, she'd seen and heard it all.

The second Jericho fired his weapon and the guy dropped, she bolted behind the dead man's car.

A shudder ran through her before she started the engine. She'd never been in this situation before. Should she report the murder? Should she talk to Jericho?

Her uncle told her to call him if Jericho went off the rails. She fished her phone from her bag, unlocked it, and tapped over to Z's personal phone number.

A wave of nausea rolled through her.

I fucked up Jericho's life once. I can't do it again. She sat there, phone in hand, for the longest time.

I can't turn him in.

She tapped the ALPHA locator app. Jericho was on the move, perhaps headed back to Jericho Road. She started her car and headed out. The situation was way worse than she could have ever imagined.

Acid churned in her stomach as she drove in a stunned silence back to his restaurant. It was just after two in the morning and the parking lot was mostly empty.

She parked near his truck, walked inside, and scanned the large room. A few waitstaff were cleaning up. Two servers were seated at the bar while the bartender chatted with them.

"Sorry," said the bartender. "We're closed."

"I'm here to see Jericho."

One of the women swiveled toward her. "I don't think he's here."

"He's been in his office all night," said the bartender.

What the hell? How did no one see him leave?

"You want me to get him for you?" asked the bartender.

"Please," Liv replied.

He made a call. "Someone's here to see you." The bartender flicked his gaze to Liv. "What's your name?"

"Just a friend," Liv replied.

"Says she's a friend." The bartender hung up. "He'll be out. You want a drink?"

"Water would be great, thanks."

He handed her a small glass and she drank a few sips, hoping it would stay down. Her guts were in knots. Watching a man die in a movie and watching him actually drop dead were two completely different things.

A moment later, *he* loomed into view, and her heart took off in her chest. The man he'd become was an overwhelming sight. This wasn't a costumed Jericho in lowlighting. It was the real deal. One deliberate step at a time, he stalked toward her.

Tall and broad shouldered with guns that had her biting back a moan. His black T-shirt hugged his V-shaped torso, forcing his granite-hard muscles to stretch against the thin fabric. Her gaze jumped to his tats. Just below the sleeve on his left arm were the words La Familia. On his right, the prongs of a barbed-wire tat jutted into view, and on the same forearm, a dagger. Each tat was black and they were all sexy as hell. She'd been so focused on sex with him, they'd gone unnoticed. His tattered black jeans clung to his perfectly sculpted thighs.

He was completely breathtaking, a little terrifying, and an alpha in every damn way.

Ohgod, so sexy.

Despite the stressful situation, heat blasted through her and she inhaled a calming breath. Didn't help.

Jericho Savage was a ruthless beast.

The coldness in his eyes snapped her back to reality. That, and the fire he was breathing out his flared nostrils. He pulled to a stop a few feet away from her and crossed his massive arms over his chest.

"You a detective?" he asked.

"No."

"Whad'ya want?"

"To talk to you."

He shook his head. "It's after two in the morning. You gotta give me more than that."

"I'm Livingston Blackstone."

The air turned frosty, the silence deafening.

He narrowed his gaze, his body turned rigid, and a low, deep growl rolled out of him. He hitched his hands on his hips and shook his head. "I don't need your condolences."

"We need to talk."

"No, we don't. I got nothin' to say to you. You had your chance, years ago." He turned and strode back to his office.

If she didn't go after him, her narrow window would close. She couldn't let that happen, so she hurried after him, but he was eating up the floor with his long strides.

"Jericho, stop."

Shaking his head, he waved her off. "Get lost, Livy."

She pushed on, undeterred by his rejection. He stopped in front of a closed door and she hastened her step. The scanner turned green and he opened the door.

She pulled up alongside him. "It's about what just happened at the warehouse," she whispered.

He glared at her so hard a shiver flitted through her. Despite that, she didn't back down. Instead, she stood tall and glared back. This was her one chance to talk to him and he was going to listen, despite the hatred rolling off him in tsunami-like waves.

"You have three minutes." He waited, she crossed the threshold.

He shut the door, sat behind his desk, and glared at her. She stood in the center of his office staring back at him.

"It's *your* three minutes. If this is how you—"

Severing their combative stare down, she eased into the guest chair. "I'm sorry about Bryan."

No reaction. Nothing. His gaze didn't soften. Just a chilly hardness glared back at her.

"You're not fit... I was hired... I... you—" She stopped and studied his face. Lines creased his eyes and between his brows. She saw deeper laugh lines. His hair was the same color, but so much longer. Full lips that she'd finally kissed the other night at the club. Yet his beautiful, soulful green eyes were as she remembered them. Only, now they were shooting daggers at her.

"Time's up," he said.

His gaze had strayed from her face to her hair—still tied in a twist—but nowhere else.

"I watch the watchers," she began. "I observe ALPHA Operatives after an especially hard mission. I trail FBI agents who are being considered for ALPHA, and Secret Service agents being considered to protect the President. My job is to write up a psychological profile to determine if a candidate is suitable for the job or if an Operative might be suffering from PTSD. I do this after observing my subject for a period of days, even weeks. Every job is different." She paused. "I was assigned to watch you after Bryan was murdered. And I saw what happened in that abandoned warehouse tonight."

Another long, ugly silence hung heavy in the air.

"Fuck," he muttered.

"If I write up my report, you'll get sidelined because the mission wasn't ALPHA approved."

"No shit."

Knock-knock.

"What?" Jericho bellowed, his frustration uncontainable.

The bartender stuck his head inside. "Sorry to interrupt. We're taking off. I'll lock up."

Jericho nodded, and the bartender shut the door.

"I'll get arrested," he bit out.

"I was told that, if you went off the rails, I was to let my contact know ASAP."

"Thanks for the heads up. Don't let the door hit you on the way out." Hatred seethed from his pores.

"My timeframe on this was fast, just seventy-two hours."

"Well, think of how much time you get back since I offed a guy in twenty-four. Aren't you a fuckin' lucky lady?"

"In two days, I'm going to turn in a report stating that you're ready to return to work. I read your ALPHA profile and I know how much you love being a sniper and doing recon—"

"So, you're up in my business now?" He looked so damn pissed, she bit back a smile. "And that's amusing to you? How in the hell is that entertaining?"

Ignoring his question, she pushed on. "I heard what that man said about being a TK. That could be the Thriller Killers gang."

His brows slashed down. "How would you know?"

"I'm an expert on gang behavior."

"Because you are…?"

"A PhD psychologist."

"Okay, Doc, I don't give a damn about your fancy degrees or your write-up—"

"How 'bout this? Show me the video of the night Bryan was murdered and I'll be your alibi for tonight."

"There is no video."

She tossed him a nod. "Sure, there is."

"I don't need you *or* your help. I don't know you. Don't wanna know you. You tanked my life once and I survived. At least, this time, you're givin' me a heads-up."

Jericho was fucked. Totally fucked. Never mind going to prison, he could lose his job as an ALPHA Op. Strange how, in the moment, the only thing that mattered was the stunningly beautiful woman sitting across from him.

Too bad she's the effin' enemy.

She shoved out of her chair and lifted her phone from her pocket. While her fingers flew over the keyboard, he took his time and checked her out.

Damn, she's smokin' hot.

Sweet, innocent, adorable Livy had changed from a beanpole to a voluptuous woman. All woman, every damn inch of her.

Needing to be closer, he pushed out of his chair, walked around, and leaned his backside against the desk. That's when he caught her familiar scent. Despite his total dislike of her, she smelled like home.

When she raised her head, he stared into her whiskey-colored eyes. He'd always loved her eyes. They had a perpetual gleam that made him happy. Years earlier, when his mom first got sick, he used to stare into Livy's eyes and pretend like everything was okay. It was dumb, but he didn't care. He'd take happiness any way he could get it.

His phone buzzed. He ignored it. She gripped her hip. He did not—*did not*—glance down at how her shirt pulled against her breast. He wanted to look. But he didn't.

"That text is from me," she said, snapping him back to the present. "Text me when you're ready to hunt down your brother's killer." She marched out, taking her fiery attitude with her.

A few seconds passed while he wrestled with his thoughts. Part of him wanted to go after her and take her up on her offer. But there was no freakin' way he'd do that. That would be him admitting he needed her help. He did *not* need her help.

He wasn't about to lose his job. He'd get sidelined for a while and probably get a lecture, but there's no way he was getting kicked out of ALPHA. He was too good. On the other hand, he might get arrested for murder.

Maybe I was too rash. Livy owes me, and I'm gonna need that alibi.

THE NEXT MORNING, Vincent called.

"How you doin'?" Jericho asked his brother.

"I feel terrible about what happened to Bryan."

"It's not your fault."

"I've got a casket for him. What funeral home?"

The reality of the situation rained down on him. His brother was going to be placed in a box, decades too soon, his life now nothing but a short-lived memory. The sadness came in waves and this one hit hard. He choked back a sob.

Jericho gave him the phone number to the funeral home.

"When is it, the funeral?" Vincent asked.

"Thursday."

"Is there a wake?"

"No, we're having a gathering at the house after Bryan is buried." A stabbing pain shot through him. "You don't have to come. You hardly knew him."

"He was my brother. I'll be there," Vincent insisted.

The call ended and Jericho went for a long run through his neighborhood. He did not want to bury his brother. He would have taken the hit himself, if he could have. His brother was going to become a lawyer, and a damn good one. Grief pummeled him.

The harder he pushed himself, the worse he felt. Running always cleared his mind and he loved going to the limit. Not today. He thought his lungs were gonna collapse in his chest. He slowed down enough to catch his breath. After a minute, he started up again, slowly.

Forty minutes later, he was sitting in the kitchen chugging water when Cooper Grant called.

"Hey, Coop," he answered.

"Checking on you," Cooper said.

"Not good."

"What can I do?"

"You guys coming to the funeral?"

"We'll be there. You need something now? Anything?"

"I could use a distraction." He glanced around. The first floor was quiet, but he walked through the living room and out onto the back patio overlooking the Olympic-sized swimming pool. "When's my next recon job or mission?"

"Let's get you through the funeral, then we'll reinstate you. I know this is killing you, but I gotta follow protocol. There will be plenty of missions and your name is always on the top of my list."

Jericho smiled. "You sweet talker, you."

"Seriously, I'm here for whatever you need. We'll talk Thursday. Sorry, not at the funeral. We'll talk Friday."

"Thursday works. I need good news and you're gonna give it to me."

"You got it, brother." Cooper hung up.

Jericho pulled off his shirt and dove into the water. It was crisp and invigorating. He swam a few laps, then treaded water in the deep end.

He swam more laps before getting out and drying off. After a quick shower, he dressed and took off for The Road. The restaurant was closed, which meant he'd have a coupla hours before the lunch crowd.

Once in his private office, he did an Internet search on the Thriller Killers. They were a U.S.-based gang with formalized groups in several major cities along the East Coast. They got the name Thriller Killers because they bragged about how thrilling it was to kill someone in the name of the gang. Anger sent a growl erupting from him. Some thug got off on killing his brother.

Jericho pulled out the police officer's business card and dialed the number.

"Officer Binkman," he answered.

Jericho asked if there was any update on the case.

"It's been turned over to homicide," he said. "I pass along your number and the detective will call you back."

Jericho hung up.

Things are moving too damn slowly.

He stared at the text from Livy. "Let me help you."

He typed, "OK", then stared at those two letters.

I don't need her help.

He deleted the text and pulled the driver's cell phone from his safe.

I'll do it my damn self.

. . .

THURSDAY MORNING had arrived. Their hearts were shattered, the loss overwhelming.

Today, they were burying the youngest Savage.

Rather than take his truck, he ushered his family into his Escalade. After helping Gram into the front seat, he waited until she buckled herself in before he shut the door. Tim, Mark and Georgia got in back. His sister-in-law, Patty, was staying behind with the kids, and to let the caterer in.

He hated that everyone was coming over after the funeral service. Hated that he had to talk to anyone. But he would do it to honor his brother.

No one had said much all morning. There was nothing to say. It was a day he never ever thought he'd see. But there it was looming over them like the angriest of storm clouds.

Over the past few days, Jericho had laid low. Besides making the rounds at his restaurants, he did nothing but spend time with his family. He didn't contact Livy and he didn't hear from her either. If she was watching him, he couldn't go after the triggerman.

If she cleared him to work, *then* he'd go after that motherfucker with a vengeance. While he hated doing nothing, at least she'd tipped him off that she'd be watching him.

But first, he had to get through the day and be strong for his family.

7

A TRAGIC END AND A NEW BEGINNING

Even though the funeral home was the largest in the area, the place was chock full. As Jericho got his family situated in the front row, he eyed the dark walnut casket surrounded by several colorful bouquets. He wanted to throw open the lid and shake his brother alive. Tell him he couldn't be dead. That he had too much living to do, too much to accomplish. He had people to make proud, adventures to have, a woman to marry, maybe even children to raise.

That damn lump in his throat returned. After kissing Gram on the cheek, he whispered that he'd be right back. He needed some air before the service began. When he entered the lobby, his friends walked in.

It was always good when the group got together, but today was not one of those events that warmed his heart. As he accepted hugs from Stryker, Cooper, and Hawk, he bit back yet another wave of sadness.

When Emerson and Danielle whispered their condolences, a few tears rolled down his cheeks.

"Sorry," he muttered.

Danielle handed him a tissue.

"No, thanks," he replied.

"Take it." She leaned up and whispered, "It'll be our little secret." He took it, wiped his eyes. "We're here for you."

"I'm sorry you're not still in the business of revenge," Jericho said. "I could use your help."

"Who says I'm not?" Danielle replied.

Despite the fact that ALPHA was a top-secret organization, the entire group was there. He made his way over to them. "Thanks for being here. It means a lot."

They each expressed their condolences before he moved on.

Georgia had pulled together family photos and pictures from Bryan's life that the funeral home had placed throughout the lobby and in one of the salons. Seeing those only fueled the anger Jericho was fighting hard to keep in check. But... when the time was right, he'd unleash it on the enemy... and he could not fucking wait.

The funeral director made his way over. After a few kind words, he suggested Jericho take his seat so they could begin.

The second Jericho entered the room, he cemented his gaze on the casket, and his heart broke all over again. He needed to get through the day and be strong for his family. Then, he could channel all the pain and loss into rage. Taking out his brother's killer would become his number one priority.

After sitting beside Gram, she clasped his hand. He peered at her small one nestled in his. She'd buried her daughter and, now, her grandson. Life was full of surprises. Not all of them good ones.

His brother, Tim, stood, buttoned his suit jacket, and walked to the podium. "Thank you for being here with us today. I'm Tim Savage, one of Bryan's brothers."

As he delivered his eulogy, Jericho thought back over Bryan's life. He'd been too young to remember their dad leaving, but when their mom died, he was six. For the longest time, he asked when mom was coming home.

Over time, the darkness lifted and life went on. Bryan was a happy child who loved school and excelled there. It was a crazy time in Jericho's life, but now, looking back, they were finding their way without their mom.

Tim finished his eulogy and introduced his brother, Mark. After Mark, Georgia said a few words. When his sister finished, she invited anyone who knew Bryan to speak. To Jericho's surprise a line formed as his friends, teachers, professors, and employers offered a kind word or a heartwarming story.

Though these stories should have helped Jericho, it only fueled his grit. He wondered what the man who'd taken Bryan's life had accomplished. What accolades had he achieved? What milestones and goals had he reached? What was his contribution to society?

Maybe everyone was considered equal in the eyes of God, but they sure as hell weren't in Jericho's eyes. By the end of the service, Jericho's resolve for revenge was so strong, he couldn't wait to hunt down the killer who took the shot… and the one who ordered it. If it took him the rest of his life, he would destroy every last one of them.

When the last person spoke and the room grew still, Gram squeezed his hand. Time to move on to the cemetery. Jericho rose and made his way to the podium, pausing to lay hands on the casket.

"Love you, Bryan."

He stood at the podium, adjusted the mic. "I'm Jericho Savage. Like my siblings and our Gram, we're thankful for your support. Today is rough. Burying a loved one is never easy, but when someone's life is ruthlessly cut short at twenty-one, it's hard to comprehend. For anyone who's interested in joining us at the cemetery, the staff will give you a card to hang from your rearview mirror. There's a QR code for directions if you fall behind. Thanks for helping us honor Bryan."

Once the room cleared, the pallbearers— Jericho, Tim, Mark, and three of Bryan's closest friends—moved into position. As they lifted the heavy wooden box, every muscle in his body ached. Not from the weight, but from the loss. They walked slowly outside and placed the casket into the waiting hearse.

The ride to the cemetery was quiet. Nothing to say and no need to fill the void.

The pallbearers carried the coffin to the grave site as the mourners began to arrive.

Several minutes later, Jericho addressed the small crowd. "It's with unbearable grief that we lay our brother, Bryan Richard Savage, to rest." He eyed the coffin. "Too soon, brother. Decades too soon. We love you and we'll carry you with us every day, for the rest of our lives."

Next, Georgia recited Psalm 23, and Mark spoke of the healing power of love and time.

To Jericho's surprise, Gram stepped forward. "Another senseless death that should never have happened." She glanced around. "Mark my words, the person who did this will not get away with it. I feel it in my bones and I know it in my heart. Bryan, honey, you're with Mama now. Rest in peace, sweet boy."

After the coffin was lowered into the ground, Gram picked up a handful of dirt and tossed it onto the casket. One by one, others paid their respects by tossing in a handful.

As he watched the procession of mourners file by, he was more determined than ever to right this horrific wrong.

When everyone had finished, Tim announced a celebration of Bryan's life at the Savage estate. Georgia told him she'd get Gram back to the truck. As they made their way toward the vehicle, Jericho spotted Livy, standing alone under an oak tree.

His heart ca-chunked in his chest while adrenaline spiked through him. His reaction to her was irrelevant.

And totally inappropriate.

Ignoring her, he turned to the casket one last time before setting off toward the SUV. Out of the corner of his eye, he caught two men in suits veering his way.

His brother, Vincent—his arm in a sling—and an older man.

No fuckin' way.

His dad, Roger Savage, looked a lot older. Less hair, more belly. He didn't remember him having a slight limp. Rather than being happy to see him, Jericho fought the urge to lash out. Now was *not* the time to get into it with him. Ignoring them, he slid on his shades and kept his eyes trained on his vehicle.

"Jericho," his dad called out.

Here we go.

Jericho slowed to a stop. Vincent hugged him with his good arm. "We're sorry for… um… your loss."

"Thank you," Jericho replied, stone faced.

"You remember Dad," Vincent said.

Jericho shifted his attention to his father and his blood turned to ice in his veins. "Not really."

"How've you been?" his dad asked.

"I'm not doing this now," Jericho bit out. "You've got a lot of damn nerve showin' up, you know that? Where the hell were you when Bryan was alive?" He glared at his dad.

"I was in Oklahoma," he replied matter-of-factly.

"This is a tough day for us," Jericho said. "I gotta to."

"I haven't seen your mom," his dad blurted. "How's she holding up?"

Ohmygod.

Jericho flicked his gaze from one man to the other. "Mom *died* sixteen years ago."

His dad's eyebrows shot up and he regarded Vincent. "Did you know about this?"

"Yeah, I told you she died," Vincent said.

"I didn't know," his dad continued. "I'm sorry to hear that."

A growl shot out of Jericho. "I'm outta here—"

"I was thinking of swinging by the house," Vincent blurted. "You know, pay my respects to Gram. Would that be okay?"

Jericho shifted his gaze from one man to another. *Whatever.* "Yeah."

"It was a nice service," his dad added.

Jericho was great at small talk. Did it every night at The Road. He was a master at saying nothing and making sure his customers had a damn good evening. Most everyone who walked into any of his restaurants was treated like family.

The man standing in front of him was a stranger. A deserter. Jericho had zero respect for him. "I gotta get the family back to the house."

His father extended his hand.

Shaking it would be the right thing to do. It would be what his mom would want, what his grandmother would expect. He glanced down at the hand of a stranger and into the eyes of a man he didn't want to remember. In the moment, Jericho had to do what *he* thought was best, and shaking that man's hand wasn't gonna happen.

"See you back at the house."

Several steps toward his family and his brain caught up with his eyes. Livy stood at the truck talking to Gram and Georgia. Hawk and Addison had joined them as well.

As he got closer, she turned in his direction and the ice melted in his veins. A blast of heat streaked through him while he checked her out. She'd left her hair down and it was *the* sexiest thing he'd ever seen. Her wavy, wild, dark mane framed her face and trailed down her back.

She'd worn a simple black dress and heels. Tasteful and modest, but she was rockin' it out.

Dammit, get it together. You can't stand her.

"Jericho, you remember Livy, don't you?" Georgia said. "She used to babysit us when you took mom to her doctor appointments."

He tossed her a nod.

"I'm sorry for your loss," Livy said.

"Oh, Jericho David," Gram said, "give her a hug, for goodness sakes. She's as pretty as a picture and she's not going to bite you, though I wouldn't blame her if she did."

Jericho offered a polite hug, but the second he wrapped his arms around her that feeling of home crept back into his soul.

"I'll take one of those," Hawk said.

"Idiot," Jericho grumbled while the two men hugged it out.

"How you holding up?" Hawk asked.

"Auto pilot," he replied, his gaze flipping back to Livy.

"It was a lovely service," Addison added.

"You guys are coming back to the house, right?" Georgia asked.

"Yup," Hawk replied, lighting up a cigarette. "You two ready to head out?"

Livy, Addison, and Hawk headed toward Hawk's car.

The Savages piled into the SUV. After Jericho loosened his tie, which felt like a noose, he took off toward home.

"I'm not in the mood for a party," Georgia said. "I mean, I was happy to see Livy, but I just want to go to my room."

"Me, too, dear," said Gram, "but we have to do this for Bryan. We have to honor Bryan's life and get through the day."

"Who were the two men you were talking to?" asked his brother, Mark.

"Vincent and Dad," Jericho said.

"That snake," Gram grumbled.

"I didn't recognize them," Mark continued.

"I don't really remember them," Georgia added. "How old was I when they left?"

"Five," Jericho replied.

"So, Bryan was only two," Georgia murmured.

"Roger Savage is not welcome in our home." The edge in Gram's voice snagged Jericho's ear.

"Vincent wants to see you, Gram, and the motherfucker is along for the ride," Jericho explained.

"I'll be civil, for Bryan's sake, but I cannot stand that man," Gram said.

They drove the rest of the way in silence. The day was already painful enough, but now his family had to suffer the afternoon by playing nice with their dad. Jericho drove down the long driveway and pulled around the side of the home and into one of the garages. They entered the home as a united front.

His brother, Tim, was already there. He glanced through the living room to see guests milling on the patio near the swimming pool.

After talking with his brother and sister-in-law, he checked on the food set-up in the kitchen and dining room.

Jericho's four-year-old niece ran over to him, her dolly in hand. "Hi, Uncle Jericho." Her sweet smile was so good for his soul. "Can you play with me?"

Jericho lifted her up. "How you doin', pip squeak?"

"I'm sad about Uncle Bryan, but Mommy says he's playing with his friends in heaven."

Jericho wasn't gonna touch that one. "You smell like chocolate, Annie."

She put her tiny hand by her mouth to block anyone else from hearing her. "I saw a plate of candy. I ate free." She held up three small fingers. "Owen ate them, too. Don't tell Mommy."

Jericho couldn't help but smile. "No more candy. Where's your brother?"

"Playing with the lady."

"What lady?"

"She has sooo much hair. Biggest hair ever!" Annie giggled.

"Let's go find him."

With her still in his arms, they left the dining room. The first floor was crowded with so many people he didn't know. Hawk, Cooper, and Stryker were outside, by the pool.

He flicked his gaze across the living room, and spotted his nephew sitting on the sofa staring up at Livy while she wiped his fingers with a napkin. Another zing of energy raced through him. Things were tough enough. He didn't need this intense reaction every damn time he saw her.

She was smiling at Owen while he chatted away. If there was anything about Livy that he lived for… it was her smile. From the moment they'd become friends, he loved making her laugh or smile.

Before he got to her and Owen, Vincent and his dad cut him off. "Is this my granddaughter?" his dad asked.

Jericho's stomach roiled.

"How many kids you got, Jericho?"

"This is Tim's daughter," Jericho said.

His dad held out his arms. "She's adorable. Come to Grandpa."

"No," Jericho bit out. "You're a stranger."

"I don't talk to thrangers," Annie added.

Jericho clutched her tighter.

Vincent glanced around. "This place is amazing. I've never been in a house this ritzy. Whose is it?"

"Mine," Jericho replied.

Surprise flashed in both men's eyes. "Oooeee, brother, you did yourself gooooood," Vincent cooed. "What's your secret?"

"I work my ass off."

"You live alone?" Vincent continued.

"I got the fam with me," Jericho said.

"I'm family," Vincent said. "Got space for me? Maybe I could crash in Bryan's bedroom for a while."

Jericho scowled. *That's harsh.*

No way would he replace his baby bro with one he hardly knew.

Vincent ran his fingers through his short hair. "My bad. Not coolio of me."

Jericho had spent two more minutes with his dad than he wanted. "Excuse me," he said to them.

As he made his way toward Livy, warmth blanketed his chest.

Despite his dislike of her, Jericho was grateful she was watching Owen. He'd just lost his brother. No way in hell was he gonna let anything happen to these little ones. The swimming pool was open and everyone was too busy talking to notice a toddler fall into the water.

When Livy turned toward him, he couldn't look away. So much stunning beauty stared back.

He knelt by Owen, set Annie down, but his gaze stayed cemented on Livy.

She had this way of touching the deepest part of him. As they stared into each other's eyes, he was transported back to a different time in his life. A time when everything was easy and everything was good.

Up close, she was even more breathtaking than he remembered.

"Uncle Jer-Jer," Owen exclaimed, snagging his attention. "My fingers are thicky."

"Not anymore," Livy said. "You're clean and chocolate-free."

"Were they here by themselves?" Jericho asked as Annie climbed on his back.

She nodded, her gaze flicking from his eyes to his mouth. That wasn't helping. Definitely not helping.

His sister-in-law came flying over. "I'm so sorry. I lost track of them..."

Livy stood. "I'm Livy—I go by Liv now—Blackstone. I used to babysit the Savage kids. Well, everyone except Jericho. I saw the children were alone, and the pool is right there, so I was watching them."

"Thank you so much. I'm Tim Savage's wife, Patty." She held out her hands for her children. "I've got sandwiches in the kitchen and Gram is waiting for you two. Who's hungry?"

"I want to stay with Uncle," Annie protested while clinging to his back.

Jericho rose and his niece shrieked with laughter. "I'm in the sky!"

Owen giggled at his sister. "I want a wich, Mommy."

Patty lifted her son into her arms and extended her hand. "C'mon, young lady."

"Noooooo!!!" Annie cried.

"I don't mind watching her," Livy said. "I'll stay with Jericho and we'll keep Annie with us."

"Thank you," Patty said. "I'll be in the kitchen if you need me."

After his sister-in-law and nephew left, Jericho hitched a brow at Livy. "Smooth, aren't you?"

"Yay!" Annie said. "I'm a monkey in a tree." When Livy smiled at her, electricity shot through him.

Damn, she's gorgeous.

"Have you made any progress on your project?" she asked him.

He shook his head.

"I'll help you." Soulful brown eyes met his. The connection was immediate and intense. "And I'm not taking no for an answer." Her gaze drilled into him. She crossed her arms, hitched a brow. Clearly, she was not backing down.

"I'll give you one shot, Livy. But I'm not interested in how you're doing or what you've been up to."

"Fine by me," she replied.

"I want to go outside," Annie stated.

With his niece clinging to his back and Livy by his side, they walked onto the patio. Despite the grief coursing through him, having her next to him soothed his tormented soul. She had always been a source of calm for him, especially while his mom was sick, and then, when she had died.

She'd been there for him, until she wasn't.

Pushing out the bad memory, Jericho made his way toward his friends.

"Hey, look," Hawk said to Annie. "Jericho's got a baby monkey on his back."

Annie giggled. "I'm not a baby!" She started climbing down, but she fell on her rump. Tears welled in her eyes.

Livy knelt. "That was an impressive landing, Annie."

"I have an owie." Getting to her feet, Annie rubbed her bottom.

"You're a strong monkey," Livy said. "You okay?" Livy offered an encouraging smile and her hand.

Annie clasped it. "Can we walk around, and I'm hungry."

"We're going for a walk, then we'll be in the kitchen," Livy said to Jericho.

"You got this?" he asked.

She nodded as Addison joined her. "I'll go with you."

After they left, Cooper stepped close. "You've been looking for the triggerman, haven't you?"

"No comment."

"Well, if you're up for some good news—"

"Hell, yeah," Jericho replied.

"You've been reinstated at ALPHA." Cooper shot him a grin. "Welcome back, brother."

Relief coursed through him while some of the tension in his shoulders released. "Who cleared me?"

"I got the green light from Providence," Cooper replied.

"Thanks for telling me." Jericho glanced around for Livy, but she and Addison had taken Annie inside. He regarded his friends. "Thanks for being here. Means a lot."

"We love you, babe," Hawk said.

"If you need help with hacking, call me," Stryker said. "I don't care if it's three in the morning. And if you need a spotter to close that loop, I'm there."

Jericho squeezed Stryker's shoulder. "I appreciate that, but I gotta do this on my own."

"That was *my* problem," Cooper said, "and it was *you* who told me I didn't need to do it alone. Whatever you need, I'm there. We all are."

"Where's Prescott?" Jericho asked.

"Out of town," Cooper replied. "He's gone dark."

Jericho's brother, Mark, came rushing outside. "Dad and Gram are going at it. It's like one of your fights at The Road."

Jericho strode inside, Hawk, Cooper, and Stryker close on his heels.

Gram was standing in the middle of the kitchen glaring at her former son-in-law. "How dare you come into my home and think I'm going to welcome you back like nothing happened! You're a good-for-nothing excuse for a human being!"

Jericho had never heard Gram this angry.

"What's goin' on?" Jericho asked.

"I was telling Gram how sad we are over Bryan," Vincent said, "and she kinda blew up at Dad."

"You come into my house and act all sad." Gram's staccato pierced the silence as guests crowded in. "How dare you, Roger Savage! Bryan was a baby when packed up and left. I applaud that, but take your family with you, you son of a—"

"Okay, Gram, you gotta relax," Jericho said. "He's not worth it."

Gram was breathing hard and clutching her chest. "Get him out of my sight."

"You gotta go," Jericho said.

"Oh dang," Vincent said. "How 'bout I hang with Gram and Dad takes off?"

This isn't a fuckin' party.

Crossing his arms over his chest, Jericho shook his head. Within seconds, Hawk, Cooper, and Stryker flanked Jericho.

Vincent and Jericho's dad regarded the men.

"Hey, guys," Vincent said. "You're Hawk, right?"

"Last time I checked," Hawk deadpanned.

"Dude, help me out," Vincent said to Hawk. "C'mon, we're buds."

Jericho took a step toward them. "Time to go."

Vincent's shoulders dropped. "Damn." Then, he eyed Gram. "Sorry things got a lil' cray-cray."

"You can come back, Vincent," Gram said. "But *he's* not welcome."

Stryker stepped forward. "Let me walk you out."

"I'm leaving," Jericho's dad snapped.

A red-faced Roger Savage left, Stryker and Hawk following closely. Vincent hugged Gram. "It's been fun, Gram—well, you know what I mean."

A growl shot out of Jericho. *Fuckin' idiot.*

Gram patted Vincent's face. "Be a good boy."

"Hey, Jericho, maybe we'll meet up at Cho." Vincent took off toward the front door.

Jericho swallowed down the bitter taste.

The room was quiet, all eyes on Jericho. "Today is for Bryan." He swept the crowd until he found his sister. "My sis put together some videos of Bryan. Georgia, you wanna start 'em up?"

"Sure." She hurried into the family room.

When the guests left the kitchen and the room cleared, Livy remained. His Livy. Only she wasn't his anymore.

She walked over and put her arms around him. The second she touched him, he pulled her close and held her. "I'm sorry," she whispered.

He tightened his hold, never wanting to let go of the lifeline he'd once clung to when his life had spun out of control.

"We'll start working together, tonight," she whispered.

"Thank you for clearing me to return to work," he murmured.

She peered into his eyes, then let go. The hug was over before he'd been able to enjoy it. But that's not why he was going to work with her. This wasn't about enjoyment. This was about revenge… and murder.

Whoever had killed his brother was already a dead man.

Liv loved being around Jericho's family. Despite their grief and their pain, they were still the wonderful people she remembered them to be. Except his brother and dad. Their bold behavior seemed out of line. While they *were* family, they were outsiders. But she wasn't there to analyze the situation, and she certainly wasn't there to offer her professional opinion.

She was there to pay a debt to someone she'd wronged and regretted hurting. She was there to put Jericho first, like he'd done for her all those years ago.

Liv had turned in a glowing assessment to Z. Jericho was ready to return to work, despite the loss of his sibling. As she sent it through the secure portal, she wondered how long it would take her uncle to learn of her lie. There was nothing that man did not know.

Nothing.

To further complicate her life, she was going to help Jericho find his brother's killer, be his alibi, and lie about it. If he was going down, so was she.

Georgia started the video and the crowd turned toward the large television in the spacious family room.

The first video was of three-year-old Bryan playing with Georgia. It was as adorable as it was heartwarming. The next one was of the entire Savage clan at the beach. It looked like utter chaos and a total blast. Liv had grown up with the strictest dad on the planet. His idea of fun was doling out reading assignments and insisting his daughters each write a detailed book report.

"Hey, that's you Livy," Jericho's brother, Mark, exclaimed, plucking her from her childhood thoughts.

Jericho had videotaped one of the times she'd babysat Tim, Mark, Georgia, and Bryan. He'd come back from taking his mom to the doctor. Like most times, Liv stayed to help Jericho make dinner. His grandmother hadn't moved in yet, and it was Jericho's responsibility to take care of them.

Liv watched her younger self interact with them. She and

Georgia were helping Bryan, who looked to be four, build with LEGO DUPLO. They were laughing and having so much fun.

Then, Jericho had called her name. She turned to the camera and grinned at him, then blew him a kiss. "I love you, Livy Blackstone," whispered sixteen-year-old Jericho. "You're the best."

Liv had never heard him say those words, but the camera had picked them up.

Oh, wow.

Liv glanced around. Jericho was standing in the back of his spacious family room surrounded by his friends. He winked, and the hardness around his eyes softened a little.

"Awww, that's so sweet," Georgia said. "We always had so much fun whenever Livy babysat us. Hey, Bryan, do you remember—" Georgia stopped, the color draining from her face. "Ohmygod, I can't do this." She jumped up and ran out of the room.

The group fell silent as the video continued playing.

Liv's heart broke for them. "I'll go." As she passed Jericho, she stopped. "Where's she headed?"

Jericho pointed toward the massive winding staircase. "Second on the left."

Liv trotted up the stairs, her thoughts on Georgia. She'd always loved watching the Savage kids, and she felt like she and Georgia had a special bond simply because they were the only girls in a sea of Savage boys.

Tap-tap-tap.

"Georgia, it's Liv. Can I come in?"

No response. Liv waited. Another few seconds passed before Georgia opened her bedroom door. She wiped her eyes and blew her nose in a tissue.

"Come in." Georgia sank into her oversized beanbag chair. Her eyes were smeared with mascara, her shoulder-length, dark blonde hair was tucked behind her ears. Liv walked into the bathroom, moistened a few tissues, and returned to clean up Georgia's face.

"I'm surprised you're here," Georgia said. "I'm happy to see you. Well, I'm not happy. Ugh, you know what I mean."

"I do." Liv threw away the dirty tissue, returning to sit on the floor.

"Jericho doesn't like you, but he never told any of us what happened," Georgia blew her nose again.

"Doesn't matter. I'm here now and I want to help you, if I can."

Georgia sighed. "Can you bring Bryan back? That's the only thing that will help."

"I know you two were close. You always looked out for him."

"I loved having a baby brother. I used to dress him up and he never minded, well, until he didn't like it anymore." Georgia cracked a little smile. "Life is so unfair."

"Yeah, it is, and a lot of time it makes no sense."

"How am I supposed to do this, you know, without him?"

"One day at a time," Liv offered. "You can pray. You can join a grief group. You can talk to a friend or a counselor. You can carry his memory with you and keep him alive that way."

Tears filled Georgia's eyes. "Those are so practical. My entire body *hurts*. I can't eat. I can't sleep."

"I know."

Frustration flashed in Georgia's eyes. "How do *you* know how I feel?"

"I lost a sister, plus I'm a psychologist, and I've helped patients through this type of loss."

"I'm angry," Georgia whispered. "I'm filled with hate toward the person who killed my brother. I want to kill him myself."

Mostly, Liv listened. That's what she was trained to do. She asked a few questions. Offered a little guidance and a few suggestions.

"Thank you for listening," Georgia said. "You're really good at it." After a pause, she asked, "So, what happened between you and my brother?"

"I made bad choices and it cost me the best friendship I ever had," Liv replied. "I'm here to offer Jericho help, if he wants it."

Georgia laughed. "He's not a talker, especially about his feelings. He'll beat the punching bag in our gym, swim a bunch of laps, or go for a run. I've tried running with him, but he's a beast."

Liv smiled. "Everyone grieves differently and they heal differently, too."

"I'm never going to be okay," Georgia said.

"You will," Liv said. "Not today or even tomorrow. You'll find a new normal. Let me give you my number. Call or text me anytime."

Georgia typed it into her phone and hugged Liv. "Thanks for trying to help me. I know Jericho would never tell you, but your being here makes a difference."

The women stood.

Georgia opened her bedroom door, stepped into the hall, and startled. "Oh, you scared me. What are you doing?"

Liv joined Georgia in the hall.

Jericho was leaning against the wall, phone in hand. He'd pulled his hair into a half-bun so the front hair was pulled back, leaving the sides and back down.

He's grown into a Savage, sexy beast.

"Livy's the best." She flicked her gaze to Liv, then back to her brother. "I'm not okay, but I will be." She turned back to Liv. "Thanks for talking with me." She vanished down the stairs.

"Get anywhere with her?" Jericho asked.

"She's hurting. All of you are." Liv studied him. Anger and pain shone from his eyes, his angled jaw set in a hard line.

He took a step closer. A shadow darkened his gaze. Unwilling to stop herself, she kissed him. Hard and deep. A growl rolled out of him, he threaded his arm around her, pulled her flush against him and kissed her back. A ravenous, needy kiss that had her gasping for air.

He broke away, sucked down a breath. "Thanks for helping my sister." Like thunder, his voice rumbled through her.

Her insides came alive, her lips tingled. She craved more. So much more. Heat blanketed her chest, spreading to her neck.

"Livy."

Having him once wasn't enough. She wanted his strong arms holding her close while their naked bodies—"

"*Livingston.*"

His commanding voice snapped her out of her fantasy. "What?"

"Where'd you go?" he asked.

"Where are we doing it?"

Another growl rolled out of him.

"I mean working. Where are we working?"

Get it together.

"At The Road."

Side by side, they descended the stairs. For as many years as had passed, they fell into a rhythm so familiar and comforting to her that she felt like that missing puzzle piece had been found.

But she was helping him because she owed him.

At the bottom of the staircase, Tim and Patty were waiting. Tim held Owen while Patty held Annie's hand.

"You guys heading out?" Jericho asked.

"I know today is the absolute worst day," Tim started. "And our timing is terrible—"

"Just say it," Jericho said. "The lead-in isn't helping."

"Can we stay here for a few weeks?" Patty blurted. "Our kitchen remodeling is stalled. The cabinets are on backorder. The room has been gutted and we're trying to cook with a camping stove and a microwave."

"The downstairs suite is open," Jericho said.

Patty hugged him. "Thank you. We didn't want to ask."

Jericho's eyebrows slashed downward. "Why the hell not?"

"It's such an imposition," Patty replied.

"Not to me. We're family." Jericho ran a gentle hand down little Owen's back. "Don't tell Vincent. He took one look around and was ready to replace Bryan."

"Ohgod," Tim blurted. "That makes me sick to my stomach."

"Who?" Patty asked.

"Our oldest brother," Tim explained. "The one who came with Roger, our shit of a father."

"Daaaaddy," Annie scolded. "Bad word."

"Sorry, honey," Tim replied.

"Can I sleep with Auntie Georgia?" Annie asked.

"We can talk about it," Patty replied before regarding Jericho. "We'll move in tomorrow." She offered a rueful smile. "You handled today well. Tim and I thought you were going to kill Roger."

Jericho lifted Annie, gave her a kiss on her cheek. "Gram was way more fired up than I was. He's not worth my time." He set the child down.

"Nice to meet you, Liv," Patty said. "Thank you for watching the kids. Those videos were lovely to see." Patty glanced from Liv to Jericho. "You've been friends for a long time. That's nice." She regarded her husband. "Ready to head out?"

"Yeah." Tim hugged Jericho. "You doing okay?"

As Jericho scraped his fingers through his beard, he slid his gaze to Liv.

"Never effin' better," he ground out.

8

THE SEARCH IS ON

"Ride with me," Jericho said. He wasn't asking. He was demanding. He waited. Livy didn't push back. That worked.

For the past hour, she'd been upstairs with Georgia, and the guests had thinned out. They found Gram on the sofa watching family videos. She looked so small against the backdrop of the massive furniture in the oversized room.

He sat next to her on his large sectional. "We're taking off."

She patted his hand before regarding Livy. "Thank you for helping out today."

"Anytime," Livy replied.

"Where are you going?" Gram asked.

"Out," he replied. After a chaste kiss on Gram's cheek, he took Livy by the arm and led her toward the door leading through the mudroom and into his garages.

He shouldn't like touching her as much as he did. But he did… a lot.

Once in the massive garage, he said, "Computer, open center garage door."

The door silently rose.

"I've never seen that," Liv said.

"We'll take my truck." He didn't open the passenger door for her. This wasn't a date. This was work.

"My security system is voice activated," Jericho explained as he backed out of the garage. "Hawk installed it."

He didn't ask her any questions, didn't make small talk. While he told himself he wasn't interested, that was a lie even he didn't believe. Having her beside him was torturous enough. The desire to sink his fingers into her wild hair and pull her close was killing him.

Not gonna make things worse by chattin' her up.

They arrived at The Road. The lot was packed with the dinner crowd, so he parked around back and they walked in through the front door. Instead of stopping at the bar, he placed his hand on the small of her back and guided her to his office. Hated that he liked touching her so effin' much, but he wasn't gonna sweat it. She was there to help him. Once she did, he wouldn't see her again.

Done.

He unlocked the door, pushed it open, waited for her to walk through. Once inside, he shut and locked the door behind them. Now, he had two problems. One, he was in a small space with an incredibly attractive woman, and, two, his ALPHA computer was in his private office.

Shifting toward her, he ignored the spike of adrenaline pounding through him.

"Going forward, everything we discuss, everything you see stays with you. Got it?"

"Absolutely," she replied.

He stood in front of the retina scanner on the supply closet doorframe, the light turned green and he entered the walk-in closet.

"Come on," he said.

"Where are we going?"

"Into my ALPHA office."

Joining him, she eyed the supplies.

"Computer, open the door," he said.

"Hello, Jericho," replied the computerized voice.

The back wall slid open and he turned back. "Go ahead."

She walked in, he followed.

"This is great," she said glancing around.

After he logged in, she stood beside him. He liked that she didn't get comfortable on the love seat. Showed she was ready to work. It would have been less torturous if she wasn't so easy on the eyes and she didn't smell so damn good. But he had to give her props for staying quiet.

He pulled up the video from Raphael's, let it run.

"Have the police seen this?" she asked.

"Yeah. I was told the case was turned over to homicide. Haven't heard from anyone."

"Can you play the video in slow motion?"

He did. When it finished, she fixed her gaze on his.

"The driver told you he was a TK," Livy began. "TK stands for Thriller Killers. They're an established gang, but they're new to the area."

He was curious about her life, but he stayed silent.

"I wish I had my laptop with me," she said.

"Not my problem."

"It kinda is. Run the tape again." He did. "Stop it... now."

He paused it. "The shooter is left handed and he's got a black tat that starts on that wrist and winds around his arm. Looks like a snake. Did the driver have a tat like that?"

"No idea."

"Can you enhance the video?"

"No, but Hawk can." Jericho pulled out his phone, dialed.

"Yo, baby," Hawk answered.

"I'm gonna drop the vid from the shooting into the portal. Can you enhance the shooter's arm? Livy wants a clear pic of his tat."

"Send it over and I'll see what I can do." Hawk hung up and Jericho uploaded it to the portal.

He called Hawk back. "Yup," Hawk answered.

"How long?"

"Fifteen. I'm five from home." Again, the line went dead.

Silence.

Jericho moved toward the door. "You wanna drink?"

"Iced tea." Liv followed him to his outer office, pulled a five from her wallet, and held it out to him.

"Save it." With his hand on the knob, he turned back to her. "You coming?"

She pulled her phone from her handbag. "I know someone who's an expert on gang behavior. He's the reason I—doesn't matter."

Curious, he decided to stick around. After shutting the door to his supply closet, he called his bartender.

"Hey, boss. Whatcha need?"

"An iced tea and a whiskey, neat. Top-shelf."

"Sugar or lemon with the tea?"

"Livy, what do you want in your tea?"

"Lemon, please."

She made a call, pressed her phone to her ear. He sat at his desk and opened email, but his attention was trained on her.

"It's Liv." Silence. "I know it's late." Her jaw muscles were clenching in her cheeks. "I need some help with a gang." As she listened, she started pacing in front of his desk. He liked her form, could stare at her profile all damn day. She raked her hand through her hair. "No, I'm not moving back and I'm definitely *not* spending a weekend with you." She huffed. "I should never have called." She hung up and stopped pacing.

"I'm gonna use your restroom." Liv was gone before he could tell her he had a private bathroom.

The bartender swung by with their drinks.

Seconds after he left, Liv returned. To his surprise, she was biting back a smile. "There are two people going at it pretty good in the Ladies room." She laughed.

Her laughter caught him off guard. Hadn't expected that. For that split second, his heart felt full, like everything was okay. But it wasn't. His brother was dead and Livy was back in his life.

He grunted out his frustration. "I need to bring a woman in with me. You up for the job?"

"This'll be a first."

As they made their way to the restroom, she asked if this type of thing happened a lot.

"I hear about it once a week, but I'm not here every day. It happens late at night."

BAM-BAM-BAM.

Jericho thumped on the Ladies room door with his fist before pushing it open. He gestured for Liv to walk in. Her smile sent a white-hot streak of desire through him.

"No way," she murmured. "You, first."

He walked in and she followed. The moans and grunts were coming from the oversized stall in the corner.

"Fuck, I'm gonna come," said a guy.

"Me, too," said a woman.

"Not in my restaurant." Jericho kicked in the stall door, stood in the frame, and glared down at them while Livy peered over his shoulder.

The man was sitting on the toilet lid and the woman was riding him pretty hard. The guy glanced over her shoulder. "C'mon, I'm so close, man. I haven't been able to get it up—"

"Get out and fuck somewhere else!" Jericho thundered.

The woman pulled off, yanked down her short skirt, and went flying past them. The guy stood and glared at Jericho. "I haven't gotten laid in months." He tugged his pants up and over himself, holding them in place with one hand while he swung at Jericho with the other.

He missed by several inches.

Jericho wanted to laugh. The drunk customer was only making things worse for himself. "Let's go, buddy. We'll call you a ride."

The guy threw another swing and missed again. He wanted to get Livy out of the bathroom, but when he glanced over his shoulder, she wasn't there. As Jericho turned back, the guy's fist was coming in fast. Jericho blocked it, grabbed his wrist and twisted him around pressing his face against the wall.

"No screwing in my restaurant."

"Go to hell," said the drunk customer.

Liv hurried back in with his GM, Jamal. "Hey," Jamal said taking the guy from Jericho. When Jamal turned him around, the customer's pants fell down.

"Pull up your pants, man," Jamal said. "You got kicked out last week. I told you not to come back. Now, I gotta call the cops."

"Fuck you," said the customer.

Jericho pulled out his phone and dialed 9-1-1. Fifteen minutes later, the guy was hauled away.

"I'll get a restraining order for him," Jamal said.

Back in his office, Jericho told Liv about his private restroom. She ducked in while he took a mouthful of whiskey. When she exited, she drank down some tea. Jericho opened his private office and they returned to his computer.

"I had no idea that went on in restaurant bathrooms," Liv said. "I've gotta get out more."

"It's disgusting," Jericho replied.

"You mean sex?" Liv asked with a smirk. He loved how her gaze had turned playful. He missed that most about her.

"Yeah, I mean sex," Jericho deadpanned. He checked the ALPHA portal. "Hawk uploaded a new video."

Jericho clicked on it, but it didn't open right away. "For fuck's sake."

She curled her fingers around his, still on the mouse. "Give it a minute. It's a big file." She squeezed his hand, but she didn't remove hers.

He stared at their hands, hers on his.

The air grew charged while blood whooshed through him. Her touch electrified him. When he peered over at her, she met his gaze. Another bolt of energy powered through him, this one landing between his legs.

Fuck, I want her.

His gaze wandered from her eyes to her long, thin nose. Her high cheekbones were turning pinker by the second and he loved that he was having that kind of an effect on her. When he dropped his attention to her mouth, her lips parted, her breathing shifted.

He waited for her to say something or tug her hand away. She did neither. The atmosphere turned turbulent like dark storm clouds rolling in to cover the bright blue sky.

"You let your hair grow long," she murmured. "I like it."

"You, too," he replied. He coulda told her he thought her hair was gorgeous, but he wasn't going there. "Looks good."

Dammit. Shut up, dummy.

"Who'd you call?" he asked.

Ah, fuck me.

He wasn't gonna ask her anything about her life.

Stupid fuck.

She took her hand off his. He fuckin' hated that. "Someone I worked with when I lived in Memphis."

He waited, hoping she'd continue.

"We dated. Lived together, actually. The relationship ended years before I left." She raked her long fingernails through her wavy hair, then as if out of habit, she pulled it into a bun on the top of her head, knotting it so it stayed there.

Hypnotized by her movement, he couldn't look away. When

she raised her hands, her breasts lifted. In seconds, she'd tamed her wild hair while igniting a flame in him.

Jesus, she's sexy.

"I was great at helping my patients," she continued, "but I couldn't help myself."

"What changed?"

"Addison visited me. Boy, did I get an earful. That woman does *not* hold back. She didn't like him and she didn't like the way he treated me."

He sipped the liquor. "She opened a club."

"Yeah, she mentioned it." Livy cleared her throat.

Jericho didn't have the degrees most of his friends had, but he did have something money could *not* buy. He had instinct. And it was never, ever wrong. Livy stunk at lying, at least with him. She knew about Lost Souls. Had she been there?

"You into cosplay?" he pressed.

"Not really," she replied. "You?"

"On Halloween."

She glanced at the screen. "The video uploaded. You gave me one chance, so I've got to make it count." She hitched an eyebrow before taking control of the mouse and clicking on the link.

As she studied the video, he studied her. She'd once been his salvation. A friend he could share his biggest fears and wildest dreams with. He'd wanted to be a Navy SEAL and she'd been so encouraging and so excited for him.

Then, his life took a turn, and that was the end of his childhood dream.

"That's definitely a snake tat." She regarded him. "I'll confirm with Detective Morales in the Alexandria gang unit. She'll know. And, no worries, I'll be discreet."

"Then, what?" he asked. "You gonna haul the killer in and offer him counseling?"

"No, *Jericho*, I'm going to help you track him down, then I'm going to be your alibi when the police come looking for you. I have to ask—" She stopped. "Never mind."

"Don't do that. Just say it."

"This could have been a gang initiation. New members are told to kill someone—doesn't matter who—in order to prove their loyalty. It could have been gang-on-gang violence—"

Frustrated, he furrowed his brow. "I'm not in a gang."

She released a sigh. "Two people were shot. Two weren't. Could this be ALPHA-related?"

"My brothers were shot because of me. I don't know who I pissed off or why, and I don't give a fuck. I keep things simple, you know that. I see a guy about to rape my best friend, I beat the livin' hell outta him. I'm all about getting' shit done. If anyone knows that, it's you."

Her mouth dropped open. He'd stunned her into silence.

"I gave you one chance. We're done." Jericho logged out of ALPHA.

Her eyebrows jutted into her forehead. "We just started."

"It's late and it's been a bitch of a day." Jericho put the computer to sleep.

"You took the driver's phone after you killed him," Liv said.

He stared at her. "You saw that?"

"I saw plenty," she replied. "We haven't even looked at that."

"We're done," he said.

"No, we're *not*," she insisted.

The ride back to his house was filled with a frigid silence. After pulling her hair out of the bun, she stared out the passenger window.

Once in his driveway, she said, "Bryan was a special little boy. From everything I heard today, it sounds like he was a wonderful man. You did a great job with him. Your mom would be so proud of all of you." She got out of his truck and headed toward her car, parked in his large, circular driveway.

Watching her go made his heart ache. It was already shattered from grief, but seeing her leave felt like a knife to his chest.

"It's better this way," he said to himself as he headed toward the house.

But it wasn't. Not really.

He'd just lost Bryan. Did he want to lose her again, too?

Friday, at eight in the morning, Liv left her condo to tail a Secret Service Agent being considered by ALPHA. Every other morning that she'd followed him, he left his house at eight thirty and drove straight to work. But, today, instead of driving east toward DC, he drove to Tysons Corner Mall, parked in the mostly-deserted garage, got into someone else's car, and they drove out.

Well, this is interesting.

The sedan pulled into the parking lot of a nearby hotel. The prospective agent got out, along with a woman. Liv snapped a few pictures of the woman, then uploaded them to a software program on her laptop. Within minutes, she had a match. He'd gone into the hotel with his boss's daughter.

Liv's stomach churned. The agent was married with children. His boss's daughter was a twenty-five-year-old sales rep. Unless the woman was bringing him with her on a sales call, those two were whooping it up in a hotel room.

While she waited, she typed up her report.

Almost two hours later, the couple exited the hotel. She tailed them back to the mall parking garage. Before the man got out, he leaned over and kissed the woman. She drove away. He got into his car, headed out of the garage, and drove to his office in DC.

"I don't think you're getting the ALPHA gig, buddy."

Liv uploaded her summary, along with the pictures, to a secure portal for Z's review. Unless she heard from him, that case was closed.

Next, she texted Jericho. "I'm going to APD to talk to my detective friend. I'll let you know what I learn." She sent it off. No dots appeared, but she hadn't expected a reply.

Off she went, in search of answers without appearing as if she were looking for anything in particular. She parked near the Alexandria PD and hurried inside where she found Detective Morales talking to a police officer.

When they finished, Mirabel said to her, "Have you got time to observe a gang member interview?"

"I'll make time," Liv replied. "Which one?"

"The Saviors."

"What's he in for?"

"Selling meth and driving a stolen vehicle."

Liv entered the room next to the interrogation room and eyed the man through the one-way mirror. He was texting on his phone. A moment later, Detective Morales and the officer joined him. She'd seen dozens of conversations like this one. The detective pushed for answers. The gang member offered very little. Liv studied his mannerisms, watched his facial expressions. He fiddled with his bracelet, shifted in the chair.

Thirty minutes later, the detective and the officer exited.

Morales walked into the observation room. "He's denying everything. What do you think?"

"He was selling the meth as a distraction to what was really going on. Were there other gang members in the area?"

"We didn't see anyone," Morales replied. "What about the stolen car?"

"That's all him. I think he stole it."

Morales nodded. "When the officer brought him in, the set-up felt staged to me. I agree with you about the car."

"You're the detective. I just analyze what I see."

"Thanks for the help. What brings you by?"

Liv glanced at the gang member in the interrogation room. "If you've got a sec, I've got a gang-related question."

"He can wait," the detective replied.

"I'm doing some research into area gangs. Do the TK's have a gang tat?"

"I don't know. Ask the sergeant's assistant if you can view some mug shots."

Liv found Sergeant Hayes's assistant, Bee, at her desk. Always friendly, she offered a warm smile. "How's it going, Dr. Blackstone?"

"Fine, you?"

"I'm leaving early today. My grandbaby turns one and we're having a weekend-long celebration."

"That sounds fun."

"Whatcha need?"

"I'm looking for a gang identifier."

"I can help you."

Liv pulled over a guest chair while the assistant toggled over to the department's online database.

"What am I looking for?"

"The Thriller Killer's tat."

"Got it." Bee started scrolling through the online mug shots. There were dozens. In addition to those pictures, the department had also started cataloguing tattoos, piercings, and other identifiers to help them ID gangs easier. After ten minutes of scrolling with no luck, Liv had her type "snake" into the search field.

Different photos filled the screen.

As Bee scrolled, Liv's gaze swept through the pictures searching for the snake tat.

"Stop." Liv pointed to one of the mugshots. "Can you open that one?"

Bee clicked and the photo enlarged. The serpent started on the back of his hand, then wound its way up his arm.

"That's it," Liv said.

"Hey, Dr. Blackstone... I mean, Liv." Liv glanced up to see

Sergeant Hayes. "What brings you by?"

"Research paper," she replied. "Just compiling some data."

"Got any plans this weekend?"

Jericho popped into her thoughts. "Hanging out with friends. You?"

"The wife and I are spending it at Deep Creek Lake in Western Maryland. I'm looking forward to some downtime."

"Sounds relaxing."

"Bee, when you have a minute," the sergeant said to his assistant.

"We're just finishing up here," Bee replied.

"Andre, maybe you can help," Liv said. "What kind of snake is that?"

The sergeant peered at the computer screen. "You want my best guess?"

She nodded.

"King Cobra."

"That's what I was going to say," Bee chimed in.

"My thoughts, too," Liv replied. "Thanks for your help."

"Any reason you're focused on this gang?" Andre asked.

"It's for a colleague who's doing his thesis," she lied. With a relaxed smile, she pushed out of the chair. "Thanks for your help, Bee. You both have a good weekend."

She'd spent her morning watching a married man go into a hotel room with his boss's daughter, then watched a gang member lie during a police interrogation. She, herself, had just lied to a detective, a sergeant, and his assistant.

As a trained psychologist, she knew that everyone lied. Some lies were bigger and more damaging, but everyone spoke falsehoods at various points in their lives. Her head was swimming with all the deceit.

On the way to her car, she checked for messages. Nothing from Jericho, but she did have one from Addison.

"Our new bartender called out sick," Addison texted. "Can you work tonight?"

"Yes," Liv replied.

Addison replied with a thumbs up and another text. "I hired a chef. She's got some great appetizer ideas."

Liv texted her back a smiley face.

Back in her car, she checked the ALPHA app for Jericho's whereabouts. He was at Jericho Road. The closer she got to his restaurant, the faster her pulse soared. She shouldn't be so happy to see him... but she was.

They weren't friends. That relationship ended years ago. They'd hooked up *once* and she'd kept her identity a secret. Their working relationship was filled with tension and they'd been reunited over grief. Not the best of re-starts, but she would take him any way she could get him.

She parked, went inside, set her sunglasses on her head. The staffers were getting ready for the early dinner crowd.

"Table for one?" asked the hostess.

"I'm here to see Jericho."

"Hang a sec." The hostess made her way through the quiet room. Rather than wait, Liv was curious about the other rooms. The only other one she'd seen had been the restroom. There was a long bar on the left and a large main dining room with tables and booths. Past that, were two small dining salons, a room with a mechanical bull, and a large room at the end of the hallway. Curious, she walked in to check that one out.

Rafters covered the high ceiling, a sound booth filled with audio equipment stood at the front, while tables and chairs crowded the left. The majority of the space was covered with a scuffed, wooden dance floor.

She'd been so busy focused on helping Jericho, she hadn't even paid any attention to the tunes coming from that room. Pausing, she thought back.

I never heard the music because his ALPHA office is soundproof.

An image of her riding him on his sofa crashed into her

thoughts. His hands roaming greedily over her heated skin while she fucked him to the moon, their cries of ecstasy heard by no one.

Her insides came alive.

"Mmm." Her moan pierced the silence.

She turned to leave. Jericho hung in the doorway, his arms gripping the top of the frame while his raw stare drilled into hers. She stilled, unable to move or breathe or think.

Her gaze dropped. Untucked blue shirt, stretched against his bulging muscles. Black jeans. Cowboy boots. Man bun.

Good God. He's so freakin' hot.

Another moan ripped through her.

He checked her out... slowly. Down to her open-toed stilettos, then back up.

Normally, when she tailed someone, she'd dress comfortably. A blouse and dress pants. Hoping she'd see Jericho, she'd worn a tight black skirt, a black scoop-neck camisole with a white shirt that she'd left partially unbuttoned. And stilettos.

In truth, she'd dressed for him.

His gaze darkened, her pulse shot up. Her body burned for him and she couldn't shut it down. It happened with so much intensity, she thought she'd pass out. Sucking down a breath, then another, she waited until the tiny yellow stars faded from view.

She moved toward him. He didn't budge.

"What are you doing here?" His eyes might be smoldering hot, but his biting tone sliced right through her.

She wasn't deterred. If anything, her resolve to win him over increased tenfold. She had to prove she wasn't the bad guy. Not this time around. She would do anything to help him, to pay him back, to show her allegiance.

"I have an update and thought we'd check the driver's phone," she whispered. "Plus, I've got an idea to move our project along."

His low, husky growl sent shock waves pounding through her. The sounds he made, the way his intense gaze never strayed from hers, had her swallowing down another moan. She wanted him, his anger, his resentment. She wanted all that overwhelming and overpowering animal magnetism so she could unleash her own pent-up desire on a man who could so easily handle it.

"Not interested. Nothing's changed." But he still didn't move.

She walked right up to him and stared into his bright green eyes. He narrowed his gaze, his breathing hitched.

"You agreed to let me help you. Now, you're stuck with me."

In an instant, he was on her, his greedy mouth on hers, their tongues crashing together in a blur of explosive passion. He had her up against the wall so fast, she was grinding hard against him before she realized he'd pinned her. One of his hands palmed her ass, the other was around her neck, cradling her gently.

Her thoughts were a mangled mess, but her body thrummed wildly. She needed him inside her, his hands massaging her breasts, his mouth biting her sensitive nipples. She couldn't stop the mewling sounds coming out of her and she didn't even care. There was no holding back with him, no filtering of her raw, gritty desire. She wanted all of him and she desperately needed him to take *all* of her.

"Take me in your office," she rasped out between kisses. "I mean... into. Take me *into* your office."

He broke away, panting hard. Wiping his wet mouth with the back of his hand, he stood there like a grizzly staring down his next meal. "Fuck, Livy. You, me. It can't happen."

It already has.

Breathing hard, she clasped his hand and marched toward his office. The door was open. She walked in.

"Why the hell won't you leave me alone?"

"Because you don't want me to." She ran her hand down the crotch of his jeans. His shaft was granite hard.

"My dick's got nothing to do with you and me."

"I get that you hate me. I hate me for what I did to you." She stared him down. "I owe you. Let me do this for you... for your family."

The seconds passed while their gazes stayed glued to each other. On a disgruntled huff, he closed and locked his office door, stood in front of the scanner. The light turned green. He opened the door.

"In," was all he said.

She entered his walk-in closet.

"Computer, open the door." The hidden door on the back wall slid open. "Go."

She walked in. He followed.

"You got ten minutes." She couldn't miss the chill in his tone.

"I stopped by Alexandria PD and got confirmation that TK's gang tat is a King Cobra," she said. "It starts on the back of the hand or inside the wrist and wraps its way up, stopping at the elbow or shoulder."

"So, what?"

He definitely wasn't making this easy for her. "Where's the driver's phone?"

After opening his safe, he handed it to her. "Password's gone."

"Nice. How'd you figure it out?"

"I got people."

She tapped on the phone icon, then scrolled through recent calls. "Did you look at these?"

He nodded, once.

"He made three calls in the hours before he went to Raphael's. Teak, Jaylah, and SJ. Did you call them?"

"I'm not using the phone until I know who I'm goin' after."

She tapped on the text message icon. There had been a few, but nothing about the hit.

"I'll find out where these guys hang out and swing by there tonight—" he began.

"I can't tonight," she interrupted.

"What the hell does this have to do with you?"

"I'm going with you."

"You? At a gang bar." He laughed. Even though he was laughing *at* her, his expression was breathtaking. "No way."

"We need a plan," she continued, unfazed by his pushback. "And I've got a couple of ideas."

He raised his eyebrows. "These, I gotta hear."

"No matter what we decide, we're doing this together, Jericho. *Together.*"

"We'll see about that," he replied.

9

LIV'S SECOND CHANCE

He loved how she said his name. Always had. He wanted to kiss her pouty lips when she finished saying it, but he wasn't gonna give her the satisfaction.

Taking Livy to a gang hangout was the least of his concerns. What he wanted to do to her now was causing him a major effin' problem. He was hard as fucking steel and no matter what they discussed, or what he tried to distract himself with, he was touting a boner that was starting to ache.

She launched into a plan. It was pretty good. Then, she told him her second one. Even better.

"Second one," he said.

"Me, too. We'll do that."

He raked his fingers down his beard. "I work alone."

"You need my help to pull this off. I can do this. I won't let you down. *Please.*"

He wanted her by his side. He craved her. Her beauty kept him anchored to her. She had a solid idea. She was smart, no doubt about that. But she was a civilian. Would she be able to pull her own weight or would she crumble under the pressure?

Only one way to find out.

He extended his hand. "Partners, this once."

Her smile sent his blood pumping through him. She shook his hand, then let him go, but her gaze never strayed from his.

He'd treat this like any other recon job. No room for error. Except now, he had to watch his own back... and hers.

No way would he let anything happen to her.

Jericho grabbed his phone, scrolled until he found who he needed. He dialed, hit the speaker button, slid his gaze to Liv. She'd worn her hair down, parted on the side, but not as wavy. Light on the makeup.

Damn, she's easy on the eyes.

"Hello," answered a woman.

"Is Buck around?"

"This isn't his number anymore. Hold on, I get calls for him all the time." A few seconds later the woman returned and rattled off a number.

Jericho called the new number.

"Buckster here."

"Yo, dawg. It's Jericho."

"Jericho, my man, it's been a while. How it's hangin'?"

Hard as a fuckin' rock. "You still plugged in to gangs?"

"Ah, no, I got outta that scene. I'm growing weed in Alabama."

"When you lived up here, where'd you hang out?" Jericho asked.

"Me and my boys played pool at CJ's in Arlington and drank for free at the Mad Dog. That used to be on—"

"Seminary Road?"

"They shut that down and opened one in Annandale."

"How's the weed business?" Jericho asked.

"Good, man. You want some of the finest—"

"I don't smoke. Thanks for the help." Jericho hung up, then jumped on his phone in search of those two bars.

Liv turned her phone toward him. "CJ's is still there."

Jericho found Mad Dog in Annandale. "If you can't go tonight, how's tomorrow?"

"That'll work," she replied. "What time?"

"Late." He gave her the once-over. "You got leathers and boots?"

She nodded.

"Wear those. And try not to look so damn sophisticated."

If she liked his comment, she didn't let on.

"We gotta talk about the motivation for the shooting," she continued.

He shook his head. "I'm not gonna even try to get in someone's head. The last thing I do is analyze—"

"Not that. Who ordered the hit and why? You… I mean, *we* kill the shooter—"

"For chrissakes Livy, there is no '*we* kill the shooter'."

"If we don't know *why* the hit happened, we're just reacting. What happens if Hawk gets gunned down next?"

He glared at her. Seconds passed. The energy shifted to combative, the need to pull her into his arms and kiss her was turning him hard again.

A growl rumbled out of him. She raised her eyebrows, stayed silent.

The hit was ordered by someone, and he—*not they*—needed to find out why.

"They were coming after me," Jericho said. "I work alone on ALPHA jobs. I don't take a spotter, don't need one. I don't wear a ski mask or use camouflage paint, or any of that bullshit. My kills are at night and I'm not seen—"

"You sure about that? I watched you gun down a man in cold blood."

Fuck, she's right again.

Her bein' right was starting to piss him off.

"Do you think someone saw you on a job?" she pressed.

"I took out a terrorist a coupla weeks back. Someone made me, but I took him out." He paused. "You know the players at ALPHA?"

"You, Hawk, and the one's I've been assigned to watch, like Cooper Grant."

She knows more than I thought.

"Hawk wondered if the guy I took out had a body cam."

"We need to check that out," she said "What about your brothers or Hawk?"

"You already asked me 'bout them," he snapped. "I said no."

"Humor me," she pushed back.

"Bryan just graduated from GW. He was going there in the fall for law." He shook his head. "There's no way someone would target him."

"Can you find out if he pissed someone off? Maybe someone cheated off him and he turned them in. Maybe his getting into law school meant one of his friends didn't."

Jericho pulled out his phone and scrolled. After searching for the dean of the law school, he dialed, put the call on speaker.

"Dean Marshall's office."

"Jericho Savage for the dean."

"Just a minute."

"This is Dean Marshall. How are you doing, Mr. Savage?"

"We're hangin' in. I'm trying to make sense of everything, so I gotta ask. Did Bryan have any enemies? You know, someone cheated off him and got kicked out?"

"I'm not aware of anything," said the dean. "Let me pull his records. Can I put you on hold?"

"Go 'head."

Jericho slid his gaze to Liv. She'd been staring at his chest, then her gaze jumped to his tats, then his hair. When her eyes met his, her lips curved at the corners. Inches away, the pull to touch her, kiss her was impossible to ignore. He wanted to tell her how beautiful she was, how much he admired her career. Instead, he hitched a brow. "Like what you see?"

She shrugged a shoulder. "Meh."

"Mr. Savage," said the dean. "There's nothing in Bryan's file that would indicate he had any enemies. He never had a run-in with a professor. He was an excellent student. I can check with a few of his professor's if you want."

"No need. Appreciate your help."

"Again, we're very sorry for your loss. Bryan was a wonderful young man."

Jericho hung up, the heartache rising to the surface. He'd come in to work to escape the pain, but Livy was forcing him to confront it.

"I can't do this," he said.

"I know it's rough."

"What do you know about losing someone?"

"My older sister died in a car accident two years ago."

Ah, damn. "I'm sorry. What happened?"

"Her boyfriend was trying to make it in the music industry and she'd gone with him to Nashville. Anyway, one night, she'd been drinking. On the way home, she crossed the median and got hit by a truck. When I moved to Memphis, we hung out on weekends and got close. I really miss her."

He covered her hand with his. "Life's a bitch, ain't it?"

"Some days, but we have to push through to get to the better ones. I'm not trying to make you feel badly about Bryan. I just can't jump to the conclusion that you're to blame for his death, that's all."

"Understood." He'd been stroking her soft skin with his thumb and gazing into her eyes. "You're so beautiful," he murmured.

Her eyes softened. "So are you."

They leaned forward at the same time, their lips coming together in a tender peck. "I can't stop thinking about you," he said, "and I'm so pissed at myself for not having any damn control."

"You're hurting." She ran the back of her finger down his cheek and over his beard. "We're falling back into old patterns."

He kissed her again, this time letting his lips linger on hers. "I don't remember any pattern like this."

"Right, there was definitely no kissing in high school."

"Not because I didn't want to."

"I was so terrified of my dad. Do you remember how strict he —" She stopped. "Sorry."

The mention of her dad soured his already dark mood.

She cleared her throat, moved away. He hated that even more.

"What about your older brother, Vincent?" Liv continued. "What's he up to?"

"He and my dad moved back here a month ago. They got a casket company in Oklahoma and they just opened an office in Chantilly. Divorced twice, no kids. He acts like he's still in high school. Into partying, drinking, women. He mentioned our dad's got a gambling problem."

"Hmm."

"Seriously?"

"People do crazy things when they're in debt."

"How would killing Bryan get him out of debt?"

"Maybe someone was sending him a message by hurting his sons."

Knock-knock.

Jericho headed toward his outer office. When she didn't move, he said, "I gotta close up here."

She shouldered her bag, followed him out, and pulled the closet door closed behind her. Back in his outer office, Jericho opened his door.

"Someone's here to see you," Jamal said.

"I'm not expecting anyone," Jericho replied. "Who is it?"

"She wouldn't say. Told me it was personal."

"Lemme walk Livy out."

"It's fine," she said. "I'll see you tomorrow."

He wrapped his hand around her arm. Their connection was immediate and intense. "I'll walk you out." To Jamal he said, "Where's the visitor?"

"At the bar." Jamal left.

"We'll talk tomorrow," Livy said. Pausing, she gazed into his eyes. "I'm sorry I betrayed you. For what it's worth, hurting you is my biggest regret." She stood on her toes and dropped a tender kiss on his cheek. "Thank you for a second chance."

Sad eyes met his before she broke away.

He wrapped his hand around her arm, pulled her close, and kissed her like she was his. No hesitation, no holding back. She groaned into him, opened her mouth, and kissed him back with an unexpected ferocity. Her fingers sunk in his hair, raked his back. Her moans turned him hard, her thrusting tongue had him tightening his hold.

Their chemistry was off-the-fucking rails.

When the kiss ended, she flashed a smile, then she was gone.

He pulled out his hair tie, raked his fingers through his hair. She was pushing all his buttons, even the ones he sure as fuck didn't need pushed. Not now. She was a distraction. A beautiful, sexy, strong-willed distraction.

I am so screwed.

He strode through his packed restaurant. As he approached the long bar, a woman he didn't recognize pushed off a stool. His attention jumped from her to the front door.

Livy turned back. A thrill spiked through him. There was never a moment she hadn't stolen his breath, even back then, when he hated her for being a wrecking ball in his life.

Her smile was a soft upturn of her lips, but it was the intensity in her gaze that kept him anchored to her. And that gorgeous, wild head of hair. She looked like the beacon he'd been searching for, for the longest time.

And then, she pushed through the door, and was gone.

Jericho stopped in front of the woman. "I'm Jericho. Whatcha need?"

"Hi." She batted her eyes at him. "I had drinks here a while back and you were behind the bar. I was with a guy, so I had to play things chill." She smiled up at him. "I'm alone. Thought we could get to know each other."

"Sorry, darlin'. No can do."

"But I'm unattached."

Livy popped into his thoughts. "I'm not."

As he returned to his office, he couldn't stop thinking about her. It was bad enough that he was even more attracted to her than when they were kids, but he'd agreed to take her with him on a recon job.

Dammit, Livy. If this doesn't work, it's on me.

Back in front of his ALPHA computer, he pulled up a website that provided background checks, and typed in Livingston Blackstone.

He wanted to believe she wasn't going to betray him again, but once burned, twice... cover your ass.

Twenty minutes later, he read the results. Her consulting company—Blackstone, LLC—was listed, along with her previous job in Memphis, but her job as a watcher was not.

No surprise there.

As he continued reading, his brain skidded to an abrupt stop.

Livingston Blackstone was co-owner of Lost Souls nightclub. Catwoman popped into his thoughts.

Tall, curvy, whiskey-colored eyes, and completely-disguised.

"No fucking way."

Liv had been serving drinks from the moment Lost Souls opened that evening. When she and Addison had been throwing around the idea, they'd done their research into cosplay and knew there would be interest. But this... this was insane.

Addison was right there alongside her pouring drinks as fast as she could, but Addison had never been a bartender, so she couldn't make the cocktails.

Hawk sidled up to the crowded bar. "Ladies, what's the word?"

Liv glanced around. No Jericho. Disappointment coursed through her.

"You should be back here helping us," Addison scolded.

He shot her a smarmy smile. "I just got off work. It's after ten on Friday and I'm ready to chill."

"How's Jericho and his family doing?" Addison asked as she served him a beer.

"His brother, Tim, and his family moved in today," Hawk explained. "Jericho said they were grilling and doing movie night for the kids."

Liv loved that he put his family first.

A man wearing reflective sunglasses slid onto a barstool. Last weekend, he'd invited her to hook up. She'd turned him down.

What's his name?

"How ya doin'? You're looking super sexy, girlie."

Inwardly, she cringed. "What can I get you?"

He lowered his shades and peered over the rims. "Name's Guapo. Remember me?"

"No," she lied.

"I wanted to get to know you, upstairs, but you turned me down. How 'bout tonight?"

"Still, a no."

The guy creeped her out, so she moved on to serve other members.

While Liv missed Jericho, she wouldn't have been able to spend a second with him. The place was crazy-busy all evening. The night flew by, last call was announced, and the crowd began to trickle out.

As soon as Addison and the bouncer went upstairs to check the suites, Guapo slid onto a stool.

Ah, crap, he's back.

"What's your name, honey?" he asked.

"Catwoman."

Shaking his head, Guapo said, "Not buying that. You ready to go upstairs now, baby doll?"

"I told you no, last weekend. Stop badgering me."

"You got a great body, plus you're all masked up. A little mystery is a total turn-on." Then, he leaned across the bar. "You're uptight and I know *just* what you need—"

Liv fisted her hands on her hips. "Out. *Now.*"

Hawk had been talking with a group nearby and made his way over. "What's the problem?"

"I'm a goner." Guapo flashed the peace sign, then strolled out.

As soon as the other customers left, Liv locked the door behind them and turned up the lights. "What a creep," she mumbled.

"I'll stick around 'til you guys close up," Hawk said.

A few moments later, Addison and the bouncer came back down. "All clear," Addison said.

"Did my friend contact you about tending bar?" Hawk asked.

"Yup, and I'm trialing him tomorrow," Addison replied. "I fired the first one before we opened and the one we've got now is hit or miss. He calls out as much as he shows up."

"You'll love my guy," Hawk said. "He's reliable."

"Gonna grab our handbags." Liv took off for the office, collected their things, and met them at the front door. Addison set the security alarm, and they left.

On the way home, Liv thought of Jericho. Since he'd crashed into her world, she'd thought of little else. After crawling into bed, she jumped on the Lost Souls app, reserved a room, and sent Jericho an Invitation to Escape for the following night at midnight. If he accepted, she was going to remove her mask. She had to come clean.

He would hate her for it, but he'd hate her more if she continued deceiving him.

She added a note to her invitation. "Escape reality with me."

Seconds later, her phone binged with his reply. "I'll be there."

10

CHASING THE TRIGGERMAN

At nine o'clock the following night, Jericho pulled around the circle at Livy's condo building. He got out, walked around to the passenger side and shot her a text. "I'm here."

If it were a date, he'd go inside and get her, but this was a job. They were partners, not lovers. He bit back a smile. *That's all about to change.*

He glanced over as a biker babe exited the building.

"Hey," she said.

"How's it goin'? he replied, not looking up from his phone.

The woman stopped in front of him. He flicked his gaze in her direction. The biker babe was Livy.

"Whoa."

She stepped back. "Did I pull it off?"

Holy fuck.

"Damn, woman."

Black leather pants, black tank top, black leather jacket. She'd pulled her wavy hair straight, wore dark sunglasses. Several necklaces of varying lengths lay against her chest, two of them disappearing in her cleavage. Large, silver hoop earrings, several silver rings on her fingers, her nails painted black. Her lips were covered in dark purple lipstick.

Livy Blackstone was pushing all his buttons.

"You look scorchin' hot, mama," he said.

"You, too."

He'd worn a leather jacket, a black shirt, tattered black jeans, and black boots.

"Gimme a three-sixty… slowly." He loved the playfulness in her voice.

As he turned around, she whistled. "That is one tight ass."

When he finished, she lowered her shades to reveal a black eye. "Gotta make this look real."

"Nice."

She removed her jacket. Her arms were covered with bruises. "Make up and a few YouTube videos."

He was impressed. She was going all-in.

"I'm staying very close to you," she said.

He was liking this recon job more and more. After he opened the passenger door, she climbed into his truck. He jumped behind the wheel and they took off for CJ's.

He wanted to tell her the gig was up. He knew she was Catwoman. But he wanted to see how she'd handle their late-night hook up.

"I gotta drop you off before midnight." He glanced over at her.

In the darkened car, her gaze met his.

"That's fine." After a pause, she said, "I've never done anything like this."

"What are you talkin' about? You saw me take the driver out."

"I'm a watcher, not a doer. It's kind of exciting—I'm sorry, that's not the right word. I haven't lost sight that Bryan is gone. I'm aware that this is dangerous and you're taking a risk by bringing me. I'm not ALPHA. Being an expert on gang behavior is great when you're writing a paper or teaching a course, but this is real life." She placed her hand over her chest. "My heart is pounding way too fast right now."

"You got this."

Sitting tall, she folded her hands in her lap and cleared her throat. "I won't screw this up for you."

"I know that."

He pulled into the CJ's parking lot. The rundown building was in need of a facelift, starting with the sign. The J looked like it was one bolt from plummeting to the sidewalk. They walked inside and scoped out the place. The bartender was talking to a couple of old-timers. A man and a woman were playing pool. There were a few people sitting at tables.

"Hey, guys, sit wherever," said the bartender.

"We're gonna chill at the bar," Jericho murmured to Liv.

He left two empty stools between him and the other customers. Close enough to strike up a conversation, without being in their business.

The bartender sidled over. "What can I getcha?"

"I'll have a beer," Liv replied.

"Two Buds," Jericho said.

The bartender popped two and set them on napkins. "Never seen you before. New in town?"

Jericho took a hearty swig from the bottle. "I'm looking for a TK."

"A what?" asked the bartender.

"Thriller Killer," Jericho replied. "Got any gang members here?"

"Not anymore. They cleared outta here years ago when I stopped feeding 'em for free." Bartender held up his left hand. His pinky was missing. "It cost me my finger, but a guy's gotta make a living."

Though Liv didn't say anything, she stiffened on the stool. The bartender slid his gaze from Jericho to her.

"What's with the shades, Miss?"

She lowered them so he could see her black eye.

The guy flicked his gaze to Jericho. "You beating her?"

"This is my brother," Liv said. "He didn't hurt me." She pointed to her eye. "This was 'cause I told my husband I'm leavin' him. He didn't like that."

She took a mouthful of beer and swallowed it down.

Nice job, Livy.

"They could be over at a new club in Alexandria," the bartender said. "Lost… um… Lost something." After a pause, he blurted. "Lost Souls."

"Ohgod, no," she murmured.

There it is. She just gave herself away.

"The other place is Mad Dog's," the bartender continued. "They might be there."

"Thanks for the help." Jericho took another mouthful before dropping a twenty on the bar.

Liv slid off the stool.

Back in the car, he said, "You did good."

"I thought I'd be nervous, but I wasn't. I feel so safe with you." She shot him a little smile. "Things were always better with you."

"Same," he'd blurted before he could censor his damn thoughts.

"Thanks for saying that."

As he started the engine, their eyes met in the darkened truck. His heart kicked up speed. Livy was doing it for him in the absolute best way.

Kissing the badass biker babe was so damn tempting, but he shoved down the desire and pulled onto the street. Tonight was all about Livy making the first move.

"Do you think gang members are going to my… um… to that club he mentioned, Lost something?"

He flicked his gaze to her. "Lost Souls?"

"Mm-hmm."

"We'll swing by sometime and check it out." He loved messin' with her.

"That's Addison's club."

He nodded. "Don't say anything to her 'til we know."

"Of course."

He stayed silent, waiting for her to reveal that she was Addison's silent partner, but she said nothing more.

So much for full disclosure.

She cracked open the window, then started fiddling with her rings.

You are so busted, Blackstone.

Jericho pulled into Mad Dog's. The place was filled with trucks and motorcycles, customers drinking in the parking lot. Jericho drove around. No spots. He drove out back. Nothing. He ended up parking a block away.

He peered over at her. "Ready, sis?"

"Definitely."

As they walked down the quiet street, he wanted to put his arm around her, pull her close, kiss her. Being around her energized him, left him wanting more of her. But they were posing as brother and sister, so he kept his hands to himself.

Once inside, his eyes adjusted to the dim lighting and smoky haze that hung over the pool table in the far corner. Clearly, no one gave a shit that smoking inside was illegal.

"Stay close," he said.

No problem with that.

This dive bar had a completely different vibe. Most of the men were in leathers. Some in T-shirts and jeans. A group of women at a nearby table were wearing leather bras and leather shorts.

Several patrons turned in Jericho's direction. He was a

commanding man, built like an armored tank with bright eyes and long, mussed hair. It was hard *not* to notice him.

A middle-aged woman moseyed over. "I got a booth open."

"That'll work," he rasped.

His gritty voice snagged Liv's attention.

Once seated, the waitress smiled at Jericho. "Whatcha drinkin'?" She didn't even glance in Liv's direction.

"Two whiskeys, neat. Make one of 'em a double."

"You hungry, honey?"

The waitress's cheeks were flushing, she was arching her back a little. Whether she knew it or not, she was blinking in rapid succession. She was attracted to him. Liv couldn't blame her.

So am I.

"Just the booze," he replied.

"Love your hair." She licked her lips before heading to the bar.

Once the server was out of earshot, Jericho flicked his gaze to her. "How ya doin' sis?" He winked.

"I'm terrified of my husband and I'm covered with bruises. So, not good."

"Nice," he murmured.

Jericho shifted from her to the room. First, he did a sweeping gaze across it, then, he circled back and studied each person individually. Liv loved watching him work.

The server returned with their whiskeys. "Here you go, baby."

"I'm lookin' for someone," Jericho said.

"You and me both." She smiled at him. "Whatcha need?"

"Lucky's cousin."

"I'm Lucky's cousin," she replied with a snicker.

"No, darlin' you ain't," Jericho bit out. "Got any TK's here?"

"Sure. I'll send someone over." She spoke to the bartender who shifted his gaze to Jericho. Jericho leaned back, hooked his arm over the back of the booth. He looked like a man in total control, sexy as hell, and intimidated by no one.

Liv leaned forward. The lighting was bad enough without the

sunglasses, but it was near to impossible to see much of anything with them on. She lowered them. "Do you have a weapon on you?"

"Three," he replied.

"Oh, wow." She was so unprepared for this.

Bartender moseyed over. "I hear you're lookin' for someone."

"I got a proposition for Lucky's cousin," Jericho replied.

"He's not here."

"My sis is in bad shape. Show 'em, honey."

Liv slid off her jacket, removed her sunglasses. The bartender gaped at her purplish bruises.

"I've got a violent husband," she murmured.

The bartender studied Jericho. "Why can't you help her out?"

"I did five years 'cause I turned a jerkoff's face into pulp, and that was just one of the guys," he lied. "Plus, I need an alibi. I'm leavin' this job to the pros. I got a friend who said Lucky's cousin is the best."

"Can you get word to him?" Liv asked. "I'm terrified my husband's gonna kill me." Tears filled her eyes.

"Hang tight. I'll see what I can do." The bartender stopped at a table in the back before returning to the bar.

Jericho caught her gaze. "You're doin' great."

"It's you," she said, her voice low. "I'm just following your lead."

A few minutes later, a guy in leathers and a skull cap walked over. He was stocky with a thick scar that cut through the middle of his mustache. He had a tat on his neck and one on his right hand.

Liv regarded him with a cool gaze.

"I heard you're in a bad way," he said to Liv. "Can I sit?"

"Pull up a chair," Jericho said.

Instead of grabbing a nearby chair, he slid next to Liv. Her skin crawled and she moved away from him.

"Someone roughed you up good. You need me to take care of him for ya?"

"I'm good," Liv replied.

"I get the job done, no questions asked. How much you payin'?" Beneath the table he placed his palm on her thigh. She shoved him. "Get your fucking hand off my leg, you son of a bitch."

On a growl, Jericho pushed out of the booth, grabbed the guy by the scruff of his jacket, yanked him out of the booth, and shoved him.

"Get the fuck away from her!" he roared.

The guy pulled out a folding knife and its blade snapped into place. "I'm not afraid of you."

Ohmygod. Liv's heart galloped in her chest.

Towering over him, Jericho whipped out his seven-inch, fixed blade fighting knife. "You should be."

The bartender and server rushed over. "Take it down, boys. We don't need the cops here."

When the guy slipped his knife back into its sheath, Jericho did the same. But Jericho looked like a beast preparing to do battle. More than his "don't fuck with me" 'tude, his flared nostrils, angry stance, and seething eyes left no doubt he could do some serious damage.

"If you think I'm playin', just try me," Jericho glowered at the gang member.

"She's your sister, not your old lady," said the gang member. "Whad'ya care if someone has a little fun with—"

Jericho clocked him with a right cross. The guy staggered backwards, banging into a table. Beer bottles toppled over and everyone looked in their direction.

Liv's mouth dropped open. She hadn't seen *this* Jericho in a long, long time. The difference between then and now? Jericho was bigger, stronger, and much, much faster.

"You're fuckin' with the wrong man." Slowly, Jericho turned to the bartender. "Where the hell is Lucky's cousin?"

"He'll meet you here tomorrow, nine o'clock."

Jericho handed a fifty to the bartender, same to the server. "I'm coming back tomorrow night and I don't want no trouble." Without waiting for a response, he clasped Liv's arm and led her out the front door.

Liv had never been so terrified and so aroused in her entire life. Jericho was the baddest ass she'd ever met and there was no way—*no way in hell*—she was letting him go.

Jericho drove out of the parking lot muttering a string of obscenities under his breath, finishing with, "I fucking knew bringing you with me was risky. I should have trusted my gut, but I can't say no when it comes to you."

He fucking hated when shit came flying out of his mouth.

She dropped her sunglasses in the cup holder. "Pull over."

He'd driven several blocks, but he was too pissed to give a fuck where he was headed. "I'm so fucking angry," he growled.

"Pull over. *Now.*"

The second he did, she was all over him. Her mouth, her tongue, her fingers in his hair. Her savageness took away his breath. In seconds, he was rock hard. He was a man on fire, the heat of their passion burning through him like a blazing wildfire torching everything in its path.

"I need you," she blurted between kisses. "So damn bad."

He ended the kiss, didn't take his hands off the sides of her face. Her wild eyes were locked on his, her lids hooded.

Twenty minutes to his house or hers. Thirty to Lost Souls. Then, his brain kicked in. He had to see how she was going to handle their club hookup. "Like I said earlier, I got plans."

Surprise flashed in her eyes. "I understand."

He glanced at the clock in his truck. It was eleven. Just enough time to drop her off, get to the club, and wait for her in the Pink

Room. *Fucking irony.* They coulda just stayed together if she'd come clean about being Catwoman.

"I'll take you home."

She pushed off him and pulled on the seat belt.

They drove the rest of the way in silence. He glanced over at her. She returned his gaze. He waited for her to tell him she'd sent the invitation. Instead, she broke eye contact, stared out the windshield.

Women were complicated, but Livy was in a class of her own. She'd knowingly screwed him. Must've liked it enough to want to do it again. They were ending up at the same location, so why not come clean and drive over there together or tell him the truth and invite him to spend the night at her place?

As he pulled up to her condo, the answer came to him.

She's afraid I'll be pissed she kept her identity a secret. And I'll stop talking to her all over again.

She grabbed her sunglasses, opened the truck door. "Thanks for including me tonight. Your world is much more exciting than mine."

"My world is exciting because you're in it."

This time, he got a full-on smile. She got out, shut the door, and vanished inside.

On the way to Lost Souls, his phone buzzed. Catwoman had sent him a message in the app.

"Tonight is for you. A massage and a happy ending."

He couldn't wait to see her, but he did *not* deserve a happy ending. He was one of the bad guys who lived by his own set of rules, and would probably die by them too.

He was meeting her because he couldn't stay away. When it came to Livy, he could never say no.

Time to forgive her and move forward... together.

11

BARING IT ALL

A mix of excitement and jitters had Liv's guts in knots as she walked into Lost Souls. Telling Jericho the truth meant accepting the consequences. The fear of losing him sent a shudder through her, but she had no other option.

As she made her way through the crowded club, she glanced over at the bar.

Two bartenders. Neither was Addison.

Up the stairs, down the hall, and into the Pink Room. Diffused pink light bathed the room in color. A massage table sat flush against a wall. Across the room stood a dark pink sofa, the cushions covered with a pink silk sheet. Next to it, a winged-back chair, also pink.

She sat in the chair, crossed her legs, and tried to relax.

Deep, slow inhale with a slow release.

She was conflicted about *when* to remove her mask and cowl. If she told him *before* they had sex, he might not want to. If she told him after, he could resent her even more.

She'd worn a sexy cat suit that she'd bought to use in a suite. The faux leather outfit had crisscross ties across the tight-fitting bodice with a zipper in the back for easy on, easy off. Attached to the back of the bodice was a knee-length coat—with a high collar—that was cut short in the front. A faux leather thong covered her pussy. It was the sluttiest outfit she'd ever worn and she couldn't wait for him to see her in it. On her feet, stilettos. Also, easy on, easy off.

The door opened. Her heart jumped into her throat. Jericho. Just Jericho. No costume, just the beast of a man in a black T-shirt, black leather pants. In his hand he held his leather jacket. All man, all machismo. Her heart raced with anticipation. She wanted to jump in his arms and kiss him for days.

He closed the door. Her insides came alive.

Please forgive me.

She rose, but she didn't go to him. She stood there, giving him a moment to take her in. So much confidence and a brooding anger radiated off him. His commanding presence was a powerful aphrodisiac.

"Holy hell, darlin', you're rockin' that outfit. So fuckin' hot."

Fueled by hope, determination and lust, she sauntered close. "Hi," she whispered, running her fingers down his triceps.

As she stared into his eyes, her thundering heart roared in her ears. Tonight could be the end. Losing him the first time was bad enough, but this time, she'd never survive without him.

Jericho was a smart man. She had every confidence he'd recognize her voice, so she stayed quiet.

She took his jacket from him, then helped him remove his shirt. Pausing, she admired his sculpted chest. All muscle. Hard, developed pecs under soft, tanned skin. Glorious waves of pleasure pounded through her as she trailed her fingers over him, pausing to tease his nipples with her fingertips.

His body was a temple, and he was her religion.

When she started unbuckling his belt, he toed off his boots. Next, came his pants. To her surprise, he'd worn black boxer briefs. Those were removed and cast aside. His long, thick, and very hard shaft saluted her. She stroked it once, then again. It would be easy to get lost in this Adonis of a man, but she would stick to her plan… no matter how desperately she wanted him.

She patted the massage table. "On your stomach," she whispered.

As he climbed on, she retrieved body oil. After pulling the pink sheet over his legs, she drizzled oil into her palm, rubbed her hands together, and began to massage his shoulders. Soft, gentle strokes that morphed into stronger ones.

"Oh, yeah," he groaned out.

She loved touching him, loved doting on him.

"Tell me about yourself," he said.

Leaning close, she whispered, "Not yet," as she rubbed through the train of knots trailing across his shoulders. Taking her time, she massaged those out before moving to his upper back, appreciating his thick, striated muscles that bowed to her touch.

Slowly, she made her way down his back to his glutes. He had the sexiest ass she'd ever seen. Tight and round.

"Feels great," he murmured.

She smiled, grateful she could do this for him. After reading his ALPHA file, she knew he worked nonstop. Missions, recon assignments, plus all the restaurants, and his family. Then, Bryan, and the pressure he put on himself to right a horrible wrong.

Inch by inch, she finished his legs.

"Can you turn over for me?" When he did, she asked, "how are you doing?"

"Damn good."

She kissed his forehead, then started massaging his chest. "Mygod, you're a sexy beast," she blurted.

Ah, crap.

She'd been so into him, she'd forgotten to whisper.

He gazed up at her, the normal divot between his eyes had been replaced with a calmness she hadn't seen in years. "Take off that damn mask."

Here we go.

She untied it and set it down.

"Better," he said. "Lose the cowl."

"Shh."

She stroked his biceps and triceps while her insides simmered with desire. He was absolute male perfection. He was more man, more alpha than anyone she'd ever imagined for herself. When she moved on to massage his thighs, he started to harden.

A blast of heat had her sighing as she imagined him inside her, his glorious rod bringing her all the pleasure while she stared into his intense green pools and kissed his full, luscious lips.

"Mmmm," she moaned.

"I'll take that happy ending whenever you want to give it to me," he said.

She was going to finish her gift to him. If she gave him a thousand massages, it would never make up for the pain she caused him, but tonight was a start. Working her way down his bulging thighs and thick calves, she rubbed his feet before finishing with a scalp massage.

Then, she pressed her lips to his and whispered, "I'm all yours to do with as you wish."

His eyes fluttered open. She hardly recognized him. Gone were the deep lines and the anger in his eyes. His jaw had stopped ticking, his lips were curved upward hinting at a smile. The transformation was remarkable.

Another moan escaped her lips. A relaxed Jericho was even sexier than the fury-filled one.

Moving slowly, he swung his legs over the side of the table. Sitting up, he pulled her between his legs, placed both hands on her cheeks, and kissed her. Slowly, gently, and with so much passion, she released a coo.

His lips curved. "Never heard that sound before."

He stood, fished a condom from his pants pocket before scooping her into his arms and walking to the sofa. He set her down, knelt at her feet, and peered into her eyes. "Thank you for an amazing massage."

For a split second, her heart rejoiced. But in a matter of seconds, it might all be over. Tears pricked her eyes. Never before had she felt this way about another person.

Never.

She wanted to make amends and earn back his trust. Until they'd reunited, she hadn't realized how much she missed him. Would he look at her like that after she told him who she was? Would he love how they'd reconnected, how they hadn't been able to take their hands off each other, or would he resent her for what he considered her latest betrayal?

Biting back the tears, she ran her hand across the silky sheet, then patted it. "Sit beside me," she whispered.

"Take your thong off."

His commanding tone sent tingles of excitement flittering through her.

He pushed to his feet and rolled on the condom. She rose, wiggled out of it, then turned so he could unzip the jumpsuit that would release the bodice.

"That stays on," he said.

When he eased down on the sofa, she straddled him. Staring into his eyes, she wanted to blurt out the truth, but fear had constricted her throat. Leaning close, she pressed her lips to his. A series of mini-explosions soared through her and she sucked down several jagged breaths.

She took her time, savoring his mouth, before deepening the kiss. His growl reverberated through her chest, landing in her pussy, already slick with arousal.

He grabbed her hip with one hand, slid the other under her butt cheek. "Jesus, you've got the best damn ass. Made for some damn good fucking."

She wrapped her fingers around his shaft. His already hard cock firmed in her grip. As if he had nothing but time, he untied the crisscross laces over her breasts. When he opened it enough to expose them, he released a low, gritty growl.

"Your tits are too much. Too fuckin' much. I could suck 'em for days." He teased her hard nibs with his fingers until they plumped from his touch, then he repositioned her so he could suck.

And, mygod, could that man pull the pleasure out of her with his talented mouth, lips, and teeth. He nibbled, sucked, and bit her until she thought she'd pass out from the euphoria washing over her.

Never before had any man been able to draw out the gritty sounds coming out of her.

"I'm gonna come," she blurted before the orgasm ripped through her. She cried out through the onslaught of ecstasy, letting Jericho do what he did best. Take care of her, thoroughly and completely.

He hadn't even touched her pussy or her clit. It was his talented mouth on her nipples that sent her flying over the edge.

Panting, she pushed onto her knees. "In me," she ordered.

With his shaft in hand, he positioned himself at her opening. He was a big boy, but she could handle him. Sliding down on his hardness, she found his mouth and tongued him with such ferocity, he roared.

The glide of his erection stole her breath, his cock rooted inside her was a perfect fit. She clung to him, stilling for a few magical seconds. As she started moving on him, she opened her eyes.

Beautiful Jericho peered back.

Jericho was on fire. Desire burned through him like a five-alarm inferno that he never, ever wanted to extinguish. Being inside Livy felt too damn good. There was no second. No other woman compared. He wasn't going to let himself come until she'd revealed herself to him. He wanted to be inside Livy, not some stranger at a kink club.

"Take. Off. Your. Cowl."

She started shaking. "I'm afraid you won't like what you see," she whispered.

"You want me to have a happy ending?"

"Yes."

"Take it off," he commanded.

With trembling fingers, she removed the head covering. His heart kicked up speed. After all these years, they'd found each other again.

His cock grew firmer inside her beautiful, supple pussy. He raked his fingers through the long, stunning waves.

"You are so fucking beautiful," he said. "Kiss me."

The kiss was filled with relentless passion. The more powerful his kiss, the harder she kissed him back. Their tongues crashed against each other. He bit her lip. She yelped and ground against him. Then, she started moving on him. Slowly, effortlessly. Like they were made for each other.

Up and down she glided on him, taking him higher and higher. Sex had always been a physical release. Sex with Livy was an experience that touched the depths of his soul.

Being with her was pure euphoria. She had the ability to steal him away from the madness so he could shut out the demons that haunted him day and night. She started moving faster, grinding harder. He loved the raw, dirty way she fucked him. Her gasps and guttural groans sent him hurtling over the edge so hard he roared like a lion.

"Fuuuuuuucck," he ground out.

Wave after wave of ecstasy soothed his rage while she rocked him through the orgasm.

The minutes following were filled with passionate kissing, then tender pecks and soft caresses. When the kissing ended, they were still anchored together in the best possible way.

She was a goddess and she was all his. Their eyes met. To his surprise, anxiety sprang from hers. His smile, then another tender kiss, softened the crease between her sculpted eyebrows.

"Hello, Livy."

She let out a long breath.

"Are you angry?"

"Not at the moment," he replied. "You fucked the fury right outta me, darlin'."

Her smile was a mix of elation and relief. "I can explain."

"No need."

"Please keep my identity a secret here."

"Got it." After a pause, he asked, "Are you Addison's silent partner?"

This question was a test. He already knew the answer.

"Yes, I am." She ran gentle fingers through his hair. "Thank you for not being angry. I saw you… had to have you… wanted to give myself to you." Then, she gave him an adorable smile. "I knew you wouldn't want anything to do with me if you knew it was me."

She was right about that.

"I hope you liked your happy ending." She kissed the tip of his nose.

That elicited another smile from him. He hadn't smiled this much since… well, since fucking forever.

I loved it because it was with you, Livy.

He dropped a light kiss on her soft lips. "It was perfect."

Their moment of Zen ended when she pulled off him. They dressed, she hid her long hair in the cowl and tied on her mask. Together, they left the club.

He wanted to stay at her place, make love to her all night long.

In the parking lot, he walked her to her car.

"Where's your truck?" she asked.

He tossed a nod toward his motorcycle, parked beside her. "That baby's mine."

"I didn't know you rode," she said.

"There's a lot of things we don't know about each other."

"Maybe it's time we change that," she said.

He dipped down, kissed her. "Maybe it is."

"What kind of motorcycle is that?"

"Indian Springfield." His phone started buzzing in his pocket. Ignoring it, he said, "I want you to ride with me sometime."

Her eyes lit up. "I'd love that." She leaned up, kissed him. "Don't you need to get that?"

"I'm hoping the person will go away." He yanked his phone from his pocket. "Yo," he answered.

"We got a problem," Cooper said.

"Go."

"There's an active shooter at the Kennedy Center."

"It's almost one thirty in the morning," Jericho replied.

"This started just after eleven," Cooper explained. "As the evening performances were letting out, someone on the rooftop terrace near the Terrace Theatre opened fire. There are over a thousand people currently in the building, sheltering in place. The shooter won't talk to a negotiator. He's demanding ten mil, plus a laundry list of other things." Cooper paused. "He's got over thirty hostages. They're on the terrace with him, on the west side, near the restaurant. The good news—if we can call it that—is that the west side faces the river."

"What do you need?"

"We need you to take him out," Cooper said. "But you can't do it alone."

"Why the hell not?"

"It requires a long-distance shot, like a mile."

"So?"

"It's dark."

"I got this."

"The job is yours, but you gotta take a spotter."

He grunted. "Where's Hawk?"

"He can be at The Road in ten. When can you get there?"

"Five," Jericho replied. "I'm going dark."

"I'm on my way to the Kennedy Center. Use your comm."

"No. I can't have chatter in my ear. You can talk to Hawk."

"Good luck," Cooper said.

"Luck's got nothing to do with this." Jericho hung up, unlocked his helmet and straddled his bike. Then, he fixed his gaze on Liv. "I was two seconds from inviting myself back to your place."

"Tomorrow," she said, leaning down and kissing him. "Is this a—"

"Sniper job."

"Be safe."

"That's the plan."

"Thank you for tonight," she replied.

"Anytime." He winked. "As long as it's you." He pulled on his helmet, flipped up the visor. "Get in your car and drive out, so I know you're on your way home."

After she did, he followed her out, then accelerated, full-throttle toward The Road.

As much as he didn't want to say goodbye to her, he had to focus up. On the short ride back to his restaurant, he visualized the Kennedy Center and its surroundings. Cooper was right. There was no place nearby where he could get a clean shot from above the rooftop terrace, which meant Hawk would have to take him across the river into Rosslyn.

As he pulled around back, near his private entrance, he spied Hawk leaning against his Mercedes, smoking. More relaxed he could not have looked.

"Ready to work?" Jericho asked as he stood in front of the retina scanner.

"I'm taking the chopper out for a spin. No work required."

They entered his private office. Jericho unlocked his ALPHA computer and Hawk jumped online while Jericho readied his go-bag. With that done, Jericho joined Hawk at the computer.

Hawk was studying an aerial shot of the Kennedy Center and

the surrounding area. "We're landing on the Deloitte building across the river. It's one mile, but the wind is in your favor. It's five miles an hour with an occasional gust to ten."

"Copy," Jericho said studying the map.

Hawk pointed to a spot on the back of the Kennedy Center. "He's outside on the Terrace rooftop, overlooking the Potomac. The hostages are sitting against the building."

"How many?"

"Over thirty."

"Jesus. Let's go." Jericho set his phone on the desk, shouldered his bag, and the men left out the back.

Ten to Reagan Airport, another five to the helicopter. Every minute mattered, but they had to check a lot of boxes if they were gonna do this right.

While Hawk ran through his pre-flight inspection, Jericho lit up the bird with his megawatt flashlight. Nine minutes later, they were seated in the cockpit. Hawk fired up ALPHA's Bell 407 with its Rolls Royce turboshaft engine.

After pulling on headphones, Jericho focused on his breathing. He closed his eyes and visualized his shot. A mile was on the far end of his sniper shots, but he'd done it one other time.

"Tower, this is Bravo King Whiskey Alpha Alpha," Hawk said. "Alpha Alpha requests clearance for lift off."

"Alpha Alpha, what's your destination?" asked the controller.

"Alpha Alpha to 1919 North Lynn Street, Rosslyn," Hawk replied.

"Alpha Alpha, did you say Rosslyn?"

"Copy," Hawk replied. "Alpha Alpha is landing on the rooftop." Silence.

"Alpha Alpha, you're cleared for lift-off," said the controller.

"Cleared for lift-off, Alpha Alpha," Hawk repeated.

"Alpha Alpha, are you crossing into DC?"

"Tower, Alpha Alpha is *not* flying into DC," Hawk replied.

"Alpha Alpha, cleared for 1919 North Lynn rooftop," tower said.

"Here we go, babe," Hawk said, lifting the helo off the ground.

Hawk was the best pilot Jericho had ever known. The chopper ascended, banked left and sailed toward Rosslyn, cutting through the clear, nighttime sky. The flight plan took them west of the Potomac River, flying over Arlington National Cemetery.

Jericho kept his sights trained across the river. Two minutes later, the Kennedy Center loomed into view. "Target in sight."

Jericho lived for these missions. They breathed life into him, pushed him to his limits. If he didn't hit his target, there were thirty innocent hostages who might take the hit, not to mention the bullet piercing one of the windows of the building and killing someone inside.

Zero room for error.

"You got this," Hawk said, setting the bird down on the rooftop.

Before he'd cut the power and the blades had stopped whirring, Jericho was out the door. He shouldered his go-bag, made his way to the east side of the building.

Across the river, the white stone and marble structure lit up the dark sky. Every interior light facing the river was on, as were the lights on the rooftop. Jericho set down the bag and pulled out the tripod, attached his long rifle, then positioned himself on the roof's rough surface.

Using the scope, he searched the Kennedy Center's roof terrace. The hostages were sitting against the building, outside the restaurant. "I count thirty adults, three children. There are four bodies on the north side. See 'em?"

Hawk knelt beside him, binoculars to his eyes. "Copy. Where's the shooter?"

A man armed with a semi-automatic assault rifle emerged from the glass-walled building. "He just walked outside."

"I got eyes on him," Hawk said. "I'm turning on my comm."

After a pause, he said, "Cooper, we're in position. Where are you?" Silence, then Hawk said to Jericho, "Cooper's been trying to work a deal with him."

The gunman started pacing back and forth in front of the hostages. Then, he broke away and walked to the edge of the terrace, pointed his rifle across the river, and opened fire.

"He's fucking insane," Hawk bit out. "Does he know we're here?"

"I don't think so," Jericho replied. "He's showing them who's boss. It's a scare tactic."

"Well, it's scaring the hell out of me."

Jericho smiled. Hawk had nerves of steel. Nothing rattled him.

"There are three children in the hostage group," Jericho said. "I don't want them to see what I'm about to do."

"We can't wait this out, bro. If he turns on them and starts shooting, that'll be the last thing those kids see."

"Copy."

Jericho repositioned, trained his gaze through the scope. The terrorist wouldn't stop pacing. He watched as the gunman walked to the far end, stopped, then walked back. The length of the terrace facing the river had to be two hundred yards. After slowing in front of the hostages, he pointed his gun at them, then continued to the other end of the building.

Back and forth he walked, twice. Then, he lifted his phone from his pocket and took a call during which he became very agitated, pulled the phone away from his ear, and started screaming.

"He's a lunatic," Jericho murmured.

"No surprise there," Hawk said, then added, "Cooper says the terrorist is allowing a swap to free the children. Cooper's going dark."

The terrorist walked over and said something to each of the children. They stood and followed him to the sliding glass doors leading into the building. Both men watched as the kids hurried inside. Second later, Cooper walked out, his arms in the air.

"Ah, fuck," Hawk bit out.

"Okay, Coop, you puttin' the squeeze on me, aren't you, bro?" Jericho murmured.

The terrorist patted him down, then rammed him in the stomach with the butt of his rifle. Cooper crumpled to the ground.

"Fuck-fuck-fuck" Hawk bit out.

The terrorist began walking the length of the terrace again. Jericho had to move fast. He heaved in a breath, let it out slowly. He rested his finger on the trigger.

"I'm gonna take him out at the far end of the building. When he gets there, he stops for two-to-four seconds, turns, and starts walking back," Jericho said.

"Copy."

The gunman started walking, got to the middle of the building and stopped. Then, he pointed his gun in Cooper's direction. Pushing off the ground, Cooper joined him. Together, they started walking the rest of the way.

Jericho's stomach dropped.

When they got near the end, the shooter stopped. Cooper stilled two paces behind him. The shooter turned toward Cooper, appeared to go on a tirade, and Cooper dropped to his knees.

This is it. Take your shot.

Jericho homed in on the small space between the terrorist's eyebrows. It was a harder shot than if he hit him in the chest, but it was lethal. Hitting him in the chest might not kill him. Sending a bullet through his brain would.

He inhaled, let out some air, then paused his breath. *Easy does it.* He squeezed the trigger, the bullet rocketed across the river.

Hawk jumped up, binos in hand. "C'mon, c'mom."

The two seconds it took for the bullet to fly across the river felt like an eternity. If Jericho missed, one of his closest friends in the world would be dead. The blood on his hands would be more than either he or Hawk could handle. He could justify taking out the bad guy, even to God himself, but he could not live if his friend died because he couldn't do his damn job.

The shooter pointed his gun at Cooper's head, then crumpled to the ground.

"He's down," Hawk said. "Beautiful shot, Jericho. Terrorist is down. Let's get outta here."

Jericho released his breath. "Confirm."

"Confirmed."

Jericho removed his finger from the trigger, grabbed his binos. Cooper put the comm back into his ear as a SWAT team ran onto the Terrace, their guns draw.

"Cooper says thank you," Hawk said.

"Tell him 'anytime brother,'" Jericho replied.

Hawk relayed the message, then asked Cooper if he was okay." After listening, Hawk said to Jericho, "Coop's good, and we're cleared to leave."

Jericho pushed off the ground and extended his hand to Hawk. "Thanks for having my back, dawg."

Hawk clasped his hand, pulled him in for a bro-hug. "Thanks for having mine, babe."

12

LIV'S NEW ASSIGNMENT

Sunday morning, Jericho was playing with the kids in the shallow end of the pool. Both were wearing arm floaties, but he had Owen in his arms and both eyes on Annie.

"Catch me!" Annie jumped in and Jericho pulled her to the surface. "Again!"

He laughed before lifting her out and setting her on the edge.

She jumped in again.

"Time for your lesson," he said.

Annie wiped the water from her eyes. "I love jumping! It's soooo fun."

"I jump," Owen said.

"Okay, buddy, you get a turn too." Jericho set his nephew on the side of the pool, held his chubby hands and counted to three. Owen jumped in and Jericho pulled him up.

He giggled. "I jump."

Jericho did this again while making sure Annie was above water.

"Who wants a swim lesson?" Jericho asked.

"I do! I do!" his niece exclaimed.

"I do!" his nephew parroted.

It was another basic lesson that he hoped would help them, but they were so little and, when it came to children, he didn't have a clue. But they were adorable and easy to manage. They were a hell of a lot easier than his complicated relationship with Livy.

After showing them how to blow bubbles, he held Owen while Annie tried it. She inhaled, held her breath, shoved her face in the water, and blew. Annie did it over and over until he held out his arm, like a bar, letting her cling on. With her face in the water, he pulled her for a few seconds, then lifted her out.

She was smiling, got water in her mouth, and started choking.

He gently patted her on the back. "Cough it up."

When she stopped, Jericho turned to Owen.

"Your turn, buddy," Jericho said. "You wanna hold your breath and put your face in the water?"

He eyed his sister. "No."

Even after Jericho demonstrated, it was a no-go for the tyke.

Jericho needed to blow off steam with laps, so he glanced around for Bryan, expecting to see him playing a game of water hoops in the deep end. But Bryan wasn't in the water. Pain slammed his chest, the harsh reality ripping his heart open all over again.

Tim walked outside. "Are you ready for a break?"

Shoving down the ache, Jericho set the kids on the side of the pool. "They're all yours."

"I don't want to stop," Annie said. "I want to play in the water."

"Me, too," Owen echoed.

Jericho left the negotiating to his brother. Pushing against the side of the pool, he began with free-style. Swimming helped assuage the anger. Water always did that for him, but not today.

The harder her swam, the more agitated he grew. Back and forth, changing from free-style to breast stroke, then butterfly. His mind wouldn't clear. He thought of Bryan and the gangbanger he'd killed. His thoughts drifted to the guy he was gonna take out next. The triggerman. Then, what? Would the deaths of these men be enough?

I'm not stopping until I kill every last one of 'em.

His lungs burned for air, so he burst out of the water in the deep end and threw his arms over the edge while catching his breath. And that's when he saw her.

Livy.

A thrill raced through him.

She and Georgia were sitting at a patio table on the other side of the pool talking. Looking super-hot in a white shirt and a short pink skirt, she was laser-focused on his sister. He soaked up her muscular thighs and shapely calves.

The pull to be near her had him swimming over. When he reached the shallow end, he stalked out of the water, wiped his eyes, and raked his hands through his soaked hair. Trailing droplets of water, he made his way over.

As they locked eyes, every bad thing in his world evaporated. There she was and nothing else mattered.

Her gaze dropped to the grim reaper tat on his chest, then to the words beneath it, "My Life My Rules". After scanning his torso, his bathing suit and legs, she flicked her gaze back to his face. He loved that she was checking him out. A hungry desire swept through him. He wanted to pull her into his arms and kiss her hello like she was his.

Because, dammit, she needs to be.

"I invited Liv for brunch," Georgia said.

Like he hadn't figured that out for himself.

"Got a bathing suit?" Jericho asked.

She nodded.

"Swim with me," he said. It wasn't an invitation. It was him telling her what he needed, what they both needed.

The corners of her lips curved upward. "I'm hanging with Georgia."

His sis rose. "You should swim. I'm going to journal. Thank

you for talking to me. You've been so supportive and super helpful." She gave Liv a hug.

Happiness shone from Livy's eyes. "I'm happy to hear that."

Jericho appreciated that she was there for his sister.

"Mark won't be home for an hour, so you two have fun." Georgia waggled her eyebrows at him, then made her way inside.

Alone with Livy.

That was quickly becoming his favorite thing. She stood and unbuttoned her shirt. Jericho didn't want to gawk, but there was no way in hell he was missing this show. It was a feast for his eyes *and* his imagination. She dropped the shirt off her shoulders, tossed it on the chair, then removed her shorts. Even though she'd worn a conservative one piece, she was rockin' the suit.

No denying those sexy-as-hell curves.

She walked to the deep end and dove in. Seconds later, she emerged, silky wet and damn hot.

"Water feels incredible," she said.

Water's refreshing. You're incredible.

He started sporting wood, so he dove in. She was treading water, her sublime body moving in perfect rhythm to keep herself afloat.

Every last fiber of his being wanted her. To touch her, kiss her, bury himself inside her. It was immediate, powerful, and unrelenting.

"Hey," he said, swimming over to her.

"That's the best you got?"

He pulled her into his arms. As their lips came together, they dipped below the water, sinking to the bottom of the pool. The kiss was an explosion of nerves, turning him hard in seconds.

After she severed their connection, they returned to the surface.

Gasping for air, she stared into his eyes. "What are you doing to me?"

"Same damn thing you're doing to me," he growled.

Jericho controlled his emotions, not the other way around. Being around her was pushing him into unchartered waters.

"I'm swimming." She moved away, the spray from her kicks splashing his face.

Back and forth they swam. The need to stay close had him swimming by her side. After several laps, she stopped at the deep end to catch her breath.

With his back against the pool, he rested his arms on the edge, tilted his face toward the sun, and closed his eyes.

Seconds passed in a comfortable silence.

"I would never have pictured you living in something like this," she said.

He moved her wet hair away from her cheek, then kissed her skin. "What do you see me in?"

"A cabin in the mountains or a lake house."

He let his gaze drift over her face. "I needed a large house for everyone, but I bought this for Gram. She and Gramps lived in an apartment for decades, then they were able to afford a small trailer. She saved and saved and, then, she gave me her life savings to open The Road. When I was house huntin', I brought her with me. When she walked in here, she fell in love. I had to buy it for her."

"You are such a good guy."

He threw his head back and laughed. "I killed a man. You know, premeditated." He leaned close enough to feel her breath on his cheeks. "I'm gonna do it again. I pulled a knife last night at the dive bar and would have used it, no problem."

"I'm surprised you haven't sliced *me* up into small pieces."

"I'd never hurt you, but I am gonna make you *shatter* into a million pieces."

Her moan ripped through him, landing between his legs.

"Jericho, I can't breathe around you." Pushing off the side of the pool, she swam away.

Jericho waited until his boner stood down to get out of the

pool. His balls were in a perpetual state of blue around her. He sat in a chaise and sipped one of the orange juices Georgia had left on the table. Livy was still in the pool, so he waited at a safe distance. If he got any closer, *BAM,* his junk would turn to steel.

Her swimming was like poetry in motion. She glided effortlessly across the water. She wasn't a fast swimmer, but she had the grace he didn't. Everything about him was functional. Watching her soothed him and roused him. It was a complicated mix of emotions, but he couldn't look away. That's how captivated he was. There was something about her... always had been.

She paused, treading water in the middle of the pool. "Why'd you leave me?" she called out to him.

"I'm right here."

One quick smile that stole his heart, then she was back to laps. When she finished, he rose and wrapped her in a towel. She was breathing hard, her cheeks flush with color. "This is paradise."

"I'm glad you like it."

She toweled off. With her beach bag in hand, she asked, "Where can I change?"

Rather than take her to the guest house, next to the pool, he brought her inside.

Before taking her upstairs, he stopped in the kitchen.

Gram and Georgia were getting ready to put cinnamon buns in the oven.

"What's happenin'?" he asked.

"Mark's twenty minutes away," Georgia, said. "Are you making pancakes?"

"Sure. Back in a few."

He brought Livy upstairs. "I'll put you in my bedroom." He couldn't miss the grit in his own damn voice.

Once there, she locked the door behind him. In an instant, the air turned electric, charged with blinding heat and desire. She was on him, her hands claiming him, her mouth on his. He palmed her ass, pulled her against him, his hardness pressing against her tummy.

"Fuck," he ground out. "I'm dyin' for you."

In seconds, their wet bathing suits were on the floor, his hands on her flesh, his mouth on her shoulder, her nipple. Her muffled moans ripped through him, turning him harder still. He needed a release, needed to drive himself inside her. But taking her, here, like this, wasn't gonna happen.

Women weren't invited here, so he didn't have any condoms in his bedroom.

She broke away, knelt at his feet, took his hard shaft in her mouth. Her growls were raw and raspy, her mouth on his cock felt like fucking heaven. Then, the guilt and the pain crashed through the pleasure. He didn't deserve to feel *this* good. It was one thing to fuck at a club, but not in his home, where his brother had once lived.

He couldn't do it.

"Stop," he blurted.

With his cock rooted in her mouth, she stilled. Slowly, she pulled him out. "Not good?"

"Fucking fantastic. I can't feel good, not when…"

She rose. "You're wrong. You deserve to have a full life. You need to do that, for Bryan."

The guilt was too much.

"Let me do this for you." Again, she dropped to her knees.

Her lustful gaze was cemented on his. When she took him into her mouth, he squeezed her shoulder. The pleasure was undeserved, but the more she sucked, the weaker he became. He couldn't tell her to stop, didn't want to. He needed her to suck him dry, needed to escape, even if only for a little while.

She stroked his balls, cradled in her hand, while she relaxed her jaw and took him in all the way. Then, she pulled him out, swirled her tongue over the head, sucking gently as she took him all the way back in again. He placed his hands on her head and guided her, slowly, then faster. She bobbed greedily over him while the ecstasy shot out, filling her mouth. He grunted through the release, the euphoria soothing his angry, broken soul.

"Fuck," he ground out. "Fuuuuuck, Livy. You are… perfect."

He pulled her to him and kissed her, hard. Their tongues swirled and pounded against each other's. He laid her sideways on his bed, then he pulled her to the end, dropped to his knees, and slid his gaze past her tummy, her breasts, until their eyes locked.

"Hold on, baby. You're gonna come hard and fast."

He ran his tongue over her soaked pussy, pulled the hood of her clit back and flicked his tongue over her sensitive, swollen button.

"Ohhhh, yes," she murmured while her hips moved beneath him.

She was so ready, so close. He licked and sucked until she started thrashing on his bed. He ran his fingers under her ass and stroked over her anus.

Her orgasm shot out of her, along with a string of garbled words, as she bucked beneath him,. He kissed her tender flesh, then her tummy, each breast, until their mouths melded in another insatiable kiss.

Breathing hard, she slowed them down, gazed into his eyes.

"We've opened Pandora's box," she whispered.

"No complaints here," he murmured.

"You're a phenomenal lover," she murmured. "That thing you did at the end. What was that?"

"I teased your anus."

Up went her eyebrows. "Hmm."

"I've got a lot of ways to make you scream my name when you come."

Oh. My. God.

He pushed off the bed and held out his hands. Gazing up at him, Liv knew.

Jericho was everything she wanted and all that she needed. He was her person, that all-important missing piece in her life.

When she placed hers in his, energy whizzed through her. In his arms, she nuzzled close. Then, she traced his grim reaper tat with her fingertip. "I admire that you live life *your* way."

"My life my rules," he said, repeating the words inked on his chest.

"Hmm."

"What?"

"I wonder if there's any—never mind. Sorry." She broke away.

He pulled her back into his arms. "Say it, woman."

She held his gaze for the longest time while the air turned electric. She wanted to ask him if there was room for an "our" in his rulebook? But the words lodged in her throat. She had to tread lightly with Jericho.

After dropping a soft kiss on his lips, she severed their connection. "Where can I shower?"

"My bathroom. Clean towels are in the closet."

Rather than leave, she watched him pull on boxer briefs, shorts, and a T-shirt. After one more passionate kiss, he pulled the door closed behind him.

Fifteen minutes later, she found his family bustling around the spacious kitchen with Jericho flipping pancakes on the stovetop griddle.

She sidled close. His gaze floated over her face, then he gently tugged on a chunk of her curls. She ran her hand down his back. Seemingly irrelevant gestures, yet they had significant meaning. She peered into his eyes.

Can he forgive me? Is that even a possibility?

"What can I do to help?" she asked.

His sister-in-law, Patty, handed her an orange juice container.

"Can you fill the small glasses with juice and the larger ones with water?"

Liv loved being a part of Jericho's family. She appreciated how well they got along, how they operated as a cohesive unit, even if it was something as simple as cooking a meal. Everyone sat at the spacious kitchen table. Jericho clasped her hand while Tim led a prayer of thanks.

As the kids dug in, Jericho raised his champagne flute. "La familia."

"Always," Mark replied.

"I miss Bryan," Georgia added. "Livy, thank you for helping me."

Liv offered her a warm smile. "Of course. Thank you for including me today."

When brunch was over, Liv spent more time talking with Georgia by the pool. Georgia was struggling with grief that came in waves. One minute, she felt like she could function, the next—and without warning—she found herself sobbing.

"It's okay," Liv said.

"But sometimes I'm at work and I erupt into tears," Georgia replied.

Liv nodded. "What about acceptance?"

"I accept that Brian is gone."

"I know you do," Liv replied. "I was talking about you. Would you feel better if you accepted your grief, even welcomed it?"

Georgia thought about it, then shrugged. "Maybe. I do kind of beat myself up when it happens at work."

"What would you tell a friend who was struggling with the loss of her brother?"

"I'd tell her that I was there for her," Georgia said. "I'd tell her to be kind to herself and not try to do everything right or perfect."

Liv offered a little smile. "That's great advice. Could you give that a try?"

Tears pricked Georgia's eyes. "Yeah, I could."

The conversation continued until Jericho walked over and kissed Georgia on the top of her head. "Hangin' in there?"

"One day at a time," Georgia replied.

"It's gonna be rough for a while," he said matter-of-factly before glancing at Liv. "I'll see ya later."

Peering up at him, she nodded.

When he left, Georgia studied Liv for an extra beat. "You've got it bad for him, don't you?"

"So, so bad," Liv replied. "Is it that obvious?"

"The only thing *more* obvious is how bad he's got it for you," Georgia replied.

That evening, Jericho pulled into Mad Dog's. For a Sunday night, the lot was almost full. He handed Liv a burner. "Use this."

She tucked the phone in her jacket pocket.

"Since I pulled a knife last night, there might be more of 'em," he continued. "If things get crazy, get yourself out." He offered her the key fob to his truck.

She refused it. "I'm not leaving without you. Plus, I'm sure you could take them all on. We're doing this together. *Together,* Jericho."

"Dammit, why do you push back on everything?"

On a huff, she held out her hand. He gave her the key fob, got out. She slid on the sunglasses and exited the truck. As he rounded his vehicle, he checked her out.

Livy Blackstone in leathers was smokin' hot. He could eat her up and love her all night long.

She'd styled her hair the same, even put the bruises in the same spots. Only difference, a sling held her arm in place. Another prop.

After he entered the busy bar, his gaze swept over the crowd. Definitely more guys, but no one stood out that he couldn't take on. Only problem? He couldn't take on twenty by himself. "Maybe I shoulda brought the guys," he muttered.

"We got this," she whispered.

The waitress stopped bussing a table and hurried over. "Hey, you're back. You gotta keep yourself in check tonight, honey. We can't have the cops here."

"I got no problem with that," Jericho bit out, "unless someone touches my sister. She's been through enough. I don't need no strangers gettin' handsy with her."

On a nod, the server led them to a different booth.

"Whatcha drinking?" she asked.

Jericho tossed a nod to Liv.

"Bottle of Bud," Liv replied.

"Whiskey, neat," Jericho added.

The server left and Jericho studied the customers, one at a time.

The bartender delivered their drinks. "You gonna be chill, tonight, right?" he asked.

"Like I told the waitress, these guys need to keep their paws off my sister. She's lookin' for a pro, so they need to fuckin' act like one."

The bartender slid his gaze to Liv. "You doin' okay?"

She lowered her shades, revealing her shiner. "No, I'm not. Is Lucky's cousin here?"

"Not yet," said the bartender. "He said he'd stop by."

Liv pushed her shades back in place before downing a mouthful of beer.

The minutes ticked by. Jericho nursed the cheap whiskey, keeping his eye on the customers. Everyone seemed chill. A few were playing pool. Several others were playing darts.

As Jericho was ordering another whiskey, three guys moseyed in. Two were average height, one was short and slender. The short one had on a leather jacket, but the other two wore T-shirts, their bare arms exposed. One had a sleeve of tats covering his right arm. The other had no tats.

They squeezed in at the bar. After the bartender set down their drinks, he pointed in their direction.

"Here we go," Jericho murmured.

Liv acknowledged him with a nod.

With his drink in hand, the skinny dude made his way over. Muscles running down Jericho's back tensed. He wanted to shove a shiv in him and end his life in exchange for his brother's, but he needed confirmation first.

Time to find out.

The man regarded both of them. "How's it goin'?"

"You Lucky's cousin?" Jericho asked.

"Yeah. I'm Slim Jim. I hear you been askin' for me."

"Grab a chair," Jericho said.

Slim Jim snagged an empty chair from a nearby four-top, spun it around, and sat facing them. "You got names?"

"I'm Reaper. My sis, Julie. She needs help."

"How'd you hear about me?" Slim Jim asked.

"I got a friend who says you're a good shot," Jericho said. "You make things look like an accident, if you know what I mean."

"I got you," Slim Jim replied. "How'd you hurt your arm?" he asked Liv.

With trembling fingers, she removed her sunglasses, revealing her black eye. "My husband's a monster. The sling is for goin' out with my brother last night. He didn't believe I was with him." Tears filled her eyes. "I'm a prisoner and I need him gone."

Slim Jim tossed back the shot, then glanced around for the server. Once he caught her attention, he held up the empty glass. His jacket sleeve rode up on his left arm revealing the head of a snake starting on his wrist.

The server made her way over. She set down a shot glass and a lowball glass of whiskey for Jericho, then left.

Slim Jim sipped the cheap booze. "How much you payin'?"

"Five hundred now," Jericho said. "Ninety-five hundred when the job is done."

"But it's gotta look like an accident or random," Liv added. "Or the cops'll think it was me."

Slim Jim eyed them. "How do I know *you* ain't cops?"

Liv removed one sleeve on her leather jacket and held out her arm. "If my shiner and my sprained arm aren't enough, these bruises are from the other day."

After eyeing them, Slim Jim regarded Jericho. "Why don't you do it?"

"Like I told the bartender, I did my time. Not goin' back. I can't stand the son of a bitch, so I'm gonna need a solid alibi when the shit goes down."

Slim Jim tossed back the liquor.

Before they could move forward, Jericho needed to see the snake tat on his arm.

As if Liv read his mind—or they were in total sync—she said, "That's a nice jacket. Where'd you get it?"

He glanced down. "Who knows? I picked it up somewhere."

"Can I see the tag?" Liv asked.

Slim Jim furrowed his brow. "What?"

"Take your jacket off and show her the tag in the collar," Jericho explained.

Chuckling, Slim Jim slipped off the jacket and handed it to Liv. A king cobra tat wound its way up his left arm.

You're a dead man, you son of a bitch.

Liv glanced at the tag before handing it back. "Thanks."

"I'll sell it to ya," Slim Jim said.

"Ten grand's all I got and I'm giving that to you," Liv said. "It's a nice jacket. You keep it. So, do we have a deal?"

"Yeah, we do."

"Let me get your number so I can text you my husband's schedule." He rattled it off, and she sent him a text from the burner.

Jericho pulled out a bundle of twenties. "Five hundred."

Slim Jim shoved the money in his jacket pocket. "When do you want this to happen?"

"As soon as I text you his schedule," Liv replied.

"Who's your driver?" Jericho asked.

"My cousin, Lucky," Slim Jim replied. "Except I ain't heard from him lately, so I gotta coupla other guys I can use."

"I'll let you know," Liv said.

With the shot glass in hand, Slim Jim pushed out of the chair. "Good doin' business with you."

As he ambled toward the bar, Jericho tossed cash on the table. "We're outta here."

Once outside, they jumped in Jericho's truck.

"You've got nerves of steel," she said as he started the engine. "Did you see me shaking?"

"I thought you were fakin' it."

"I don't know how you do those ALPHA jobs."

"I'm not afraid," he replied. "That helps." He pulled onto the street. "You think he's our triggerman?"

"I think he's the SJ in Lucky's phone." She turned toward him. "Are we headed to The Road?"

"No."

"Where are we going?" she asked.

"Your place."

She curled her hand around his thigh. "Drive faster."

The kissing started at the traffic light, then continued in the elevator. By the time she unlocked her front door, she was ready to maul him. She couldn't keep her hands, or her mouth, off him. The air cracked with frenzied energy, their need to mate uncontrollable.

Liv "unleashed" was something she couldn't process, so she just enjoyed the hell out of him. Clothing was gone in the living room. They were pressed together, staring into each other's eyes when a smile brightened his.

"Aren't you going to give me a tour?" he asked.

She grinned up at him. "You're a fast learner. You'll figure it out on the fly." She jumped into his arms and wrapped herself around him like a blanket. "Am I too heavy?"

That made him laugh. "You're joking, right?"

"I'm no Skinny Minnie."

"You're all woman with curves that do not end. I appreciate every beautiful inch of you."

She kissed him, pointed down the hall. "Bedroom."

With her still holding on, he dug out a condom packet from his jeans pocket and handed it to her. Then, he held her tight and strode down the hall. "Where am I going?"

"End of the hallway."

He walked in and stood in the dark room. She detached, turned on a beside light. "Get in my bed."

He flashed a smile. "You're bossy."

"I'm making up for lost time. So much lost time."

"Don't look back," he said as they crawled into bed. "Be in the moment or look forward. We can't change the past. We can only learn from it."

He'd always been her rock. Some things never changed.

He leaned up on his elbow and gazed down at her. "Talk to me, Livy. What do you like? What arouses you?"

This wasn't a hookup at a club. This was a side of him she'd never seen. Tender, attentive, doting.

"You," she said. "I just want you."

Jericho cupped her cheek, kissed her. Her breathing shifted while she appreciated the way his tongue dipped inside her mouth. She ran her fingers over his shoulders, down his back, over his ass. Between kisses, they stared into each other's eyes. Everything was happening in slow motion, as if they had nothing but time. Everything in their world felt right. They were together.

He moved from her mouth to her shoulder to her chest. When his mouth found her nipple, she watched as he sucked and licked.

She was on fire, her insides throbbing with unrelenting desire. Jericho caressed her skin, ran his fingers inside her thighs, teasing her pussy with a glance as he ran his fingers across her tummy.

The build was slow, but the desire thrummed through her as she flew higher and higher.

"In me," she groaned.

His lids were heavy, his gaze unwavering. With his cock in hand, he inched his way inside while she accommodated his thick shaft. The pleasure so intense, she dug her nails into his back. "I love having you inside me. You feel so right."

He stilled.

I shouldn't have said that.

A smile tugged at the corners of his sexy mouth. "I missed you, Livy." He pressed his lips to hers and her heart overflowed. This —*him*—was what had been missing from her life.

He started moving inside her, the friction a glorious eruption of euphoria. A million-pleasure points exploded inside her, the thrill of their connection tying her soul to his.

They weren't fucking at a club, they were making love in her bed.

The boy she'd once adored was the man she was falling deeply in love with.

Falling in love with Livy was the easiest thing Jericho had ever done.

Monday morning, Liv made her way through the corridors of DOJ en route to her Uncle's hovel. Why a man of his stature chose to work underground when he could have been on the executive floor was one of life's great mysteries.

Despite being less than a year apart, her Uncle Z and her dad couldn't be more different. Her father was large, intimidating, and overbearing. When they were kids, Liv and her sisters nicknamed his unblinking gaze the Death Stare. As children, that Death Stare terrified them. That's why she tried to excel in *everything*. She didn't like playing the violin, but she was a star student. Same with her grades. Anything to avoid her father's disapproval, long lectures, and that nightmare-invoking Death Stare.

Her mom was the only person who would laugh at him or scold him for his tyrannical behavior. Because of her mom, she got to quit violin lessons. Not once had she picked up the instrument since that delightful day.

In stark contrast, her Uncle Z was short and slender. He spoke quietly, never said much when he did speak, and he never forced Addison or her siblings to do anything when they were kids.

Liv pulled to a stop in front of his office.

Knock-knock-knock.

"Come in," Z said.

She opened the door. Her uncle was on the phone. She waited for him to wave her in or shoo her out. He pointed to the guest chair. She shut the door and sat.

"Who confirmed the source of the death threat?" While he listened, he tapped his fingers on the metal desk. "I'm looking at his rap sheet now. It goes back thirty years." More listening and more finger tapping. "I'm sending it to ALPHA." More listening. "I concur. A kill mission."

The call ended, Z slid his gaze to Liv.

"You're having someone *assassinated*?" Liv blurted.

"You didn't hear a thing because you were never here," Z replied nonchalantly. "This office doesn't exist and I don't work here." With a sly smile, he added, "I'm retired and I spend afternoons in my vegetable garden. I read and take Pooches for long walks in the neighborhood."

Liv cracked a smile. "Who's Pooches?"

"My imaginary dog."

"You're one of the most ruthless men in America, and yet, one of my absolute favorite people."

This smile touched his eyes. "I feel the same way, my dear." He pushed out of his chair. "I sit too much. Let's take a walk."

"You mean, you actually leave your office?"

His soft laugh followed him into the quiet, dimly lit corridor. They started strolling down the hall.

"I'm concerned there's a leak in the Alexandria Police Department," Z began. "DEA suspects an area gang is involved in drug trafficking, so they teamed up with APD to assist with the bust. When they went in to make the arrests, no one was there. They suspect the gang was tipped off by someone at APD."

"Why not someone at DEA?"

"This is the second time it's happened. Different DEA team, but the same gang unit."

She and Z rounded the corner, continuing their stroll.

"Since APD is one of your clients, I need you to get in there," he said.

"Who am I watching?"

"Unfortunately, I don't know, but I'd start with the gang unit's detectives."

"What can you tell me about the two DEA cases?"

"The first bust was supposed to happen three months ago at an abandoned warehouse in Fairfax," he said. "When DEA and APD got there, the place was empty."

"And the other one?"

"Two weeks ago, a different group of DEA Agents and the APD gang unit swarmed a house in Falls Church. It was four in the morning, but no one was there. Looked like whoever was living there grabbed what they could and cleared out."

"Got it," Liv said. "Which gang is it?"

"Thriller Killers," he replied.

Ohmygod. The gang that murdered Bryan.

"And if I find no one?"

"Then, that'll be your answer."

They continued walking in silence. They could have talked about family, but Z never mixed the two. When she was there, she was an employee. If they got together for a family event, she was his niece. That worked for her.

At the elevator, he offered a warm smile. "You do a good job, Livy. I'm proud of you. I know your dad would be, too, if he knew about your *real* job."

Pride filled her heart.

"Where are you headed?" he asked after pushing the up button.

"I'm teaching a class at APD on the latest trends in gang behavior."

Z's lips ticked upward. "Perfect timing."

The elevator doors opened and she stepped in. When she turned back, he was gone.

An hour later, she stood in front of the group of officers and staff in the large conference room. This course was an easy way for them to earn continuing education credits, so it was another standing-room-only workshop.

While Liv discussed the increase in gang violence and how DMV gangs were branching into additional types of crimes, she studied her audience. She didn't know everyone by name, but she recognized all of them.

The leak could be anywhere from the Captain all the way down to a rookie.

"Dr. Blackstone, can you give us examples of other types of crimes gangs are turning to?" asked one of the officers.

"White-collar crimes like phone scams or Internet scams," Liv explained. "Smash-n-Grabs have also seen an uptick in popularity."

Three hours later, she opened the floor to questions. When the event concluded, the group filed out. Liv needed to make some notes to follow-up with some of the officers, the rookie, in particular, who asked a lot of questions.

Sergeant Hayes moseyed over. "Nice job, Liv. We had a packed house today. These classes are working out great."

Liv slid her laptop into her bag. "I hope so. Lots of good questions. Who's the rookie cop?"

"Which one?"

"The one who asked all the questions."

Sergeant Hayes chuckled. "Brad Brown. He's a rising star. Very hard worker. He expressed interest in my unit."

"Already?" Liv asked.

"An overachiever is better than someone who phones it in, right?" Andre offered a warm smile. "Got lunch plans?"

Liv glanced at the time. It was after one. "No."

"C'mon, I'm taking you to my favorite Italian restaurant. It's nearby."

"It'll give us a chance to catch up," she replied.

She dropped her laptop in her car before they walked the two short blocks to an adorable eatery. The waitstaff knew Andre by name. When the hostess seated them, she only handed a menu to Liv.

After the hostess left, Liv held out the menu so Andre could see it.

"Don't need it," he said. "I either get one of the daily specials or lasagna. The lasagna is always good, so it's a win-win no matter what I order."

The server stopped by, filled their water glasses, and rattled off the specials. "Sergeant, you're having the chicken marsala, aren't you?"

Andre nodded. "How'd you know?"

"You got it the last time Chef made it. Iced tea today?"

"Thanks."

"Ma'am, what can I get you?"

"Andre raved about the lasagna, so I'll have that."

"Excellent choice. Iced tea as well?"

"Water's fine."

The server took her menu and left.

"I noticed a few new faces in the precinct, today," Liv began.

Andre set his napkin on his lap. "We were given the green light for more hires."

"Can you pull anyone up to the gang unit?" she asked.

"Unfortunately, no."

"How's the caseload for your team? About the same or busier than usual?" Liv asked before sipping her water.

She didn't want to pummel the sergeant with questions, but she didn't want to miss an easy opportunity to dig deeper. Maybe someone on his team was behaving strangely or having financial problems.

"We're always chasing the latest gang crime," Andre said. "We've made some arrests that were a direct result of your expertise, Doc."

The server returned with the sergeant's iced tea and a plate of sliced mozzarella and tomatoes with fresh basil. "From the chef. Buon appetito." He topped Liv's water and moved on.

"How's morale at the station?" she asked.

"The new crop always comes in with a great attitude and an ego that says, 'Bring it on.' One negative cop can tarnish a good group of hard-working people. I always check back with them after their rookie year, then, again after their second. Most love what they do. For others, the job becomes a grind."

"That can be the same for any job, though not every job has the level of intensity that yours can have," Liv said.

"We've got one officer who's seven years in. He's already counting down to retirement." Andre paused. "If he's already thinking of leaving, it's not the right fit."

"Where are you in all of this?"

"Got a decade before I retire, but I love what I do. Always have.

I wanted to be a detective since I was ten." He smiled. "I'm living my dream. How 'bout you?"

Their easygoing conversation continued through lunch.

If anyone in the department was tipping off the Thriller Killers, Liv would have to interview each of them to determine who it was. This would pose a challenge. Never before had she needed to step up to the front line and interact with her targets. She was a watcher, clean and simple. Going forward, she'd need to come up with reasons to check-in with everyone, without making it look obvious.

The server delivered the check and Liv pulled out her wallet.

"My treat," Andre said, tucking his credit card into the leather billfold.

"Thank you for lunch," she said. "We've never done this before. Next time, my treat."

When they left the restaurant, Andre said, "I've got to make a stop at the end of the block. Why don't you come with me?"

"I was planning on—"

"It'll take five minutes. There's someone I'd love for you to meet."

Outside, she slipped on her shades as they made their way down the busy sidewalk, passing boutiques and other small specialty stores. Andre pulled to a stop at a gallery on the corner.

"Here we are." He opened the front door.

The cozy space was filled with artwork hanging on the walls. Small pedestals were perfectly placed around the room boasting small statues and sculptures.

A beautiful piece captured Liv's attention, so she walked closer to check it out. It was an oil painting of a stunning lake sunset where beautiful homes peppered the water's edge. Two children played in the sand while a man and a woman sat nearby watching them.

Liv's attention was diverted when the woman behind the counter picked up a medium-sized painting wrapped in plain brown paper, walked around the counter, and handed it to a couple. After the man took it, she escorted them to the front door.

Once they left, the woman with light, blonde hair and fair skin smiled at Andre.

"Hello, honey," Andre said, kissing the woman on her cheek.

"Did you have lunch at Ciao Bella's?" she asked.

"Every chance I get." Andre regarded Liv. "This is my wife, Brenda. Honey, this is Dr. Blackstone. She's the psychologist I brought in to consult with the department."

"Good to put a face with a name," Brenda said.

"Is this your gallery?" Liv asked.

"Guilty," Brenda replied. She eyed the painting Liv had been admiring. "That just came in a few days ago. The artist is local, which is always nice. I try to support area talent whenever I can."

"It's beautiful. The colors are breathtaking and the scene is lovely."

"I'm happy to put it aside for you," Brenda said.

Liv glanced at the price of the artwork. It was ten grand.

"I can't even afford to be looking at it," Liv said with a smile.

Andre chuckled.

"We've got some smaller pieces scattered throughout," Brenda said. "You're welcome to take a look around."

Liv meandered around the gallery for a few minutes, but nothing caught her eye. She wound her way back to Andre and Brenda, chatting by the front door.

"Are you here late tonight?" Andre asked.

"Probably," Brenda replied. "I've got a prospective buyer coming in at eight."

"If I'm still at work, we can have a late dinner together," Andre said. "Liv, are you headed back to the station?"

"I am," Liv replied. "You?"

"I'll be along in a few," he replied.

After saying her goodbyes, Liv left thinking about the job her uncle had tasked her with and the challenge of trying to figure out if there was a dirty cop amongst the sea of good ones.

As she neared the station, she saw Detective Mirabel Morales heading toward the precinct parking lot.

"Detective Morales," Liv called.

The detective didn't turn, so Liv quickened her step, catching her before she rounded the corner. She was on her phone. When Mirabel saw her, she stopped.

"No, I'm not changing my mind. I gotta go." She hung up and rolled her eyes. "Sorry, what can I do for you?"

"Got a minute?" Liv asked.

"I'm on my way to question a witness. You want to head back inside?"

"I was hoping we could chat in private," Liv replied. "What about the little park down the block?"

After crossing the street, Liv asked, "You doing okay?"

"You mean in general or that phone call?" Mirabel asked.

"Both, but we can start with the call."

"That was my ex-boyfriend. He broke up with me 'cause he wanted to date someone else."

They walked over to a park bench and sat.

"Gotta give him props for not cheating," Liv said.

"I'm not sure he didn't cheat. Anyway, he ended it three months ago. Things didn't work out with the other woman and he's crawling back to me. I'm not interested."

"Do you miss him?" Liv asked.

"I did. The first couple of weeks were rough. We'd been together for over a year." Mirabel cracked a smile. "It's kind of satisfying that he wants me back, and that I'm strong enough to say no."

"You've always come across as super level-headed to me."

"I try." She paused. "How are things with you?"

"I recently reconnected with someone from high school. We had a pretty bad falling out, so I'm not so sure he trusts me."

"Men," Mirabel said and both women laughed.

"A couple of weeks ago, you started to tell me something," Liv said, "but you had to leave with the sergeant. Everything okay?"

"Hmm, I don't remember."

"You said, 'Just between you and me,'" Liv reminded her.

Mirabel nodded. "Oh, I remember. A few months back, I was working with DEA on a drug trafficking case. We'd gotten a tip from a CI and we'd gone to raid a warehouse in Fairfax." She leaned close. "It was crazy. The place was cleaned out."

"That happens though, doesn't it?" Liv prodded.

"It does, but the same thing happened two weeks ago, only this raid was at a house in Falls Church. Whoever lived there had grabbed what they could and bolted. One failed bust, I can buy that, but twice? I was concerned the agents thought I was tipping off the gang."

"Why? Because you were at both?"

"Right."

"Anyone else at both raids with you?"

"Detective Kutchner," Mirabel replied. "Sarge told me not to worry, but the Captain called me into her office and asked me a bunch of questions about the raids."

"Which gang?" Liv asked.

"TK." The detective's attention was snagged by a mom hurrying through the small park after her toddler while pushing a stroller. The child was heading for the street.

"Aiiiiieeeee, ohmygod! Justin, STOP!" screamed the mom.

Mirabel flew off the bench, running fast. She grabbed the little boy just before he stepped off the curb.

Liv hurried over as Mirabel returned the child to his mom. With tears in her eyes, the mom hugged her.

"Thank you so, so much. I told myself I'd never be one of those moms who puts her child on a leash, but now that I've got two—" Liv and Mirabel peeked into the stroller at the sleeping infant— "I don't have a choice." She hugged the detective again.

"Can I give you a little cash?" asked the woman.

"No, but thank you," said Mirabel. "I'm grateful I was in the right place at the right time." She knelt down next to the boy. "Stay close to your mama. Those cars are going fast. You have to stop before crossing a street, okay?"

"Uh-huh," said the tyke.

Mirabel rose. "Hold on to the stroller and help your mom with the baby. You're a big brother now. That's a very important job."

The little boy grabbed the stroller with his hand, and the mom and her children headed toward the swings.

"I've got to go," Mirabel said. "I'm concerned we've got a snitch in the precinct and I don't want this pinned on me. Please keep this between us."

The women set off toward the parking lot. "I won't say anything," Liv replied. "I appreciate your confiding in me. Any idea who the snitch could be?"

"Kutchner's new and he's kinda private. Maybe he's slow to warm up, but he doesn't strike me as a team player." Mirabel stopped behind an unmarked police car. "Thanks for listening. Please don't—"

"Not a word," Liv replied. "Thanks for trusting me."

Liv wanted to head back into the police station in search of Detective Kutchner, but she had to play this cool. Z didn't expect her to root out the snitch in a day.

Nice and easy, she told herself as she slid into her car. As she waited for traffic to pass before pulling out of the parking lot, Sergeant Hayes walked past her.

"Good seeing you, Liv," he said.

"You, too, Andre."

"Come back, anytime."

She smiled. "I'll be back before you know it."

13

VINCENT THE DRUNK

At just after six that evening, Jericho trotted down the stairs and made his way toward the kitchen.

He spotted Tim on the phone in the living room, Mark was sleeping on a chaise by the pool. He entered the kitchen to find Gram, Patty, and the kids. Georgia was at work, managing his upscale restaurant, Carole Jean's.

Jericho was meeting Vincent at The Road for dinner. Felt like a time suck, but he was doing it for Livy. Crossing his brother and dad off his list meant he didn't have to deal with them going forward. They'd exited his life years ago and he saw no reason to bring them back in now.

Jericho was confident his brother had nothing to do with the shooting. How could he? He was new in town, worked at a casket company, and came across as somewhat of an idiot.

The bright spot in this? Liv had agreed to meet him there.

Patty was pulling chicken thighs from the oven while potatoes boiled on the stove.

Jericho eased down beside the kids, busy coloring at the kitchen table. "What trouble have you two urchins gotten into today?"

"None," Annie replied. "I was good."

Jericho smiled at her. "Were you with your mommy, today?"

"I had school."

His niece spent three afternoons a week in pre-K. "Learn anything?"

"Uh-huh," she replied before switching out the red crayon for the purple one.

"What about you, Owen?" he asked.

"I played. Me and Mommy had paint class."

"Nice. Where's your artwork?"

He pointed at the fridge with his pudgy finger.

Patty plucked if off and handed it to Jericho.

"This is good stuff, buddy," Jericho said as he eyed the paint splotches.

"Tanks."

"Where's Gram?" Jericho asked.

"Outside, by the pool," Patty replied.

"Is she okay?" he asked.

"Not really, but she's putting on a good show," Patty replied.

"I'll go talk to her." Jericho pushed out of the chair. "I'll see you two tomorrow," Jericho said to the kids.

"Bye," Owen said while he continued coloring.

"Where are you going?" Annie asked.

"To my restaurant to have dinner with friends," he replied. "Do you remember the pretty lady with the big hair?"

Annie smiled. "Uh-huh."

"I'm taking her to dinner."

"We have food," Annie said.

"Should I invite her to have dinner with us, sometime?"

"Okay," Annie replied.

Jericho tossed Tim a nod as he strode outside. Mark had just woken up and was on his phone.

Gram sat alone at one of the round tables, poolside. Bryan's death had changed her. She looked small, frail, and sad.

Jericho sat beside her. "How you doin'?"

"I miss Bryan."

He held her small hand in his large one. "Me, too."

"Have the police contacted you about his case?"

"No," he replied.

"Have you called them?"

He shook his head, but he stayed silent.

"Jericho, we need answers," she pushed. "People have to pay for this. They have to be punished."

"When I was a kid, you used to tell me to be patient. You'd say, Christmas is coming, Jericho. Be patient. Or if I wanted it to be my birthday, you'd tell me to enjoy the time leading up to it because once the day passed, I'd have to wait another year all over again."

She offered a rueful smile. "I didn't know you were listening to me."

"Patience, Gram. I'm workin' on it. But not a word to anyone."

"Whenever a friend asks about you, I tell them you take good care of your family. Beyond that, it's none of their damn business."

"Good answer." He patted her hand. "I'll be home late. Should I tell you not to wait up?"

"I always sleep better when all my babies are home." Sadness touched her eyes. "Now, without Bryan, sleep doesn't come so easily."

Pain pierced his chest. For years, she'd been a source of strength and guidance. Now it was his turn to be hers.

"It will, once we have justice." He kissed the top of her head and left.

He made his way into his garage, tapped the remote, and the door rose. Despite the warm weather, he'd worn his leathers so he could ride his bike. His phone rang with a call from Jamal.

"Yo," he answered. "What's up?"

"I've got a customer who's run up a six-hundred-dollar bar tab. He said you're paying and he's buying everyone drinks."

"On my way." Jericho pulled on his helmet, jumped on his bike, and started her up.

After driving out, he said, "Computer, close garage door."

As soon as the garage door folded down, Jericho opened the throttle and thundered toward The Road.

Thirty minutes later, he strode in, helmet in hand. Pausing, he spoke to the hostess before continuing on. Most everyone in the bar was singing Vienna by Billy Joel. Jericho hollered to the bartender, "Where's Jamal?"

"Trying to get a drunk customer off the Beast."

Jericho moved through his eatery, his feet eating up the floor. A server, carrying a full try of food over her head, came flying out of the kitchen. Jericho swerved, barely missing her, but she startled and lost her balance. The tray of plates, loaded with entrées, toppled to the floor.

CRASH!

The restaurant grew silent. A man staggered out of the mechanical bull room clapping. "Bravo! Bravoooo! Way to gooooooo!"

Ah, fuck. It's Vincent.

The diners burst into laughter and applause while staff rushed over to help the red-faced server pick up the mess.

Jericho knelt beside his employee. "You okay?"

"I'm fine," she replied. "Embarrassed, but I'll survive."

"My fault," Jericho said. "Shake it off."

As he stood, Vincent stumbled toward him, then stopped and gaped at Jericho before he broke into a lopsided grin.

"Hey, brooooother! Heyyyyyooooo! "I found yur wessern bar! "This place is rad, man. I rooooode da beeeeast." He laughed. "It's sickkkkkk." He threw his arm around Jericho. "How ya doin'?"

"I gotta sober you up." Jericho grabbed him by arm and led him to his private booth. "Sit."

Vincent slid onto the leather bench. His eyes were glazed and he was mumbling to himself.

A server hurried over.

A pitcher of water, two burger platters," Jericho said.

Vincent started to slide out. "I gottttaaaa—"

"*No!*" Jericho did not have the time or the energy for this crap.

"Whooooppsie." Vincent shoved himself to the center of the horseshoe booth. "I'm stayin'. Doan git mad."

"What the hell is going on?" Jericho bit out.

"I found yur place. Cho." Vincent snort laughed. "Short for Jerrrrrrichoooo. I git it!"

"You ran up a six-hundred-dollar bill and told my GM I'm payin' for everyone's drinks." Jericho growled. "Not cool."

"Oooooh, okay. My bad." He struggled to pull his wallet from his pocket. "I kin pay. I git money."

The server returned with the pitcher and glasses. "I put a rush on the food." She poured Jericho a full glass and his brother half a glass.

Jericho acknowledged her before she left, then said to Vincent, "I gotta sober you up."

"Have ya met my girlie? You gotttta meet her. Yeah, you gots to meet my ladyyyyyy."

"Is she here?"

"Yuppers." He looked around, then shrugged.

Jericho raised his arm and the dutiful server hurried back over. "Can you find his girlfriend? What's her name, Vincent?"

"Brennnndaaaaaaa."

Jericho grunted his frustration as he flicked his gaze to the server. "Did you understand him?"

"I think he said Brenda," she replied.

"Find her."

Liv couldn't wait to see Jericho.

Could. Not. Wait.

As soon as dinner with his brother was over, she knew he'd want to kick off their plan to take out Slim Jim. While she did *not* agree with his form of justice, she'd agreed to help him.

So, she would.

As she entered the noisy restaurant, butterflies zoomed in her belly and her heart beat faster.

Pausing at the hostess stand, she asked for Jericho.

"Are you Dr. Blackstone?" the hostess asked.

Liv bit back a smile. *What's up with that?* "Yes."

The hostess grabbed a menu. "I can bring you back to his booth."

"That's fine," Liv replied taking the menu from her. "I got this."

As she approached Jericho's booth, their eyes met. He pushed out, then strode in her direction. Her heart jumped into her throat at the sight of him in his leathers, his beautiful, untamed hair framing his ruggedly handsome face.

She loved that he was checking her out. She'd worn a halter sundress and strappy sandals. It was impossible to second guess Jericho, so she'd left a pair of jeans, a shirt, and sneakers in her car.

"Hey," Jericho stepped so close his warm breath brushed her forehead. "You look beautiful."

"Heyyyyooooooo," Vincent twisted around in the booth. "Come over."

"He was trashed out of his mind and acting like a fool," Jericho murmured. "His girlfriend got him to eat something and he's sobering up."

"What's with the hostess calling me Dr. Blackstone?"

He dropped a tender peck on her lips. "It's sexy as hell."

"I missed you today."

"Me, too."

"Heyyy, come join us," Vincent hollered.

"Ready to meet the idiot?" Jericho asked her.

She bit back a smile. "Absolutely."

As they made their way over, Liv could only see the backs of their heads. They stopped at the booth.

"How's he doin'?" Jericho asked.

Liv shifted her attention from Vincent to his girlfriend.

No effin' way.

Liv didn't want to gawk, but she couldn't look away. It was Sergeant Hayes' wife, Brenda.

"There he is!" Vincent said. "Hey, brother."

Jericho gestured for Liv to slide into the booth. She stood there, her gaze sliding from Vincent to Brenda while the color drained from Brenda's rosy cheeks.

"Livy," Jericho said.

Liv shifted to Jericho. "You go first. I'm probably gonna run to the bathroom."

"You wanna go now?"

"Sit, Jericho."

Jericho's eyebrows jutted up before he slid in. Liv eased down and slid so close to him, their thighs butted against each other.

His gritty, sexy growl rolled out of him and into her. She forced what she hoped was a friendly smile across the booth.

"Hi, I'm Liv."

"Good to meet you." She swallowed hard. "I'm Brenda."

"This is my woman," Vincent said. "Are you Jericho's?"

She didn't know how to answer that.

"Yes," Jericho replied. "She is."

Adrenaline surged through her. Beneath the table, she rested her palm on his massive thigh. Despite the mayhem, his answer touched the deepest part of her soul.

I'm his.

Gaining composure, she asked, "How'd you two meet?"

"A friend," Vincent replied. "I took one look at her and it was all over." He grinned at her. "Bren's something special."

Brenda's forced smile did *not* touch her eyes.

For all Liv knew, Andre and Brenda could have an open

marriage. He might know she had a lover. Vincent and Brenda could be just friends. There were numerous possibilities. As a therapist, she'd been trained to keep an open mind. Judging interfered with her ability to treat a patient.

She offered what she hoped was a warm smile.

The server appeared. "I'm sorry, Jericho. I got busy—"

"Relax," Jericho said.

"What can I get you, ma'am?" The waitress asked Liv.

"Coffee, black."

"Same," Jericho said and the server bustled off.

"You stopped slurring," Jericho said to his brother. "And you're in the clean plate club."

Vincent stared at him. "The what?"

Jericho's shoulders dropped. It was subtle, but Liv felt the shift.

"Mom used to say that to us," Jericho said. "You don't remember?"

"Nah, I got shit for a memory."

"You ran up a six-hundred-dollar bill," Jericho said. "Remember that?"

What the hell!

"No way!" Vincent said. "How much did I drink?"

Brenda laughed. "Too much."

"You were buyin' drinks for everyone," Jericho said. "You do that again, I'm gonna throw you out. I flagged you, so no one's gonna serve you without my signing off."

"C'mon, dude, I'm your brother," Vincent said. "Plus, I seen where you live." He shifted toward Brenda. "You gotta see his digs. It's a mansion. Biggest house I ever saw. When did you get so uppity? Chandeliers, expensive-looking furniture, oh, and a swimming pool to fuckin' die for. I mean, you can just write my six-hundred-dollar bill off."

The server returned with a pitcher of water, filled with lemon chunks, and two coffees.

While she topped off everyone's glasses, Jericho said, "Write what off? I gotta eat it."

"Okay, okay, sorry," Vincent said scowling.

"Mr. Jericho, are you all ready to order?" asked the server.

"Livy, what would you like?"

Liv opened the menu. There were so many options. "I'd love a steak salad."

"Make that two, but double the meat on mine and use filet for both," Jericho instructed. "Add a baked potato for me."

She nodded before turning toward Vincent and Brenda. "Can I get you both anything else?"

"What kinda pies you got?" Vincent asked.

The server ran through the list.

"Apple with a side of ice cream and two forks," Vincent said.

"Charge this to my account," Jericho said.

"Like I said, it's a write-off," Vincent said with a laugh.

After a quick nod, the waitress left.

"So, Vincent, where do you work?" Liv asked hoping to calm some of the angry energy rolling off Jericho.

"My dad owns a casket company and I kinda run it. Boring as fuck, but it's a living."

"What do you do for fun?" Liv asked.

Vincent grinned. "She's sittin' right next to me."

"Besides Brenda," Liv said.

"I got a small gun collection. I head to the shooting range once or twice a week."

"You and Jericho should do something together, you know, just the two of you."

Jericho squeezed her thigh. "I'm kinda busy," he pushed back.

She craned toward him. "You should get to know your brother, don't you think?" Beneath the table, she clasped his hand.

"Sure," Jericho grumbled. "We can go shooting together."

"Yeah, man, that sounds coolio. After, let's stop by here, so I can ride the Beast. That was like bein' back home."

"It's a date," Liv said.

"Maybe you and Bren could chill together while weez guys hang? Get your nails done or something?"

Another low-level growl rumbled out of Jericho.

"Can you excuse me?" Liv pushed out of the booth.

"Are you going to the Ladies room?" Brenda asked.

So much for a moment alone. "Yeah."

Brenda nudged Vincent. "Wait for me."

"Easy, woman," Vincent said. "I got a raging headache." As soon as he stood, Brenda scooted out.

The women made their way to the restroom. Once inside, Liv retreated into a stall. When she exited, Brenda was retying her ponytail while another customer washed her hands. Liv walked over to a nearby sink.

"Oh, wow, your hair is gorgeous," the stranger said to Liv.

Liv glanced over. "Thank you.

The woman punched the air dryer. Liv tapped the one next to her. When the customer finished, she left.

"I don't know what to say," Brenda murmured. "This has never happened to me before."

Liv waited.

"I've never had an affair. It's wrong, I know. Please don't say anything to Andre. Ohgod, I'm freaking out right now."

"I'm not telling your husband, Brenda. It's not my business and I *don't* want to get in the middle of your marriage."

Brenda threw her arms around Liv. When she broke away, she clutched her chest. "Thank you so much. This relationship with Vincent should never have happened, but I can't control myself around him. I'm elated, ashamed, and dying of guilt. I'm such a mess, I can't sleep."

A customer entered and glanced over on her way to a stall.

Liv didn't want to get involved. She wasn't Brenda's therapist or her friend. The less she knew, the better. "We should get back out there."

When they returned, Vincent was focused on eating his pie-a-la-mode while Jericho checked his phone.

As she slid in beside Jericho, she swallowed down the frustration. This was Jericho's opportunity to get to know his brother. From what she could tell, neither man was putting forth much effort.

"Dig in or there won't be any left," Vincent said. "Good pie."

"I'm fine," Brenda replied. "That's all you."

"Great," Vincent said while shoveling in a spoonful of ice cream.

Liv waited to see if anyone else would attempt to make conversation. She peered at Jericho. His gaze met hers. The divot between his brows was there, but she expected that. Then, his gaze softened and he kissed her cheek.

She melted.

Vincent set his spoon down and patted his stomach. "Damn, that was good. I don't remember eating the burger. What else did I have?"

"Slaw and fries," Brenda replied. "And most of my food."

Vincent laughed. "Good thing I wasn't stoned, too, or I woulda eaten more."

Another awkward pregnant pause.

"We're gonna take off," Vincent said, pushing Brenda out of the booth. "She's driving, well at least some of the way, but I'm sober." Vincent extended his hand to Jericho. "Thanks for being so coolio about this. I owe you, dude."

Liv pushed out of the booth, Jericho followed and shook his brother's hand.

"Take care of my bro," Vincent said to Liv.

She nodded.

"Good to meet you both," Brenda said. "Thanks for dinner."

Vincent and Brenda took off through the crowded restaurant toward the front door.

Liv waited until they were out of sight. "What a cluster."

"You're tellin' me." Jericho slid into the booth. "I do *not* wanna spend any more time with him."

Liv scooted beside him. "It's for Bryan," she murmured.

"Vincent's too stupid to be behind the shoot—"

The server delivered their dinners and they grew silent. After she left, they started eating.

After a brief respite, Liv said, "Brenda's having an affair."

Jericho eyebrows slashed down. "How do you know? Didn't you just meet her?"

"She's married to Sergeant Andre Hayes, Alexandria PD. He heads up the gang unit. I met her a few days ago when Andre and I went to lunch near the station. She owns an art gallery nearby called The Hayes. That's why she joined me in the bathroom, to ask me not to say anything."

"I thought that was a thing women did."

She laughed. "Sometimes, but I'm a big girl when it comes to peeing."

"I liked Vincent more when he was drunk. I fuckin' hate cheaters."

"So, you're good being an assassin, but you draw the line at cheaters," she murmured.

"You got it."

"You're serious."

"I told Vincent you're mine. I meant that. I'm not even gonna look at another woman—"

She laughed. "Oh, c'mon. You would so look. Humans look. It's what we do."

He shook his head before forking in salad. After swallowing, he said, "Not happening."

"I love being yours," she replied. "Goes both ways."

He leaned over. "Kiss me, woman."

With a smile, she did.

"Are you telling the sergeant?" he asked.

"No." She studied him. "What would you do? Would you tell him?"

"Are you two friends?"

"Not really. We talk shop when we're together. I'd never had lunch with him before the other day when I met Brenda."

"I agree," he replied. "Say nothing."

They finished dinner and the server returned to inquire about dessert. They declined. After clearing their plates, she left.

"You ready to get to work?" she asked.

"Yeah, but there's something we gotta do, first."

They exited the booth. He grasped her hand and dropped a kiss on her forehead before leading her through the packed restaurant toward the back, the country music growing louder with each step.

She loved being his, loved that he showed affection in public without going overboard.

Instead of veering into his office, he walked to the end of the hall and into the large room. "Dance with me."

Then, he kissed her again. This time, letting his full lips linger on hers. Her pulse soared while a whisper-soft moan fluttered out of her.

"Please," he murmured.

She grew up with a father who never gave her a choice. There wasn't even so much as a forced choice. It was never, "You can have a friend over or we can go to the movies." It was, "Thirty more minutes with the violin, then, we'll do a geometry theorem."

Despite Jericho's commanding presence and bossy attitude, she always felt like she had a choice. In part, because she was a grown woman, but because they were equals. He *was* bossy, but he wasn't the boss of her.

Standing tall, she kissed him. "I'd love to."

Into the room she floated, their hands entwined. The DJ was spinning a love ballad, the clusters of couples pressed together, all swaying to the slow beat of the country crooner.

He pulled her onto the dance floor and into his arms, while a sea of people clamored in their direction. Strange, she never thought of Jericho as a public figure. The showman tossed a nod or said hello to them by name. He was the king of the manor and she loved being his queen.

Once the surge passed, he fixed his gaze on hers. "Hello, Livy."

She kissed his cheek, then pressed herself as close as she could get. As they moved as one, their breathing fell in line. His chest expanded, then hers against his. He rooted his fingers behind her hair, curling them around her neck.

Everything and everyone faded away. Being with him was all that mattered to her. When the song ended, the DJ returned and started chatting about an upcoming tune and his recommended line dance.

Liv had never line danced. Jericho broke away and pulled her next to him as lines formed.

Rather than blurt out, "I can't, I don't know what I'm doing," she started following the person in front of her.

It was an ugly, semi-uncoordinated, first attempt at who-the-hell-knows-what, but she did not care. She was happy being with him.

The group turned, she followed, slowly starting to pick up the recurring steps. When they turned again, Jericho was in front of her, so she mimicked him until she realized half his moves were legit, the others were a Jericho-rendition of the actual dance.

In that moment, she realized that doing it perfectly did *not* matter. All that mattered was getting her ass out of the chair and doing it. Graceful, sloppy. She was with someone she cared about and that meant everything to her.

The song ended and she went to him, throwing her arms around him and kissing him. "I haven't had that much fun in a while."

"Not the sex?"

She laughed. He actually looked hurt.

"That's in a category of its own." This time, she took his hand. "Let's get to work."

14

GUNNING DOWN THE TRIGGERMAN

Jericho could have stayed on that dance floor with Liv all night. He loved that she faked the dance steps until she caught on. Loved how she didn't back out or make an excuse. She just did it.

That's how he lived his life. Half the time, he didn't know jack, but he did it anyway. Figured it out as he went. Sometimes mistakes would slow him down, but he'd find a way.

He brought her into his office, shut and locked the door, then ushered her through the closet and into his secret office. After logging in, he unlocked his safe and grabbed Lucky's cell phone.

"What's our plan for Slim Jim?" she asked.

Acid churned in his stomach. "We? No. I'm doin' this one alone, like I did the first one."

"Hawk made sure Lucky showed up alone. What happens if Slim Jim brings people with him?"

"I'll take 'em all out."

"I'll stay in the car and let you know if he's alone. If something goes wrong—which it won't—I couldn't live with myself if I wasn't there to help you."

He glanced at the computer clock. Ten-twenty. "I'm taking him out, tonight."

"You got a vest for me? What about a weapon?"

He gaped at her, then shook his head. "No."

"Well, I can't go without a vest."

"Dammit to hell, Liv!"

She crossed her arms, glared at him.

"You willing to go to prison for this?" he asked.

"I'm *not* willing to let you die, that's for fucking sure!"

They were on each other, the heat of her touch burning through him. He couldn't kiss her hard enough or pull her close enough. She clawed his back, her groans ripping through her. Then, her soft hands sandwiched his face. She slowed the kiss, then ended it.

When he opened his eyes, so much love stared back.

"I told you, we're in this together," she said, after catching her breath. "I'm not backing down."

"You can't go dressed like that."

"I brought pants, a black shirt, and sneakers. They're in my car."

"I'll get them."

She handed him her car keys. Two minutes later, he returned with her backpack. As she changed, he crossed his arms and watched.

"Are you enjoying the show?" she asked.

"Abso-fuckin'-lutely."

When she finished, he handed her a Kevlar vest. "The vest does not come off. Understood?"

"Ever?" She smirked at him. "Seriously, I *won't* remove it."

"What is it about you that I can't say no to?"

She shot him an adorable smile. "I cast a spell on you a long time ago. My only regret is that I screwed us up. But… we're partners, now, and I *won't* let you down."

"Know how to fire a gun?"

"I learned during grad school. I don't go to the shooting range much, but I have a SIG Saur P365 in my safe at home."

"Not gonna do you any good in your safe. You shoulda learned that lesson fifteen years ago."

She held his gaze. "You're right."

He scrolled through Lucky's cell phone until he found the thread with Slim Jim. Liv pulled up his number on her burner.

"They're a match," she said.

"Time to die, triggerman. I'm sending him a text from Lucky's phone so he thinks it's his cousin," Jericho explained. He typed, 'Heyo, I got a prob. Got questioned at work by a cop about a job. Should I leave town? We gotta talk."

He showed Liv the text.

"Scroll back so I can see Lucky's older texts to him."

After he did, she said, "He doesn't use punctuation and he sends a few short texts rather than one long one. The sentence that starts with 'Got' needs to be shorter."

He retyped, "Heyo got prob", and sent it.

Then, he typed, "Cop had questions about a job" and sent that one. Next, he texted, "Should I leave town". His last test, said, "We gotta talk".

No dots appeared. Another moment passed while they stared at the phone.

"Come home with me tonight," she murmured.

He ran the back of his finger down her soft cheek, leaned in, kissed her. "I'm like a stray dog. You invite me over, I'm never gonna leave."

Lucky's phone buzzed with a text from Slim Jim. "Where you at?"

"Driving and freaking out," Jericho texted back.

"You gotta calm the fuck down," Slim Jim texted. "I'll meet you somewhere safe."

Jericho pushed out of the chair. "Suit up," he said to Liv. "We're taking Slim Jim out."

She slipped the vest over her shirt. He went into his closet in search of a black cap. He found one and walked over to her. Tie your hair up and cover it with this."

While she did, Jericho yanked off his shirt, threw on the Kevlar vest, then pulled his shirt back on. He retreated into the closet for his holster, which he fitted under his arm, then checked his Glock before holstering it. He attached his ankle holster, slid his smaller weapon into it, then confirmed the knife was in the sheath on his belt loop. After shoving the silencer into his pocket, he pulled out a gun for Liv to use.

She was staring at him with great intent.

"Now, you're seein' the *real* Jericho." He handed her the weapon.

"You're a bad ass."

"I'm leaving my cell phone." He dropped it and his wallet on the desk. If something goes sideways, call Hawk. If he doesn't answer, call Stryker Truman.

"I don't have Stryker's number." He rattled off both numbers and she typed them into the burner.

He pulled two comms from the desk drawer. "Put this in your ear and we'll test them." He turned them on before handing her one.

"Can you hear me?" he asked.

"Yes. You're standing two feet away from me."

He bit back a smile, walked into his closet, and shut the door. "How 'bout now?"

"Yeah. Can you hear me?"

"Copy." He exited, shoved Lucky's cell phone in his pocket. Then, he shrugged into his black leather jacket, concealing the holstered Glock.

"Where are we going?" she asked.

"There's an abandoned gas station a few miles away. We'll text him from there."

She left her handbag, and headed toward his outer office. He wrapped his arm around her. "No, this way."

Out the back exit they went, and into the ALPHA SUV parked at the curb. Seconds later, they were on the main road. On the short ride over, Jericho clasped Liv's hand, glanced over at her.

"You doin' okay?"

"Of course."

"Not too late to back out."

His comment was met with silence as he parked in the lot across the street from the rundown building.

"Keep the weapon in your hand," he instructed. "But first, get behind the wheel in case you need to get out fast."

"I'm *not* leaving you."

"Then, you could die with me."

"Understood."

Wow, she's really puttin' herself out there.

He cupped her chin, peered into her eyes. "We got this." After a second, he typed a message to Slim Jim. "Abandoned gas station on Kilby." He sent it, then typed another. "After we talk I'm leaving town."

"Relax," Slim Jim texted back. "Be there in ten."

"As soon as he pulls in, let me know." He scanned her face. If she was afraid, she hid it well.

She dropped a soft kiss on his lips. "You're gonna do great. I've got your back."

He pulled on his black gloves, got out, and grabbed the million-watt flashlight from the back seat.

Liv moved into the driver's seat.

"Lock the doors." As soon as she did, he jogged across the quiet street.

The front door of the empty building was locked, so he strode around back. The employee entrance was also locked. He attached the silencer—

POP!

—and shot out the lock, shoved the brass in his pocket, and

entered the dark room. The full moon offered enough light for him to check out the place. Rats scurried for cover in the three empty bays. He made his way to the front door and unlocked it. Then, he moved to the back of the room to avoid headlights, shoved his Glock into the back of his pants, and waited to avenge his brother.

A few moments of silence passed before Liv broke it. "Jericho," she murmured through the comm.

"Yeah, babe."

"I'm so sorry for what I did to you in high school."

Her voice was a whisper in his ear, yet the power of her words was like a trumpeter echoing off a mountainside.

"I know."

"I've missed you so much," she whispered.

"Me, too."

His heart had been closed off for years.

"I love you," she whispered.

I love you, too, Livy.

"And I will never betray you again," she continued.

"Thank you, babe."

He'd waited years to hear the words he used to dream about. Now, he could forgive her and move forward. Despite how he felt about her, he had to focus up. One careless mistake and things could fly off the rails too damn fast.

Four minutes passed.

"Here comes a car," she murmured. "Not him." He glimpsed the headlights as it drove past.

Another two minutes.

"Here's here," she said. "One car."

As Jericho predicted, Slim Jim parked out front, his headlights illuminating the dark interior. Jericho waited.

The lights went dark, the engine went silent. A car door opened.

"Someone's stepping out," Liv whispered.

Jericho's fingers curled into fists. "This is for you, Bryan. Time to even the score."

"Slim Jim's alone," she murmured.

The front door opened. "Lucky, where you at?"

"Hiding," Jericho replied, altering his voice as best he could.

The door closed.

"Come on out," Slim Jim said.

Jericho stepped out of the shadows, flipped on the megawatt flashlight, and shone it in Slim Jim's face.

His hand flew over his face. "Fuck, that's killin' me."

He lowered the light, lifted his Glock, aimed, and fired.

POP!

"Aiiiiieeee" Slim Jim grabbed his arm, blood spilling through his fingers. Jericho strode over, peered down at him, and shone the light in his direction.

"What the fuck! You're the dude from Mad Dog's. Where the hell's my cousin?"

"I ask the questions," Jericho rasped. "You did a drive-by with Lucky a coupla weeks ago. Four guys comin' out of a restaurant in McLean."

"Fuck, my arm hurts. What the hell is goin' on? You some kinda fucked up weirdo or somethin'?"

"Answers or blood," Jericho growled. "Who ordered the hit?"

Fear shadowed Slim Jim's eyes. "My boss, El Jefe."

"Is he one of Abdul Al-Mazir's guys?"

"I dunno his real name."

"Why'd he order the hit?" Jericho asked.

Slim Jim chuckled. "You never been in a gang, have ya? I don't ask, I do."

"Gimme your cell phone."

"Fuck you. I'm fucking bleeding here. You think I'm gonna help you?"

"Were you the triggerman that night?"

Slim Jim puffs out his chest. "Hell, yeah."

"Lucky said it was a scare job. Who were you tryin' to scare?"

"I don't owe you nothin'. You said you had a job for me. Now, you're just wasting my time. I answer to El Jefe, not you."

"Last chance." Jericho raised his gun.

Wincing, Slim Jim yanked a gun from the back of his pants, raised his arm—

POP!

Jericho hit him between the eyes and he dropped. After collecting the shell casing, he pulled Slim Jim's phone from his pocket and turned it off.

"Rot in hell for killing my brother."

He walked across the quiet street. Liv unlocked the doors. Jericho opened the door to the back seat, set the flashlight and gloves on the floor as Liv moved to the passenger seat. After shoving Slim Jim's phone in his pocket, he got behind the wheel.

"Stay quiet," Jericho said as he pulled a burner from his center console and turned it on. He dialed 9-1-1.

"What's your emergency?"

"I heard gunshots."

"Where are you?" asked the emergency dispatcher.

"On Kilby Lane in Alexandria, near the abandoned gas station."

"What's your name?"

"There's a second body on Graybill at Springfield Industrial Park. Both are Thriller Killers." Jericho hung up and turned off the burner.

After starting the SUV, he rolled out.

"Are you okay?" Liv asked.

Jericho pulled onto the main road and flipped on his headlights. "Of course not. I just killed a man."

She sighed. "You got your revenge, so we're done, right?"

Silence.

It would be easy to lie to her, move forward without her ever knowing. But he'd never lied to her before. Wasn't gonna start now, especially if this was the start of something good.

"Jericho, tell me we're done."

"I'm taking out the gang leader."

"The killing has to stop."

"They both told me it was a scare job. I'm not stopping 'til I get some damn answers."

"Why'd you call in both shootings?"

"Word'll travel fast once the cops get involved. TK's leader is gonna hear about his guys gettin' gunned down. He might think someone's comin' for him. But he might not."

He let the silence hang for a second. "Either way, he's a dead man."

Liv wanted Jericho to put this nightmare behind him, but she knew he wasn't walking from this. He was a take-charge man who had no intention of waiting for law enforcement to do its job. He didn't care about the "right" way to do it, and he wasn't concerned about the consequences.

The words etched in ink on his pec—"My Life My Rules"—popped into her head. More than ever, those words rang true.

Part of her wanted to tell him that if he didn't stop, she couldn't continue down this path, but she would never use coercion as a tool or make an empty threat. Truth was, she wasn't going anywhere. She meant it when she told him they were in this together. Eyes wide open, she knew what she was getting herself into.

The ride back to The Road was quiet. She'd spoken her mind. She couldn't imagine any part of this ending well, for either one of them.

He pulled into the parking lot and parked the ALPHA SUV around back. The lot was empty, the club was closed. He killed the engine.

She regarded him. "I don't want tonight to end."

He clasped her hand, rested it on her thigh. "We're each other's alibis."

She nodded.

"Does your condo building have surveillance?" he asked.

"Yes, but my unit doesn't." Then, she thought about that for a second. "You know, I don't think it does, but I'm not sure."

"You don't know?"

"I rent it from my uncle. It never occurred to me, but there could be cameras hidden in it."

"That's creepy. You want me to ask Hawk to sweep the place for you?"

"That would be good, thanks."

"Well, we can't go there," he said.

"I packed an overnight bag," she said with a sly smile, "in case I got an invitation for a sleepover."

He leaned over, kissed her. "Finally, something good. We'll stay in my guest house."

She kissed him back.

"We gotta go back inside through my private entrance, then out the front door," he explained. "That way, it's like we never left."

"Ohgod," she bleated.

"What?"

"This is definitely premeditated."

"I always use this entrance for my ALPHA missions," he explained.

"This *isn't* an ALPHA mission."

In silence, they went inside. Once in his private office, he dropped Slim Jim's phone in his safe. She changed back into her halter dress and strappy sandals.

With her backpack slung over his shoulder, they made their way to his outer office. Together, they walked through the restaurant, now closed. It was quiet, clean, and ready for the next day's customers.

She slid into her car and waited while he mounted his bike. Jericho Savage on a motorcycle was the sexiest thing she'd ever seen. All man. All muscle. All alpha.

She was falling in love with a complicated man.

But her heart wanted who it wanted. She could walk away, but she never would. Losing him as a friend had wrecked her. She'd never survive a break up now.

Twenty minutes later, they parked at his estate. He took the overnight bag from her trunk, ushered her inside. The house was dark and quiet. He led her through the living room and out through the sliding glass door. On the other side of the pool was his one-story guest house.

Another scanner at the front door cleared him to enter.

"Computer, lights on low," he commanded.

"Welcome home, Jericho," the computer replied.

Off to the right sat a living room with casual beach furniture. Beyond that, a bright, white kitchen. On the other side of the home were three open doors.

"I know you're stressing over what I'm doing," he murmured. "I shouldn't have brought you with me tonight. I knew better."

"I insisted on going," she replied. "I can't tell you we're in this together, then struggle with the outcome."

"Sure, you can," he replied matter-of-factly. "I do that all the time. I'm always at war with myself." He captured her chin in his hand, kissed her. "We can talk about it after we sleep."

With her overnight bag in hand, he led her into a bedroom.

"Computer, bedroom lights on low," he commanded.

"Lights on low, Jericho," the computer replied.

Both lamps on the night tables flicked on, bathing the room in soft, yellow light. The cozy bedroom with its light-wood furniture and king bed felt like the perfect getaway spot to unwind.

He helped her out of her clothing. She did the same for him. Once naked, he pulled her into his arms, but he didn't kiss her. He stared into her eyes, tucked a chunk of her curls behind her ear.

"Let's get some hot water on your tight muscles."

"I'm fine," she protested.

He stepped behind her to massage her shoulders. "No, you're not."

She loved his touch. He'd always filled a place in her heart no one else could. Now, it was so much more. She needed him beyond a friendship. She craved him as a lover. Even now, mired in angst, she wanted him.

He nuzzled her neck, a moan rumbling from his chest. "I love the way you smell. Always have."

Seconds passed. She closed her eyes, relishing their tenderness. This felt right. They were naked and vulnerable. There was no agenda, no plan, no mission. Just the two of them, the way it was supposed to be.

She turned to face him, stared into his eyes. Even at this late hour, they were bright. Only the etched lines between his brows gave away his tension.

His kiss was tender. One led to several until they deepened the embrace. Being with him felt like the best extension of herself. She ran her fingers down his back and over his backside.

Their breathing shifted. There was no denying how she felt. In the intensity of their mission, she'd blurted out those three little words—I love you.

I do love him.

And when he didn't reciprocate, she wasn't deterred. She would earn his love, like she was earning his trust.

The kiss slowed, ending as tenderly as it began.

He stared into her eyes. "Shower with me."

They entered the en suite bathroom with its white double vanities and two opposing showerheads. He turned on the water, pulled two hair ties from a drawer, and offered one to her.

With their hair out of the way, they stepped into the shower. The pounding water helped relax her, but it was Jericho's touch she needed.

He collected the bar soap and sudsed his hands. Strong, soapy hands massaged her shoulders. She closed her eyes, melting into his touch. After a few minutes, he slowed to a stop.

She turned. "Thank you."

"I want to spoil you," he murmured. "All the time."

Those words, coupled the love pouring from his eyes, made her heart happy.

With lathered hands, she washed him, taking her time to explore and cherish. From the expanse of his shoulders to his perfectly sculpted eight-pack abs, from his striated thighs and calves to his large feet and elongated toes. She loved touching this man.

When finished, they dried off. She pulled her toothbrush from her travel bag. In an easy silence, they brushed their teeth. An everyday task that, with Jericho, was something she could see themselves doing together every single day for the rest of their lives.

After pulling out his hair tie, he stood behind her, wrapped her in his arms and stared at them in the mirror.

"Feel better?" he asked.

"Much."

For a few seconds, they stared at each other's reflection. "You read my file," he said. "You know what I do, what I am. You gotta be at peace with it if we're gonna make a go at this." With gentle hands, he turned her toward him, kissed her forehead. "I lost you once. I would understand if you couldn't be with me now."

"Years ago, I made a choice. It was the wrong one. This time, I'm making the right one."

He folded his ripped arms around her, held her against his chest. This was the best place in the world.

In his arms.

"I got us something." She broke their embrace, wrapped her fingers around his triceps and led him into the bedroom where she dug out a condom box and handed it to him.

"I like *your* premeditated much better than mine," he said.

She smiled, grateful he could lighten the mood. "I know the condoms at the club are too small for you, so I bought these, hoping they'd work."

"I don't bring women home with me, so I don't have any here." He read the tag line aloud. "For the giant man in your life."

"The cashier asked me if I was having sex with Bigfoot," she said. "I told her I was, but it wasn't your foot that was going in the condom."

They burst out laughing.

"This is what I missed," he said, pulling her close. "Us—the laughing—you. Jesus, Livy, I never stopped—"

Silence.

The energy shifted, the desire to tell her how he felt threatened to explode out of him. He loved her, never stopped, but he'd let the hate consume him. As they peered into each other's eyes, he wanted to tell her, but those three little words were lodged in his throat.

With a gleam in her eyes, she pulled back the linens and crawled into bed. "Hurry," she said. "The sheets are cold. You gotta keep me warm."

With a condom packet in hand, he got into bed, and turned to face her.

"Mygod, you're beautiful," he said. "If I look really hard, I see a couple of faint freckles on your nose."

"Ugh, I hated those."

"I loved them, especially when you'd scrunch up your nose at me. They'd all run together."

Her smile was filled with love.

She ran her fingernails over his shoulder and across his chest, then down his eight-pack. "You filled out." Then, she wrapped her hand around his cock. "In all the right places."

He loved the gentle way she caressed his shaft, running her fingertip around the head.

She leaned close, kissed him. He drew her to him and let go, turning off the constant thoughts running through his head. And he focused on Liv.

His Livy.

The girl he'd crushed hard on, the one who shredded his heart with her betrayal, and the death of a friendship that had once consumed him.

Within seconds, they were on each other. He couldn't stop touching her, appreciating her sexy curves, her beautiful body, her luscious mouth. Back in high school, they'd never kissed. But now, now he couldn't stop kissing her. Their tongues crashing together, stroking and teasing. The build with Liv was fast, the desire to bury himself inside her a constant pull.

But he took his time, appreciating her coos and moans that turned to groans and growls. He laved her firm nipple, sucking it into his mouth. Her body bowed to his, her breathing erupting in a series of gasps and whimpers.

He kissed his way to her other nipple, then down to her soaked sex. He teased and prodded, but he didn't take her over the edge.

"You're torturing me," she groaned, "and I love it."

Then, he wound his way back to her mouth. The connection was real and intense and so damn electrifying. The thrumming in his cock and the tightness of his balls had him breaking away.

"Ohgod, Jericho, inside me," she pleaded.

On went the condom.

"Better?" she asked.

"Oh, yeah," he replied.

"C'mon on in, Bigfoot."

They shared a smile before he rose over her and, with his cock in hand, pressed into her. Her groans ripped through him, the initial slide making him roar with pleasure.

She wrapped herself around him while they found their rhythm. He wanted to take his time, but she was moving fast beneath him.

"Hard," she commanded. "And deep."

"Babe,"

"Kiss me, I'm gonna come," she moaned.

He pounded into her, thrusting again and again while she bucked against him. They were wild and uninhibited, biting and clawing while he tunneled into her. She convulsed and cried out through her orgasm.

"Here I go, baby," he growled.

The ecstasy pounded through him while she kissed him through his release. More pleasure than he deserved. He wasn't one of the good guys. Wasn't even pretending to be. He was a sniper, an assassin, a killer of killers.

Evil chasing evil doesn't make anyone a good guy.

Yet, as he stared into Liv's eyes, he knew that she would be able to save him from himself.

Her savage kisses had him ravaging her until they were spent.

In the aftermath, he spooned close, wrapping his arm around her and cupping her breast. Their breathing was in sync. The only difference was an occasional sigh that floated from her and hung in the air over them.

He wished they could stay there, retreating into a paradise for two. But reality had a way of creeping back in, even now.

He hated leaving her, even for a minute. "Be right back." As he made his way to the bathroom, she caught up with him. While he cleaned up, she peed. Was this the beginning of their forever?

Sure as hell feels like it.

Back in bed, he laid on his back and she snuggled close, her head on his chest. A tangle of arms and legs connecting in every place where skin could touch.

She caressed his chest with her fingernails, her touch both arousing and comforting.

"Why the mask at Lost Souls?" he asked.

"When I first started watching the watchers, an FBI agent cornered me at a coffee shop and asked why I'd been tailing him. I denied it, but I learned my lesson. The DMV is a large region, but a small town. Plus, I do a lot of consulting with law enforcement. I didn't know if any of my clients would come to the club, and I didn't want them recognizing me. I wanted to keep my professional and personal lives separate."

"Got it."

"Plus, when Addison and I decided to do this, I wanted to play in complete anonymity. I didn't want anyone I'd hooked up with to know anything about me, not even what I look like."

"How'd that go?"

"Since you're the only one I've been with, I'd say, not so good."

They shared a laugh that fell into a comfortable silence.

Pushing up on her elbow, she peered into his eyes, then regarded the 5 • 31 inked above the La Familia tattoo on his bicep. As she traced the date with her finger, she asked, "Why is five thirty-one important?"

"May thirty-first is the day I won guardianship of my brothers and sister. Keeping us together meant everything to me."

Tears pricked her eyes. "I've never known anyone so fiercely loyal." And then, she broke down and cried. "I'm so sorry, Jericho."

The desire to keep her safe, to ensure her happiness, and to put her first, had him wiping away her tears. He tilted her face toward his. "I forgive you, Liv."

He would always remember this moment. Part relief, part joy sprang from her eyes, but it was the way that she smiled at him that told him everything he needed to know.

This was it. He had found his forever love.

"I started to tell you something earlier," he murmured. "You know, at the gas station."

"I remember," she whispered.
"I never stopped loving you, Livy," he said.
And I never will.

15

BLINDSIDED

Jericho woke nose to nose with Liv. His thigh was over hers, her arm across his chest. Light streamed in between the closed blind slats. He wanted to make her breakfast, then lounge the day away, but he couldn't. Like most days, he had a chock-full schedule.

Her eyes fluttered open and he was rewarded with her sleepy smile. Everything in his universe shifted. She was back in his life. Not only that, she was in his bed, and they were entwined like clinging ivy.

Then, the stark reality crept in. Bryan was dead, his entire family was hurting. He was on a mission to find out who the gang leader was trying to scare.

"I can see you thinking," she whispered. "Your dreams must be intense."

He smiled. "I rarely remember them."

"That's because you've probably killed your muse," she said with a chuckle.

"I don't have a muse."

"I'm sure you do. He's just toting around a machine gun and inspiring your next mission."

She kissed him, then pushed out of bed.

"Where you going?" he called after her.

"It's almost eight. I've got a training class in DC this morning and another one in Bowie this afternoon. I gotta get going."

He joined her in the bathroom. "Breakfast?"

"Raincheck. If I bolt, I've got just enough time to get home, get ready, grab a bite, and go."

"I loved last night," he said.

"Which part?"

"The second half.'"

She rinsed out the toothpaste, then sidled close. "I'm glad I rate higher than a kill mission."

He kissed her. "We gotta do something fun together."

She caressed his bare ass. "Okay."

"I'm gonna take you somewhere nice. We'll have a normal evening, like other couples."

"I would love that. Does that mean you're done… never mind." She cupped his shoulders. "I love you for you."

One kiss that was much too short, then she got dressed. Five minutes later, she was gone.

He dressed, returned to the house. Voices in the kitchen drew him into the room. Everyone, but Mark, was eating breakfast.

Owen lit up. "Uncle, play wif me!"

He mussed the boy's head of blond hair. "I can't right now, buddy. I gotta go to work. We'll play when I get home."

"Are you just getting back?" Georgia asked.

"I was in the guest house."

Silence.

Everyone, but the kids, looked at him.

Tim squinted. "Why were you—"

"*Tim*," Patty scolded. "Think."

"Was it Liv?" Georgia asked.

"How is it that everyone lives here for free and I'm the one getting bombarded with questions?" He flashed a smile. Truth was, he loved when his family ribbed him.

Since Bryan had been killed, everyone had been so sad, he was more than happy to get teased if it meant a few moments of levity.

"Georgia Renee Savage," Gram began. "Mind your business."

"Uh-oh," little Annie blurted. "Gram only uses whole names when we're in trouble."

Everyone started laughing.

"Hey, so on a serious note, the final inspection of the wine cellar at Carole Jean's is later today," Georgia said. "Can you swing by and sign off?"

"I'll be there," Jericho replied.

After breakfast, Jericho got ready and returned to the kitchen. Gram was alone, cleaning up. Jericho cleared the remaining dishes and glasses, setting them on the counter next to the sink.

"I can do that, Gram."

"It's fine, dear." She glanced over. "Are you heading out?"

"Yeah."

She tapped off the faucet and tugged off her dishwashing gloves. "I'll walk you out."

Once outside, she stood in the shade of the covered front door. "Are you making progress?"

"Gram, you gotta trust me."

"I lie awake wondering if his killer is going to come after someone else in our family." Her gaze was unblinking and unwavering. For a small woman, her presence was enormous.

"You trust me, right?" he asked.

"I have, so far."

He smiled. "I'm not gonna let anything happen to us."

"Something already has."

The guilt he carried around jumped to the surface. Was he to blame for Bryan's death? Two more men were dead and he still didn't have answers.

"I'm workin' on it," he said. "And I can't say anything else."

On a harrumph, she glared at him. "Will you tell me when you know?"

"I'll tell you what I can," he replied. "Sometimes it's safer *not* to know."

"Not this time." She patted his chest and retreated inside.

On the way to work, he called Hawk. "I need your help."

"Talk to me, babe," Hawk replied.

"I've got a cell phone that's probably password protected."

"No problem. Use my software," Hawk said.

"Can you swing by Liv's place and sweep for hidden cams?"

"Also, no prob. What else?"

"I need twenty-four seven protection on my fam," Jericho said.

"Got it."

"I'm gonna have a job."

"On or off the books?"

"Off."

"Team or the two of us?"

"We'll talk in person," Jericho replied.

"I'll swing by The Road tonight." Hawk hung up.

That evening, the doorbell rang and Liv swung open her front door. Hawk stood in the hallway, a backpack slung over his shoulder, a helmet on his head with night vision goggles in the up position. Per Hawk's instruction, she'd turned out every light in her condo and closed the blinds.

Hawk handed her a pair of goggles, lowered his, then walked inside. She shut the door and, using the goggles, returned to her living room. Hawk unzipped his backpack and pulled out two electronic devices. One, he set on the floor, plugged it in, and turned it on. The second was a handheld.

He returned to the foyer and walked through her entire home. He checked closets, the pantry, the drawers in the kitchen and in both bathrooms. He jumped on her kitchen counter and checked the tops of the cabinets. He opened the drawers in her dresser, checked every lamp, every piece of furniture, even the sofa and chair cushions. If there were tiny cams or bugs hidden in that unit, Hawk assured her he would find them.

Ninety minutes later, he strolled into her kitchen. "I'm gonna turn on the light."

"Okay," she replied.

"Take off the goggles or you're gonna be blinded by the light." Then, he started singing the classic rock song by Manfred Mann's Earth Band.

While singing his off-key rendition, he flipped on the kitchen light. She turned on the table lamps in the living room as he pulled a laptop from the bag.

Several clicks later, he tossed her a nod. "You're all clear."

"Thank you for doing this." She paused. "Are you sure?"

"Check this out."

She stood next to him. "This is my report. I scanned everything. There's nothing."

Every line item had a zero next to it.

"Could they be in the ceiling?"

"This isn't a false ceiling," Hawk replied. "How long have you lived here?"

"Six months."

"Why do you think the place is bugged?"

"I just wanted to confirm, that's all. What do I owe you?"

That made him laugh. "Owe me? We're friends."

"Thank you for doing this. I'm making chicken. Can you stay for dinner?"

"Thanks, but I'm headed to The Road." He shouldered his backpack, made his way to the front door. "You know, there *is* something you can do for me."

"Sure," she replied.

"Do *not* break Jericho's heart. He won't admit it, but he's a goner." With a wink and a grin, he opened the door. Heading down the hall, he started singing Blinded By The Light.

That man doesn't have a care in the world.

Jericho returned to The Road after paying the remaining balance on his new state-of-the-art wine cellar at Carole Jean's, his upscale restaurant in Tysons. Before getting out of his truck, he called his sister.

"This wine cellar is uh-mazing.",' she answered. "I'm never leaving."

He chuffed out a laugh. "It better be. That baby cost me a mil."

"Shut. Up."

"Hey, I forgot to check the schedule. Make me a res for tomorrow. Dinner for two at eight in the Copper room."

"How romantic," Georgia replied. "You do know we're booked like two months in advance?"

"I know, but see if you can squeeze a table in."

"Hold on." After a long wait, she came back. "I'm moving a few things around. Hold two seconds." He waited. "Okay, done."

"Thanks, sis. Enjoy your million-dollar wine cellar."

"Jericho—"

"Yeah?"

"I love you. I regret not telling Bryan more."

"I love you, too, darlin.'"

When he walked into The Road, the bar crowd was singing along to a song he kinda recognized. As he pushed his way through, he spotted Hawk, sitting on the bar, belting out the tune, while a harem of women formed a tight circle around him.

When the song ended, the entire room broke into a rousing applause that only bolstered Hawk's already massive ego. When the clapping subsided, Jericho whistled. Those near him stopped talking. He whistled again, louder. The place grew quiet.

"Yo, I'm glad everyone's havin' fun, but I gotta steal the travelin' singer away from you," Jericho boomed.

Several women booed him.

"My bro," Hawk pushed off the bar and made his way over.

"Hawk, call me," yelled one of the women.

"Me, too," hollered another.

"They love you," Jericho said.

Hawk waggled his eyebrows. "And I let 'em show me, every chance I get."

The two men pushed their way through the crowd. As they passed the dining area, Hawk received another round of applause. And, in true Nicholas Hawk form, he waved and grinned like a damn movie star. Jericho got enough attention for owning the most popular restaurant in the area. He didn't need Hawk throwing fuel on the fire.

In his office, he locked the door.

"You know, sometimes you sing off key," Jericho said.

Hawk laughed. "Life's too short to give a fuck. We oughta know. We're the ones doing the shortening."

Jericho stood in front of the scanner, the light turned green, and the two men made their way back. Hawk dropped his backpack on the love seat.

"Liv's place is clean," Hawk said.

"Thanks for doing that."

"Who owns the condo?"

"Her uncle."

"Who's that?"

"Didn't ask."

"Uh, don'tcha think you should, considering what you *really* do for a living?" Hawk asked.

"Not now." Jericho unlocked his computer and the screen brightened. "I took out the driver and the triggerman. Now, I'm goin' after the gang leader."

"Hmm, a gang hit?"

"Unless some guy callin' himself El Jefe is taking orders from Al-Mazir, then, yeah, it was a gang hit."

"What gang?"

"Thriller Killers," Jericho said.

"Never heard of 'em." Hawk walked around the standing desk and eyeballed the computer screen. "What are we looking at?"

"I've been geolocating El Jefe's phone." Jericho pulled up a map that provided locations where he'd been that day. "Every time as I think I got a hit on where he lives, he goes somewhere else. Once we know, I need you to set up surveillance. I have no idea what this guy looks like and I need him alive when I take him."

"Why not a clean hit?" Hawk asked.

"I gotta find out why he shot at us. If it's not me they're after, and it wasn't Bryan, is it you? Are you in danger? Is it Vincent? I don't know shit about him."

Hawk tossed a nod at the screen. "He's on the move."

After a few minutes, Hawk said, "I love ya, man, but this feels like watching paint dry. You eaten?"

"No."

"C'mon. I'll buy you a burger."

Jericho locked up and they left his office. As they eased into his private booth, he vowed he wouldn't rest until he found this man and got some damn answers, preferably by beating them out of him.

Friday morning, Liv entered the APD in search of gang unit detective Mark Kutchner. She found him at his desk, talking to Sergeant Hayes.

"Hey, Liv, how's it going?" Mark asked.

"You've got a big fan in my wife," Andre said. "She told me she wanted to have lunch with you sometime. Just the girls. She thinks you two are a lot alike."

I don't think so.

Liv forced a smile. "That's so nice." She addressed Kutchner, "Detective, I'm compiling data for a research paper I've been working on. Any chance we could chat for a few when you and the sergeant finish up?"

"We're done." Andre pushed out of the chair next to Mark's desk. "I can only put off paperwork for so long. Good seeing you Liv."

"You, too, Andre."

Mark gestured. "Have a seat."

"How have you been?" she asked as she sat.

In a previous conversation, he'd mentioned having two children. Since Z had assigned her the APD case, he'd given her access to the personnel files. After reading Mark's, she learned he was in his forties and separated. Years earlier, when he was a rookie, the precinct had received an anonymous call that he'd taken a bribe. The matter had been investigated, but no evidence had been found.

"Hanging in," Mark replied. "Work's been keeping me busy." His phone buzzed and he glanced at it.

"Wanna take that?" Liv asked.

"No, it's fine. What do you need?"

"I'm compiling stats on the stress levels of law enforcement personnel. Do you mind if I ask you a few questions?"

"As long as you don't put my name in your paper, I'm happy to help you."

"No names."

His answers to the questions were somewhat irrelevant. Liv was more interested in his non-verbal reactions to them. She pulled out a small notebook.

"How do you handle a particularly stressful day?" she began.

"Go for a run, spend time with my kids, you know, like play with them, show them they're my priority. I try to mentally separate when I leave here, but if I've got a really stressful or difficult case, it follows me everywhere. Sometimes I wake up in the middle of the night thinking about it."

She asked several more questions. Mark was easygoing, made decent eye contact, and mentioned his children a lot. He confided he'd started seeing someone, but it was casual. His phone had rung a few times, but he'd let it go.

When it rang again, she said, "I've taken up enough of your time. I appreciate it, Mark."

"Good seeing you, Liv. Good luck with your project." He answered the phone. "Detective Kutchner."

Moving away from his desk, she glanced around the busy room. There were uniformed officers, detectives, and support staff. It would take her weeks to question everyone. She didn't expect this case would be easy, but as far as she could tell, the people she'd talked to—Sergeant Andre Hayes, Detective Mirabel Morales, and Detective Mark Kutchner—were not the snitches.

As she made her way toward one of the homicide detectives, her phone rang with a call from BLOCKED CALLER.

"Hello," she answered.

"My office. *Now*," Uncle Z said.

The line went dead.

Dread made the hair on the back of her neck prickle.

On her way into DC, Jericho called her. "Hey," she answered, her thoughts still on Z's abrupt call.

"Have dinner with me tonight."

That got her full attention. "I'd love to. Your place?"

"No. Carole Jean's. It's my two-Michelin-starred restaurant."

"You, in a suit. I'm so there."

He laughed. "Only if you're in a little black dress."

"Absolutely. I look forward to it."

Silence.

"You okay?" he asked.

"My—yes." She wasn't about to dump this on him. That call from Z was probably nothing. "I'll see you tonight."

She hung up and rubbed her chest, but the tightness wouldn't lift. She'd been summoned to DOJ numerous times since accepting the job, but never by phone. Always with a text.

Relax, you're fine.

She made her way into the district, then through the maze of DOJ to Z's basement office.

Knock-knock.

"Enter."

She opened the door.

"Come in and close the door." He did not smile.

She sat on the edge of the guest chair.

Z sighed. "Livingston, I can't decide if I'm more angry or more heartbroken."

He never calls me Livingston.

Her stomach dropped. "Why?"

"I trusted you. You betrayed me when you let your past interfere with your present."

"What are you talking about?" Playing dumb was a pathetic Hail Mary. A last-ditch attempt to avoid the inevitable.

"Don't make this worse than it is," he hissed. "You're smart and hard working. You have the education, the background, the expertise. But I hired you because I *trusted* you. You've broken that trust. And you've left me no alternative."

God, no.

"You're fired."

"Because?"

His spine stiffened. "Are you going to make me say it?"

"I have a right—"

"You lost that right when you lied on your report about Savage." His voice was tight, each word pronounced, his eyes small and beady. "He was *not* ready to return to work and he should never have been reinstated. Two gang members were found dead. I'm confident one of them killed Bryan Savage. While law enforcement has no idea Jericho does anything beyond owning several restaurants in the area, I am well aware of what he *really* does for a living—more importantly, what he's *capable* of doing. I just read the police reports and was surprised the dead men's limbs weren't ripped from their bodies."

He raked his fingers over his forehead, sighed again, then shook his head at her. "I am beyond disappointed in your choice."

He's going to be a hell of a lot more disappointed when he learns I'm Jericho's alibi for both murders.

"The condo was a perk that came with this job," Z continued. "Since you no longer work for me, you need to relocate. I'm sorry, Livy."

Liv opened her mouth to protest. No words came out. They were running rampant in her head, but they were all pointless. He was right. She'd falsified a report. She'd let her broken relationship with Jericho affect her decision. And she was willing to lie again when the police questioned him. Her gut had been right… this had not ended well.

"Thank you for the opportunity," she said. "I loved being a watcher. It was unlike anything I've ever done. And I appreciate your opening doors for me with the PDs."

A sad smile touched his eyes. "I hope, going forward, you make better decisions where Savage is concerned."

"I'll be out of the condo as soon as I can."

He nodded, turned back to his computer. She'd been dismissed for good.

With a heavy heart, she made the slow trek back through the building. Once outside, she called Jericho.

"Hey, babe," he answered. "I was just thinkin' 'bout you."

"Where are you?"

"The Road. You comin' to see me?"

"Yeah. Just a heads-up. The police will probably be stopping by to question you."

"I'll be ready."

Silence.

"Livy, you there?"

"I'm in DC. Be there shortly."

As she made her way to her car, she glanced over her shoulder.

If Uncle Z labeled me a traitor... is there a watcher watching me now?

Jericho waited at the bar, nursing a cuppa joe. Every time the door opened, he flicked his gaze toward the bright light. He couldn't wait to see Liv. He was *that* pussy-whipped.

The door opened, a man entered and approached the hostess stand. She escorted him in Jericho's direction. He was average height, dark skin, with a short Afro and stylish beard and mustache. He wore a blue button-down, a blue striped tie, and navy pants.

Here we go.

"Jericho—" said the hostess.

"Sergeant Andre Hayes, Alexandria PD," he said, flashing his badge. "Are you Jericho Savage?"

"You got 'im. Tell me you caught the SOB who killed my brother." Always on the offense, Jericho was gonna push for answers before he gave a damn inch.

"We have."

Jericho narrowed his gaze. "Who did it?"

The bartender sidled over. "Can I get you something to drink?"

"I'm good, thanks," Hayes replied. "Mr. Savage, is there somewhere we can talk in private?"

Jericho tapped his fingers on the bar. He didn't want to bring the guy to his private booth. That was for friends and family, and Hayes was neither.

"My office." He led the way toward the back of the restaurant, slowing to say hey to the regulars.

He left his office door open, gestured to one of two chairs

across from his desk before easing down in his worn, leather chair. Then, he waited.

Hayes sat in the chair. "We were able to recover the stolen vehicle used in the drive-by. Fingerprints ID'd both men in the car. They were members of the Thriller Killers gang, known as TK. The bullets that killed your brother matched the gun used in the drive-by."

"Where's he being held?"

"He's dead, killed execution-style along with the driver."

"Sounds like they got what they deserved."

"Maybe so, but I need to investigate all three murders. We don't have a motive for your brother's death, so I need to ask you a few questions. Have you ever had anything to do with the Thriller Killers, or any other gang?"

"You gotta be fucking kidding me."

"No, I'm not. Not long after your brother was killed, both of these men were murdered."

Damn straight they were and my killin' spree isn't over.

Jericho regarded the sergeant with a cool indifference.

"No reaction?" Hayes asked.

"You're the expert. Don't gang members get killed every day?"

"They can."

"I gave the homicide detective space to do his job," Jericho bit out, his eyes drilling into the sergeant. "I didn't call. I kept telling my anxious, concerned family to chill. We'd hear something, at some point. Looks like today is that day. You got two dead gang members who gunned down my brother." Jericho sucked down a breath while his hands curled into fists.

Take it down a few.

"Did you, or either of your brothers, have anything to do with the TKs?" Hayes asked.

"I sure as fuck don't," Jericho ground out. "My brother, Bryan, graduated with honors from GW and was headed to law school in the fall. I hardly know my older brother. He left years ago."

"Where you were on the nights these two men were killed?" Hayes rattled off the dates.

Silence.

Jericho pushed out of his chair, walked around his desk, and leaned his ass on the worn wood. "You think I killed two men I couldn't pick out in a lineup."

"Both men were killed with the same gun. Do you own any firearms?"

Jericho glared at him. "You have got some fuckin' nerve comin' into my restaurant and askin' me where I was. Are you tellin' me I'm a suspect?"

"I can't rule anyone out."

"When you figure out *why* my brother was gunned down, you let me know. Now, get outta my face and don't come back until you have some damn answers!"

The tension in the room was thick. Jericho's frustration had reached a boiling point.

Liv appeared in his doorway. Her gaze flitting from Jericho to the sergeant, then back to Jericho. He was impressed. She hid her reaction well.

"Liv." Hayes' expression brightened. "This is a pleasant surprise."

"Absolutely. Are you handling Bryan Savage's case?"

"I am," Hayes replied.

"Do you have any suspects?" Liv asked.

"I can't discuss the case with you," Hayes replied. "I'm sorry."

Liv slid her gaze to Jericho. "I'll wait for you in your booth."

"The sergeant stopped by to let me know that two gang members killed Bryan," Jericho said to her as he eased back down in his chair. "Hayes, here, wants to know where I was the night they got killed."

"Two nights, Mr. Savage."

Jericho's stomach soured. Seemed like the cop was more interested in the thugs than his brother.

Rather than leave, Liv stepped into the room. "What dates?" she asked.

"I can't discuss—" Hayes protested.

"I might be able to help," she pushed back.

The sergeant rattled them off.

"I was here that first night," Jericho replied.

"And what about the night of the second murder?" Hayes asked.

"Jericho was with me," Liv said. "We were here, then we went to his house."

She rattled that off like it was the truth. But the crease between her eyebrows was deep with worry.

He hoped the sergeant didn't know Liv like he did, or it would all be over in an instant.

16

THE INTERROGATION

Jericho needed the sergeant to leave him alone so he could go after the gang leader.

Now that the case had been assigned to the gang unit, Jericho expected they'd be all up in his business. Next, they'd question his family. Though he'd brought this all on himself, he had no regrets.

None.

"Small world," Hayes said. "Liv, would you mind if I asked you a few questions?" He regarded Jericho. "Alone."

Jericho was about to jump in, but his gut told him to shut the hell up.

"Sure, but Jericho stays," Liv replied. "His youngest brother was killed and his other brother was also a victim of gang violence." She eased down in the second guest chair.

"How do you know Mr. Savage?" Hayes asked.

"Childhood friends, and I babysat his four younger siblings when Jericho would take his mom for her cancer treatments."

While Hayes made some notes, Liv didn't fidget. She didn't look his way either. She just waited, not rushing to fill the silence. Jericho appreciated her chill vibe.

"Where were you the night in question?" Hayes repeated the date.

"Like I said, we were here, then at his home."

"What time did you leave?"

Her gaze jumped to Jericho. "Would you say around three or three-thirty in the morning?"

"Sounds about right, but I wasn't looking at the time," Jericho replied.

"Where'd you go after you left here?" Hayes asked.

"To Jericho's guest house, on his property in McLean," she replied

"Until?" Hayes asked Liv.

"Around nine that morning," she replied.

"Why were you here so late?" Hayes asked, his gaze cemented on Liv.

Her lips curved up. "Use your imagination, Andre."

On a nod, Andre slid his gaze to Jericho. "And the surveillance will verify this?"

"Yup," Jericho replied.

"Why did you stay in your guest house?" Andre asked Jericho.

Jericho's blood pressure was on the rise again. He was done answering questions, finished talking to the cop. A growl rumbled from his chest.

Liv caught his eye and shook her head ever-so-slightly.

He took a beat, and a breath. Rather than lose his shit, he'd answer the question before he kicked the sergeant out.

"Privacy. My entire family—grandmother, siblings, niece and nephew—live in the main house."

"How long have you two been seeing each other?" Hayes asked.

"I reached out to him after Bryan was killed."

More note taking by Hayes.

"We'd been close friends, so our being together again isn't really a surprise," Liv explained. "Not to me anyway."

Hayes nodded, his gaze flitting from her to Jericho.

"Can I get a copy of your surveillance for the nights in question?" Hayes asked.

"When you serve me with a warrant, you get a copy." Jericho leaned back, crossed his arms over his chest. "I don't hear from anyone until two gang members get killed. Now, you're up in my face. What happened to my brothers in all of this?"

Hayes closed his notebook. "I'm sorry for your loss, Mr. Savage. A homicide detective was in charge of your brother's case until the gang members' prints were found on the stolen vehicle and we were able to ID them from the surveillance. I'm just following the evidence."

"And what evidence do you have that I'm involved in their deaths?"

"None, but I've got to be thorough in my investigation."

Jericho grunted. Nevertheless, he was impressed. The sergeant had wasted no time finding the gangbangers' killer.

"Thanks for your time." Hayes stood. "I'll be in touch." He swung his gaze to Liv. "Good seeing you, Liv."

"You, too."

Hayes walked out, and Jericho peered at Liv. She was waiting, the intensity in her gaze not lost on him. The sergeant would be back with a warrant, but the surveillance would show he hadn't left his club... until they walked out the front door, together.

Going forward, he'd make sure he covered his tracks... More importantly, he'd shelter Liv from this madness. If he was going down, he was *not* taking her with him.

She shut the door. He stood and went to her. Holding her in his arms helped diffuse his anger, but a punching bag would do wonders right about now.

"I'm sure you're not okay," she said.

"Thanks for being my alibi." He kissed her.

"I'm trying to keep us both out of prison," she whispered.

He dropped a peck on her forehead, then gestured for her to

sit on the sofa. When she did, he sat beside her, scooped her hands in his. "What brings you by?"

"I got fired from my job as a watcher."

His head started pounding. "Fuck. It was because of me, wasn't it?"

She nodded.

"I can make this right. Let me help—"

She pressed her finger to his lips. "I chose to lie. I deserved to get fired. The PD gig is great, but it's not enough. I'll figure it out, but not right now."

"I'm sorry," he said. "I know you loved that job. You have to fight—"

She patted his thigh. "The person who hired me doesn't trust me. I didn't want to tell you the news tonight and ruin our dinner, so I thought I'd stop by. I'm glad I did. Andre trusts me. Plus, the surveillance shows us here."

"Why the hell is he coming after me?"

"I don't know." She stood, held out her hand. He clasped hers and she pulled him up. "I've got to start looking for a place to live."

"Can't afford the condo?"

"It was a perk of the DOJ gig."

"I fucked this up."

"Jericho, stop. I wanted to make things right for you. I know how much you love your job. You'd lost Bryan. I didn't want you to be sidelined at work, too."

He placed his hands on her face, dipped down and kissed her. "You are the best thing to ever happen to me, Livy Blackstone. I will make this right. I don't even know who you work for or how I can help, but you'll get your job back."

"It's over. I'm moving on." She cleared her throat. "Am I meeting you at the restaurant?"

"Hell, no. It's a date. I'll swing by at seven. Are you packin' an overnight bag, or should I?"

"Your place is definitely more fun than mine. I love your

family." She kissed him, then opened the door. Before sailing through it, she turned. "Seeing you is the best part of my day." She blew him a kiss and was gone.

I'm gonna marry that woman.

That evening, just before seven, Liv couldn't calm the butterflies flitting around in her tummy. Her heart was pounding, her mouth had gone bone dry. It was absurd. She knew it, but she couldn't stop the jitters. There was something about going on an actual date with Jericho that turned her inside out.

They'd been drawn to each other at the club, then been reunited through grief. She'd wanted to prove her allegiance to him, so she helped him hunt down the triggerman. She'd lost her job and gotten evicted.

Dinner seemed too normal to be real. Could they function as a couple? Is that what they were becoming? She had no idea, but she was excited to find out.

Knock-knock-knock.

Ohgod, he's here.

She finished her glass of water, pushed off the kitchen barstool, and made her way to the front door. When she swung it wide, he stood there holding an oversized bouquet of red and pink roses. He'd pulled his hair into a man bun and was rocking a black suit.

Her heart jumped into her throat. "Wow," she whispered.

They stood there staring at each other for so long, Jericho arched an eyebrow. "Can I come in?"

"Oh, right, sorry." She stepped out of the way.

He entered, shut the door, and kissed her. "Mygod, you're stunning. Out of my league. You look phenomenal."

She modeled the off-the-shoulder little black dress that showed off some cleavage without turning it into the girls' night out. It hugged her curves, but not like the latex cat suit. To finish her outfit, she'd worn a strand of pearls and her favorite black stilettos. Rather than pull her hair straight, she'd left the waves cascading down her back.

He kissed her cheek. "I am the luckiest man, to be with you."

"I'm the lucky one. Turn around. I gotta see the full package."

He turned, slowly, and she soaked up all that male beauty. The tailored suit hugged his bulging muscles. "Take off the jacket and do it again."

"We're never gonna get outta here if you're planning on stripping me naked."

She smiled. Being with Jericho was as easy as breathing.

"I just need to see that nice, tight ass of yours," she said. "A preview of coming attractions."

"First, these are for you." He offered her the flowers.

She inhaled the aromatic fragrance. "Thank you. They're beautiful. I hope I have a vase."

He slung his jacket over his shoulder and strutted into the living room where he stopped, posed, and turned.

"You check all the boxes," she said, "and boxes I didn't even know needed checking. You clean up well."

"I thought about shaving."

"For me or for you?"

"You."

"I love your beard and mustache." She sauntered close, stroked his whiskers with her fingertips. "So sexy." She dropped a soft kiss on his lips. "Mmm, yummy, too."

"What about a trim?" he asked.

"I'll allow that," she said with a smirk. After another peck, she retreated into the kitchen.

He eased onto a barstool while she went hunting for a vase. She couldn't find one, so she had to use a tall, plastic container.

"Not the best, but it'll work." She regarded him across the

counter. "There's so much going on that isn't good, but everything gets better when we're together."

He stilled, his unwavering gaze fastened on hers. "I get that. You ready to head out?"

She collected her clutch and made her way toward the front door.

"Whoa, mama, I thought you were staying with me tonight."

"I am." She was drawing a blank.

"Are you wearing that dress in the morning?"

"Oh, right." She collected her overnight bag from the sofa.

After he took it from her, they left.

An Escalade was parked at the circle. "This is nice," she said as he offered a hand and helped her step into it.

"It's a share toy," he said, once behind the wheel. "Well, that pretty much goes for everything I own."

"How did you become your sibling's legal guardian?"

He turned on the engine, pulled onto the street. "After my mom died, I was didn't want us split up and sent to different foster homes. Fortunately, I'd just turned eighteen. I hired a lawyer, petitioned the court, and went through the long process of getting guardianship. It was just me and the kids for a year."

"Wow, that musta been a challenge."

"It was a crazy time, but worth it."

She loved hearing about all the parts in his life she'd missed. "How did you end up being a restauranteur?"

"I'd been workin' as a handyman, but I needed to be around when the kids got home from school. When my mom died, Bryan was only six and Georgia was nine. A year later, Gram moved in after my Gramps passed. That's when I started bartending. When she gave me her savings to open a restaurant, I opened Jericho Road."

He drove into the parking lot and up to valet parking. Carole Jean's was emblazoned in lights on the front of the stand-alone restaurant.

A valet opened Liv's door. "Welcome to Carole Jean's, ma'am."

Jericho walked around the truck. "Mr. Savage, how are you doing?"

He handed the valet a folded bill. "How's it goin', Rick?"

"Very well, sir. It's a packed house. Enjoy your dinner."

The valet opened the door and they breezed inside. While Jericho checked in with the maître d', Liv took in the sights. Amber lighting set the romantic mood, and brightly colored short-stemmed bouquets adorned each table, surrounded by tea candles. Crisp, white linens finished the table settings. Servers dressed in all black flitted through the large dining room made cozy with the deep, red walls covered in abstract artwork.

Jericho returned to her side. "Our table is ready." He grasped her hand. Together, they followed the maître d' across the main dining room, through a closed door, and into a smaller salon in the back of the restaurant. Both rooms were filled to capacity.

On the back wall, a large gas fireplace threw dancing flames on the shiny black hearth while copper-tiled walls reflected the warm glow. More amber lighting, tea candles, and bouquets filled this smaller dining space.

They stopped at a table for two tucked near the fireplace. Jericho pulled out her chair.

"The air conditioner keeps the salon a little colder than our main dining room to balance out the heat from the fire," explained the attendant. "If you're chilly, please let us know. We have a shawl for your comfort, ma'am."

"Thank you," Liv replied before sitting.

Jericho pulled out his chair, eased down across from her.

"It's wonderful to see you dining at your restaurant, Mr. Savage," said the attendant. "Let me know if you need anything." He handed each of them a menu and left.

"This is amazing," Liv said. "It's a feast for the eyes."

"No, babe, that's what *you* are." He reached across the table and she clasped his hand.

She loved this side of him. Romantic *and* relaxed.

Their server appeared, discussed the evening's specials and pointed out a few of the entrees. After they ordered, he suggested a bottle of wine.

"We'll have the Domaine de la Romanee-Conti Montrachet from my private collection. The sommelier will know where that is."

"I'm sure Miss Georgia will as well, sir," said the server. "She's become quite the wine expert. Would either of you like a cocktail?"

They both declined.

"We'll have the wine now," Jericho said.

Shortly after the server left, the sommelier appeared with their white wine and two glasses. Jericho asked that they both taste the selection. She loved that he wanted her input, that he wasn't deciding what she would drink.

She sipped the luxury wine and smiled. "I've never tasted wine like this. So smooth."

Jericho drank from the crystal glass. "Do you like it?"

"It's delicious," she replied. "I taste a hint of honey, vanilla, and orange peel."

"You have a sensitive palate," Jericho said before nodding to the sommelier who poured their glasses, then left.

"Join me at my next wine tasting," he said.

"I'd love that," she replied.

Jericho raised his glass. "I'm grateful you're in my life, Livy."

"I feel the same way," she replied.

After they'd eaten their shared hors d'oeuvres and their small plates were removed, Georgia stopped by. Liv rose and hugged her.

"You look beautiful, Livy," Georgia said.

"Thank you. How are you doing?" Liv asked.

"Better. I love working here. The food, the vibe, everything about this place makes me happy."

After pushing out of his chair, Jericho hugged his sister. "Thanks for making tonight happen."

She grinned at him, then at Liv. "You two are too cute. How do you like the wine?"

"It's amazing," Liv replied, sitting back down. "I've never had wine like this."

Georgia nodded. "Jericho has an impressive collection."

He sat. "Are you cleaning out my wine cellar?"

"I did open one of the more expensive bottles," she confessed. "I was curious what a thousand-dollar bottle of wine tasted like."

"A thousand?" Liv murmured.

"This one's way more than that," Georgia replied tapping the bottle chilling in an ice bucket.

"*Georgia,*" Jericho scolded.

Georgia grinned at Liv. "Enjoy your dinner."

"That's insane," Liv said to Jericho after his sister left.

Jericho eased back into the cushioned chair. "Not for you. I love sharing my wealth with people I care about."

"Thank you." She squeezed his hand.

"I thought you might bail tonight," he said.

"Why?"

He leaned forward. "You had a rough day."

"I put everything in perspective," she said. "I can teach, I can counsel. I'm not willing to live with strangers, so if Addison can't help me out, I'll find a one bedroom."

"Stay in my guest house," he said.

She shook her head. "I can't do that?"

"Why the hell not?"

Jericho knew he was an intense man. He also knew he got tunnel vision when going after a goal. Only, Liv wasn't a goal. She was his destiny.

She'd grown quiet. Either she was surprised by his offer or she didn't want to live in his guest house.

The server delivered their entrees. Jericho had ordered the Wagyu beef striploin with summer squash tartlet, fondant potatoes, and a glass of cabernet sauvignon. Liv had selected the quail stuffed with foie gras, Castroville artichoke, and spätzle. After refilling their water goblets, he left.

She tasted the artichoke. "Mmm, this is unbelievable." She forked a piece of quail with artichoke and held out it out. "Try this."

He opened his mouth and she fed him, gently pulling the fork from his mouth. It was delicious, but he expected it would be. His evening was special because it was with Liv.

His Livy.

"Excellent," he said, slicing into his protein and offering her the first bite.

His cock stirred as she closed her luscious lips around the utensil. The food might have been a culinary masterpiece, but being with Liv excited *all* of his senses.

"Livy," he said. "I...the past few weeks... since we've..." Words weren't his thing. He peered into her eyes and spoke from his heart. "I've fallen in love with you."

Her joyous smile lit up her face. She pushed out of her chair, and kissed him. Happy, bright eyes stared into his. As she sat back down, he stood and guided her chair back into position.

An attendant hurried over with a clean, linen napkin. He offered it to her, then knelt and picked up the one that had fallen from her lap.

"How is everything?" asked the attendant.

"Excellent," she replied.

"Mr. Savage?"

"Couldn't be better," Jericho replied.

After the attendant left, Liv said, "I'm in love with you, too."

Rather than feeling over the moon, his stomach dropped. *Tell her.* "You could do better than me."

She laughed. He did not.

"You can't be serious," she replied, furrowing her brow.

"I'm not sure we're right for each other."

"Based on what? We like each other. We love each other. I respect you. Do you respect me?"

"So much." He sipped the red wine. "You earned a PhD. I got a high school diploma. You're sophisticated. I'm a salt-of-the-earth guy."

She nodded. "First, have you seen yourself tonight? Drop. Dead. Gorgeous. You're the epitome of sophistication. Two, I love you *exactly* the way you are. I'm so into you because you're real. You're grounded. Anyone can get an education. Look at all your success and everything you've accomplished."

"I'm the bull in a china shop."

She set down her silverware. "I'm surprised this is an issue for you. You're the most confident, fearless man I've ever met." She leaned forward. "I'm braver because of you."

"I'm insane."

She smiled. "You're not. You don't fit the clinical description. If anyone should be concerned about the differences between us, it should be you, about me."

He took a bite of his Wagyu and waited for her to explain.

"You're wealthy," she continued. "I'm not. You're very close with your family. I'm not that close with mine, except for Addison. You're a man of action. I analyze."

"So?"

"Exactly," she replied. "These differences create balance. I admire how you've worked hard to achieve your success. I care more about your character and how you put your family and friends first."

"Thank you," he replied.

"So, you love me, huh?"

"Crazy love. I never stopped. Only now, it's better. There're more perks."

She laughed. "So many more. Jericho, I love you *for* you."

No doubt, she's the one.

When they finished, their dishes were cleared. The server combed away the crumbs, then returned with their shared dessert. A raspberry and white chocolate soufflé and two coffees.

When the server scooted off, a couple walked over to their table.

Liv glanced up, surprise flashing in her eyes. "Mom, Dad."

Ah, fuck.

The fluffy, white cloud Jericho had been floating on evaporated in a gust of wind, dropping him flat on his ass.

Reality sucked.

"Mom, Dad, you remember Jericho Savage."

A frosty silence hung like icicles overhead.

Jericho rose, buttoned his jacket. "Mr. and Mrs. Blackstone." He did not extend his hand, didn't call her dad judge, either.

"Jericho, it's been a long time." To his surprise, Liv's mom gave him a warm embrace. He offered a stiff hug, in return.

Jericho's two-hundred-dollar entrée started to sour in his stomach. Nothing like ruining a perfect evening by running into two people who flat-out hated him.

Her mom slid her gaze to Liv. "I didn't know you and Jericho had gotten reacquainted since you've been back."

Jericho caught the eye of a nearby attendant who rushed over. "Yes, Mr. Savage, sir, what can I help with?"

"Two chairs for our guests," he replied.

"Not necessary," Liv's dad blurted. "We can't stay."

Works for me.

"How was your dinner?" Jericho asked them.

"It was delicious," his mom replied. "This is our favorite restaurant. We come here all the time."

"Next time, let the maître d' know you're friends of mine,"

Jericho said. Seeing Liv's dad agitated the hell out of him. The guy had put him through hell, but he'd take the high road... for Liv.

"Why would we do that?" her dad asked.

Liv stood. "This is one of Jericho's restaurants."

"Figures," his dad bit out. "I'm going to miss coming here."

The tension creeping up Jericho's spine grew teeth and snapped at him like a rabid dog. He bit back a growl.

"Bernard, that is rude," Liv's mom scolded. "Livy is having a wonderful dinner with an old friend. Can't you leave it at that? Jericho, how is your mom doing?"

"She passed."

"I'm so sorry," her mom said. "How are your siblings?"

He hesitated.

"His youngest brother, Bryan, was killed a few weeks ago," Liv murmured.

"Ohmygod," said her mom. "I'm sorry for your loss. Are you okay?"

"It's been rough," Jericho replied.

"We should get going," her dad said.

Doesn't get any colder than Judge Blackstone.

"You're unkind, Dad." Liv hugged her mom, then sat down.

Again, Jericho refused to extend his hand. Same with Liv's dad. Her mom smiled warmly at Jericho. "Your restaurant is exquisite. Have a fun evening." Her mom slipped her hand around her dad's arm and they headed toward the exit.

Jericho sat back down, sipped his lukewarm coffee. Their server descended with a fresh pot and two clean mugs.

"Thank you," Jericho said. "The service has been outstanding."

"It's my pleasure, sir."

"I'm so sorry, babe," Liv said.

And just like that, Jericho was grinning like a happy fool.

She laughed. "What?"

"You called me babe."

"Well, look at you. You're a total hottie and you're mine. All mine."

"I gotta hand it to you," he said. "You know how to redirect me away from all the things that piss me off."

"I can think of something in particular that will take your mind off everything and even soothe my Savage beast."

"Is Bigfoot involved?"

With a smile, she nodded. "Most definitely."

On the drive back to his house, he wrapped his fingers around her thigh. She blanketed his hand with hers. The sunroof was open, the evening air refreshing. He loved having Liv in his life. Loved that, in spite of everything going on, they were falling in love. But he couldn't shake the dark cloud that hung over him, the one that he'd be forced to face every single time he was around her dad.

"Babe," he said breaking the silence. "If this is gonna work, you gotta make things right between me and your parents. You know that, don't you?"

"I do," she replied.

Sunday afternoon, after brunch with his family, Jericho dropped Liv at her condo.

"Thank you for an amazing evening," she said. "A night I'll never forget." She kissed him. "I'm in love with an amazing man."

"My family adores you," he said.

"What about the handsome man in my arms?" She stood tall, kissed him again.

He held her close, kissed her good. "You're the best thing to ever happen to me. I love you somethin' sick, Livy Blackstone."

She grinned up at him. "I love you back." One more kiss before she broke away and vanished inside her condo building.

As Jericho headed out, he called Hawk. "You ready to work?"

"Born ready, baby," Hawk replied. "We meeting at The Road?"

"Yeah, I'll be there in fifteen."

He and Hawk arrived at the same time.

"We should be on your boat," Hawk said. "What the hell are we doing inside with weather like this?"

"'Cause I need your help and—"

"I'm the idiot friend who never says no."

Jericho slapped him on the back. "I'd do the same for you, dawg."

They made their way inside, stopping at the bar to order food. They entered Jericho's ALPHA office and Hawk pulled up the surveillance cameras he'd installed at El Jefe's.

Geolocating the gang leader's phone had paid off. He lived in a house in Springfield.

"How'd it go when you scoped out the neighborhood?" Jericho asked.

"I swung by in a HAWK Security van, parked on the street, and opened up the back. I stayed long enough for neighbors to notice the van."

"Nice."

"I went back at three in the morning, in an ALPHA SUV, parked a block away."

"Was the house dark?"

"No, the house was pretty lit up. A couple of guys had just arrived."

"How'd you do?" Jericho asked.

"I left three cams in trees across the street and two on neighbors' houses. They're so small, no one'll see 'em. I checked a few times since putting them in. The house is definitely a hub with guys coming and going. It gets quiet between four and nine in the morning."

"I appreciate you, brother," Jericho said.

"Anytime," Hawk replied. "What's the plan?"

Knock-knock-knock.

They returned to Jericho's outer office. Jericho took the tray from the server and the guys ate while they watched the live cams.

After ten minutes," Jericho said, "Here come a coupla guys."

Two men exited the house. A tall man with long hair, his face hidden by a baseball cap and sunglasses, and a short heavyset guy. A car pulled up, parked on the street. Three men got out and joined them. They each acknowledged the taller one with an unusual hand clasp before he got in the back seat, while the other two rode up front.

"What do you think?" Jericho asked. "Tall one's the leader?"

"I'm thinking, yeah," Hawk replied.

Using the geolocation system, they tracked the car. It drove to a nearby fast-food joint, then on to a stand-alone building. Jericho opened a new window, entered the coordinates, and zoomed in.

"What the hell?" Jericho said. "He's with a psychic."

"She could be reading his palm... or blowing him."

Twenty minutes later, the car was on the move again. Just as the vehicle was en route back to the house, another car pulled up there. Rather than go inside, a brunette leaned against her vehicle and waited.

El Jefe's car pulled into the driveway. One of the guys opened the back door and the tall one stepped out. The woman hurried over and they kissed.

"His old lady, maybe?" Hawk asked.

"Have you seen any women at the house?" Jericho asked.

"Two, but neither stayed."

The dark-haired woman went inside with the men.

"What's your plan?" Hawk asked.

"We'll do the hit at four in the morning," Jericho began.

"That's gonna be tough with just the two of us," Hawk said. "Especially if he's got a full house."

"I'll call Stryker." Jericho picked up his phone. "What about Coop—"

"Cooper's no vigilante," Hawk pushed back. "If the hit isn't ALPHA approved, he won't touch it."

"What about Sin?" Jericho asked.

Hawk pulled out his phone. "Him or Dakota."

After they had their team, Hawk said, "I'll be back at two tomorrow morning. What a fucking crazy way to start the week."

"You know me—"

"Catch 'em by surprise," Hawk replied.

"And I can't fuckin' wait."

17

VANISHED

At two in the morning, Jericho shut down the surveillance cameras at The Road. One by one, the guys showed up. Hawk, first. Sin strolled in, then Stryker last.

All dressed in black, all carrying black go-bags.

They sat in Jericho's private booth while he brought them up to speed on the first two hits, Lucky and Slim Jim.

"I want everyone taken out but the leader." Jericho showed them a picture of El Jefe from the surveillance. "I got questions. He's got answers."

"And if he won't talk?" Sin asked.

"I'll start with his fingers," Jericho replied. "I'll sink a knife into his guts. Whatever it takes."

"From what I know about Al-Mazir's terrorist group, they've got no connections to the Thriller Killers," Sin said.

"Why aren't you taking out the leader?" Stryker asked. "It's not your M.O. to ask questions. You never give a fuck."

"This is personal," Jericho replied. "This wasn't a random hit and Bryan wasn't their target. It was a scare job."

"How long you wanna torture him?" Stryker asked.

"Until he breaks," Jericho said.

"We gotta be outta there before dawn," Sin said.

"If I don't get answers by then, I'll take him out," Jericho replied. "Hawk, you turning off the surveillance outside his house?"

Hawk plucked a cigarette from the pack. "Just before we leave, I'll deactivate them, then grab 'em while we're there." He lit up and inhaled.

"One more puff, then put that damn thing out," Jericho said.

Hawk flipped him off.

They discussed the situation going sideways. They talked about worst case scenarios. Jericho fucking hated reviewing these, but they had to run through every possibility, even the ones where none of them came out alive.

When the conversations ended, they made their way to Jericho's office. Once there, they pulled on their Kevlar vests, slid comms into their ears.

"Anyone need a weapon?" Jericho asked while Hawk smeared camouflage paint on his cheeks.

No one did.

Jericho checked El Jefe's whereabouts one final time. He was at home. Next, Hawk fast-forwarded through the last hour of surveillance, confirming that there were eleven men in the house, no women or children. Then, Hawk killed the surveillance cams.

"Thanks for taking the risk with me," Jericho said.

"Anytime, brother," Stryker replied.

A growl rumbled from Sin. "I'm doing this for Bryan. He was a good kid."

"We'll get you answers," Hawk added.

With their go-bags in hand, they left through Jericho's private exit. Once outside, they tested the comms before jumping into Jericho's SUV, parked out back.

They drove in silence.

At half-past four in the morning, Jericho killed the headlights and turned onto El Jefe's street. He drove past the two-story house. It was dark. The black sedan sat in the driveway, five more vehicles were parked at the curb. Jericho parked at the corner. Sin and Stryker pulled on black ski masks. All four wore helmets with night vision goggles and black gloves.

"Last chance to back out." Jericho knew they wouldn't.

"No way," Hawk said.

"Time to take out the bottom feeders," Sin added.

"For Bryan," Stryker replied.

"Jericho, where's your mask?" Sin asked.

"I want that fucker to see me when I torture the answers outta him," Jericho replied.

Stryker handed him a hair tie. "You're too easy to ID."

Jericho secured his hair out of the way.

With silencers on their Glocks and their weapons in hand, they made their way toward the house. Jericho and Hawk in the front, Stryker and Sin taking up the rear. Jericho would take a bullet for any one of these men. Death didn't scare him. It was the eternity in hell that he wasn't looking forward to. Still, that hadn't stopped him so far, and it wasn't stopping him now.

Rather than split up, they stayed together.

Despite the nice weather, the windows on the first floor were closed. None had curtains or blinds, so Jericho peered through a front window. A man slept on the sofa.

During their discussion, they agreed they'd breach the house through the front. Once inside, they'd split up.

Sin tried the door. Locked. He pulled out his pick set and got to work while a breeze rustled through the nearby trees. Seconds later, the lock clicked open. Sin turned the doorknob. Opening it might trigger a house alarm. They'd have mere seconds to take out as many of the gang members as possible. With guns at the ready, Sin whispered, "Three, two—"

He threw open the door, they all rushed in.

Jericho aimed at the sleeping man on the sofa.

POP!

And hit him between the eyes.

Then, he took out two more men on the first floor—

POP! POP!

Stryker and Sin disappeared up the stairs.

Revenge fueled Jericho. He was laser-focused on finding the man with the long hair. His goggles gave him the visibility he wouldn't have otherwise. He strode through the quiet kitchen—

"Two down, upper level," Sin said through the comm.

Hawk opened a door. "Basement," he whispered through the comm. Down he flew.

A shadow rounded the corner. Jericho bolted after him. Then, someone flicked on the living room lights, temporarily blinding him. Jericho flipped up the goggles, his gaze sweeping left and right.

BANG!

A bullet whizzed by him. Unfazed, Jericho went after him. The man turned and started firing in Jericho's direction.

BANG! BANG! BANG!

Jericho got hit in the vest, the force sending him flying backwards into the wall. He raised his arm and returned fire.

POP! POP! POP! POP!

The gang leader grabbed his thigh. "Motherfucker!" he roared as he hurried outside, favoring his wounded leg.

Jericho had to let him go. He couldn't take this fight outside. From the driveway, a car peeled out, and was gone.

"Fuck," Jericho bit out. "I need status."

"Basement," Hawk replied. "Three down. I need help clearing."

"Two more down," Stryker added. "We're clearing the top floor."

"I'm heading to the basement." Jericho flew down the stairs, flipping down his goggles. Hawk stood in the middle of the finished basement. There were three dead men. One on a sofa, two in chairs.

"You hit?" Jericho asked.

"In the vest," Hawk replied. "He got out, didn't he?"

"Yeah," Jericho bit out. "I hit the son of a bitch in the leg and he still managed to drive off."

After clearing the closets and the storage area, and finding no one, they returned to the first floor where Stryker and Sin waited by the front door.

"Upstairs cleared?" Jericho asked.

"Confirmed," Stryker replied.

"We got ten out of eleven," Jericho said.

"Confirmed," Hawk said.

They left the house.

Once outside, Jericho said to Hawk, "We gotta leave a cam so I can track if El Jefe comes back."

Hawk climbed the tree and tossed the small cameras down to Jericho. After retrieving all but one, they jumped in the car and drove away. When they hit the main road, Jericho flipped on the headlights and floored it.

"I reactivated the camera we left behind," Hawk said.

"You guys okay?" Jericho asked.

"Hey," Hawk said. "You got hit."

Jericho glanced at him, then down at his blood-soaked arm. "Ah, fuck. The motherfucker shot me."

"Pull over," Stryker said.

"I'm fine," Jericho replied.

"Do it," Hawk bit out.

Jericho pulled over, got out. The guys surrounded him, checking him for injuries.

"Yeah, you took one in the arm," Stryker said.

"Safe house," Sin said.

"That's ridiculous," Jericho growled. "I'm fine."

"In the back seat," Stryker ordered.

On a growl, Jericho climbed in. Stryker shut his door, jumped behind the wheel.

On the way, Sin made a call. "Jericho was hit. I need the

medical team. We're twenty minutes from the safe house." He hung up.

"That's just fuckin' great." Jericho gritted his teeth. "The asshole shoots me *and* he gets away. What a cluster."

"What happened?" Hawk asked.

"He blinded me by turning on the lights," Jericho replied.

"You gotta apply pressure," Sin said.

"If I bleed out, one of you can fill me back up. Then, we'll really be blood brothers."

The guys laughed.

"You're the only man I know who gets shot and jokes about it," Hawk said.

Stryker jumped off the beltway, following the main road. After several turns, he made his way onto a dirt road, nestled in a wooded area of Great Falls, and pulled up to the warehouse-looking structure. Stryker drove around back, the oversized garage door opened, and he drove inside.

Jericho opened the SUV door and winced. They each had to stand in front of the scanner before the light turned green. When it did, Sin led them into a triage room.

"You gotta take off your vest and shirt," Sin said.

A bullet had pierced his biceps, but the wound had clotted. "Damn," Jericho said through the pain. "Good thing it's my left arm."

"You want me to let her know you got shot?" Hawk asked after Jericho sat on the edge of the hospital bed.

"The surgeon and nurse are here," Sin said.

When Sin strode out, Jericho leaned back on the propped pillows. "She's gonna flip out."

"Who're we talking about?" Stryker asked.

"Livingston Blackstone," Hawk replied.

Stryker furrowed his brow. "What are you talking about?"

"I'll fill you in later," Hawk said.

Sin returned with a man and a woman. "Dr. Joyce Ferguson and Nurse Baker Deen."

Jericho tossed them a nod. "How ya doin?"

The surgeon approached him. "I'm Dr. Joyce."

"Jericho."

"How'd this happen?"

"I was trying to take out a gang member, but it didn't go as—"

Her eyes grew large and she glanced over at Hawk, his face still covered in camouflage paint.

"I'm just messin' with you," Jericho said. "I'm an assassin. You should see what we did to the other guys."

She shook her head. "Have you had anything to drink, Jericho?"

"No."

"Have you done any kind of recreational drugs or are you on any prescription meds?"

"No."

"Any food in the past few hours?"

"Nope."

She offered a warm smile. "I'll have Nurse Baker prep you for surgery—"

"Whoa. I don't need surgery."

"How else do you expect me to get the bullet out?"

"Leave it there."

She shook her head.

"Just reach in and grab it."

"I'll see you in the OR." The surgeon spoke with the nurse before exiting.

"When I get outta here, that son of a bitch doesn't stand a chance," Jericho bit out.

"I'll call Liv," Hawk said to Stryker and Sin, unlocking his phone. "Maybe she can shut him up."

Liv's ringing phone pierced the silence. She jerked awake. "Uh, hello," she answered.

"Hey, babe, it's Hawk. Whatcha doing?"

"Sleeping."

"I'm coming to get you."

She bolted upright. "Ohmygod, something happened to Jericho, didn't it? I can be ready in five minutes." Phone to ear, she flew into the bathroom.

"He's fine," Hawk said. "It's all good."

Liv's heart had jumped into triple digits. "What happened?"

"I'll explain on the way." Hawk hung up.

Liv was pacing in the lobby when Hawk pulled into the circle. She hurried outside and into his car. "What's all over your face? Is that camouflage paint?"

"Yeah."

"What happened?"

"Take a deep breath," Hawk said. "He's okay. He's in surgery—"

"*What?*"

"He got shot—"

Liv leaned back, put her hand over her chest. "I'm gonna pass out."

"Woman, you gotta breathe. He's okay. He got hit in the arm. It's not life threatening. Just take a few and get yourself together. I need you chill around him."

After several minutes, she'd calmed down. "Sorry. I really care about him and I panicked."

"No shit."

"He was cutting it up with the surgeon and we're concerned he's talking too much, so you need to tell him to zip it."

"Okay," she said. "I'm not sure he'll listen to me, though."

"Pussy-whipped Savage will do anything you tell him."

That made her smile. "I love him, too."

"I did *not* use the L word."

"What's he saying?"

"He told the medical team he was going after a gang member. Then, he said he's an assassin. Pretty much everything. We're not sure she believed him, but we gotta make sure he stays quiet."

"Being in ALPHA means everything to him. Maybe he was nervous."

Hawk chuckled. "Jericho gets angry. He gets even. He doesn't get nervous."

"I didn't know he was going after the gang leader tonight—well, this morning."

"He probably didn't want you to worry," Hawk replied. He grew quiet until he turned onto a dirt road. "You're being taken to ALPHA's safe house. You're not supposed to know this exists."

"No worries. All I do is keep secrets."

Hawk drove around to the back of a warehouse in what could have been Great Falls or Mclean. She hadn't been paying close attention. In the hangar-like garage were a fleet of black SUVs.

Her racing heart had stopped thumping in her ears, but her mouth had gone bone dry and she couldn't stop shaking. Rather than stand in front of the scanner, Hawk made a call.

"Let me in."

"Is that one of your scanners?" Liv asked.

"Yup."

"Is it broken?"

"Nope."

She stared at him. "Then, why—"

"You're with me and you're not cleared to enter. The scanner knows there's two people, so it's not gonna let either of us enter. I designed it that way, in case someone's brought here against their will. No one gets in."

"Brilliant," she said as Sin pushed the door open.

"Sinclair Develin, Liv Blackstone," Hawk said.

Sin tossed her a nod and she acknowledged him with a tight smile.

As Hawk led her down a hallway lined with closed doors, she asked, "Can I get some water?"

Hawk brought her into a break room where Stryker Truman and Cooper Grant were sitting around a table. Sin re-joined them. Liv had stepped into the center of ALPHA territory. Though she could have been thrilled, she was too anxious about Jericho to care. After Hawk introduced her, he handed her a bottle of chilled water, then scrubbed off his face paint at the sink.

The surgeon walked in, acknowledged everyone, but addressed Sin. "He did great. It was a clean hit, so I was able to remove the entire bullet. He'll be in a sling—"

"Not Jericho," Stryker blurted.

"He'll be sore and the sling will help, but that's his call."

"Did he finally stop talking?" Sin asked.

"You know, I've been asking for years what you do, and why I'm *always* called here in the middle of the night. I finally thought had my answer until he kept changing his story. Just before he went under, he told me he owns a slew of restaurants. Jericho Road, Carole Jean's, Raphael's, Kaleidoscope, the list went on and on. I liked his first two answers better." She poured herself a coffee. "He's groggy, but you're welcome to go in. Nurse Baker is with him now." The surgeon sat. "I'll stick around for a while to make sure he's okay."

Sin gestured to Liv. "You wanna go first?"

She nodded, then slid her gaze to Hawk. "Come with me."

"You okay?" Hawk asked as they made their way down the hall.

"I freaked. Sorry about that."

He put a comforting arm around her. "Our boy's gonna be fine."

Liv walked in to find a groggy Jericho sipping water through a straw. He had blood on his chin and chest, his hair was mussed, but he was propped against the pillows scowling.

When he saw her, his sleepy smile settled her down.

She went to him, kissed him. "You scared the hell out of me."

She held out a shaking hand. "I'm a mess, Jericho Savage. Do not blindside me like that again." Then, she kissed his forehead. "How do you feel?"

"Relaxed, pissed." He glanced at Hawk. "Aren't you gonna kiss me, too?"

Hawk shook his head. "You are such an idiot. How you doing?"

"My arm hurts. I told them no painkillers."

"Why not?" she asked.

"Pain motivates me. Now, he's a dead man."

The nurse returned with more water. "I'll be in the break room if you need anything."

"I'm ready to get outta here," Jericho replied.

"Not yet," said the nurse. "Rest for now."

Nurse Baker left and Liv sat on the edge of the bed. "Why don't you take a nap?" She held his hand, stroked his skin. "I'll stay with you. Hawk, too."

"I'm so fired up. I wanna rip that SOBs heart out."

"And we'll help you," she said. "But you have to chill for five minutes, then we'll put together a plan.

Jericho handed her the cup and closed his eyes. "Wake me in five."

She held his hand until he fell asleep, then carefully removed hers. Moving slowly, she got off the bed, sat in a chair next to Hawk.

"Okay, tell me what happened," she whispered.

When Hawk finished, she took a minute to let everything sink in.

"Did you see what happened between him and the gang leader?" she asked.

"I was in the basement."

"I can tell you, babe," Jericho said, his eyes still closed.

Hawk slid his gaze to Jericho. "I thought you were sleeping."

Jericho opened his eyes. "Playing dead." He paused. "The gang leader shot me in the arm. I hit him in the leg, but the SOB got away. From where I'm sittin', that motherfucker is already dead. All I gotta do is find him."

Later that morning, the surgeon came in to check on Jericho. "How are you feeling?"

"Never better," he said, his voice heavy with sarcasm.

As Liv watched him interact with the doctor, she studied his face. The crease between his brows was deep, his jaw muscles hadn't stopped ticking, and his hands were balled into fists. She was worried. He'd morphed from a man hellbent on revenge to full-on beast mode.

And she wasn't going to say a word to him about letting it go. It would be futile. She knew, from the moment she watched him assassinate the driver, what she was dealing with and who he really was. If she wanted a relationship with him, possibly even a life with him, she had to accept him for who he was.

An ALPHA Operative. A hit man. An assassin. A sniper. A killer. A vigilante.

And she flat-out adored him anyway.

Sin and Stryker walked in.

"Jericho, you need to rest until the anesthesia wears off," said the surgeon. "I was able to remove the bullet, so go easy until your arm heals."

Jericho tossed her a nod. "Thanks, Doc."

"I'll walk you out." Sin and the doctor disappeared out the door.

When Sin returned, Jericho regarded each of the men. "Thanks for the assist."

"If you need help finding El Jefe, I'm in," Sin said.

"Ditto," Stryker added.

"You got your A-team, so Stryker and I are taking off," Sin said.

After they left, Jericho said, "Pull up the surveillance of the house."

Hawk pulled his phone from his pocket, tapped and typed, then pulled over a chair and sat next to him.

Jericho patted the bed. "Sit next to me, Livy."

As she did, Hawk pulled up the live feed of the house. Though the home was dark, there were four cars parked on the street and three in the driveway. They watched for ten minutes, but there was no external movement.

"Jericho, I am so fucking pissed at you," Hawk growled.

"What the hell for?"

"You weren't wearing a mask. You wouldn't even use camouflage paint. If he made you, he's coming for you."

"Good," Jericho replied. "I'll be ready."

"I got protection on your fam, but give me twenty-four so I can add more guys," Hawk said.

"He can stay with me, tonight," Liv offered.

Jericho raked his fingers through his hair. "Pull up the video after everything went down."

A few clicks later, and they were watching what happened an hour after the siege. Under cover of darkness, cars arrived. Men scurried inside, removing the bodies in bags.

"I shot El Jefe," Jericho said. "Someone had to remove that bullet. Can you geolocate his phone?"

"I don't have his number," Hawk replied. "We'll do it at The Road."

"Is El Jefe TK's gang leader?" Liv asked.

"Yeah." Jericho drank down some water.

"I might be able to help ID him," Liv said. "If you've got a clear pic, I can see if there's a mugshot at APD."

"Let me pull something up," Hawk replied.

A few minutes later, he handed her his phone. "Tall guy, scraggly hair."

She stared at it for a long minute. "Does he always wear a baseball cap and sunglasses?"

"Yup," Hawk replied.

Jericho's growl hijacked their attention. "I'm gonna rip his heart out."

"I think I recognize him," she said.

"*What?*" Hawk exclaimed.

"That could be the guy from Lost Souls who wanted to hook up with me. I wasn't interested, but he kept hitting on me every time he was there. He goes by—"

"Guapo," Jericho hissed. "He had on shades at the club too."

"Did he see you there?" Liv asked Jericho.

"No idea," Jericho replied. "I had my eyes on you."

Liv checked her phone. "It's after ten." She stood. "I need to leave."

"Where you going?" Jericho asked.

"To the police station," she replied. "We have no idea who this gang leader is. I can access the mugshots and see if he's got a rap sheet."

"You can't go alone," Jericho said. "You're not safe."

"She didn't even drive here." Hawk pushed out of the chair. "I'll take her. We'll be back in time to pick you up."

"Get me my phone, so I can watch his house," Jericho commanded.

Liv fetched it from his pants pocket, kissed him goodbye. "You need to sleep."

"I need to track this man down and take him—" Nurse Baker sailed in and regarded Jericho. "To dinner," Jericho blurted. "I need to take him to dinner."

"Too much chatting," the nurse said setting Jericho's phone on the bedside table. "Please, rest."

"He's not gonna listen to you," Hawk said. "We'll be back."

"Don't let her out of your sight," Jericho replied.

Thirty minutes later, Hawk parked at the Alexandria police station. "There's no way in hell I'm walking into that building."

"Why not?"

He hitched an eyebrow at her. "I take out bad guys for a living. I'll stand guard outside."

Liv left him smoking in the parking lot. After checking in at the front desk, she headed toward Homicide. As she walked into the department, she swept the room in search of two people. Bee, the sergeant's assistant, and Detective Mirabel Morales.

Bee wasn't at her desk, but Mirabel was. Liv made her way over, caught the detective's eye and offered a friendly smile.

"Hey, Liv, how's it going?"

"Been busy?" Liv asked.

Mirabel nodded. "I'm taking a few days off, so I'm trying to take care of as much as I can before I leave."

"My timing is terrible, but I'm hoping you can help me."

"Whatcha need?"

"To view gang mugshots."

"You can't use them for any of your workshops, you know that, right?"

"I know," she replied.

"I'll help you. Who are you looking for?"

"The TK gang." Liv pulled a chair next to her and sank down.

Several clicks and Mirabel had accessed the mugshots. She entered Thriller Killers into the search field and dozens of pictures filled the screen.

"How far back do you want to go?" Mirabel asked.

"Current," Liv replied.

Mirabel regarded Liv. "What's going on?"

Liv leaned close. "I'm a member of Lost Souls. It's a cosplay club. Anyway, I think a gang member has been trying to hook up with me. I like to be super vigilant when I play."

Surprise flashed across the detective's face. "Got it."

"I'm a pretty private person," Liv whispered. "But you confided in me, so I feel comfortable doing the same."

"Absolutely." Mirabel changed the dates in the search field and the photos on the screen changed again. "What happens at the club?"

"We hang out, dance, drink. The only difference is that most everyone wears a costume. There's an exclusive area for elite members who want to act out a scene or play in private."

"I gotta get out more."

Liv smiled. "You're welcome to come as my guest."

"Maybe when I get back from vacay." Mirabel pushed out of her chair. "I've gotta run to a quick meeting."

"I'll put your computer to sleep if I leave before you're back. Thanks for letting me look."

Mirabel headed toward the conference room and Liv started scrolling. Some gang members had been arrested for petty theft. Others for selling drugs. A few for assault. One for rape. Two for murder.

What a lovely group.

Each gang member's file contained a traditional mugshot along with a second picture featuring their gang tat. Most of the men were in their twenties. Some looked even younger. She was trying not to rush, but she didn't want anyone to swing by to say hello, then ask her what she was doing.

She continued scrolling—

Her brain came to a screeching halt while a jolt of adrenaline shot through her.

Ohmygod. No way.

She broke into a cold sweat.

A photo of a man with one brown eye and one blue eye stared back at her. She was transfixed while the memories came rushing back. Forcing them out, she read his file.

Perry Pinter. Caucasian. Male.

She glanced around. Everyone was busy working. She snapped a picture, then dropped her phone back into her bag. Everything felt like it was happening in slow motion, except for her pounding heart. That was happening in triple-time.

As she stared at his photo, fear started to take hold. But she wasn't a sixteen-year-old teenager. She was a grown woman with a vigilante boyfriend. Forcing out the anxiety, she scraped her fingers through her hair and steeled her spine.

She exited out of the system and put Mirabel's computer to sleep. Then, she headed toward the door as Sergeant Hayes walked in.

"Liv, I've got a search warrant for Mr. Savage."

Fisting her hands on her hips, Liv glared at him. "You're wasting your time, Andre," she began. "His mom died when he was about to enlist in the Navy. His dream, for as long as I'd known him, was to become a SEAL. Instead, he got legal guardianship of his four younger siblings so they wouldn't be placed in foster care and split up. That man gave up a career he wanted more than anything to keep his family together. He works his ass off at all his restaurants. There's never a time when he isn't working or doing something nice for his family. You gotta back off. I was with him. What more of an alibi do you need?"

She huffed out an exasperated breath.

His mouth fell open. "Wow, Liv, I've never heard you so adamant about something."

"You can search for whatever, but you won't find it. Serve the warrant, but you're going after the wrong guy." Without waiting for a response, she strode outside.

On the way to Hawk's car, she called Jericho.

"Hey, babe," he answered.

"I know who El Jefe is… and so do you."

18

PAST AND PRESENT COLLIDE

Jericho pushed out of bed. After removing the sling, he got dressed using his right hand.

"Fucking pain in my ass," he grumbled.

He was louder than he realized because the way-too-attentive nurse hurried in. "Oh, no, no. Back in bed you go."

"I'm outta here. My ride'll be here in thirty. It's been a ton o' fun, but I'm good."

"I haven't discharged you."

Jericho sat on the bed's edge. "Better get to it, then."

A disgruntled Nurse Baker checked his vitals, then his suture. "Where's your sling?"

"On the bed."

"Are you always this difficult?"

"Every chance I get."

The nurse shook his head as he got busy on the tablet. "You're cleared to leave. I'm gonna grab my backpack. You have to escort me out."

As Baker picked up his backpack from the break room, Jericho headed toward the hangar in the back.

"What is this place?" asked the nurse.

"A building."

"What's it used for?"

"You tell me and we'll both know."

"So, you were totally joking about being an assassin, then?"

"I own a bunch of restaurants. Jericho Road, Carole Jean's, to name a few." Jericho pushed open the door and walked into the hangar with him. Then, he opened the oversized garage door and waited while the nurse got into his car and drove away.

He pressed the garage door to close it. The door started to fold down, then stopped and reversed direction.

It's El Jefe.

On instinct, Jericho reached behind for his Glock, but it wasn't there.

Hawk and Liv drove in, and the door closed behind them. She hopped out. "What are you doing?"

Hawk followed up with, "Where the hell are you going?"

"The nurse left. Didn't you see him drive away?"

"Why'd he discharge you so soon?" Hawk asked.

"I checked myself out. We got a shit-ton to do and it's not getting' done from that hospital bed."

"Where's your sling?" Liv asked.

"Don't need it. Let's get outta here."

"I gotta let Cooper know." Hawk made a call. "We're closing up." He listened, then said, "No, but I wasn't here to argue with him." Hawk tapped the speaker. "Coop wants to say hey."

"Hey, my brother," Jericho said.

"Get your ass back in bed," Cooper barked.

"Love the accommodations. Five-stars all the way, but I gotta go."

"Dammit, Jericho," Cooper asked. "How are you doing?"

"My arm hurts, my chest hurts, and I'm totally pissed that I didn't catch the SOB and beat the livin' devil outta him, then slit his throat."

Liv gasped.

"Sorry, darlin'. I didn't mean that literally. Gotta go." Jericho ended the call.

"You're insane," Hawk said.

"According to Dr. Blackstone, I'm not," Jericho quipped.

Liv and Hawk exchanged glances.

"Technically, he's not," Liv replied.

"Okay, where are you staying?" Hawk asked.

"He'll stay with me until we can figure out next steps," Liv said.

They left the safe house. Jericho laid down on the back seat for the ride home. After Hawk dropped them off, they walked into Liv's condo building and into a waiting elevator.

On the ride up, she clasped his hand. "Don't scare me like that, ever again," she whispered.

He kissed her forehead.

In her condo, she brought him over to her sofa. "You chill."

"What are you gonna do?"

"Make us dinner."

"Thank you, 'cause I'm about to tear off my arm and gnaw on that."

"Why don't you lay down?"

Instead, he sat on a barstool. "I'll watch you. That's better therapy than any damn nap."

She poured him a glass of water, which he guzzled down. She defrosted chicken thighs in the microwave, pulled potatoes from her pantry. Once the chicken and potatoes were in the oven, she got busy making a salad.

"I didn't know you could cook."

"I'm not sure this counts as cooking, but I'm gonna fill your stomach. I heard it growling on the ride home. And that was over your snoring."

"Snore? I don't snore."

"Hawk said you'd say that, so he recorded you."

"You gonna tell me about El Jefe?"

"Food first."

He loved watching her cook… watching her do anything. And it went beyond her physical beauty. He loved being around her. There was something about her that calmed the anger raging inside him.

"You got a beer?" he asked.

She refilled his water glass, slid it over. "Water today. Beer tomorrow."

"Bossy."

She flashed him a smile.

"Come here," he said.

She stopped slicing the cucumber and walked around the counter as he swiveled toward her. She was in his arms, holding him gently.

"I love you," she whispered. "So much. I've never felt this way about anyone. Ever." When she pulled back, tears filled her eyes. One spilled down her cheek and he brushed it away.

"I got you," he said. "And you got me. It's that simple. I never stopped loving you, but I hated you for a long time." She kissed him, letting her lips linger on his. "I don't hate you anymore." His kiss was soft, yet his grip strong. "I love you, Livy."

"I love you, babe."

"Now, why don't you tell me who El Jefe is?"

She broke away. "As soon as dinner's on the table."

Jericho let out a growl. "Dammit, woman."

She finished tossing the salad. The timer beeped and she pulled out the chicken and the potatoes.

"What can I do?" he asked.

"We'll eat at the table, so have a seat."

She plated his food, giving him double what she served herself. Within minutes, he was chowing down. "This is so good."

"The food'll help."

They ate in a comfortable silence for several bites. Then, she fixed her gaze on his. "The gang leader of the Thriller Killers—this El Jefe guy—is Perry Pinter."

He drew a blank. "Don't know him."

She set down her fork. "He's the guy from the party... the one you pulled off me."

As her words sunk in, his long-held hatred of Pinter jumped to the surface. "I'm gonna rip his heart out and shove it down his fuckin' throat."

He stared out her picture window at the city across the river, the nighttime lights casting a warm glow. But the picturesque vista did nothing to calm him. Every muscle in his body had turned to steel, the fury coursing so hard and fast through him that he pushed up from the table, knocking his chair to the floor.

"Jericho, take your anger out on *him*. Letting it out now isn't gonna help us. Can you sit down?"

He couldn't, so he leaned his backside against the windowsill. "Are you sure?"

She showed him his mugshot.

"I don't recognize him."

"I didn't either until I saw his eyes. That's when I knew it was him."

"What about his eyes?"

"He's got a brown one and a blue one. He's blind in the brown eye. His brother accidentally shot him in the eye with a BB gun. The iris turned brown."

"How do you know that?"

"He was in the grade above ours and all the girls thought his eyes were so cool. Someone told me his story. I'd never talked to him before that night."

Just thinking back to that horrific night made his blood pressure soar. "His mother must be so proud," he bit out. "He's a gang leader."

"Do you think he's coming after you?" Liv asked.

"For something that happened sixteen years ago? Seems kind of extreme. Why Raphael's on that night? I'm at The Road most nights and I've never seen him there. Did he look like that in high school?"

"He had short hair, no facial hair. I don't remember him being so slender. I recognized his eyes, then his name. He sent me a hookup request at the club the same night you did. I told him no."

Jericho sat back down, sliced off chicken, and forked it into his mouth. As he chewed, he thought about the night of the hit. "You think he saw us together at the club and this is a revenge hit?"

"Maybe. He had to have seen you at Lost Souls."

"Why?"

"You're six three, you're built like a tank, and your hair trails down your shoulders. You're gorgeous and you've got an attitude that screams, 'I'm in charge'."

He shook his head. "Why scare me? Why not kill me and get me out of the way?"

They went around and around, coming up with no logical conclusions.

"If the scare job wasn't you and it wasn't Bryan or Hawk, then it's gotta be Vincent," she said. "What do you know about him?"

"Besides the casket company, his affair, and his interest in guns… nothing."

"You guys agreed to go shooting together. You gotta get to know him. Maybe he and Pinter are friends."

"My brother is a lot of things, but he's not friends with a gang leader."

"Jericho, stop pushing back and do it."

"Bossy."

She kissed his cheek. "Do it for me."

"I have zero interest in hangin' with Vincent."

She caressed his cheek, ran her fingers through his hair. "I know, honey, but if you can't find Perry Pinter, or you kill him before you get answers, you'll never know why Bryan was gunned down. Maybe Vincent is the missing link."

He nodded. "You're right. I'll do it."

That evening, they stripped out of their clothes and crawled into bed. Liv snuggled close, ran her fingers over his chest and down his abs.

"I love your touch," he murmured. "You feel so good."

She continued her tender caressing, taking her time as she made her way down his strong, hard body. When she cupped his balls and fondled them, he sighed. She would have been perfectly happy massaging him until he fell asleep, but when she stroked his semi, it firmed in seconds.

"Mmm," he sighed. "You're what I need."

Though he was sore, tired, and breathing fire, she wanted to help him relax. So, she continued stroking, slowly and gently, then leaned up and kissed him. One loving kiss that built to a searing kiss that had her writhing against him.

She slowed the kiss until it ended. Her body was so primed, so ready for him, but tonight wasn't about her. It was for him.

"Do you want me to keep doing this or to straddle you?"

"I love kissing you *and* looking at you."

"Do you want to be inside me?"

He smiled. "Is that a trick question? The answer is always yes."

She rose up and straddled him. "If anything hurts—"

"Nothing hurts when we're together."

She rose up and placed him at her opening.

"No Bigfoot condom?" he asked.

Leaning down, she kissed him. "I'm clean and I don't want anything separating us."

"Me, too, baby."

She rose up, took him in hand, and guided him to her core. She sunk down, letting him fill her slowly and completely. When he'd reached her end, she stilled and stared into his eyes. A loving smile shared between two lovers, then she leaned down and kissed him. Being with him, connecting with him in this way, completed her. He wrapped her back with his good arm, caressing and stroking her skin with his massive hand.

Then, she sat up. He fondled her breast, teased the firm tip of her nipple until the sounds she made sounded foreign, even to her.

She couldn't stop gliding on his hard shaft. Nothing separating them in the most intimate of connections. His growl set her insides on fire, the desire building as she moved faster and faster.

"I don't want to come before you," he said.

"This is for you, my love," she whispered. "I want to make you happy."

He released into her with a roar, while the emotion spilled out of her, the tears sliding down her cheeks. She loved him to the depths of her soul. Loved what they were becoming… what they could become. She'd never felt this way about someone and she choked back a sob.

"Oh, fuck, Livy. I hurt you."

Jericho's concern snapped her back to the moment.

She kissed him, dotting his lips, his cheeks with tender pecks. "No pain, just love. I love you, Jericho, and I panicked when Hawk told me you'd been shot."

"Woman, you scared the fuck out of me."

She laughed. "Sorry. I'm fine."

"You didn't come."

"That's okay. Being with you feels amazing."

"That's bullshit. No woman of mine is gonna stop short of her happy ending. Not when I can give it to her."

"But you're injured," she protested.

"Not that injured. Lie next to me."

She hated separating, but she pulled off and snuggled close.

"Switch sides. I gotta use my right hand."

When they repositioned, he kissed her while he ran his fingers over her opening, pausing to play with her clit, then sliding his finger inside. Then, he broke away to lick her nipple, flicking his tongue across her hard nib. Her body bowed to his, the passion flowing through her like a waterfall over a mountaintop.

She began moving, thrusting as his fingers slid inside her. He played her like he owned her. In many ways, he did. She was his… all his. In all the ways that mattered.

The orgasm started deep inside, bursting forth with a jolt as the waves of ecstasy powered through her. "So good," she blurted as she came into his skilled hand.

When she stilled, he cupped her chin in his hand, and kissed her with such tenderness. "You. Are. Mine," he murmured.

She smiled at him. "Yes, I am."

The following morning, while Liv made breakfast, Jericho's phone rang. "Savage," he answered, not recognizing the number.

"Mr. Savage, it's Sergeant Hayes with Alexandria PD. I've got a warrant for your surveillance videos. When can I get them?"

"Take a pic and text it to me," Jericho replied.

"That's not how I—"

"You do that, I'll text you access to the videos. It's a win-win, Sergeant." Liv whipped her head in his direction. "Then, you can leave me the hell alone."

Silence.

Jericho fixed his gaze on Liv.

"Expect the picture," Hayes said.

The line went dead.

"Pain in my ass," Jericho bit out.

"It's actually a good thing," Liv pointed out. "The time stamps show you at the club, then us at the club."

His phone binged. He opened the attachment and read it. "He's only asking for the video, so I'll do this now and get him off my back." He glanced around. "It's easier on a laptop."

She left the kitchen, paused long enough to kiss him, then

retrieved hers from the living room. After setting it on the counter, she unlocked it, and spun it toward him.

He jumped online, pulled up the videos in question, created private links for them, and sent them off.

"Hayes needs to move the hell on," Jericho said.

"He will," she replied. "The video doesn't lie."

"You're in love with a bad, bad man."

"I'm in love with a vigilante."

"Same thing." He scrolled through his phone. "I'm gonna text Vincent."

"Thank you," she replied.

"Yo, it's Jericho," he texted his brother. "Wanna meet at the shooting range?" He gritted his teeth, sent the text. "Babe, I don't see how my brother is involved—"

"Maybe your dad is," she said. "What do you know about him?"

"Even less."

"The last thing I want to do is send Perry Pinter an invitation to get together at Lost Souls," Liv said. "The. Last. Thing. But I trust you and I'm doing it for your family. They deserve answers and the truth."

"Say what?"

"I'm going to lure Pinter to the club."

"You, as bait? No fucking way."

She slid the scrambled eggs onto two plates. The toaster binged. "Can you get those?"

He pulled out the four pieces. "Got peanut or almond butter?"

"Cupboard." She pointed. "Not butter?"

"Protein, darlin'." He retrieved both jars.

"So, that's the secret to those big, strong muscles." She poured juice, then sat beside him. "Are you feeling any better?"

"I'm gonna need more Livy love tonight."

She patted his thigh. "No argument from me. So, about my idea for Pinter—"

"It's not happening, but if it did, we'd need as many guys as I could get."

"We can't do it while the club is open, but we could do it after it closes."

"You're killin' my appetite."

"Check with your guys on this. I think it's a good idea."

Jericho's phone buzzed. "Vincent replied to my text. He wants to know if I'm free today or tomorrow."

"What about your arm?" she asked.

"It hurts. So?"

"You're a beast."

"I have a high tolerance for pain, plus, my woman asked me to do something, so I'm gonna do it."

Jericho texted his brother. "How's three today?"

Dots appeared, then Vincent's reply. "Two. I'm meeting Brenda at three thirty." He included a smiley and an eggplant emoji.

"He's getting laid by the sergeant's wife at three thirty," Jericho told Liv, "so we're meeting at two."

"Two works," he texted back. "Henninger Security."

He set his phone down, bit into the toast. "I fucking hate cheaters. If he's cheating, what else is he doing?"

"He might not know she's married," Liv pointed out. "If she told him she's unattached, it's all on her."

"It still doesn't make it right."

She caressed his back. "His lack of morals isn't our problem. All we care about is the truth. Then, you and your family can start to heal."

THAT AFTERNOON, as Jericho headed toward the entrance to Henninger Security, he found Vincent leaning against the building, talking on his phone.

"Dammit, baby," Vincent said. "I'm horny. What about tonight, then?" After listening, he said, "I gotta go. Talk to you later." He shoved his phone in his pocket and regarded Jericho. "How ya doin?"

"Woman problems?"

"Brenda can't get away," Vincent said. "She's got a client coming in to look at a painting."

Jericho forced himself to pull his brother in for a hug. "Why can't you see her tonight?"

"She's got a thing with her husband." Vincent opened the front door and held it for Jericho.

After they entered the building, Jericho said, "Is she leavin' him?"

"Nah, they've been together for a while."

"Why are you wastin' your time with her?"

They signed in at the front desk, then made their way to the shooting gallery.

"I'm just looking for a little fun," Vincent explained. "Every woman I ever got with was cool at first, then they wanted serious. And babies. No thanks. Brenda's hot, she's into sex. She's already got a husband, so we're chill. It's perfect."

A real winner.

Jericho's opinion of his brother sunk further. But he pushed on. The range was busy, but not crowded, so they had no problem finding two lanes, side by side. Jericho's arm was sore, so he'd go easy. Plus, he wasn't about to show his brother what he was capable of.

Smarter to play dumb.

He pulled on his goggles and slid on his body armor before opening his case and extracting his personal firearm, a Glock 17. He got in position, aimed, and fired off two shots, purposefully missing the target completely.

Vincent, who didn't bother with goggles or a vest, stepped up and fired. He hit the target, but not the bullseye. After firing off several more shots, Vincent tapped on the glass, then pointed outside the booth.

Both men stepped out.

"Can I give you some pointers?" Vincent asked.

"Bring 'em on."

"Try widening your stance and hold steady. It looks like you're jerking your arm."

"Got it." Jericho returned to his station and followed his brother's suggestions. He hit the target—but not the bullseye—every time.

Vincent gave him a thumbs-up, then went back to shooting. Jericho glanced over at him. His brother's gun was a shiny-blue metallic piece. He'd never seen a blue firearm. After moving the target back, Jericho purposely missed each shot.

Tap-tap-tap.

As Jericho expected, Vincent offered more help. They met outside the galley again where his brother rattled off more pointers. "That's a cool gun you got," Jericho said. "I've never seen a bright blue gun before."

Vincent's face split into a smile as he held out the piece. "Give it a try. It's got a fantastic release."

Jericho stepped into the booth and fired off a few rounds. His brother was right, the release was smooth and there was minimal kickback after firing. It was lightweight, too. He exited the booth. "Nice weapon." As Jericho turned it over, he spotted a logo of a lion's head with a full mane on the grip. "What's this?"

"The emblem? No idea. Dad gave it to me years ago."

What's it made of?"

"Aluminum," Vincent replied. "Weighs nothing."

"What's with the color?"

"Coolio, huh?"

Jericho handed it back to him. "You're pretty good. You do any hunting?"

"Nah, I just love guns. Got a nice collection, but I left most of them when we moved. I got my own target practice at work. You wanna come out sometime and shoot with me?"

Not really.

"Sure. You can give me a tour."

Vincent snort-laughed. "It's the most boring fucking tour you'll ever get, but, yeah, sure. Dad would love to see you."

"Whatever," Jericho grumbled. "Hey, I gotta ask—"

Vincent's phone buzzed in his pocket. He extracted it. "Hold on, it's my girl." He answered. "Hey, Bren, what's up?" As he listened, his face brightened. "I can't wait." He hung up and fist-pumped the air. "Brenda moved her client to tomorrow. She's the best."

Jericho clenched his jaw to keep quiet.

"What were you saying?" Vincent asked.

"I'm still struggling with Bryan's death. Would someone want to hurt us because Dad's in debt? Does he own money to loan sharks?"

"It kills me that Bryan died, but we were at the wrong place, wrong time." He placed his gun back in its case. "I gotta run. When can you come out and shoot with me?"

Jericho pulled out his phone and checked his schedule. "I got time tomorrow."

"See ya then." Vincent took off and Jericho released the pent-up growl he'd been holding back pretty much the entire time.

He returned to his car, grabbed his sniper bag, and strode back inside. He left out the back of Henninger, made his way over to one of the buildings, and jogged up the stairs to the roof.

Within seconds, he was set up on the roof's surface, long gun in his arms. "I don't need your fuckin' pointers." Using the scope, Jericho aimed for the farthest target. One inhale. He held his breath, eyed his target, and released.

The bullet pierced the bullseye dead center. "That's how it's done, brother."

19

UNFORGIVEN

Liv wouldn't use Lost Souls to lure Perry Pinter without full disclosure to Addison. It was risky telling her the truth, but deceiving her was *not* an option. Initiating a Girl's Night In, Liv volunteered to pick up carry-out from their favorite Mexican restaurant, a quaint eatery located in a small strip center nestled in Addison's neighborhood. When Addison invited her over, Liv accepted.

Every other time they'd gotten together, it had either been at a restaurant or at Liv's condo. She was looking forward to seeing where her cousin lived and hoped Addison had a spare bedroom where she could crash until she found her own place.

The restaurant was hopping busy when she arrived. Since she'd been teaching an all-day workshop, she asked Addison to call in their order.

"I'm picking up an order," Liv said to the hostess. "Name's Addison."

The hostess checked. "Hmm, I don't have anything with that name. Could it be under something else?"

After running through all possibilities and coming up empty, Liv placed the order, then waited at the bar. While sipping her iced tea, she jumped on an apartment-finder app. She'd been dragging her heels, hoping her uncle would have a change of heart and rehire her. Since she hadn't heard from him, it was time to move on. She plugged in her criteria and began searching.

"Liv, hey." She glanced up. Sergeant Hayes was smiling warmly at her. "Are you eating alone?"

The last time she'd seen him, she'd told him to back off regarding Jericho. She was surprised he'd even stopped by.

"I'm waiting for take-out."

"Brenda and I just ordered cocktails. Come join us."

"That's not a good idea. Jericho Savage is a person of interest in a case where I'm his alibi. I'm gonna pass on the invite, but thanks."

"I looked at the videos," the sergeant said. "They put him at his place of business during the time of the murders. He's no longer a person of interest in either case."

Relief flooded her. "Does he know?"

"Not yet."

"I'll join you once you tell him."

"Playing hard ball," Andre said with a smile. "Call him and I'll tell him."

She dialed. He answered. "Hey, babe."

"I'm picking up dinner and ran into Sergeant Hayes."

"That sucks."

She smiled. "He wants to talk to you. Do you have a sec?"

"I'm workin' out. Hold on." A few seconds later, he said, "Put him on."

Liv handed Andre her phone.

"Mr. Savage, it's Sergeant Hayes. You're no longer a person of interest in the gang murders." Andre listened. "Yes, this is an official call. Yes, I reviewed the videos." More listening. "I'm here with my wife. We saw Liv waiting for carry-out, so we asked her to sit with us while she waits." More listening. "Okay, I'll put her back on." He handed Liv the phone.

"I'll talk to you later," she said.

"Even though I've been cleared, don't discuss the case," Jericho told her.

"Of course." She hung up, slid off the stool, and collected her iced tea. "Let me tell the hostess I'll be in the dining room."

After doing that, she reluctantly walked over to the table. Brenda smiled, but she looked as uncomfortable as Liv felt.

"Hi Liv," Brenda said. "Good to see you again."

Liv eased onto the chair. "How are you doing, Brenda?"

"Been super busy at work," Brenda replied, color flushing her cheeks.

And super busy with Vincent.

"I'm impressed, ladies," Andre said. "I *never* remember people's names. I gotta see them a few times before it sinks in."

Brenda's nervous laugh caught Liv's ear. "Liv, do you live around here?"

"My cousin does," Liv replied. "I'm in Arlington. Do you both live around here?"

"Not too far," Andre replied. "This is one of our favorite restaurants."

Brenda was fiddling with her cocktail napkin while her foot bobbed beneath the table so fast, she was practically bouncing on the chair.

"What's new in the exciting world of art?" Liv asked Brenda.

Andre's phone rang and he pulled it from his pocket. "Excuse me." He rose, answered, and beelined toward the front door.

"I think the universe is telling me to stop seeing Vincent," Brenda whispered. "He told me he hung with Jericho at the shooting range earlier. Now, here I am, running into you. My stomach is in knots."

"I can imagine," Liv replied. The situation was beyond awkward, and Liv regretted sitting down with her.

"You should swing by the gallery," Brenda said. "I'm having a huge sale. Everything is thirty-to-fifty percent off. Didn't you like one of the paintings?"

"The one with the family at the lake," Liv replied.

"That's right," Brenda replied. "That's a lovely one."

The hostess appeared with a large bag of food. "You're Liv, right?"

"Yes."

"You're all set." The hostess set the bag on the empty chair and left.

Liv rose. "It was good seeing you Brenda." Then, she smiled. "I have a feeling I'll be seeing you again."

Brenda laughed. "Maybe I'll be clearheaded when we do."

Liv collected the large bag and walked outside.

Andre stood on the sidewalk, two stores down, talking on his phone. Rather than head to her car, she made her way toward him. For a reserved man, he sounded angry. Even though his back was to her, she heard him.

"How many are we talking about?" Andre turned around and startled. "Hold on."

"Good seeing you, Andre," Liv said.

"You, too," he replied. "Enjoy your dinner."

As she stepped off the sidewalk, she heard him say, "That son of a bitch!"

Liv jumped in her car and drove away, wondering what had ticked the sergeant off so badly.

She got to Addison's small, brick-front house and rang the doorbell. A moment later, Addison swung open the door. She eyed the large carry-out bag and grinned. "I'm starving. Was it crowded?"

Liv walked inside. "They didn't have our order."

Addison frowned. "Oh, I'm sorry. I completely forgot." She took the bag. "C'mon in."

The small home was lovely. Modern furniture in the living room along with a piano. "I didn't know you played."

"I'm not very good, but it's fun to tool around on it when I have the time."

Liv followed her into the kitchen. Light counters, white cabinets and appliances. Small, clean, no clutter. No papers, no opened mail.

"I can't believe I've never been here before," Liv said.

"I'll give you a tour that'll take four minutes." Addison pulled out plates and silverware. "But we gotta eat first."

After sitting at the table, they opened the appetizer and the main dishes, and dug in.

"Are you coming to the club this week?" Addison asked after a few bites.

"Yes. How's the chef working out?"

"She's great. I think things are really falling into place. I'm surprised you haven't been playing there more."

"So, there's something I need to talk to you about," Liv said. "It's pretty serious, but you need to know. You can't say anything to anyone."

Addison stilled, her mouth full of food. "Are you okay?"

"I've been helping Jericho go after the men who killed his brother."

Addison stared at her. "What do you mean... *you've* been helping Jericho?"

"I can't get into details, but the gang leader is the guy from the club who's been hitting on me. The one who calls himself Guapo."

Her eyes grew large. "Are you for real? The drive-by was gang related?"

"We know it was a scare job, but we don't know who they were trying to scare. We're luring the gang leader to the club with an invitation from me for a private party. Jericho's going to have some of his... er... um... friends there to help get answers from this guy."

Addison nodded. "Got it."

"So, you're okay with it?"

"Totally."

"But you can't be there."

"No worries," Addison replied. "Sounds like you guys have everything covered. When are you planning on doing it?"

"Since the club is closed on Tuesdays, we're doing it tomorrow night."

"Be careful," Addison said. "He sounds super dangerous."

"So, how are you doing?" Liv asked.

"Me? I'm fine." She forked enchilada into her mouth.

"You know, you never talk about your job. How's it going?"

"I'm a consultant. Nothing much to talk about." Liv scooped up a mouthful of rice.

"I thought you were an analyst."

"I was a number cruncher for an accounting firm, but now I consult with companies on financial management and reporting. I like it way better. I'm out and about all the time. I used to sit at my desk all day."

When they finished eating, Addison gave Liv a tour. Her home was neat, with a few pieces of abstract art on the walls. "I met the owner of an art gallery in Alexandria. The Hayes. You'd probably love some of her paintings."

"I did these," Addison replied matter-of-factly. "Hawk and I took an art class a while back and I kinda got hooked."

"Wow, you're so talented. You could sell these."

Addison laughed. "I'm not sure about that." She entered her bedroom, Liv close on her heels.

A queen bed sat tucked in the corner with a white comforter and several brightly colored pillows propped on the bed.

Liv laughed. "What's with the pillows?"

"I love them, except at night. It's annoying to remove all of them, but I love how it looks when it's made."

As they headed back to the living room, Liv stopped in front of a closed bedroom door. "Is this a spare bedroom?" She tried the handle, but the door was locked. "I was hoping you had room for me."

"I use that for storage," Addison replied. "Why are you moving?"

Liv couldn't tell Addison that her dad had evicted her because Addison didn't know she'd worked for him. "The owner has other plans for the condo."

"Bummer. That's such a nice place."

"Jericho offered me his guest house," Liv said as they returned to the living room.

"So, how's that going?" Addison asked.

Just thinking about Jericho made her smile. "Great. I wouldn't be surprised if we stayed together for a long time."

"Why don't you just move into his guest house?"

Liv collected her handbag. "I don't want to rush things, you know? Seems kind of fast."

"When you know, you know," Addison said giving her a hug. "Love you, cuz."

"Love you back. Thanks for finally having me over. I love the artwork. You're super talented."

As Liv walked to her car, she checked texts. Her heart skipped a beat when she saw one from Jericho. "I'm home. Come over after dinner. I miss you."

She sent a heart emoji, got in her car, and drove to her condo. After packing a small suitcase, she left for his place. Once there, she admired how the spotlights were perfectly placed in the yard, illuminating the front of the estate.

It looks like something out of a fairy tale.

She rang the doorbell. A moment later, Jericho opened the door. His long hair was pulled into a half-bun. He was dressed in a T-shirt and shorts, and barefoot. A zing skittered through her. That man was a whole lotta yummy.

So sexy.

"There's my woman." He pulled her close, lifted her up, and kissed her. When he set her down, she went to collect her suitcase.

"If the offer is still open, can I crash in your guest house until I can find—"

He stopped her with a kiss. "Hell, yeah. I love it."

"Thank you." She kissed him back.

He wheeled her suitcase through the living room. Outside, a few people were hanging at a table, poolside.

"I didn't know you had company," she said.

"A few of my guys and their women are here," Jericho said. "We're figuring out the best way to catch El Jefe."

"Did you tell them my idea?" Liv asked. "Addison's okay if we use the club tomorrow night. It's closed and I thought we could throw a fake invitation-only party."

"C'mon in and we'll throw that one into the mix," Jericho replied. "You want somethin' to drink?"

"I'll just grab a water."

With her glass in hand, they walked outside. The air was balmy, the night still. As they approached the table, the conversation stopped.

"This is Liv Blackstone," Jericho said. "You met Stryker. That's his fiancée, Emerson Easton. You know Sin, and this is his wife, Evangeline.

"Good to meet you, Liv," Evangeline said. "I've heard a lot about you."

Jericho gestured for Liv to take his chair while he pulled one over for himself.

Liv sat. "I was thinking of inviting the gang leader to an invitation-only party tomorrow at Lost Souls."

"Too dangerous for Liv," Jericho said.

"That's solid, babe," Hawk pushed back. "We'd be there, plus several other Operatives."

"Has he been back to his house?" Liv asked.

"No," Hawk answered. "And he turned off his phone, so we've got no way to track him."

"We've tossed around several ideas," Sin added. "I agree with Hawk. Liv's idea is the best one."

Stryker nodded. "We'll have enough people there to keep her safe. It's not like she'll be alone with him."

Jericho released an audible growl.

Liv pulled her phone from her handbag, opened the Lost Souls app, and scrolled until she found Pinter's photo. She tapped on Invitations to Escape, typed out a message, then read it to the group. "We're having a private party Tues. I'd love for you to be my guest."

"Short and sweet," Emerson said.

Jericho scraped his fingers over his beard. "Send it."

As soon as she did, Jericho pushed out of his chair, leaned down, and kissed Liv. "Who's swimmin' with me?"

"I don't have my suit," Liv said.

"I am." Stryker stood. "Em, you coming with me?"

"I didn't bring mine either," Emerson replied.

"Wear your bra and panties," Stryker suggested.

"I'm not wearing a bra," she replied. "I'll hang with Liv."

"No one will look," Hawk added, and everyone laughed.

"I got extra bathing suits for the guys." Jericho retreated inside, returning in a bathing suit and carrying a few.

Liv's brain shorted as she soaked up all that male hotness. His black suit hugged his massive thighs and she could not wait to glimpse his tight ass. Bulging biceps stole her attention as she raked her gaze over them, before plain old gawking at his chest. Then, she whistled.

He stuck a pose and flexed his muscles.

Everyone started laughing.

While Hawk, Stryker, and Sin changed in the guest house, Emerson asked Jericho, "How's your arm doing?"

"It's good," he replied. "How's *your* arm doin'?"

The women laughed.

"I wasn't shot in mine," Emerson replied.

The guys emerged from the guest house and all four men dove in. They played nerf basketball and had a diving competition. There was a lot of ribbing… and laughter. Liv loved seeing Jericho with his friends. Less angst, way more chill.

Emerson and Evangeline moved closer to Liv. "I'm sorry you lost your job," Evangeline said. "I heard you were so good at it, too."

Liv flicked her gaze from one woman to the other. "I… um… what are you—"

"Sin told me Z fired you," Evangeline confided. "No worries, he's excellent at keeping secrets. He does it for a living, but we tell each other everything. We don't believe in keeping secrets. They can be a marriage killer. Plus, these guys are like brothers."

"It's true," Emerson added. "We're family. Everyone's close. Everyone gets along. It's a special group of people."

"Thanks for clarifying," Liv said. "I was super disappointed, but I falsified a report."

Evangeline offered a warm smile. "Maybe Z will change his mind."

Liv laughed. "I know him pretty well and I *definitely* don't see that happening."

She loved hanging with Evangeline and Emerson. They were both so nice, so welcoming into their tight-knit circle. At one point, she felt eyes on her. She glanced in the pool. Jericho was floating on a raft—on his stomach—and peering over at her. "Hey, baby."

Stryker flipped him off the raft.

With everything that had been going on, their playfulness was a much-needed respite.

Liv's phone buzzed with an incoming message from Lost Souls. "I'll be there," Pinter replied. "I can't wait to get to know you better." A chill shot down her spine and goosebumps covered her arms.

As if Jericho could sense her uneasiness, he was out of the pool and by her side. The only thing better than Jericho in a bathing suit was a soaking-wet Jericho in a bathing suit.

She rose and whispered, "You are so gonna get laid."

His smile lit up his face, then he dropped a soft kiss on her mouth.

She showed him her phone.

"Hey, team, it's a go for tomorrow," Jericho called out. "Party at Lost Souls."

Jericho pulled up to the Chantilly building with an effin' chip on his shoulder. He did *not* want to spend any more time with his brother, and he sure as fuck didn't want to see his dad. But the team had agreed with Liv. He needed to vet the family he didn't know.

The sign — **Midwest Caskets** — was the only indication he'd come to the right place. The building was nondescript, the parking lot filled with a couple dozen cars.

Pushing out of his truck, he strode to the front door.

Let's get this over with.

He pulled and almost yanked his arm out. It was locked. He would have gotten in his car and left if he hadn't agreed to do this.

No buzzer, so he banged on the glass. When no one showed up, he walked around the side of the building. The loading zone was busy with workers carrying long, rectangular boxes onto a white truck with the company name plastered on the side.

"What the fuck is wrong with you, Vincent?" their dad bellowed. "You're loading the boxes all wrong! You stupid, fucking moron."

Jericho pulled to a stop. Vincent flipped his dad the finger before speaking to one of the workers.

"Can't you do anything right?" their dad yelled before vanishing inside.

As Jericho made his way over, Vincent flicked his gaze to him, shot him an enthusiastic grin, and jogged over.

"Hey, you made it. Welcome to the death shop. We make a home for your bones." Vincent barked out a laugh.

Jericho chuckled. "That's quite a slogan you got there."

His smile fell away. "It's a job."

"What's with all the yelling?" Jericho asked.

Vincent furrowed his brows. "What yelling?"

"Dad was screaming at you pretty good. I've never heard him holler like that before."

"That's the new and improved version of himself. He's pissed at me because I didn't show for a sales meeting this morning."

"Why not?"

"Two words. Over slept."

"That's one word," Jericho corrected.

Again, Vincent laughed. "I love it. You're a grammar whore."

"It's not grammar, but let's move on."

"Yeah, dude, I was out partying last night. I got a friend who gets me this weed. It's the best. But last night, I did Molly. It was a crazy good time. Anyhoo, Dad flipped the fuck out." Vincent dusted his shoulder with the back of his fingers. "Rolls right off me."

His brother opened the door next to the loading dock. "For all I know, he lost ten grand at the tables last night. Lemme show you 'round."

They had a small staff that consisted of a customer service person, an accountant, and a logistics person.

"Who sells the caskets?" Jericho asked.

"I've made a few calls, but Dad's the hustler. He's pretty good at it, but how hard is it to sell a wooden box?"

Vincent stopped in front of a closed office door. "Dad's office. You wanna say hey?"

Not really.

"Sure."

Not bothering to knock, Vincent opened the door. His dad was on leaning back in his chair, talking on the phone. His gaze darted from Vincent to Jericho. "I'll call you back." His dad hung up and stood.

"Jericho, I didn't know you were coming out." He extended his hand. "Good to see you. How you been?" Then, he glared at Vincent. "A little heads-up woulda been nice."

Jericho did the obligatory handshake. "It was a last-minute thing. Vincent's givin' me a tour."

His dad puffed out his chest. "It's a satellite office and small distribution center. Our home office is in Norman, Oklahoma."

"You do a lotta business around here?" Jericho asked.

His dad regarded Vincent and the warmth faded from his eyes. "Things are picking up. It's a hard market to break into, you know, being that we're the new kids on the block."

"We're going out back to shoot," Vincent said.

"What about loading the shipment?"

"The guys are on it."

"Jericho, stop by on your way out," his dad said.

Vincent swung into his office. Standard desk and chair, no guest chair. Nothing beyond a computer and a small stack of papers.

"This is where the magic happens," Vincent indicated with a sweep of his arm.

"What's your job?" Jericho asked.

"I manage the assembly and distribution. I'll show it to ya on our way outside."

"I forgot to grab a weapon."

"No worries. I got you."

His brother led him toward the back of the building and

through a door marked **WAREHOUSE** where over a dozen workers were building caskets from prefab wood. The sheer noise from the hammering made it impossible to hear.

Extra pairs of ear protectors were lying on a nearby table, so Jericho grabbed two, pulled one on and offered the second to his brother. Vincent waved it away as a few of the workers regarded them. First, he led Jericho over to the hammering team, then to the second group who were lining the caskets.

When Vincent pointed, Jericho realized he'd been talking the whole time, despite Jericho's inability to hear a word he was saying.

What an idiot.

He led Jericho to a glass-enclosed office at the other side of the warehouse. Once inside, Jericho removed the ear protection.

"The noise doesn't bother me." Vincent pointed toward the assembly line. "The caskets come in sections already cut and stained. The team puts 'em together, lines 'em with foam, then covers that with either polyester, satin, or velvet. You wanna try one out?"

What the fuck? "You mean, lay in one?"

Vincent snort-laughed. "Yeah, I take my best naps in 'em. They're great."

Jericho fought the urge to roll his eyes. "I'll pass."

Vincent opened a stand-alone cabinet with an array of guns lining the shelves. He pulled out his blue metallic one, then stepped out of the way. "Pick whatever you want."

Jericho pulled a Glock. It looked like a Glock, but it was lighter. "What's this?"

"A Glock knock-off." Vincent waggled his eyebrows. "It's lighter, easier to manage."

Jericho examined it, noting it had the same logo—the head of a lion—on its grip, same as Vincent's aluminum gun. "What's with the lion logo?"

Vincent shrugged. "No idea. Guns are like women to me.

They're all about the release, the weight, the feel in my hands." Another cackle from his brother, who was clearly entertained by that one.

He's a piece o' work.

Jericho lifted a rifle from the cabinet. "Nice."

"Bring it."

Jericho nodded toward the employees. "Don't you need to lock these up?"

"They ain't gonna use 'em. They make coffins for a living, dude. It's the last place they wanna end up." With their weapons in hand, Vincent led Jericho toward the exit.

There was a closed door on the other side of the room. Rather than head in that direction, Vincent directed him to the exit by the loading dock.

Jericho pointed toward the door. "What's in there?"

"Storage and shit."

They went around back to an open field overgrown with grasses and weeds where Vincent had set up a basic shooting range. They took turns firing off the weapons, but unlike the first time where Jericho didn't shoot well, he put forth a little effort today. In the seven shots he took, he missed the bullseye once.

"Bro, whad'ya have for breakfast? No, wait, you got laid last night. You're definitely shooting like a marksman, fo' sure."

"It's the gun," Jericho replied. "She's doing all the work for me."

"Like I said, it's how I like my women. I lay back and let 'em do all the work."

Get me the hell outta here.

Jericho tried the rifle. The release wasn't as smooth and it jerked more than he liked. Even so, he hit the target every time.

"What do you think of that one?" Vincent asked.

"It's okay." This one didn't have a logo. "What is this?"

"A rifle."

Jericho scraped his fingers down his whiskers. "Yeah, I got that part. Who makes it?"

"Dunno. Anyone can put these things together."

"How's Brenda?"

"Ah, man, she's good."

"You know, she's married to a cop."

"Yeah, he's cool. We went shooting a coupla times."

What the hell. "Does he know about you and his wife?"

"Fuck, I hope not." Vincent fired off a shot, then another.

"You miss livin' in the Midwest?"

Vincent shrugged a shoulder. "Norman's my home, but it's coolio 'round here. We gotta grow the biz. Might as well be here."

They fired off a bunch more rounds. Thirty minutes later, Jericho was done. The conversation wasn't flowing and Jericho had run out of questions… and patience.

"I gotta take off."

"Thanks for coming out to see the castle. A real shit hole, but it's a job. You want me to drop you at Dad's office so he can blow smoke up your ass?"

Jericho didn't have a relationship with his father and his brother clearly didn't like the one he had.

"Sure."

"I'm gonna shoot for a while longer," Vincent said. "You know your way back?"

Jericho pointed. "Through that door."

Vincent pulled him in for a bro-hug. "I hope you're still not guilting yourself over Bryan."

"Why would I feel guilty?"

"Well, he was killed outside *your* restaurant."

What the fuck?

"Do *you* feel guilty about Bryan's death?" Jericho asked.

"Bad things happen to good people. Whatcha gonna do? Gotta keep on keepin' on, right? One day, I'm gonna be in a casket taking my eternal nap."

Jericho held his gaze. "I don't think Bryan's death was an accident."

Vincent huffed. "Dude, it was terrible, but you gotta let it go."

I'm never letting it go.

Jericho held out the rifle and the Glock knock-off.

"Drop those in the cabinet for me, will ya?" Vincent turned around and started shooting.

As Jericho made his way inside, he wondered what his mom would have thought about the way his brother had turned out.

She woulda hated it.

Jericho returned the weapons to the cabinet, then watched the casket workers build the wooden boxes. He left the distribution center and stopped in front of his dad's open office door.

Roger Savage glanced up from his computer. "Come on in, Jericho. It's good to see you, son."

Gritting his teeth, he eased into a chair. "How do you like being back in the area?"

"I work all the time, so I wouldn't know. I did contact your Gram to see if I could spend a little time with her."

"Why her?" Jericho bit out. "She's not even a blood relation."

"I upset her at Bryan's funeral. I want to apologize."

"Apologize to your children for walking out on them." Anger had him clenching his teeth.

A bitter silence fell over the room.

"I am sorry," his father said. "I shouldn't have left, but I wasn't happy."

Despite the frustration coursing through him, Jericho needed answers, so he pushed on. "Why so tough on Vincent?"

"If I don't stay on him, he'll spend every day shooting those damn guns. He's almost thirty-five years old. Time to grow the hell up and work for a damn living. You wouldn't understand. We've got a complicated relationship."

"At least he has one with you."

"Have you come here to guilt trip me, Jericho?"

Jericho glared at him. "I don't know a thing about you. You into guns, too?"

"I hate the damn things."

"Vincent said you like to gamble."

Surprise flashed in his dad's eyes. "Yeah, so?"

"You got that under control?"

"What the hell? Is this the damn inquisition? Did that son of a bitch tell you I had a gambling problem?"

"Relax," Jericho said.

"I had debt, but it's paid off… *and* it's none of your business."

Jericho pushed out of the chair, placed his palms on the desk, and narrowed his eyes. "You abandoned your wife and six kids. Mom died when I was eighteen. I wanted to be a SEAL since I was ten years old. I had to give up *my* dream and petition the court for legal guardianship of Tim, Mark, Georgia, and Bryan, so they wouldn't be put in foster care. I gave up my dream for my family. What did you do? You walked out on yours! Fucking walked out. I had to go to Plan B, which I had to invent on the fly because I had no fucking Plan B!"

Rage clouded his thoughts.

His dad sighed. "I made a selfish mistake."

"Bryan was gunned down by a coupla thugs. I won't stop until I can choke the life out of anyone who had *anything* to do with it. If you owe people money and they wanted to scare you by killing your sons, I will find that out. Then, I will rip your fucking heart out of your chest and shove it down your goddamn throat."

A growl blasted out of him.

Stiffening, his dad narrowed his eyes. "Get. Out."

"I'll never forgive you for what you did, but at least you taught me how *not* to treat my family." Jericho stormed out and bumped into Vincent. He kept going, his feet eating up the floor. He had to get out, or his fist would make contact with someone's jaw.

"Whoa, man, you okay?" Vincent called, but Jericho kept moving.

When he pushed through the door and into the parking lot, he could breathe. Being around those two was like stepping into a fucking nightmare. Memories long buried had risen to the surface like an angry volcano spewing hot lava in every direction.

He had no idea if either of them had been involved with Bryan's murder, but he was done trying to find out. Despite his attempts, he'd learned nothing. They'd been dead to him since the moment they walked out the door and they were just as dead to him now.

20

GOING AFTER THE LEADER

Dressed in her cat suit, Liv stood in front of the scanner at the front door of Lost Souls. The light turned green and she sailed inside, locking the door behind her. The private party kicked off at ten, but she'd gotten there forty-minutes early to make sure she was the first to arrive.

She flipped on lights, stashed her bag in the manager's office, returned to the main room and startled. Addison walked in, dressed as Trinity from The Matrix. Her black latex suit hugged her, but it was her full-length black leather coat that caught Liv's eye.

"You look phenomenal, but you're not supposed to be here," Liv said.

"Someone needs to pour drinks." Addison pulled back the full-length coat revealing a gun in her hip holster.

What the hell?

Liv flicked her gaze from the weapon to Addison. "You're armed? I didn't even know you owned a gun."

"I'm staying... and I got your back."

Her cousin had a point. She couldn't bartend if she'd invited

Pinter as her guest. A shudder skirted down her spine, but she shook it off, determined to help Jericho get answers.

Jericho and Hawk arrived next. Jericho in a Batman costume made her heart pound hard and fast. His suit clung like a second skin. He was completely covered, save for his mouth.

She went to him, threw her arms around him, and hugged him. "Perfect disguise."

Hawk, dressed as a gladiator, looked like he was ready to do battle. "Looking good," Liv said to him.

"You doin' okay?" Jericho asked her.

"All good. I'm gonna wait with Addison." She moved behind the bar and over to her cousin.

"Are you nervous?" she murmured.

"No." Addison appeared calm and in control. "You got this."

"I hope so."

At five past ten, a group of people entered the club. She recognized Stryker and Emerson, Sin and Evangeline, Cooper and Danielle. Sin's twin was also in the group. He was holding the hand of a woman with short, dark hair.

Her churning guts settled down. Over the next several minutes, guests kept arriving. Liv grew concerned that word had leaked about their closed party. There had to be thirty costumed people. Then, Liv spotted a woman with purple hair and recognized her immediately. It was Amanda Maynard. Nickname, Slash. Slash had been her first assignment as a watcher. She'd just come off an intense ALPHA mission and Z wanted to make sure she wasn't suffering from PTSD.

These are ALPHA Operatives.

Her gaze flicked to Addison.

Is my cousin one, too?

Jericho and Hawk made their way over to the bar. "How 'bout a coupla beers?" Hawk asked.

Addison popped the tops and set the bottles on the shiny bar. Slowly, the group made their way over. Most ordered non-alcoholic drinks, but poured into lowball glasses. Sin's twin and his woman approached the bar.

"Staying out of trouble, Addison?" he asked.

Addison offered nothing more than a cordial smile. "This is my cousin, Livingston Blackstone," Addison said. "Dakota Luck and his wife, Providence."

"I hear you're hanging with the wild man," Dakota said to Liv.

"If you mean Jericho, then, yes, I am," Liv replied with a smile.

"We love Jericho," Providence said. "He's a good friend of ours." After collecting her non-alcoholic drink, she added, "You're gonna do great tonight."

Liv assumed they were with ALPHA, but she didn't know in what capacity. Not having access to everyone's files was a definite disadvantage.

At midnight, when Pinter still hadn't shown, she went into the office, pulled her phone from her bag, and sent him a message. "You're missing a great party."

She waited, but he didn't respond. As she was leaving, Jericho appeared in the doorway. "Any word?" he asked.

"How'd you know what I was doing?"

"I haven't taken my eyes off you since I got here."

She slunk over, leaned up, and kissed him. "Thank you for making sure I'm safe."

"Always, babe."

"You, in that costume, would make for a fun evening," she said, peering up at him. "And you, out of that costume, would be even better." She caressed his back. "Why are you so tight? Are you nervous about tonight?"

"No, darlin' I live for these missions."

"Then, what?" She searched his face. "Oh, I know. Vincent and Roger Savage."

Jericho had been in a perpetual state of pissed-off all afternoon. He couldn't shake the rancid taste in his mouth from spending time with his brother and his dad. His conclusion? His brother was too stupid to be involved with a gang, but his dad might have gotten in too deep with loan sharks.

For the moment, he needed to focus on the woman standing inches away. Keeping her safe was his primary goal. Getting answers from Pinter would be easy, but only if he showed.

Initially, he thought that would be the easy part... now he wasn't so sure.

"What does Dakota do?" Liv asked.

"He co-runs ALPHA with Providence, but he had to step away, so Cooper took the lead."

"Wow, I can't believe you told me that. Thank you."

"I trust you, Liv."

She caressed his arm. "Thank you. I won't let you down."

"I know." He stared into her eyes. "You better get back out there. He might be waiting for you."

After shutting the office door, she left him alone in the hallway. When she turned back, he was waiting.

One brief smile and she returned to the main room.

They waited until one in the morning, but when Pinter didn't show, everyone filtered out.

Frustration burned a trail to Jericho's guts. He was out of options. His brother and dad were dead ends.

Pinter was untraceable and had vanished. That made him twice as dangerous.

The next morning, Liv got ready before Jericho was even awake. She loved spending the night with him, loved waking up curled around him or sprawled across his chest. That morning, they'd been holding hands beneath the covers. Even in their sleep, they found each other. Her heart melted at how connected they'd become.

Jericho rolled over. "Are you sneaking out on me?"

"I'm going to make you breakfast in the main house, plus I was hoping to see Georgia."

"Gram's gonna have questions."

"Fine by me. I'm here until I find something permanent."

His sleepy smile warmed her heart. "You like me too much. You're not going *anywhere*."

"Cocky." One kiss and she was out the door.

On the short walk to the main house, she appreciated the warm summer morning. The kids were eating breakfast at the table with Tim while Georgia and Gram were looking at a phone.

"Good morning," Liv said.

"Hey, Livy," Georgia said. "Good morning."

"Good morning," said Gram.

"Hi." Owen held out a Cheerio. "Here."

She took it from him and popped it into her mouth. "Thank you, Owen. Those are yummy."

"You can have some of our cereal," said Annie.

"Thank you, Annie. I would love some. I'm going to make something for Jericho, first."

"He can have cereal too!" she grinned at Liv.

She's adorable.

"We'll have some as soon as he gets here," Liv replied.

"Can I make anyone else eggs?" Liv asked.

Georgia popped up. "I'll show you where everything is."

Liv appreciated how at-home they made her feel. She felt a little awkward, only because she was living in his guest house and he'd been staying there with her since she moved in.

She made plenty of scrambled eggs while Georgia cooked sausage links and cut up a watermelon.

Being with his family felt so right.

"Yo, fam," Jericho boomed as he entered the room dressed in shorts and a T-shirt.

"Uncle, sit wif me," Owen said. "Can we play?"

Jericho kissed both children on the tops of their heads. "Sure, buddy, I got time for you after breakfast." He flexed his bicep and the kids giggled. "Food for energy, right?"

Liv pictured a life with Jericho, with children and all the mayhem that came with it. Before him, she'd never imagined a future with anyone.

"Liv. *Livy.*" Jericho plucked her from her thoughts. "Do you want to play a board game with us?"

"Absolutely."

After everyone had finished eating, Liv cleared the table and started cleaning up. Gram hadn't moved from her spot at the head. Jericho helped her, then went to find the kids. Tim had gone upstairs to finish getting ready and Georgia had gotten a call about a restaurant delivery.

As soon as Liv finished cleaning up, Gram said, "Come sit with me for a second."

Liv eased down catty corner.

"Do you love him?"

Wow, she's definitely direct.

"I do."

"You were the only girl he ever told me about. How you were best friends, then you broke his heart."

She bowed her head in shame. "I know. I regret what I did and I'm earning his trust again. I'm not a scared teen. I'm a grown woman and I know myself. He deserves my absolute best."

She scooped Liv's hand into her own. "I'm happy to hear that. Jericho is the rock for this family." She leaned close. "Don't hurt him."

Liv regarded Gram for a beat. "I would marry him if he asked me. I'd have his children and build a life with him. I love him fiercely. Can you keep a secret?"

Gram nodded.

"I lost my job because of him."

Gram sat back and stared at Liv. "Why is that a secret? Doesn't he know?"

"He does, but it's not something I can talk about with anyone else."

"I see." Gram pursed her lips, then relaxed them. "I'm sorry about your job, but I am relieved you have real feelings for him. He never stopped loving you, Liv."

She patted Gram's hand. "Now, I'm mature enough to love him back."

"I feel better." Gram offered a smile. "Thank you for talking to me. No worries, your secret stays with me, dear."

Liv went in search of Jericho and found him sitting in the grass by the pool playing a game of Chutes and Ladders with the kids.

"I'm winning!" Owen exclaimed.

"That's great," Liv replied.

She sat and watched them play, which consisted of a small meltdown when Owen, on the road to victory, hit the mother slide and ended up back at the beginning.

"I quit!" Owen proclaimed.

"Don't be a baby," Annie scolded.

"No name calling," Jericho said sounding sterner than she expected. "What is it that I always say?"

"We're together and that's good," Annie replied.

"Good job." He high-fived Annie, then held up his hand to his nephew.

Owen glared at him. "I don't want to."

Jericho held up his hand to Liv and she high-fived him.

"C'mon, buddy," Jericho said. "You can do it."

"But I want to win," he whined.

"We all like winning, but we don't win every game, every time," Jericho explained.

Liv smiled at Jericho. "You have a very smart uncle."

Excusing herself Liv retrieved her phone from the guest house. She'd been putting off sending the text, but she had to respect her Uncle's wishes. She typed out a message.

"I'll be out of the condo by Sunday. Thanks for letting me stay there and for the opportunity to work for you. It was my all-time fave job. Sorry I ruined our relationship. You are my fave uncle, too."

As soon as she sent it, her phone rang.

It was Addison. "Hey, I've gotta head out of town for a meeting. Can you fill in for me tonight?"

"Absolutely," Liv replied. "It'll be way less stressful than last night."

"Last night was a piece-o-cake," Addison replied. "Nothing happened."

LOST SOULS WAS nonstop busy all evening. Jericho told Liv he'd try to swing by, but he had to deal with an issue between his chef and his sous-chef at Raphael's, then head to The Road since hump nights there were always crazy-busy.

Liv and the bartender spent the night working side by side, but she'd step away to sign up a new member every chance she got.

"Last call," the bartender announced as Liv returned behind the bar.

"I feel like I just got here," she said. After the final flurry of activity, the club started clearing out.

When the last member left, the bouncer came inside to clear the suites.

One at a time, he and Liv checked each room, including the en suite bathrooms. The Blue Room had two men re-enacting a Star Wars scene, half in and half out of their costumes. After the couple left, Liv and the bouncer finished checking the suites.

Back in the main room, the bouncer and bartender headed for the door. "You coming?" asked the bartender.

"You guys go ahead," Liv replied. "Make sure the front door is locked."

"Always do," replied the bouncer who lowered the lights before they left.

Alone in the club, Liv grabbed her handbag from the office and texted Jericho. "Wanna play at the club? I'm here all alone…"

When he didn't respond, she called him.

"Hey, baby," he answered. "Are you on your way over?"

"I'm all alone," she said, her tone playful. "I was hoping we could play in a suite."

"Oh, mama, you're killin' me. I'm short two bartenders and we're gettin' slammed."

"I'll help you," she said. "Be there soon."

She changed out of her cat suit and into a pair of Capri pants and a black shirt, pausing to fluff her flattened hair. With her phone in hand and her handbag over her shoulder, she left the office.

As she headed for the front door, movement caught her eye. A man stepped out of the shadows by the bar, sending dread spiraling through her.

Perry Pinter glared at her. "Sorry I couldn't make it last night."

"Get out," she snapped, trying to conceal her fear, despite her racing heart.

"I've been hiding in the damn toilet for the past hour. Do you know how hard it is to squat on a fuckin' toilet lid? The least you could do is offer me a drink."

"No."

"Relax. I'm not interested in you. Not anymore. I'm looking for your boyfriend. Where's he at?"

"Fuck you," she hissed.

From behind his waist, he pulled a gun and pointed it at her.

"I'm not messing around, sweetkins. He stuck his nose where it don't belong and he needs to go. Get him here."

"I just—sure. No problem. I'll call him." She hated that she was luring Jericho into a trap, but she would warn him. Somehow.

"You tell him I'm here and I blow your head off," Pinter threatened.

With trembling fingers, she dialed, put the phone to her ear.

A few rings in, Jericho answered. "Hey, babe, you on your way?"

Liv swallowed, hard. "I want you to come over here so we can play. I'm all alone."

"I can't babe, I'm sorry."

"Oh, that's great," she said. "When can I expect you?"

"Liv, what are you talking about?"

"I'll unlock the front door—"

"No!" Pinter interjected, his staccato tone making her startle. "Tell Savage to knock when he gets here."

"That's not gonna work, you know, 'cause I'm here alone," she said to Jericho. "Knock, and I'll let you in."

"Fuck. *Fuck*," Jericho hissed. "Is Pinter there?"

"Absolutely. I've got the club to myself, so we can do whatever."

"I'm on my way." The line went dead.

"Tell him to come alone," Pinter said.

Jolts of adrenaline wouldn't stop firing through her, her chest was tight, and she couldn't catch her breath. Fearing she'd pass out, she grasped the back of a chair. "Babe, you're coming alone, right?"

She waiting, pretending like he was still on the phone with her. "I know that's a silly question, but I just wanted to make sure it's just us, okay?"

Flicking her gaze to Pinter, she nodded. "Can you leave soon?"

Again, she waited, imagining his strong, husky voice in her ear, telling her that everything would be okay.

"See you in ten. I can't wait." She set the phone on the table.

Pinter pulled out two zip ties from his pocket.

"No," she protested.

"Shut up." He strode over, pointing the gun at her face. "I don't like shooting a lady, but I will if you force me to. Sit the fuck down."

Her heart was thumping in her ears. "I said, no."

He smacked her across the face, her cheek stinging from his assault. She tried to knee him, but he jumped back, then grabbed her arm and twisted it, forcing her to spin around.

"Aiiiieee," she screamed.

"Sit or I'll *really* hurt you."

Feeling helpless, she folded into the chair. He zip-tied her wrists and her ankles. Then, he pulled up a chair, swung it around so the back faced her, and sunk down.

She narrowed her eyes and glared at him.

"Do you remember me?" he asked.

Refusing to give him the satisfaction of an answer, she said nothing.

"Back then, I had no manners," he began. "I climbed on girls, did whatever. He held up his left hand, displaying his thumb and two fingers. "I learned my lesson. Some crazy bitch cut off two of my fingers." He laughed. "What a fucking bloody mess that was, but she told me I was lucky she didn't cut my dick off. I got the message."

He straightened up, puffed out his chest. "I'm a businessman now. Got me some money, a lot of associates working for me. I got ladies falling all over me, all the fucking time. Since they're offering their pussies to me, I don't have to go after some girl who doesn't want to give it to me. You get what I'm saying?"

"I'm sorry she *didn't* cut your dick off." Hatred dripped from her tongue.

"Ah, c'mon, no hard feelings." He stroked his beard. "Be happy.

I'm not gonna rape you, but I am gonna kill you after I'm done with your boyfriend."

Liv needed to stall him for as long as possible. Though she was shaking, she pushed on. "Why do you want to kill him?"

"He's hurting my business by taking out my guys. Things were going good before Savage got involved. Maybe you don't know, but him and his buddies came into my house—*my house*—and took everyone out. I 'bout shit myself, but I got outta there. My guys weren't so lucky. So, I'm moving the enemy outta my way."

"Why was Jericho targeted the night his brother got killed?"

Pinter walked behind the bar and poured himself a glass of scotch. "He wasn't. I hadn't thought of yous since high school when I got away with trying to rape you." He tossed back the booze. "Savage ain't got what it takes to outsmart me. I sent my guys to that restaurant to scare him. The SOB fell right back in line like a good little soldier." Pinter's lips split into a menacing smile. "You can't do business with me, then try to fuck me behind my back."

Pinter poured himself more scotch.

Her phone buzzed on the nearby table. Leaning over, she read the text from Jericho. "I finally found someone to cover for me. Leaving now. See ya in ten."

Her erratic heart beat thundered in her ears. She hated that he was coming, hated that he was walking into a trap.

"Who's it from?" Pinter asked from behind the bar.

"Jericho," she replied. "He's on his way."

"I can't fucking wait to take him down."

Pinter's eerie smile sent a terrifying chill careening down her spine.

Jericho had already checked the front and back doors of the club before texting Liv that he was on his way. Both were locked. Next, he'd called Hawk and told him what he was dealing with.

Despite the fury coursing through him, his thoughts were laser-focused on Liv. He was going to get her outta there alive and, then, he was gonna make that monster pay for what he'd done.

His phone buzzed in his pocket. Hawk was calling him back.

Jericho answered. "I'm about to breach the back door."

"I turned off the surveillance," Hawk said. "The circuit breaker is in their office. I overrode the system so you can get in there."

"Copy."

"I'm on my way." Hawk hung up.

Jericho shoved his phone in his pocket, aimed his Glock, and fired.

POP!

The silencer muffled the gunshot, but didn't eliminate it. Without a second to waste, he opened the door, slipped inside, and closed it silently behind him.

Then, he stilled.

He could hear a male's voice coming from the front of the club. Heat blanketed his chest.

Hang in there, baby.

In stealth mode, he made his way down the hallway. The office door was closed. He tried the handle. Locked. He stood in front of the scanner, the light turned green and he slipped inside.

Without making a sound, he opened the metal door covering the circuit breakers, found the main, and flipped it off, plunging the building into pitch-black darkness. He flipped down the night goggles on his helmet, strode down the hallway, and entered the main room.

Liv was sitting in a chair, her ankles and wrists zip-tied together. Relief pounded through him. She was alive. Her head was turned toward the bar.

He followed her gaze. A single lowball glass and a bottle of scotch sat on the bar. No Pinter.

He's hiding behind the bar.

Jericho took a step. And another. One more and the floor creaked. Pinter sprang up and fired.

BANG! BANG! BANG!

The bullets whizzed by his helmet. Jericho zeroed-in on his target and fired.

POP! POP! POP! POP! POP! POP!

21

MAKING THINGS RIGHT

Pinter dropped.
Jericho bolted to Liv, knelt down, and took her hands. "Babe, are you okay? Are you hurt?"

"Ohmygod, thank God. I can't see anything."

"Babe, you gotta confirm you're okay."

"I'm fine," she replied. "Were you hit?"

"No."

"Is he dead?"

"He oughta be. I pumped him pretty good. I've got night goggles, so I can see everything. He's behind the bar. Was he alone?"

"No one else showed up while he was here, but he was hiding in a toilet stall and we missed him when we cleared the place."

He laid a hand on her thigh. "I gotta leave you for a second to check on him before I turn on the lights. You gonna be okay?"

"Yes. Go."

Jericho jumped on the bar and stared down at Pinter. He was shot multiple times in the chest and once between the eyes. He didn't need to feel his carotid to know he'd taken him out.

He pulled his knife, knelt by Liv, and cut her free. "I'm so sorry," he murmured, pulling her to her feet and into his arms.

She pressed into him so tightly, he could feel her heart pounding hard and fast. "Thank you for saving me from him," she whispered. "Then *and* now."

"I'm gonna turn the breaker back on. Can you stand or do you need to sit back down?"

"I can stand."

Jericho bolted to her office, flipped up his goggles, and turned on the breaker. Light flooded the club. As he strode back to her, the anger in her eyes surprised him. He drew her flush against him and caressed her back, her warm body reminding him that she was okay. He hadn't been too late. He hadn't been able to save his brother, but he'd gotten to Liv in time.

"Thank you." Gazing up at him, she offered a little smile. "I knew you'd kick his ass. You did it once before."

Strangely, that made him laugh, though there was nothing funny about what had happened all those years ago… or now.

He broke away, called Hawk.

"I'm two minutes out," Hawk answered. "Stryker and Emerson are ten-to-fifteen minutes. Status?"

"Pinter's down. Liv's okay. I need clean up."

"How bad is it?"

"I pumped him full of bullets and he's bleedin' out pretty bad."

"Got it." Hawk hung up.

Jericho went behind the bar, staying clear of the blood. He pocketed Pinter's gun and his phone, then hurried back to Liv. She hadn't moved.

"I shouldn't have left you alone here," he said, wrapping her in his arms.

"If it's any consolation, he wasn't going to rape me. He was going to kill me after he killed you, but I knew you'd take him down. I'm just grateful you knew to come to the club. I was concerned you'd think I'd lost it."

"I knew something was wrong when you asked me to come over again."

"Are *you* okay?" she asked.

That stopped him. He just stared at her. "Do you want my canned answer or the real one?"

"I want you, raw and unfiltered."

"I'm pissed as fuck," he ground out, "but I'm relieved he didn't hurt you."

"You're so strong, all the damn time. I'm here for you, you know that, right?"

"I do."

"I'm here for as long as you want me to stick around," she murmured.

"I *never* want us to end."

She pushed on her toes and kissed him. "Then, we won't."

"It's that simple?" he asked.

"This time around, it's that simple."

The clean-up was fast and efficient. Pinter's body was rolled in a tarp and taken out the back by Jericho and Hawk. Moments later, Jericho returned with Stryker and Emerson in tow, but no Hawk. While Stryker and Emerson scrubbed the floor where Pinter had bled out, Liv logged in to the surveillance system so Jericho could delete all the surveillance videos from the entire evening. With that task completed, they wiped down every surface.

It was like nothing Liv had ever experienced and something she'd not soon forget.

When Hawk returned, he brought supplies to fix the back door where Jericho had blown out the lock.

She worked alongside trained ALPHA Operatives who were skilled at their jobs, even the illegal parts. When they finished, they placed their latex gloves and surgical masks in a bag, which Stryker took.

They said their goodbye's in the club, then left in silence. On the way home, Jericho stopped at The Road. Together, they went in through his private entrance in the back where he deposited Pinter's phone and gun into his safe.

Just before dawn, they returned to Jericho's guest house.

After showering, they crawled into bed. Jericho wrapped her in his arms and was asleep in seconds. Liv lay awake processing what had just happened. It was a lot to digest.

She woke just after eight, slipped out of bed, and dressed. Jericho hadn't stirred, so she left him to slumber. She eased onto a lounge chair by the pool and stared into the still water, last night's events still so vivid in her mind.

Without a doubt, Jericho was the love of her life. Being with him made her soul happy and completed her in so many ways. But could she spend her life with an ALPHA Operative? Could she accept him for who he was and what he did?

Would I be okay if the body rolled into a tarp was Jericho's?

Pain slashed through her chest and she rubbed it away with a soothing hand.

The door to the guest house opened and a bare-chested Jericho, wearing shorts and shades, made his way outside. His tousled hair made her smile.

He dragged a chair over, eased down beside her. "What's going on, babe?"

"Just thinking."

"You wanna talk about it?"

"I have questions."

He popped his sunglasses on his head. "Ask 'em."

"Where did Hawk take Pinter's body?"

"To a crematorium."

"Where did Stryker and Emerson take everything we used during clean up?"

"Crematorium."

"How do you know they won't use that evidence against you?"

"It's an ALPHA-run facility."

Ohmygod.

"Okay." She stared into his eyes. "I'm afraid that could happen to you."

"It won't."

"Jericho."

"Baby, we can't live our lives in fear. We gotta live like today is it. Not dwell on the past, not look too far ahead."

"I'm not always good at that."

"That's okay. Be *your* best you, whatever that is. What I don't want is you spending time stressing over things that might never happen." He took her hand, kissed her palm. "We're gonna grow old together. Kids, grandkids. I'm gonna love every minute with you. Every. Fucking. Minute. But, there're two of us and you gotta be okay with my life. I'm not good sittin' behind a desk. I love the restaurants, but I'm an Operative. That's who I am. What I'm meant to do."

She stared into his eyes, alight with confidence. She loved that about him.

"I'm trying to wrap my brain around everything. It's a lot to take in."

"I don't want to lie to you about anything, but I can keep things vague if you need me to."

She stroked his hand, held it in hers. "I want to be a part of your life, not the watered-down version. It's just gonna take some time, that's all."

"And I will be right there for you, the whole time."

Peering into his eyes, she knew. Living without him was *not* an option.

She kissed him, savoring his lips on hers. "With everything going on last night, I wanted to wait before I told you… I got Pinter to talk."

His eyebrows shot up. "Nice work."

"He said you weren't the target. Then, he said, 'Savage ain't got what it takes to outsmart me. I sent my guys out to scare him and the SOB fell right back in line behind me.' He added, 'You can't do business with me, then try to fuck me behind my back.'"

Jericho broke eye contact. His brows furrowed, his jaw ticked. She stayed quiet, giving him space to make sense of it.

Then, his eyes cleared. "You want something to eat?" He pushed off the chair.

She rose. "What are you thinking?"

"You were right. It's Vincent or my dad."

"Now, we've got to figure out which one… and why."

LIV NEEDED TO right a wrong that should have been fixed decades ago. After breakfast, she retreated into the guest house to make a call.

"Hello, honey," her mom answered. "How are you doing?"

"I wanted to swing by and talk to you and Dad."

"We'd love to see you. Dad's taking a couple of days off, but he's running an errand. He'll be back soon. Come by, we'll have coffee together."

"Be there shortly."

Liv found Jericho in the pool with the kids. He was so good with them. For a man who could be so ruthless, he was so patient and loving with the little ones.

"Play wif us!" Owen exclaimed, clinging to Jericho's back.

"I would love to, but I have to run out for a little while," she replied.

"Got a training class?" Jericho asked.

"Not today," she replied. "What's your schedule?"

"I'm at Kaleidoscope later this morning, then I might head to the casket company this afternoon."

She blew him a kiss.

"Oh, no," he boomed. "No virtual kissing." He pulled Owen over his shoulder and held him in one arm while he wrapped his other arm around Annie. Holding both, he walked through the shallow end and out of the pool.

Owen started crying. "Noooooo!" he wailed. "Swim!"

"Why aren't we having a lesson, Uncle Jericho?" Annie asked.

"I'm kissing Livy goodbye, then we'll swim."

"Yay!" Annie exclaimed as Owen settled back down.

As he made his way over, a trail of water followed. Inches away, he leaned down, and kissed her. She kissed him back. "I love you," he said.

"I love you." She kissed him again before addressing the kids. "Have a great lesson with Uncle Jericho. I can't wait to see what you learn." She grabbed her handbag and headed out.

On the drive over, she ran through what she'd say. By the time she pulled up to the house, she was ready to tell them the truth. It was long overdue.

She found her dad sipping coffee and reading something on his laptop at the kitchen table.

"Livingston, your mom said you'd be coming over."

"Hi, Dad." She dropped her handbag on a chair at the counter.

As she poured herself a coffee, he asked, "Aren't you working today?"

"I'm teaching a course tomorrow, in Gaithersburg." She set her mug on the table, held out the carafe. "More coffee?"

"Thank you."

She poured, returned the pot, and sat across from him. While she wasn't nervous per se, she wasn't looking forward to this conversation.

"Why aren't *you* working today?" she asked.

Her mom entered the room and smiled at Liv. "This is such a nice surprise." She poured herself coffee and sat next to Liv's Dad.

It felt like they were holding court.

"Mom and I have news," her dad blurted.

"Honey, Liv came by to talk to *us*."

"She'll get her turn." He regarded Liv. "I'm retiring at the end of the summer and your mom and I are moving to Bethany Beach in Delaware."

She slid her gaze from one to the other. With a smile, her mom clasped her dad's hand. Liv rarely saw them displaying any physical affection. Not only did her dad return the smile, he kissed her mom's cheek. Liv's gaze flitted from one to the other. It was like she'd been dropped into an alternate universe.

"Wow," Liv said. "Congratulations on retiring. That's huge. And a move, too. You guys *have* been busy."

"Your mom convinced me to do this. We're both pretty healthy. We don't have any grandchildren to keep us here—"

"Bernard, you promised me you wouldn't say anything negative," her mom snapped.

"It's a fact," he replied. "At the moment, we have no grandchildren."

Her mom pursed her lips.

"And we like visiting our friends at the beach," her dad continued, "so, we bought a condo and we close on it next week."

"I'm happy for you both," Liv said.

"We hope you'll come for a visit," her mom said. "There's plenty of room."

"I'd love that," Liv replied.

Here goes.

"So, I need to talk to you both about something... something important."

"Okay," said her mom.

"Did you decide to date Stanley?" her dad asked. "He's very interested in you, Livingston."

Ignoring that, she pressed on. "Something happened in high school and I lied about it. I'm here to tell you the truth."

"Hmm," said her dad.

Concern flashed in her mom's eyes. "All right."

"Do you remember junior year when Jericho Savage beat up some kid and they pressed charges against him?" Liv began.

"I remember that boy had two black eyes, a broken nose, and his jaw got busted," her dad said.

"I remember how withdrawn you were for months, and how sad you were when your friendship with Jericho ended," her mom added.

Liv regarded her parents. "I didn't tell you the truth. I lied because I was terrified of you, Dad. I was freaked you wouldn't pay for college, or you'd punish me for disobeying you. I made a terrible mistake that I've regretted for years."

Scowling, her dad set down his mug. "What are you talking about?"

"Jericho beat the living hell out of that boy because he was going to rape me."

Silence.

She waited, letting them absorb what she'd just told them.

"Ohmygod," her mom murmured.

Her dad stared at her, stone-faced.

"Tell us what happened, Livingston," her dad uttered. She recognized that tone. It was his "judge" tone, devoid of emotion, but the pain in his eyes told her how he was really feeling.

Even Judge Blackstone couldn't hide his anguish.

"I was never allowed to go to parties," she began. "One night, there was one in our neighborhood, just a street over, so I snuck out and went. I'd had a few beers and was pretty tipsy. I stayed close to Jericho most of the night, until I went to talk to some girlfriends. After a little while, I split off from them to use the downstairs bathroom. I'd been waiting in line when Perry Pinter, who was a senior, started talking to me. He told me there was a bathroom upstairs with no line, so I followed him up—"

"Oh, no," her mother whispered.

"He led me into the parent's room and over to their bathroom. As I was leaving their bedroom, he grabbed me and had me against the wall." Liv started shaking. She hated thinking about this, let alone talking about it.

After taking a few seconds, she continued.

"Jericho noticed I was gone, so he went looking for me. When he found me, he pulled the guy off me and beat him. He saw that I wasn't okay, so he told me to run home, so I wouldn't get in trouble. I did, never thinking Pinter's parents would press charges. When they did, Jericho told his mom and the police the truth. When they came here, to talk to you, you told them I was in my room all night." Her stomach was in knots. She hated herself for what she'd done. "I should have come forward to clear Jericho's name and to keep him out of juvi, but I was too afraid. Jericho never talked to me again and I lost my best friend."

Deafening silence for several long seconds.

"Were you sexually assaulted?" her dad asked.

"No. Jericho pulled him off me before he'd done anything." She broke into a cold sweat. Pushing away from the table, she dumped the hot drink in the sink, then filled a glass with cold water and drank it down before returning to the table.

"I shouldn't have gone to the party, but I wanted to know what I was missing out on. I should have stayed with Jericho all night. I made so many bad decisions, but the worst one I made was not standing up for someone I cared about, someone who'd been there for me. I failed him completely and I regretted it."

To her surprise, tears filled her dad's eyes. "I treated Jericho horribly. He saved you from hell, Livy." Choking back a sob, her dad walked out of the room.

Tears streamed down Liv's cheeks and her mom got up and hugged her. Ugly, sobbing tears poured out of her. Decades worth of pain, guilt, and the loss of a loyal, faithful friend.

When she finally stopped crying, her mom brought her a box of tissues. She was a mess, but at least they knew the truth.

"I have more to tell you both," Liv said.

"I'll go get Dad."

"I'm here," her father said from the doorway. "Sorry about that." He sat back down.

"When Bryan Savage was gunned down, I reached out to Jericho to offer my condolences. He forgave me for what I'd done, but he asked me to make it right with you. We've fallen in love and I would marry him today, if he asked me. You needed to know that he was my hero that night, not the villain." She smiled. "And he's my hero, now, too."

"I see," her dad murmured.

"After his mom died, he gave up his dream of becoming a Navy SEAL, requested guardianship of his four younger siblings. Initially, he raised them on his own, until his Gram could move in to help him. He bought her this absolutely stunning estate in McLean, and his siblings still live with him. I've never met anyone so loyal, so loving, so fierce. He's the most amazing man I've ever met. Dad, I want you to treat him with the utmost respect and not be rude to him going forward.

"We owe him an apology and our gratitude," said her mom. "I feel terrible."

"Why don't you both come for dinner tonight?" her dad suggested.

Both women gaped at him. "How nice, Bernard," said her mom.

"Dad, I'm not sure about that."

"I'll grill."

"It's not the menu I'm worried about," Liv said.

"I will be *very* nice to him," her dad insisted. "It's the least I can do."

That evening, Jericho opened the passenger door of the Escalade for Liv, then realized she was waiting for him at her car.

"I'll drive," she called over.

"Works for me." He got in beside her, slid the seat back and opened the window. "You gonna tell me where we're going?"

"Eventually." She drove up the long driveway and onto the street.

"You look beautiful," he said, resting his hand on her thigh. She'd worn a black skirt, a bright pink shirt, and sandals. She'd dressed more conservatively that he expected, but he had no idea where they were going.

She shot him a little smile. "You look handsome. I love when you wear your hair like that."

He'd worn a casual shirt and long shorts. Rather than leave his hair down, he'd pulled it into a half bun.

She nibbled on her finger. He hadn't seen her do that in years. "How are you handling everything that went down with Pinter?"

"I thought I'd be a wreck, but I'm not. There's been so much that's happened since we've been together, it's become one overwhelming blur. Rather than try to analyze every little thing, I'm just going with it."

"Wow, that's a change."

She flashed a smile. "Small steps, right?" He squeezed her thigh in acknowledgment. "Did you talk to your brother today?"

"No. I'm swinging by ALPHA tomorrow to talk to Cooper. He's always been a good sounding board."

They drove in a comfortable silence until she pulled into an upscale neighborhood in Potomac.

"Who lives here?" he asked.

"My parents," she replied.

He laughed. "If you think I'm gettin' out of the car, you don't know me."

"When I left this morning, I came here and talked to them." She parked out front, glanced over at him. "I told them the truth."

He wasn't expecting that. "Okay."

"The entire truth," she continued." Everything." She cut the engine, shifted toward him. "My dad cried. He had to leave the room. He felt terrible about what he put you through. He suggested we come over for dinner."

"If he says one thing—"

"We'll leave," Liv said. "Today was cathartic for me. Telling them the truth freed me." She leaned over, kissed him. "I'm sorry for everything I put you through. My dad became the bad guy, but it was my fault. I blame myself." Silence for a few beats. "If you don't want to go in—"

Jericho had to do this, for Liv's sake. He had every intention of being in her life for a long, long time. He didn't want things to be tense between him and her parents every time they got together. Family meant everything to him. He had to give them a chance.

He kissed her. "I wish I'd known. I woulda brought a bottle of wine."

"This time, I've got your back." She opened the door, pulled a wine bag with handles from the back seat. "It's their favorite." After she handed him the decorative bag, he pulled out the wine, examined the bottle. "This is good." He stashed the wine back in the gift bag. "Thanks for doing this, babe."

With a tight smile, she threaded her fingers through his. Up the driveway they walked. The garage door was closed, so they made their way down the walkway. Before opening the front door, she turned to him. "You deserve their gratitude and respect." Standing on her toes, she kissed him.

Loving Livy was getting easier and easier. "Thank you for telling them the truth."

"You ready?"

"Absolutely."

She opened the front door.

"We're here," she called.

Liv's mom walked into the foyer, a strained smile on her face. "Hi, honey. Jericho, thank you for coming to dinner."

Normally, an offensive player, he would let them do all the heavy lifting. "Hello, Mrs. Blackstone."

"Please, call me Valerie."

Liv's dad ambled toward him. While Jericho was taller and more solid, the judge was a formidable man. He kissed Liv on the cheek, then extended his hand to Jericho.

This time, Jericho shook it, then offered the wine to both of them. "For you."

Her dad took the bag, pulled out the bottle. "Thank you. This is our favorite. Let's have a glass."

He led them toward the kitchen.

Jericho was good at reading people. They looked like they'd heard the truth and it had sunk in. Once the wine had been poured, Liv's mom suggested they sit on the screened porch. Normally, Jericho led a conversation. Not by talking about himself, but by asking questions. Tonight, he stayed silent.

Liv and Jericho sat together on the sofa. Liv's mom and Dad got comfortable on cushioned patio chairs nearby.

"Jericho, I take full responsibility for what happened," Liv's dad began. "I was a very strict father. Today, I learned that my daughter was terrified of me." He cleared his throat. "I had an absentee dad, so I went overboard in the other direction. Trying to balance the scales backfired. Valerie and I are beyond grateful that you stopped Perry Pinter from raping Liv. For years, you'd been a good friend to her. I should have dug deeper, spoken to you myself. I regret my harsh manner toward you. I was myopic in my ability to make the right decision in this particular case."

"Thank you," Jericho said.

"I regret misjudging you and I am truly sorry."

Jericho acknowledged him with a simple nod.

"I, too, want to apologize to both of you," Valerie said. "As a mom, I should have asked Livy why she'd become so withdrawn, and why you stopped coming around. I should have been that safe space, that person she could confide in, but she was so scared of Bernard she didn't tell me her secrets. I failed you both, but I won't make that mistake again. I'm deeply sorry."

"Thank you," Jericho said.

"Thanks, Mom," Liv added.

"I made a few calls today after Livingston left," her dad said. "I'm going to make sure your juvi record gets expunged. I will make it up to you—to *both* of you. I don't know how or when, but I know why."

"Thank you, Dad."

After a pause, Liv took Jericho's hand in hers and turned toward him. "I've apologized to you, but I need to apologize again in front of my parents. You were my hero that night and I treated you horribly. I regretted it all these years, but I never once came forward to right the wrong. I was living with a lie and with the guilt of doing the wrong thing. I'm sorry for not being your friend, especially when you needed me the most. I will *never* make that mistake again."

She leaned up, dropped a soft kiss on his lips.

The hatred and contempt Jericho had been carrying with him all these years fell away. It was a good start to helping mend his broken relationship with her parents.

Pushing off the sofa, Jericho extended his hand. Valerie rose and hugged him. When she let go, tears welled in her eyes..

Bernard stood and held out his hand. Jericho shook it. "You make my daughter very happy. I appreciate that you forgave her and I hope you'll do the same for us."

"In time," Jericho replied.

During dinner, they both asked him a lot of questions about his restaurants. They were making an effort, and he appreciated that. After dinner, Liv stacked the dishes.

"I've got some Davidoff Signature Series cigars," Bernard said. "Interested in a smoke?"

"Sure," Jericho replied.

"I'll get them." Bernard retreated inside.

"I made a strawberry shortcake," Valerie said. "I'll put on a pot of coffee."

As Liv and Valerie disappeared into the house, Bernard returned with the cigars.

The tobacco was top quality, the draw smooth. After a few puffs, Jericho said, "I want you to know my intentions with Liv. She means everything to me and I'm going to ask her to marry me."

"I don't have to ask if you'll put her first, or keep her safe, or provide for your family. You've already shown us how much she means to you. You're a good man, Jericho."

"Thank you."

"I'd be damn proud to call you my son-in-law."

After a few more puffs, Jericho said, "I'd like to tell Valerie." He set the cigar in the ashtray.

"You can send Livingston out here."

On a nod, Jericho retreated inside to find the women sitting at the kitchen table talking. "Babe, your dad asked for you."

She kissed him before heading toward the porch.

"Tell me about your family," Valerie said.

"Before I do, I want you to know my intentions with Liv. I'm asking her to marry me. While it might seem fast—"

Valerie smiled. "That's wonderful news. I remember how close you two were. You always brought out the best in her."

"Goes both ways."

"Thank you for being so gracious tonight. You have a lot of reasons to hate us."

"I have more reasons to let it go," Jericho replied. "I never stopped loving Liv and she'll always be my top priority."

"She's a lucky woman."

"I'm the lucky one, Valerie."

"I'd say you're a great match."

That made him smile. "I gotta agree with you on that."

22

TAKING HIS SHOT

Liv's all-day workshop in Gaithersburg had been a successful one. After stopping by the captain's office to thank him, she left the precinct. It was almost six thirty in the evening. With phone to ear, she called Jericho.

"Hey, babe," he answered. "You headed back?"

"Just leaving."

"How'd it go?"

"Great. Lots of good questions and feedback. Where can I find my man?" She opened her car door, stashed her things.

"I'm at The Road. We're having new mechanical bull installed."

"Fun. Are you gonna be the first to ride?"

"The only one I'm ridin' is you, darlin'."

She laughed. "I can't wait. Should I swing by?"

"After the new Beast is in, I'm heading to Carole Jean's to sign off on a hundred grand of specialty wines and champagnes for the new cellar. Swing by for wine tasting with me and Georgia."

"I'd love that. What time?" She got behind the wheel, turned on the engine, and cranked up the air.

"Around nine."

"Perfect. That'll give me time to stop by your place and change."

"We gotta talk about that."

"I know. I need to find my own—"

"No way are you leaving," he interrupted, "but I don't want you livin' in the guest house. We'll figure it out. I gotta run, babe. The guys are here for the install. I'll meet you at Carole Jean's."

She hung up, checked the map app. With traffic, she was an hour from Jericho's house. As she pulled out of the parking lot, she thought about moving in with him and his family.

Will I fit in? Will they be okay with me living there?

The miles crawled by as she slogged her way through traffic. Forty minutes in, her phone rang with a call from Sergeant Hayes.

"Hey, Liv, it's Andre. How's it going?"

"On my way back from a full-day course with Gaithersburg PD."

"They're a great group. How'd it go?"

"Very well. What's going on?"

"Brenda and I have been talking about you and Jericho. I feel terrible that I went after him. You and I had a great working relationship and I kinda derailed that. To get us back on track, Brenda and I want to gift you the painting of the Family on the Beach."

Wow.

"Andre, thank you, but I can't accept that. You were just doing your job."

"I was, but I got this one all wrong. Brenda's the one who suggested we gift you the painting. She said she's been going through some stuff and you've been there for her."

Liv wanted to tell him the truth. She would want to know if Jericho had stepped out on her, but she didn't want to insert herself into something that wasn't her business. And certainly not over the phone.

"You there, Liv?"

"Sorry, yeah. I don't feel comfortable accepting such a generous gift."

"When Brenda makes up her mind, watch out. Why don't we do this? You and Jericho swing by the gallery tonight, eight o'clock. Just look at it. You don't have to take it. Jericho might not even like it."

"I don't know…"

"We'll have some wine. Bren will give you a private gallery showing. It'll be fun. I'm not taking no for an answer. See you then." The line went dead.

There's no way I'm taking a ten-thousand-dollar painting.

She returned to Jericho's to find Gram, alone, in the kitchen. "Where's everyone?" Liv asked.

"Georgia and Jericho are working. Timmy, Patty, and the kids are having dinner with friends. Mark is at the hospital."

"Have you eaten?" Liv asked. "I can make us something."

"I'm having dinner with friends."

"That sounds fun."

"One of my friends drives at night and she's picking me up. Where are you headed?"

Liv checked the time. "I'm meeting Jericho at Carole Jean's, but first, I'm stopping by an art gallery to see a friend."

The doorbell chimed and Gram rose. "That's my ride." She patted Liv's arm. "Have a fun evening, dear."

"You too."

On her way toward the guest house, she called Jericho.

He answered. "Hey, babe."

"I'm making a quick stop at Brenda Hayes' art gallery."

"What for?"

"Andre called. He and Brenda want to extend us an olive branch. She wants me to have a painting I fell in love with. I'm not taking it, but I told him I'd stop by."

"When you get to Carole Jean's, tell the maître d' you're here to see me."

After showering, and dressing in a sundress and open-toed heels, she left. Thirty-minutes later, she arrived in Alexandria. The neighborhood, a bustling mecca of workers during the day, cleared out in the evening. She street-parked a few storefronts down from The Hayes and made her way to the gallery.

Andre was inside, toward the back, on his phone.

Knock-knock-knock.

He didn't hear her, so she rang the doorbell. He shot her a wave as he strode toward the front door. Before opening it, he pocketed his phone.

"Come on in."

She stepped inside and he shut the door behind her.

"What happened to Jericho?" he asked.

"Unfortunately, he couldn't make it on such short notice."

"No problem," Andre said. "More wine for the three of us."

He led her though the gallery "Brenda's upstairs in her office. I warned her you aren't going to take it, so she marked it down to a hundred dollars."

"What about the artist who painted it?"

"Brenda will make up the difference."

He led the way up the worn wooden stairs. On the second floor, paintings rested against both walls of the hallway, three rows deep.

"Lots of inventory," Andre said as he headed toward the open doorway, the light bleeding into the hallway.

They entered Brenda's office. The lake painting was leaning against the desk.

"Where's Brenda?" she asked.

"She must've stepped into the restroom."

As he shut the door behind her, the hairs on the back of her neck prickled. When Andre turned back, he pointed a gun at her. Dread pounded through her.

"Andre, what are you doing?"

In that second, everything became crystal clear.

Sergeant Hayes was the leak Uncle Z had wanted her to find. He'd been working with the Thriller Killers to ensure the DEA arrests didn't happen. She thought he was one of the good guys. Clearly, she had him all wrong.

Andre walked into the middle of the room. "Have a seat."

She lunged toward the door. He got there first, blocking her only escape route. Wrapping a firm hand around her arm, he led her to the wooden chair in the middle of the room.

"Sit."

She didn't want to cooperate. She wanted to fight him. Yanking her arm away, she made another attempt to flee. This time, he grabbed her arm, shoved her into the chair, and pointed the barrel of the pistol at her face.

"Don't make this harder on yourself, Liv."

Fear had her heart pounding hard. Every muscle in her chest tightened and she couldn't breathe. Little stars floated into her vision. Sucking down a breath, she shook away the fear as best she could.

He glared down at her. "Your little boyfriend has fucked with me for the last time. He needs to be moved out of the way and you're gonna help me do that."

"What are you talking about?"

"An associate of mine named Pinter has vanished. A few days before he went missing, he told me that Jericho took out everyone in his house. My gut tells me Jericho got to him, too."

"Jericho runs restaurants, Andre. You've got the wrong man."

"I'm one damn shipment away from a once-in-a-lifetime payout. This time, tomorrow, I'll be a rich man... and the next day, I'll be relaxing on a tropical beach. Jericho has been a pain in my ass ever since his brother got killed. This time, he is *not* getting in my way. You and your boyfriend need to be silenced... for good.

Jericho watched as crates of wine were delivered to Carole Jean's restaurant cellar.

"This is so exciting," Georgia said.

"This is so expensive," Jericho muttered.

His sister laughed. "We've got a Michelin-starred restaurant with some of the best wines in the world. Makes perfect sense to me. Is Livy doing the tasting with us?"

"Yeah. She'll be here soon," he replied.

The maître d' trotted down the steps and hurried over. "Mr. Savage, your brother, Vincent, is asking for you."

I don't have time for this.

"What does he want?" Jericho asked.

"He wouldn't tell me, but he doesn't have reservations and he's not dressed appropriately."

"Do you think Vincent wants a free meal?" Georgia asked.

"Probably," Jericho replied.

"You want me to handle it?" Georgia asked.

"I'll go. Can you manage this?"

"Of course," his sister replied.

Jericho and the maître d' found Vincent waiting upstairs. While he *was* wearing a white button-down and pants, he had no jacket. No jacket, no service. No exceptions.

"Whatcha need?" Jericho asked.

Vincent threw his arms out. "What kind of a greeting is that for your fave bro?"

Not amused, Jericho folded his arms over his chest. "I'm in the middle of something, Vincent."

Brenda walked over. "That restroom is to die for. Absolutely stunning. Hello, Jericho."

"Hi, Brenda," Jericho said, then his brain shorted. "What are you doing here?"

"We was hoping to have dinner," Vincent said, "but your butler here—"

"No," Jericho said, cutting him off. "Brenda, why aren't you at your gallery?"

"Why would I be there?" she replied. "It closes at six on Fridays."

His blood turned to ice.

"Where's your husband?"

"I, er... um—" stuttered Brenda.

"Answer the question," Jericho roared.

Several customers looked in his direction.

"He's at poker night."

Every muscle in his body tensed. *Fuck, no.*

Jericho whipped his gaze to his maître d'. "Escort them out. Tell Georgia I had an emergency."

Jericho ran into the parking lot, jumped in his truck, and peeled out of the parking lot. On his way to The Road, he called Liv. Her phone rang. "Come on, come on. Pick up."

She didn't. He hung up and hit the gas. He flew into The Road parking lot, drove around back, and strode inside through his private entrance. He opened his go-bag, confirming everything was in there. With his duffle in one hand, he bolted.

He'd been on dozens of missions for ALPHA, but this one mattered the most. This one was personal. His mind on full thrusters, he ran through scenarios, liking each new one less and less.

If he's already killed her—

Refusing that option, he screeched to a halt a few doors down from the gallery and spotted Liv's car parked nearby.

The street was quiet. Despite the warm evening, this part of Alexandria had little foot traffic because everyone headed over to Old Town. With his go-bag in hand, he glanced over at the gallery. The downstairs was dark, but there was a light on upstairs. He assumed there were surveillance cameras outside, so he couldn't risk trying the door without being seen.

What the fuck is going on?

Jericho flicked his focus to the building across the street.

I gotta get a visual.

He hot-footed-it across the street and ran around the back of the building. The second he eyed the fire escape that ran the height of the building, he turned off his phone.

Time for stealth mode.

With his go-bag draped across his shoulder and over his back, he climbed up the old, metal stairs, hoping his weight wouldn't bring him crashing to the ground. At the rooftop, he hurried to the edge, set down his bag and extracted his binos. Liv was sitting in a chair, facing his direction. Andre sat across from her, partially blocking his view of her.

The sergeant rose. Jericho's greatest fear was realized. Andre held a gun in his hand.

Andre had been rambling about him and Brenda spending the rest of their lives relaxing on a sunny beach. Earlier, her phone had buzzed in her handbag. She hoped that call had been from Jericho, but when her phone hadn't buzzed again, her hope had fizzled.

He's not coming.

She'd have to figure out a way out by herself… or die trying.

"Andre, we're friends," Liv said after he'd stopped ranting. "You've been so good to me by helping me launch my consulting business. I don't know who your associate *thought* he saw, but it wasn't Jericho. Jericho's got a brother who's moved back to the area. Maybe it was him."

"Vincent? Yeah, I know him. He's not taking out the TKs."

"How do you know, Vincent?"

"We met at a shooting range. Had a few beers together."

She sucked down a breath. "Did Brenda meet him?"

"He came to the house one night for dinner."

She needed to get Andre on her side. Make him believe she

was his ally. She had a risky plan that could work, but it might backfire if Andre decided to take his anger out on the messenger.

Here goes.

"Vincent is having an affair with your wife."

Andre laughed. "Vincent?" He shook his head. "There's no way."

"I saw them together at Jericho Road. That's why Brenda wants me to have the painting. She's trying to buy my silence because she's worried I'll tell you."

Crossing his arms, Andre glowered at her. "That's not possible."

"It's the truth, Andre. Where is she now?"

"At home."

"Why don't you let me call her, so you can hear for yourself?"

His eyes turned beady, his lips slashed in a thin line.

"Get my phone and I'll make the call," she said.

He fished out her phone. She told him her password. He punched it in, dialed his wife's number, put the call on speaker.

"Hello?" Brenda answered.

"Hi, Brenda. It's Liv Blackstone. Did I catch you at a good time?"

"Your boyfriend just threw us out of Carole Jean's. I'm so bummed."

"Are you with Andre?" Liv asked.

"No, Vincent."

"Hey," Vincent said. "Bren put you on speaker. I thought Jericho and I were buds, but he wouldn't seat me. What's up with that?"

"Fuck," Andre muttered under his breath. "That son of a bitch."

"What happened?" Liv asked.

"I called for reservations but they're booked months in advance," Brenda explained. "Vincent thought Jericho would give him special treatment, so we went there. I got a new dress and everything."

Despite the anxiety coursing through her, Liv's heart broke for Andre. First, surprise flashed in his eyes, then sadness. Now, his jaw ticked and his eyes were black with anger.

She hoped her plan wasn't about to backfire on her.

"Where are you now?" Liv asked.

"I don't even know. Some chain restaurant. What's up? Why are you calling?"

"Take me off speaker," Liv said.

"Yeah, you're off. What's going on?" Brenda asked.

"You've been so conflicted about your affair, I was worried about you. I thought maybe you decided to break it off with Vincent."

"Ugh, I don't know. Vincent's so sexy. I can't keep my hands off him. But I love Andre and we've been together forever. Our food's here. Gotta go." Brenda hung up.

"What a bitch," Andre seethed. "What a fucking little bitch."

Jericho had been laying prone on the rooftop, locked in position, for five minutes. Every time he thought he had a clean shot, Andre would move out of his frame, leaving Liv in his crosshairs. Then, Andre dialed a phone and held it out for her. She spent three minutes on a call. When the call ended, Andre threw the phone on the floor.

Then, he started pacing, back and forth in front of the window. Liv was talking, but he couldn't read lips. Finally, Andre stopped in front of her.

Take the shot.

Then, Andre raised his arm, pointed his gun at Liv.

Everything went into slow-mo. Jericho homed in on Andre. Slow inhale, hold. He pulled the trigger.

BANG!

Andre fell to the ground.

Jericho shoved his gun and tripod into his bag, threw it over his back, and flew down the fire escape. Bolting across the street, he tried the front door. Locked.

He kicked it in, then went charging up the stairs, two at a time, and burst into the room.

Liv was kneeling next to Andre.

Their eyes met and he breathed again. She ran to him, threw her arms around him.

"Thank you," she whispered, clinging tightly.

"I got you," he said. "Are you injured?"

"No." She broke away, knelt by Andre. "Please tell me he's not dead."

Despite what she'd been through, she was putting the sergeant first. Jericho felt his pulse. It was silent.

"I'm sorry," Jericho murmured. "He's gone."

With a shaking hand, Liv closed Andre's eyes as she choked out a sob while tears flooded her cheeks.

"I liked him," she whispered. "He was so good to me. Such a nice guy. I'm so grateful you got here in time, but—" She stopped. "I wish this had had a different outcome, that's all."

"I'm sorry, Livy. He had a gun and he pointed it at you."

"I know." She rose.

"Let's get you downstairs."

On the first floor, Jericho made a call.

"Hey, bro," Cooper answered.

"Coop, I need your help," Jericho replied.

23

GONE MISSING

The case Liv's Uncle Z had hired her to do—before he'd fired her—had been solved. She'd found the leak in the Alexandria PD. Never once had she suspected that Andre Hayes had been that person.

Despite the ordeal he'd just put her through, Andre had opened doors for her professionally. He'd been easy to work with, was positive and friendly, but behind the scenes he'd been cozying up to Perry Pinter and taking money for shipments. He'd also been alerting Pinter about the gang raids so Pinter's guys weren't getting arrested.

While Andre was a good man, he'd been a dirty cop.

When Jericho hung up with Cooper, he told her that Cooper would be calling the police. They arrived on the scene first, then Cooper and Danielle showed up sporting DEA badges. They were there on official ALPHA business.

Not long after that, the crime scene techs arrived.

"I'm sorry you got caught up in all of this, Liv," Cooper said. "How are you doing?"

"I'm okay," Liv replied.

Danielle finished up with a call and returned to the group. "A homicide detective from a different precinct will be handing the case. APD will be undergoing an internal investigation to determine if Sergeant Hayes was working alone."

Though Liv's gut told her he had been, she stayed quiet. No one but Jericho knew she'd been a watcher—or that such a position even existed. She'd already dug her grave with her uncle, no need to make things worse for herself.

"If you experience any symptoms of PTSD," Cooper began, "we can help you find a therapist."

"She *is* a therapist," Jericho said.

"Well, she can't treat herself," Cooper quipped.

"I'm fine, really," Liv said. "I liked the sergeant. I'm sad he got caught up in everything. Who tells his wife?"

"Two of the responding officers," Cooper replied.

"That's gonna be hard for her," Liv said.

"She was cheating on him," Jericho replied. "How hard is it gonna be?"

Liv ran her hand down his back. "Honey, just because she was doing something that we don't agree with, doesn't mean she didn't love her husband. Relationships are complicated, you know that."

"Spoken like a true psychologist," Cooper said.

One of the crime scene techs came downstairs with a bag and joined the group.

"Excuse me, Agent Grant, I wanted you to see this." With a gloved hand, he removed the gun from the clear, plastic bag. "The sergeant was using a ghost gun. These guns have become really popular with gangs. Since you're dealing with a lot of drug-related arrests, I wanted you to see this before we take it to the station."

The tech displayed the handgun on his gloved palm. Cooper and Jericho crowded around as if he were doling out candy.

"The majority of ghost guns are similar to popular handguns, but without a serial number." The tech pointed to something on the gun's handle. "I've never seen this before."

"What is that?" Cooper asked.

"It's a logo," Jericho replied as he and Cooper exchanged glances. "Coop, I gotta fly."

Cooper offered a single nod.

Those two were operating on a completely different level that came from years of knowing each other, working together, and having each other's backs.

It was after midnight when Jericho ushered Liv to his truck.

"My car is here," she protested.

His eyebrows shot up, crowding his forehead. "You okay to drive?"

"I don't want to come back here tomorrow."

"After I take you home, I'm heading to The Road."

"I'll follow you there."

"You sure you're up for this?"

"We can sleep *after* we get to the truth."

He wrapped his arms around her, drew her close, and stared into her eyes. "I promise you, this is *not* how our lives are going to be."

"It's definitely more intense than when I was a watcher, but I wouldn't trade any of this. If I did, there would be no you. There would be no us."

He kissed her, peered into her eyes. "Our life, our rules."

"What happened to my life, my rules?"

"A brilliant, beautiful woman once told me, 'No matter what we decide, we're doing this together.'"

Her heart leapt. "You sure about that?"

"It's *our* life now, babe, and we're gonna write our own rules."

She hugged him. "I love you so much, Jericho."

Holding her tightly in his arms, he murmured, "I love you, Livy, with everything I am."

Fifteen minutes later, they entered The Road through his private entrance. In his office, he asked her if she wanted something to eat.

She loved that he was always thinking of her, always putting her first. "I can't eat. My stomach's in knots."

He gestured for her to sit on the sofa. After she did, he eased down beside her. "You gotta be healthy. I don't want you stressing. I'm concerned this is too much for you."

"Thank you for loving me so fiercely." She offered a grateful smile. "I'm okay, well, okay enough." She regarded him for an extra beat. "Something happened when you saw Andre's ghost gun. I saw it in your eyes, and I saw you and Cooper exchange glances."

"I've seen that logo before," Jericho replied.

Jericho retreated into his inner sanctum and withdrew the Thriller Killer's guns from his safe. His hunch proved right. He set them down on the sofa cushion between them.

"These are Lucky and Slim Jim's guns," he explained. "And this is Pinter's." He showed her the black logo on all three weapons.

She studied it for a few seconds. "Is that a lion's head?"

"Yeah. Guns have serial numbers. These don't. They're ghost guns. I never even looked at the guns. Just shoved 'em in my safe. It never occurred to me that they were ghost guns. Fucking rookie mistake."

"Was that the logo on Andre's gun?"

He nodded as the anger took hold. "You know where I first saw that logo?"

She shook her head.

"On a metallic blue gun my brother used when we went to the shooting range."

"Ohmygod."

"I asked him about it because I'd never seen a metallic blue gun or one with a logo. Ghost guns are unidentifiable. That's why they're called ghost guns. People can order kits, make 'em at home. Criminals love 'em because they're untraceable." He held up one of the ghost guns. "Except for these."

"Because of the logo," Liv said.

"Right."

"Do you think Vincent got his ghost gun from Pinter?"

"He told me our dad gave it to him. I think Roger Savage is doing business with the Thriller Killers as a way to pay off his gambling debt."

Liv's phone started buzzing in her bag. She fished it out. "It's Brenda."

"You can't tell her you know anything or that he was holding you hostage," Jericho warned. "She could be his accomplice."

"Got it." Liv put the call on speaker. "Hello."

"Liv," Brenda said between sobs. "It's Brenda Hayes. Andre's dead!"

"Oh, no! I'm so sorry," Liv replied. "What happened?"

Liv slid her gaze to Jericho. He caressed her back, the need to touch her, to comfort her always in the forefront of his mind. Even now, despite the tension, all the lives lost, and so many unanswered questions, there was an invisible force pulling them together.

"The police just left," Brenda continued. "They asked a lot of questions, but couldn't tell me anything because the investigation is open." She started crying again. "This is so shocking. I know you worked with him, so I wanted you to know."

"I'm so sorry for your loss," Liv said. "Do you have a friend or family member you can stay with for a few days?"

"Vincent was here earlier, but he left. He's on his way back over. We'd talked about getting out of town together and starting over."

Liv stilled while the silence hung like stagnant air over them. Jericho nudged her, snapping her back to the present.

"I'm surprised to hear that," Liv said.

"I decided to leave Andre," Brenda said. "Vincent said he

missed being in the Midwest and was sick of having to deal with his dad. Sounds like they don't get along. Anyway, I'm sorry to call so late, but I wanted you to know."

"Thank you for telling me," Liv said. "I'm here if you want to talk again." She hung up and peered over at Jericho.

"Andre told me something, but I didn't want to mention it in front of the police," Liv said. "He said he was one shipment away from a once-in-a-lifetime payout and, by this time tomorrow, he'd be wealthy."

"Hmm."

"He had no idea Brenda was having an affair and he didn't believe me when I told him."

"Was that the phone call he made?" Jericho asked.

"Yeah. You saw that?"

"I was across the street on the rooftop, trying to get a clean shot. You know, babe, your plan could have backfired. He could have shot you."

"I was buying myself time and trying to come up with a plan." She clasped his hand, threaded her fingers through his. "I tried to escape, twice, but he was faster and stronger. Fortunately, my hero saved me... again."

"Always." Jericho kissed her cheek, letting his lips linger on her skin.

Touching her calmed him. Knowing she was safe allowed him to breathe easier.

"I called Brenda and put her on speaker," Liv continued. "When Andre heard her talking about your brother, it was difficult to watch." Scooting close, she placed both hands on his cheeks. "I will love you for the rest of my life, but if I'm not enough, tell me. Honesty, no matter how difficult it is to hear, is better than lies and deception."

He pulled her onto his lap, kissed her. "You are my dream girl. You will always be more than enough. Always. I will tell you the truth, but I know how I feel about you. You're stuck with me."

She smiled, kissed him. "You're stuck with me, too."

The air crackled with intensity as they stared into each other's eyes.

This is it... forever.

Then, with her in his arms, he lifted off the sofa, and stood. Then, he set her on the floor. "Let's go home and catch a few hours' sleep."

It was after two in the morning when they pulled down the street. As he drove down his long driveway, he blurted, "What the hell?"

Every front-facing light in the house was on. They parked out front and hurried inside. The family was huddled together in the family room. Georgia broke from the group and rushed over.

"Oh, thank God you're back," she said. "We're been calling you for hours."

Jericho pulled his phone from his pocket, eyed the missed calls and texts. "What's going on?" His gaze swept from Tim to Patty, then to Mark—still in his scrubs. His dad stood in the corner, phone to ear. The kids weren't there and neither was Gram.

"Gram is missing," Tim blurted.

Jericho stilled. He flicked his gaze to his father, then back to Tim. Then, he went into mission mode. Laser-focused, he called his grandmother's cell. The call rolled right to voicemail. Either her phone had been turned off or it was out of juice.

"Walk me through the timeline," Jericho said.

Everyone started talking at the same time. Jericho held up a hand. "Who was the last person to see Gram?"

"I was," his dad said, joining the group.

He eyed his father. Dark circles under his eyes. His shoulders were slumped. At first glance, Roger Savage looked anxious, but just because the man appeared worried didn't mean jack.

Jericho gritted his teeth. He needed information, so rather than go off on the man, he lasered in on him. "What happened?"

"Gram had a book club meeting and I offered to drive her," his dad began. "I came by at six. I was early. She was ready, so we sat in the kitchen and talked."

"What about?" Jericho asked.

"How is that relevant?" Tim blurted.

"Shh," Georgia said.

"I asked her about the book she'd read for her meeting. I asked about her health. She talked about all of you. I asked about your mom, but she wouldn't talk about her."

Again, Jericho fought the urge to rip into him. His dad had no right asking anything about a family he'd abandoned.

"What else?" Jericho prodded.

"I told her about my business. We left at quarter to seven and got to the home in Tysons ten minutes later. Gram said she was fine walking in alone, but I walked her to the door and said hello to the man who answered. Gram knew him. It was her friend's husband. I told Gram I'd be back to pick her up. She told me the meeting ended at nine, but they'd be chatting until about nine-thirty. I told her I'd be there by nine-fifteen, and I left."

Jericho's mind was filled with possibilities, none of them good. "Where'd you go?"

"The mall."

"Which one?" Jericho asked.

His dad stared at him.

"There are *two*." Agitation tinged his tone. Minutes mattered. Jericho needed a detailed summary in two minutes, not ten. "Tysons Corner Center or Tyons Galleria?"

His dad shrugged. "I haven't lived in the area—"

"What did you do there?" Jericho asked, cutting him off.

"I ate at the food court, then checked in with the Norman team. That's the facility in Oklahoma. It was six-thirty, their time, and I knew a few of them would still be there. Then, I walked the mall. I left at quarter to nine, but when I got to the car, I had two flat tires. I had a spare, but needed a second tire. By the time I got to the house, it was an hour later. The woman said Gram had already left."

Jericho's stomach dropped. He flicked his gaze to his siblings. They looked as concerned as he felt. "Who picked her up?"

"The woman said that Gram went outside with one of the other ladies and the hostess didn't see who picked her up," his dad explained.

Jericho stalked over to his dad. "I will kill you if you did anything to her." He glared down at him. "If you made up that story—"

"Jericho!" Mark yelled. "Dad didn't do anything to Gram. You gotta take it down a few."

Jericho cracked his neck, but the tension wouldn't release.

"Did anyone check the hospitals?" Jericho asked.

"Hours ago," Mark replied. "Nothing."

"What about the surveillance cameras on the house where she went?"

"No one has the number," Georgia replied. "I think she went to Millie's tonight."

Jericho swung his gaze to his dad. "Go back there and ask them," he growled.

"Now?" Georgia asked. "It's almost two thirty in the morning."

"I'll fucking do it," Jericho boomed. "Gimme the address."

"We'll go," Patty said. "The kids are both asleep. Can someone be here in case they wake up?"

"No," Jericho said. "I'll do it."

It was too soon to file a missing person's report, but Jericho didn't want the cops involved. Taking Gram wasn't random. It was targeted.

He brought Liv outside with him. "Keep an eye on Roger. I don't trust him and I'm not convinced he's telling the truth."

"I'll talk to him," she replied. "No worries, I'll play the part of a caring therapist."

He kissed her. "Thanks."

He plugged the address into his map app and took off. On the drive over, he ran through options.

Think, dammit. Who would take her and what're they after?

Is it someone in the TK gang? Was it Roger Savage? What would his dad stand to gain? Why would he hurt his former mother-in-law when he'd been working so hard to rebuild their relationship?

He called Hawk. "Yeah." Hawk's gritty voice cut through the silence.

"Gram's gone missing."

"*What?*"

After Jericho gave him the twenty-second version, Hawk inhaled a long drag of a freshly lit cigarette.

"Put out the cancer stick," Jericho said.

"I'm online," Hawk said. "I've pulled up surveillance cams on the main road outside the neighborhood where Gram went. I'll see if I spot her."

"Whoever took her could have forced her to lie down on the back seat." Jericho paused. "Or put her in the trunk." Anger pulsated through him. "I cannot fucking believe this is happening."

"I'll let you know if I find anything." Hawk hung up.

Jericho continued to the address. The house was dark. He rang the doorbell. No response.

BAM! BAM! BAM!

"It's Jericho Savage, Joan's grandson. Please open the door."

A long moment later, a man answered in a bathrobe. "Can I help you?"

"I'm Joan's grandson, Jericho Savage. She's gone missing."

He was invited in. The couple was concerned and helpful, but they didn't have surveillance cameras and they hadn't seen anything. The wife made a call to the woman Gram had walked outside with. That friend hadn't noticed the driver.

Jericho left their house more frustrated than when he'd

arrived. By the time he returned home, the fury had taken hold. He'd kill the motherfucker on the spot.

Tim and Patty were dozing on the sofa, Georgia slept on a different one. Mark was on his phone. Liv and his dad were sitting outside by the pool.

How much could his family endure before they broke? Losing Bryan was difficult enough, but Gram?

His fingers curled into fists. He couldn't do nothing. Waiting wasn't an option either. He walked back out front, unearthed his phone. In all the years he'd been an Operative, he'd never called in a favor. That was about to change.

"Hey," Cooper's groggy voice was a godsend.

"Gram's been taken." He paced.

After Jericho brought him up to speed, Cooper said, "I'll look into it, check with ALPHA's informants. You think it's gang related?"

"I took out thirteen TKs, including the leader. I took out the dirty cop. There's a good chance someone wants to even the score."

"Why not go after you?" Cooper asked.

"Maybe the SOB wants to watch me suffer. My dad's gotta be involved. I don't trust him."

"I'll start with him. See what I can dig up. I can't make this an official kidnapping under FBI jurisdiction until we hear from the kidnappers or we get confirmation she was taken. I'll keep you posted. Try not to kill anyone, especially your dad."

"Why the hell not?" Jericho growled.

"Because if he's involved and he's dead, there's no way we'll find her." Cooper hung up.

Jericho walked back inside and into the kitchen.

"I made coffee," Mark said. "I don't know what to do, how to help."

"Go to the hospital," Jericho said. "They need you there."

"Feels like we're falling apart."

"I got you. I got this. I'll find her."

Mark sighed. "We're not kids anymore. You shouldn't have to be our rock."

"What else would I be?" Jericho forced a smile and squeezed his brother's shoulder. "Go save some lives."

After pulling Jericho in for a hug, Mark left.

Jericho made his way through the family room, turning off lamps. Georgia jerked awake, sat up ramrod straight. "Did you find her? Is she okay?"

"I didn't find her, but I will. Go back to sleep."

As he headed out back, he studied his dad, lit up by the glow of the pool lights. He wasn't getting a read on his body language. Hopefully, Liv could.

They turned in his direction. He dipped down, kissed Liv. Being around her helped diffuse some of his anger, but not even lovely Liv could make this problem go away. He eased onto a patio chair, but the angry energy coursing through him had him rising to his feet. Everyone relied on him, always had.

This time, he had no answers, not even a fucking clue to go on.

"Did you find out who picked her up?" his dad asked.

"No, they don't have security cams and they didn't see. No one did. But she got into someone's car. When I find that SOB, I'm gonna choke the life out of him." Jericho wrapped his fingers around the arms of his dad's chair, leaned down and got in his face. "Do you know where she is?"

"I don't, Jericho," his dad bleated. "I swear. For once, I was doing something nice. Even that backfired. I'm sorry."

Jericho pushed off the chair. "Why don't you go home, get some sleep?" Jericho couldn't stomach seeing his father. Roger Savage was an unwanted distraction.

His dad stood. "I'll check in in a few. Call me if you hear anything. Should I file a report with the police?"

"I'm handling that. Do nothing."

"I'm sorry." His dad walked through the house. The front-door chimed as he exited.

Liv took Jericho's hand, stroked his heated skin. "He appeared genuinely sorry," she began. "His posture was tense, but I expected that. I know you think he took her, which he could have, then put himself in the middle to find out what you know. Then again, he could be telling the truth. I'm sorry I don't have something definitive to tell you."

He stood, held out his hand. "Let's take a nap on the sofa."

She clasped his hand and stood. "You won't sleep."

"No, but you will, even if it's just for a few."

Once inside, he sat beside her on the sofa. "We'll find her," Liv whispered.

She held his hand and rested her head on his shoulder. Within minutes, her soft, steady breathing took hold.

After all we've been through together, I won't fail you, Gram. I promise.

The doorbell rang, jolting Jericho awake. Liv bolted upright. He strode to the front door, his feet eating up the marble floor. He flung open the door to find a young man standing there.

"Got a package for Jericho Savage."

"I'm Savage." Jericho took the package. It had no return address. "Who are you with?"

"Flagship Courier."

"I need to find out who this is from."

He checked his handheld scanner. "I don't know. You gotta call our office."

Jericho signed and the courier ambled toward his car.

Liv and Georgia were standing together in the family room, waiting. He opened the small package, pulled out an envelope and a phone. He tore open the envelope. Inside was a typed note on a standard piece of white printer paper.

We have Joan. You get her back alive for $1 million. You have 24 hours.
We will text you on this phone with instructions on where to bring the money.
No money? No Joan.

Fuck.

Jericho's worst nightmare had been realized. Gram had been taken.

24

BANG! BANG!

Using the burner, Jericho called his personal phone. Armed with the burner's number, he called Hawk.

"Yo," Hawk answered. "I got nothing."

"What do you mean?"

"No car exited the neighborhood with Gram. I saw her and your dad drive in, I saw your dad drive out alone, then return to pick her up, but drive out alone. She could have been in the trunk of his car or lying on the back seat. There's another way out of the neighborhood and I'm checking that."

"The kidnapper sent a ransom note and a burner phone. Can you run the number?"

"Give it to me." After Jericho rattled it off, Hawk said, "Burners are hard to track."

"I gotta exhaust everything." Jericho hung up, called Cooper and brought him up to speed.

"I'll open a case and launch a BOLO," Cooper explained. "ALPHA can supply half a mil in counterfeit. You want it?"

"I want Gram alive and I'm not willing to risk it with fake money."

"Only a counterfeit specialist would be able to detect—"

"I'll use my *real* money, but thanks. I'll let you know once he calls me for the drop." Jericho hung up and stared at the burner, willing it to ring.

He felt helpless and manipulated by some motherfucker who'd gone after the heart of their family. The anger that had been thrumming through him threatened to explode in a sea of rage. He wanted to break things, beat the hell out of a punching bag, go for a hard run.

"Uncle, can we have a swim lesson?"

Jericho turned toward the light-hearted voice. Annie stood there grinning, her dolly clutched close. Next to her stood Owen already in his bathing suit, a toy in his small hand. Tim and Patty stood behind them.

"Sorry," Patty mouthed. "We didn't say anything."

Tim stepped close. "If they ask, Gram's at a sleepover with her friends."

On a nod, Jericho released the agitation in a whoosh of an exhale. It was seven thirty in the morning. He needed access to his financial accounts.

"Of course, we can have a swim lesson," Jericho said.

His answer sent the kids jumping up and down with glee as their parents ushered them into the kitchen.

"I have to make one phone call and change into my suit. Gimme five minutes." With phone in hand, Jericho scrolled through his address book, then dialed.

His wealth manager answered. "Hey, Jericho. Isn't it a little early for you?"

"I need you to liquidate a mil to cash," Jericho said.

"Okay, it'll take me a day or two."

"I need it today, in one-hundred-dollar bills."

His financial advisor chuckled. Jericho did not. "Are you for real?" his advisor asked.

"Yeah. I'll pay for an armed guard to bring it to my house by COB."

"You got another wine cellar or restaurant you're buying?"

"Something like that, and it's worth a lot more than the mil." Jericho hung up and went to find Liv.

She was eating cheerios with Owen, one at a time, and making faces. He was giggling hard, his belly-laugh a bright spot in the mayhem.

"You two look like you're having fun," Jericho said.

"Livy funny," Owen said and started giggling again.

Liv smiled up at him. "Everything okay?"

"Money's on its way. I'm gonna go change."

After the swim lesson, Jericho swam for forty minutes, but he kept jumping out of the water to check for texts. Liv slipped into the water and started swimming. He appreciated that she didn't hover, didn't encourage him to talk. She knew that he was a man of action. Talking wouldn't bring Gram back.

At eleven, the doorbell rang.

"It's Vincent," his brother called out as he rushed into the kitchen. "Dad told me about Gram. What happened?"

"Not sure," Jericho replied. "She's missing and there's no sign of her."

"What do the police say?" Vincent asked.

"I haven't talked to them."

Vincent's eyes widened. "Seriously? Why not? Do you want me to file a missing person's report?"

"I got this, Vincent." Jericho's harsh tone had everyone looking in his direction.

"Can I talk to you for a quick minute?" Vincent asked.

"You already are," Jericho snapped.

"Alone."

The two moved outside. "Dad admitted to embezzling money for his gambling debt," Vincent explained. "He told me a coupla days ago. I'm not sure how much longer we're gonna be in business."

"What does this have to do with me?" Jericho huffed. He didn't have time for Vincent, Vincent's problems, or their father.

"If he had anything to do with Gram going missing, maybe he's looking for a big payout." Vincent shrugged. "Anyway, I'm here to offer my support. What can I do? You want me to grab lunch for everyone?"

"The only thing you could do is bring Gram home."

Vincent snort-laughed. "Well, kinda hard since I don't know where she is. But I would if I could. You want me to keep an eye on Dad?"

"No." Jericho checked to see if any texts had come in on the burner. Still nothing.

"I haven't eaten," Vincent said. "Mind if I grab myself something?"

"Go ahead," Jericho replied.

Vincent made himself a sandwich, wolfed it down. "I think you gotta let the police know. An old lady is missing, for chrissakes."

Jericho growled. *Back the fuck off.* "I *said* I got this."

Vincent held up his arms. "Sorry, look, I know everyone's worried—"

"You *don't* know." Annoyance clung to his every word. "This is killing us."

"I should get outta your hair. Who can I check in with, you know, so I don't bother anyone?"

"You can text me," Georgia said. "I'll let you know."

Vincent showed himself out and Jericho released another growl. "Things were fine until those two came back to town. I was living a normal life, then, fucking mayhem ensued."

"Uh-oh... naughty word," Annie called out from the middle of the floor where she'd been playing with her dolls.

With the burner in hand, Jericho strode outside. He couldn't breathe. He couldn't jump into action. He couldn't fucking *do* a damn thing. All he could do was wait for the kidnapper to contact him with instructions. The minutes ticked by like a damn eternity.

Just before noon, the burner buzzed with a text.

"Leave the money in an unmarked duffle at Lakeview park by the entrance. 1AM. Come alone. No cops. If you don't do this exactly, Joan dies."

He didn't know who the hell he was dealing with or if Gram was even alive. His thumbs flew over the keyboard. "I need proof she's alive. No proof, no money." He sent the text.

Nothing happened.

Nothing. Fucking. Happened.

Ten minutes passed. Still nothing.

Another ten.

"I gotta get outta here," he ground out.

Liv caught up to him as he powered out the front door and over to his truck.

"You've got to find a way to detach," Liv said.

"*What?*" he snapped.

She raised an eyebrow and waited.

"I'm sorry."

"If this was a mission, what would you do?"

"I'd execute a well-laid-out plan and take the motherfucker out."

"You're letting your feelings get in the way this time and it's not helping. Treat this like a mission."

"What am I supposed to do?"

"Get your team ready for the drop-off. You've got to catch the kidnappers and you have no room for error."

The burner phone buzzed with a video of Gram.

"It worked." He hit play.

"Hello," Gram began. "I have not been harmed. Please, Jericho, if you pay the money, my captor will let me go." Gram held up a piece of paper with today's date. Then, she glanced up at the person holding the phone. "How was that? Did I do a good job, de—"

The video ended.

Liv had been studying Gram's expression. She didn't appear scared, in fact, just the opposite.

"Let's go inside so I can watch this again." Liv wrapped her arm through Jericho's. "Come with me. This might offer us some clues."

They didn't want the kids to see the video, so they retreated upstairs to his bedroom and shut the door. She sat on the upholstered bench at the end of his bed. To her relief, he sat beside her. He didn't say anything, didn't appear tense of frustrated. She hoped her suggestion that he detach was working and he was moving into mission mode.

"She knows the person holding her prisoner and she wants us to know that," Liv said. "Watch her when she looks up at her kidnapper and listen to how her tone changes."

Liv played it for Jericho. "Yeah, so?" he asked.

"She's very monotone while she recites what she's been told to say," Liv explained. "Look how flat her eyes are, but there's no fear in them."

"She's a kick-ass grandmother. Nothing scares her."

"Maybe so," Liv said, "but watch her expression change when she looks at the person videoing her. She says, 'How was that? Did I do a good job, de—'. She's asking how she did and whether he or she approves."

"Okay," Jericho replied.

"She ends the video with the kidnapper's name, De— or maybe she's calling them dear. She says that all the time when she's talking to you guys. Also, I hear a background noise." Liv played the video again.

"Oh, fuck me," Jericho bit out. "How'd I miss that?" He fixed his attention on Liv. "That's hammering."

"Hammering what?"

"Caskets. My gut tells me she's at my dad's casket company."

"Ohmygod," Liv blurted.

"If she is, that son-of-a-bitch has gone too fucking far."

Jericho tucked the comm into his ear, waited for Liv to do the same, then walked into his outer office at The Road. "Can you hear me?"

"Yes, I can," she replied from his ALPHA office.

It was half past midnight. The beat of a country tune filtered in from the line dancing down the hall, but he and Liv had something else planned for their evening.

In addition to body armor, he'd given her a helmet with night vision goggles, and a Glock. As they made their way out through his private entrance, he turned back. The determination pouring from her eyes spurred him forward.

Before taking off, he filled Cooper in on his plan. As Jericho drove out of the parking lot in the ALPHA SUV, he called Hawk.

"Hey," Hawk answered. "We're on our way. I've got a tracker on the bag and several hidden amongst the stacks of bills."

"You got on a ski mask?" Jericho asked.

"Absolutely. I'm not you."

"No, you're not," Jericho replied.

"I'm much, much prettier," Hawk said and Liv laughed.

"Hey, Liv, you ready to kick some ass?" Hawk asked.

"I'm leaving the ass kicking to Jericho," she replied.

"Are you driving?" Jericho asked.

"I can't drive *and* pilot the drone," Hawk replied.

"Who's driving?" Jericho asked.

"I am," Addison replied.

"Ohmygod, Addison, what are you doing?" Liv blurted.

"I'm driving," Addison replied. "That's way, way less dangerous than what you're doing, missy."

"We've got comms," Hawk said. "When we hang up, we're switching to those."

"Thanks for the assist," Jericho said.

"Always, brother." Hawk hung up, the chatter replaced with silence.

As Jericho drove west, he clasped Liv's hand, rested it on her thigh.

When they pulled down the quiet Chantilly street, he cut the headlights. Then, they rolled into the casket company parking lot. He drove around back and cut the engine.

In the vehicle, they stared into each other's eyes.

"Ready to find Gram?" he asked.

"Absolutely," she replied.

They slipped silently out of the SUV, shut the doors quietly, and made their way to the back door. The area was eerily dark, so they flipped down their goggles. Armed with his tool pick kit, Jericho got busy working the lock. On the third try, the pin gave way. He opened the door, prepared for an ear-piercing alarm, but silence awaited them. He stepped in first, Liv next. Without making a sound, she closed the door behind them.

"Jericho," Hawk murmured through the comm. "The duffle bag and drone are in place. Addison and I are parked on the residential street outside the park."

"Copy," Jericho whispered. "We breached the building."

With their weapons drawn, he and Liv entered the distribution center where the caskets were assembled. Seeing coffins in various states of completion sent a shiver through him. This was not where he wanted them to end up.

"I'm going down that hallway," she whispered.

"Stay with me," he replied.

Ignoring him, she took off down a pitch-black corridor and vanished into an office. Adrenaline pumped through him. His instinct was to go after her, protect her.

"I'm okay," she whispered through the comm. "No Gram here."

"The bag was picked up," Hawk murmured. "White woman, super blonde hair, maybe in her late thirties, early forties. I launched my drone. Traffic is light, so we're putting a little distance between us and her vehicle."

"Copy," Jericho whispered as he checked the large room for a closet or a door. He found one, turned the handle, opened it. It was a large supply closet.

Liv moved from office to office, searching for Gram. Remembering Jericho's secret door in his supply closet that led to his ALPHA office, she checked to make sure there were no false backs in the closets. Despite her fast-pounding heartbeat, determination kept her moving forward.

At the end of the hallway, she found a janitor's closet. Nothing more than brooms, mops, cleaning supplies, an old vacuum. The bottom of an unfinished coffin had been propped against the back wall. She left the closet, heading back down the hallway.

Move that wood.

She hurried back in and tried lifting it. It was heavy, but she dragged it out of the way. With the large piece of wood gone, a door handle loomed into view. She tried it, and it turned. She opened the door, peered inside the closet-sized room illuminated by a night light. Her heart jumped into her throat. Lying on a cot was Gram.

Please, please be alive.

"Gram," she whispered. "It's Liv."

Gram rolled over. "I knew you'd find me."

"Are you hurt?" Liv whispered.

"No, but I *am* madder than hell," Gram replied.

Still in the distribution center, Jericho made his way toward a group of thirty coffins. Ten rows of neatly arranged caskets stacked three high. Shoving his Glock behind his waist, he opened a lid, hoping Gram wasn't inside. It was empty, the pine odor filling his nose. The second casket was lined with white satin. He opened the third.

No fucking way.

Packed on foam padding sat fifteen handguns. He peeled back the layer of foam revealing another layer of guns resting on more foam.

"Jericho, I found Gram," Liv whispered.

"Great work," he whispered. "Is she hurt?"

"No. Where are you?"

"Main room, in the corner," he murmured. "At the stack of coffins."

"On our way," Liv replied.

"Hawk, call Cooper," Jericho murmured. "They're not movin' drugs. They're gun runners."

"Copy," Hawk replied.

Jericho lifted one out and ran his hand down the grip. Even with the night goggles, he couldn't see the logo, but he could feel the embossed emblem.

I got a mil ridin' on a lion's head.

He opened another casket. Two long rifles rested on the foam insert. He lifted the pliable foam. Two more guns beneath. The anger he carried around with him burst into a raging inferno.

What the hell is Roger Savage up to?

The lights in the warehouse flicked on, temporarily blinding him. In one fluid movement, he flipped up the goggles, grabbed his Glock, and stood.

"We got company," Jericho murmured.

His dad walked into the room, hatred shooting from his eyes. "What the hell are you doing here?"

"I thought abandoning your family was bad. You're making

ghost guns and selling them to gangs. You're the scum of the earth."

"You don't know what you're talking about. You need to leave. *Now.*"

"Were you behind Bryan's death? Did you fuck up and the Thriller Killers wanted to teach you a lesson, so they shot up your sons?" A growl exploded out of him. "I wanna kill you so fucking badly."

"You're in over your head, Jericho."

"You don't know the first thing about me."

"Get out," his dad said. "If you don't, you'll be left for dead."

"You gonna take me out with one of your fucking ghost guns?"

His brother stepped out of the shadows. "He won't, but I sure as fuck will." Vincent pointed his gun at Jericho. "Drop it or I'll blow your goddamn head off, then I'll unload on Gram."

Fuck. Fuck me.

Jericho set his weapon on the floor.

"Kick it away," Vincent's gruff voice snagged Jericho's ear.

Jericho did.

"You've been a pain in my ass from the moment Bryan was killed," Vincent snarled.

"What are you talking about? Dad's behind this."

"No, Jericho, I'm not," his dad replied.

"I'm a pretty convincing idiot, aren't I? But I don't give a fuck about any of you." Vincent glared at their dad. "Daddio here had a wicked gambling problem that put us so fucking far in debt, he was seconds away from declaring bankruptcy. I paid his debts, got our stupid, fucking company out of the red by building ghost guns. I sold *thousands* to gangs in the Midwest. A connection introduced me to El Jefe. We started doing business together, so I made Dad open this satellite office. Then, that damn Sergeant Hayes got in the middle of my business deal and threatened to arrest us if we didn't cut him in on the *real* business. Gun running.

"But you got greedy, didn't you Vincent?" their dad spat out.

"Shut up, old man," Vincent snapped. "I struck a deal with TK's rival gang and Hayes told El Jefe. That son-of-a-bitch gang leader is a crazy motherfucker."

"*That* was the scare job," Jericho bit out.

"Bingo!" Vincent said. "El Jefe didn't like me doing business with a rival gang, so he sent me a message." Vincent shrugged. "Oops."

Fury enveloped Jericho in a blackness that had him taking a step toward Vincent. He didn't need his fucking gun to kill him. He'd do it with his bare hands.

Vincent waved his gun. "Not one more step, *brother*."

"We were days away from our biggest payout," Vincent continued. "So fucking big, I was gonna be set for life. Me and Brenda were gonna jump on a plane and vanish. Get the hell outta here. When El Jefe went missing, his gang didn't know which end was up. I needed that mil, so I grabbed Gram. You had the money, I knew you'd pay. Now, I'm gonna kill you both and meet Bren at the airport. Adios suckers!"

Years of pent-up rage exploded from Jericho. "You were the reason Bryan died," he roared. "You and your fucking gun-running operation."

"Shut the fuck up!" Vincent screamed.

BANG!

Vincent fired his gun, hitting Jericho in the chest. He staggered back, the Kevlar absorbing the bullet. Jericho lunged for his gun as Liv flew into the room. Heads whipped in her direction.

"Get out!" Jericho screamed.

Liv raised her gun. "No fucking way!"

POP! POP! POP! POP!

She unloaded into Vincent, and he crashed to the floor.

25

TOGETHER FOREVER

Liv ran over to Jericho. "Ohmygod, are you okay?"
Jericho scooped up his Glock, then banged the hard vest. "I'm good." He regarded his brother, lying in an expanding pool of blood. "I did not expect that from you."

"I'll always have your back," she said.

"Hey," Hawk said, "what the hell happened?"

"Man down," Jericho replied. "Where's the team?"

"Five minutes out," Hawk replied.

"You trailing the woman?" Jericho asked.

"We thought she was on her way to your location, but she jumped on the Dulles access road, heading for the airport."

"We got a rabbit?"

"Looks that way," Hawk said. "She's taking the money and dumping the boy toy. "We're staying on her. I got a team meeting us at the airport."

"Nice work. I gotta deal with things here." Jericho pointed his gun at his dad. "How'd you know we were here?"

"Silent alarm."

Jericho motioned with his gun toward the hallway. "Move." Once there, he said, "On the ground, face down."

"What for?" his father bleated. "I didn't kidnap Gram."

"You're an accomplice in a nationwide gun-running business. You're manufacturing illegal guns, selling them to gangs. The list is long and you're goin' away for a while."

"Is this a joke? You own restaurants. How can you arrest me?"

"You don't know anything about me. Face down, on the floor, Roger Savage." He waited while his dad laid down. "You have the right to remain silent. Anything you say, can and will be used against you in a court of law. You have the right to an attorney."

A sense of relief flowed through him as he mirandized the scumbag of a man who walked out on them all those years ago. As he finished, Liv returned with Gram.

Gram's face lit up as she made her way over to him. He dipped down, kissed her cheek, then wrapped her in his arms and hugged her. "How you doin', Gram?"

"Did Vincent get away?" she asked.

"No," Jericho replied.

"Where is he?" Gram said, heading toward the distribution center. "I want to give him a piece of my mind."

Jericho wrapped his hand around her arm and gently pulled her to a stop. "He's in there, Gram. You don't need to see him."

She peered up at him. "He's dead?"

Jericho nodded.

His dad craned his head. "Gram, what are you doing here?"

"Vincent kidnapped me," she replied dryly.

"Ohgod, I'm so sorry," his dad said.

Gram rolled her eyes before redirecting her attention on Jericho. "How'd you find me?"

"It was all Liv," Jericho answered.

Gram looped her arm through Liv's. "This lady's a definite keeper."

"She sure is." Jericho slid his gaze to Liv's. Even in the midst of the mayhem, an intense love flowed between them.

"Gram, how'd Vincent kidnap you?" Liv asked.

"He showed up at my friend's house and told me Roger had two flat tires," Gram explained. "I didn't think anything of it and got in his car. "He brought me here and into that secret room. Did you get your money back?"

"Vincent's girlfriend is trying to skip town with it—"

"You have to stop her!" Gram exclaimed.

"I got a team who'll catch her at the airport."

With a knowing smile, Gram patted his back. "I knew you did more than run restaurants."

Cooper, Danielle, and Slash rushed into the room, local law enforcement arriving close on their heels. Jericho was impressed by Gram's inner strength. She gave her statement to Cooper and again to the police, then told them she would be available to testify against her former son-in-law. Even after being kidnapped, she was unshaken.

He loved that the women in his life were smart, strong-willed, and so damn fearless.

"I could never understand why you left the FBI," Gram said to Cooper. "You loved that job so much. I'm surprised you left for ATF."

Cooper nodded.

"Or maybe you never left at all?" Gram shot him a little smile before cementing her gaze on Jericho. "I'm proud of you, dear. Your job sounds very exciting, like something I'd read in one of my book club novels." She paused. "Can I go home now?"

"Absolutely," Cooper replied.

"Let's get the hell outta here," Jericho said, putting his arms around Gram and Liv.

"Amen to that," Gram added.

On the drive home, Gram slept.

His phone rang with a call from Hawk. "What's the word?" Jericho answered, putting the call on speaker.

"Brenda was arrested at the ticket counter," Hawk said. "Boy, was she pissed."

"How'd she take hearing about Vincent's death?"

"She was more upset that she'd been caught. We got a bagful of money, so Addison and I are going shopping."

Jericho laughed. "You kids have fun. Bring me back the change."

On a chuckle, Hawk hung up.

Clasping Liv's hand, he drove them home in a peaceful silence.

As soon as he parked in front of his house, the family rushed outside. As they ushered Gram in, she told them how Vincent had taken her to his gun-making facility.

Jericho needed a moment alone with Liv. Clasping her hand, he led her through the house to the pool. He didn't have a speech planned, didn't even have a ring.

"You saved my life, Liv," he said. "You were very brave."

She shot him a little smile. "I did it purely for selfish reasons." Then, her happy expression fell away. "You have an intense job. I loved being a part of it, loved helping you, but being a watcher was more my speed. I'm not an adrenaline junkie, but I admire you so much for what you do. I'm probably going to worry about you more than I should, but I will always be your biggest supporter. You were made to be an ALPHA Op."

He pulled her into his arms, kissed her, then peered into her eyes. "This is just our beginning. I want to build a life with you. Livingston Blackstone, marry me."

She kissed him, then kissed him again. "You know I will."

He grinned at her. "I don't have a ring."

"I don't need one."

He lifted her left hand, kissed her palm. "I want to spoil you, starting with an engagement ring."

She smiled up at him. "I'm gonna marry you either way, Jericho Savage."

"One of my regulars at Carole Jean's owns a high-end jewelry store in Chevy Chase. I'll see when he can meet us to help us pick out that perfect ring."

She kissed him. "Liv Savage. I love the sound of that."

"So do I, baby." He glanced into the house. "Wanna share our news?"

Liv headed toward the guest house. "Not until we have our own private celebration, just the two of us."

They stripped down, crawled into bed, and loved each other with relentless passion. Jericho had fallen in love with a girl he could never have, but now, as he gazed into the eyes of the woman she'd become, his soul was complete.

That afternoon, while the family slept, he and Liv met the owner at his upscale jewelry store. After being buzzed in, a woman greeted them.

"We're meeting Nico," Jericho said.

A robust man walked out from the back. After a hearty hug for Jericho, he shook Liv's hand. "Congratulations!" He smiled warmly at Liv. "You've got your hands full with this one."

Liv slid her arm around Jericho and ran her hand down his back. "I look forward to the challenge."

Nico led them to two cases filled with engagement rings. "These are very popular types of rings, but I can also design one for you."

After Liv picked out a few, Nico brought the rings over to a small desk and gestured to the two guest chairs. They examined all the rings and Liv fell in love with the cushion-cut diamond.

"What size carat is that?" Jericho asked.

"That one is one and a half carats," Nico replied.

"It's beautiful," Liv said.

"I'm thinking we double the carat size, then add a couple of the —what are those called?" Jericho asked.

"Halos," Nico explained.

"Babe, what do you think about two bands of halos around the center stone?"

"That'll look stunning," she replied.

"I'd like to add small cushion-cut diamonds down the sides of the band," Nico suggested.

Jericho nodded. "Liv?"

"I love it," she replied with a smile.

"This will be a stunning ring," Nico said. "I look forward to creating it."

In the parking lot, Liv slipped her arms around him and kissed him. "Thank you. You didn't have to go all out."

Jericho dipped down, kissed her. "Sure, I did. My gorgeous woman deserves a stunning engagement ring."

After they hopped in his truck, Jericho drove to a motorcycle gear store.

"What are we doing here?" Liv asked.

"You've got leathers, but you need boots and a helmet. We gotta get you suited up. I'm taking my Livy for a ride in the country this afternoon."

She grinned at him before opening the truck door. "I can't wait."

THE FOLLOWING MORNING, Jericho met Sin in front of the Department of Justice Building in DC.

"Got a badge?" Sin asked as he pulled to a stop beside Jericho.

Jericho flashed his ALPHA-assigned FBI badge. "Let's make this happen."

The men sailed inside, passed through security, and headed toward the elevator bank. Once there, Sin pushed the down button.

"Excuse me," said a man standing nearby. "There're no offices in the basement."

"We're part of the custodial team." Sin replied. He and Jericho exchanged glances.

The man eyed their suits. "Yeah, right."

"We're expected to blend in," Jericho told the stranger.

Two women sidled over.

"Hi," said the first one. "I know this is kinda forward, but maybe you guys would like to meet us for coffee after your meeting."

"I'm married," Sin replied.

"I'm engaged," Jericho answered.

"Damn," the second woman mumbled.

"You two are fine-looking men," said the first. "Eye candy for sure."

An elevator binged, doors slid open. "That's us," Sin said with a wink.

Both men entered and the elevator descended.

"Congratulations," Sin said. "When'd you propose?"

"Yesterday."

"No rest for the weary," Sin said with a chuckle.

"We went ring shopping, too."

"Don't you sleep?"

"Here and there," Jericho replied as the doors slid open. "Does he know I'm coming with you?"

"No, and he *hates* surprises." Sin's lips curved upward. "That'll teach him for fucking with me."

Jericho laughed. "A code I live by. Never ever fuck with Develin."

Sin led him down one dimly-lit hallway then another, pulling to a stop in front of a closed office.

Knock-knock-knock.

A few seconds passed before Z opened the door. He was a slender man in a suit, his short brown hair parted on the side. All Jericho knew about this man was that he controlled a lot of what happened in law enforcement.

He eyed both men, then narrowed his gaze at Sin. "You shouldn't have brought Jericho with you."

"It's important," Sin replied, his tone relaxed.

Z left the door open, returned to his chair behind the metal desk. Sin entered and gestured for Jericho to sit in the second chair. As Jericho eased down, Sin shut the door.

Sin sat, crossed his legs, cemented his gaze on Z. Instead of friendly banter or perfunctory small talk, Sin let the awkward silence hang in the air. Jericho had no idea what kind of fucked-up mind game these two men were playing, but it was odd... to say the least.

The office was barebones. A metal desk, a few chairs, an ugly desk lamp and a computer. The monitors on the wall were dark.

Jericho shifted, putting Sin in his peripheral vision. He sat there still and stone faced. Jericho made a mental note to never play poker with him.

Several more seconds passed.

Z sighed. "You want me to reinstate her, don't you?"

"Yes," Sin replied.

"She broke the rules. She put her life and Jericho's life in danger, not to mention putting the entire ALPHA organization at risk."

"What's the flip side?" Sin asked, folding his hands in his lap.

"Livy helped bring down one of the biggest gun-running operations in the country *and* she found the leak in the APD."

Sin nodded, once.

"I'll reinstate her this afternoon," Z said. "This conversation never happened."

Sin rose. "I'll be back after I walk Jericho out."

Jericho stood. "She deserves this."

Z offered a tight smile. "You're an excellent sniper, Jericho. I'm glad you're on *our* side."

In silence, the men walked down the hall. They rode alone to the lobby, the doors slid open, and they exited the elevator.

"Z is Liv's Uncle," Sin said.

"Is he Addison's dad?" Jericho asked.

"He is, but very few people know that."

Jericho extended his hand and Sin shook it. "Thanks for making that happen."

Sin's face split into a grin. "On occasion, I like to remind him who's *really* in charge."

Liv had been working in the guest house, finishing up a call with the Fairfax County PD where she'd booked a series of workshops, when her phone buzzed with an incoming call. She said goodbye to the Liaison Officer and clicked over.

"Hello?"

"Livy, it's Uncle Z."

"Hi. You know I moved out, right?"

"I do. I wanted to congratulate you on finding the APD leak and for being a part of a mission that brought down one of the largest gun-running operations in the country. I'd also like to apologize for firing you. I made a terrible mistake and would like to hire you back, if you're still interested."

Yes!

"I'd love to. When can I start?"

"Excellent," he said. "How's next week?"

"That'll work."

"Swing by my office Monday and we'll talk then."

The line went dead.

Jericho made this happen.

She wanted to give Jericho a thank you he wasn't expecting, so she hopped on the Lost Souls app and jumped to his online profile. So much had changed since their first hookup. She'd definitely gone far outside her comfort zone by partnering with him, but her loyalty had paid off. She'd won his heart and she was going to spend the rest of her life with him, have his babies, and maybe even work with him again… one day.

Her heart soared.

She sent him an invitation for that evening. "Thor, it's been a while," she typed. "I'd love to make a fantasy come true for you. If you're interested, I'll be the slutty cheerleader waiting in the Purple room." She sent the message.

A few moments later, Jericho walked into the guest house. Their eyes met across the room. She hurried over to him, threw her arms around him, and kissed him hello.

"Thank you for getting me my job back," she murmured.

"I wish I could take credit, but it was all Sin."

"How do you know?"

"Because I was with him. We ambushed Z at his shithole office."

She laughed. "He probably took a look at the two of you and realized he'd never be seen again if he didn't cooperate."

Jericho chuffed out a laugh. "Were you working?"

She nodded.

"It's a great day to ride. Can I steal you away?"

"There's nowhere I'd rather be," she replied, pressing her lips to his.

His phone buzzed and he lifted it from his pocket. He read her message from the Lost Souls app, then winked at her. "All my fantasies start and end with you, babe."

"Mine, too," she replied with a smile.

EPILOGUE

One month later

Liv leaned into the turn, her arms wrapped around Jericho. She loved riding on the back of his Indian Springfield, loved holding on to her man. It was early Sunday morning and they'd left before the family had woken up.

He pulled into a beautiful Annapolis neighborhood, turned down another tree-lined street, and slowed to a stop in front of a pretty two-story home with a manicured flower garden and a pink dogwood tree in the front yard. She hopped off, removed her helmet. "Are we having breakfast with friends of yours?" she asked.

Jericho removed his helmet. "No."

Rather than walk to the front door, he grasped her hand, brought her around back to a breathtaking view of the Chesapeake Bay. Nothing but water for miles.

"This is beautiful." She peered over at him. "Why are we here?"

"I know we've moved into the main house, but we don't have that much privacy."

She shrugged. "I don't mind. I adore your family."

"Tim talked to me last night and asked if they could stay a little longer," Jericho said. "Patty's pregnant and they've been talking about buying a bigger house."

"I love them, too, especially the little ones. They're so adorable."

"So, you don't want to move out?"

"No, what made you think that?"

"My entire fam lives with us. Not normal."

She laughed. "No, we're not normal. I love that about us."

"You wanna go inside?" he asked.

Liv nodded. "Sure. Who am I meeting?"

"You'll see."

As soon as the front door loomed into view, Liv spotted the lockbox. "Hmm, Jericho Savage, you're up to something."

He punched in a code, the lockbox opened. After keying the lock, he pushed open the door and waited for her to enter.

The home was lovely. It wasn't large, but it wasn't small either. Hand in hand, they meandered from room to room. It had been staged perfectly. Just enough furniture to make it looked lived in, but not so much that it appeared cluttered.

"What do you think about a weekend place or a getaway home?" he asked.

"Are you serious?"

"It's close enough to be here in about an hour, but far enough away to feel like a vacation."

She draped her arms over his shoulders. "I absolutely love it. What realtor are you working with?"

"It's Dakota's real estate company, Goode-Luck. That's why there's no realtor in tow. He gave me the code to a bunch of homes in the area, if you wanna check 'em out."

She leaned up, kissed him. "I would want to get married here, or at whichever house we buy. I would love a simple ceremony.

Just close friends and family. It could be in the backyard if the weather is nice, so we could do it as early as October."

He pulled her close, kissed her. "Making me wait 'til the fall, huh?"

She smiled. "You'll be okay, I'm sure of it."

"We need a house with a dock for a boat," he said.

"Are we buying one of those, too?"

"My friend, Jett St. John, and his wife, Cassidy, own a yacht that's docked at a boat club. They—"

"The movie star, Jett St. John?"

"Yeah, that one."

"How come you've never said anything?"

"We've been kinda preoccupied with chasing gangbangers, so talking about Jett slipped my mind."

"He won an academy award for *K Street Conspiracy*."

"I was in that movie, along with Jericho Road."

"Are you for real?"

"The director wanted me and my western bar in the movie."

She smiled. "Well, I know what movie I'm watching tonight."

"Jett would love it if I kept the boat. This place has a dock, so it's perfect. They come back here every few months, but they're usually so busy, they don't take it out much."

"Wow, a boat."

"The Doris is a forty-foot Prestige. She's a beauty."

Liv laughed. "The Doris?"

"That was her name when Jett bought her. He never changed it."

After sharing another loving kiss, they walked through the home again, then meandered around the property. "This is definitely a keeper," Liv said, "but we should see everything on your list."

Over the next few hours, they toured all of the properties Dakota had found for them. All of them were lovely, but none boasted a view like the first one.

Jericho called Dakota. "What did you both think?" Dakota asked.

"The one on Happy Trails Court," Jericho said.

"That' would've been my first choice, too," Dakota replied. "Great water view. I'll put in an offer."

Instead of heading home, Jericho rode to the first house and brought Liv around back.

There, with the breathtaking view as their backdrop, he dropped to one knee, and pulled a ring box from his pocket. "You are the love of my life, Livy Blackstone. Marry me and make all my dreams come true."

He opened the small velvet box and the dazzling diamond ring caught her eye, but only for a second. The man kneeling before her was all she really wanted.

She grinned at him. "You're the love of my life, too. I want it all, Jericho Savage, as long as it starts and ends with you. I will absolutely be your *official* fiancée."

He slipped the stunning engagement ring on her finger. She placed her hands on his scruffy face, leaned down, and kissed him.

He stood, snaked his arms around her, and kissed her with so much passion, she grew breathless. "You so do it for me," she said. "Wow. We have *definitely* got the kissing down."

With a smile, he kissed her forehead. "Ready to head home?"

"I already am," she replied. "Home is wherever you are."

February, the following year

Jericho and Liv walked inside the Chantilly building and glanced at the guests milling around. Every trace of the casket company was gone, replaced with a beautiful two-story lobby and a first-class facility that was already booked to capacity.

Georgia hurried over. "I was starting to worry," she whispered. "You guys almost missed your own opening."

"You coulda handled it, sis," Jericho said.

"Uh, no. I don't think so," she replied. "It's about time to start, so you should probably head into the gathering room."

Jericho helped Liv off with her coat, then his own. After hanging them on a nearby coat rack, he clasped her hand and set off into the crowd.

"Hey!" called Hawk. "There they are!"

Jericho grinned as they joined his close-knit group of friends. Hawk, Stryker and Emerson, Cooper and Danielle, and Addison. "Thanks for being here."

"Wouldn't miss it," Stryker said.

"The building is beautiful," Addison added. "We got here a little early and Georgia took us around."

"We're happy with the way it turned out," Liv replied.

"We gotta go to Carole Jean's after," Cooper said. "When was the last time we were all together—"

"—and this dressed up?" Danielle added.

"Our wedding," Jericho replied.

"That was back in October," Stryker said.

"I'm one step ahead of you," Jericho replied. "I reserved the back room at Carole Jean's for us."

"I was thinking we'd head over to The Road for line dancing," Danielle said.

"We can do dinner at Carole Jean's," Liv replied, "and line dancing after."

"Love that," Emerson added.

"It's time to get started." Jericho led the group toward the double doors of the spacious room across from the lobby. They made their way to the reserved rows at the front, where Liv's mom and dad were waiting.

"Congratulations, this is incredible," Bernard said.

"Very impressive," Valerie added. "You did a great job."

"It was definitely a labor of love," Liv replied.

Liv's mom held out an envelope. "This is for your center."

As Liv took it, her dad said, "I promised you both I'd make it up to you." He smiled. "Go on, open it."

Liv peeked inside. "Oh, wow." She showed it to Jericho.

The bank check was for a quarter million dollars. "That's too much," Jericho said.

"We insist," Valerie added.

"You have our full support." Bernard thrust out his hand.

"Very generous," Jericho said. "C'mon, big guy, let's hug it out."

Though Bernard rolled his eyes playfully, Jericho pulled him in for a hand-clasp hug. After hugs all around, her parents took their seats behind them.

Once Jericho and Liv were seated in the front row, Jericho clasped her hand, leaned over, and whispered, "How are you feelin'?"

"I'm good," she replied, giving his hand a little squeeze.

Ten minutes later, the room was filled to capacity. Georgia walked over and whispered, "You're up."

Jericho and Liv made their way to the podium. After the chatter quieted down, Jericho stepped up to the mic and smiled out at the crowd. "Hey, everyone, I'm Jericho Savage. Welcome to Bryan's House."

He waited until the applause ended.

"My brother, Bryan Savage, was gunned down by gang members. If you've ever lost someone to gang violence, then you know how heart-wrenching it is. Bryan's death left a hole, but our family wanted to do something to make a difference. This one-hundred-bed safe house is a place where men—who are trying to disassociate themselves from gangs—can live while they put their lives back together. We open next week and we're already full."

He paused while the room exploded in applause.

"My wife, Liv Savage, is the organization's executive director. She's much better at speaking to crowds, so please put your hands together for my amazing better half."

She smiled at him before setting her sights on the audience.

"Hello, I'm Liv Savage, but I'm definitely not Jericho's better half. I'm simply his other half. We want to thank so many people for helping us make this happen, but there's one person in particular who we're honoring today."

Jericho walked to the front row on the other side of the aisle and held out his hand to Gram. She rose and walked to the podium.

"If you know anyone in the Savage family," Liv continued, "then you know Gram. While it's alleged that her first name is Joan, *everyone* calls her Gram. The idea to open a facility was hers. She wanted to find a way to honor her grandson that went above and beyond… a legacy that could help many people get out of a situation they no longer found beneficial. The house isn't for everyone, but for the men who want to be here, they'll be offered education and alternatives." She smiled. "We're naming the Gathering Room, Gram's Place, in honor of her and what she means to our family."

She paused while the audience applauded.

"On a personal note," Jericho added, "We wanna let everyone in on some news." Jericho beamed out at the crowd before pulling a tiny onesie from his suit pocket and holding it up.

"For those of you in the back of the room, Jericho's holding up an infant onesie that says, 'Little Savage,'" Liv explained.

"We're havin' a baby!" Jericho announced.

The audience broke into more applause.

"Thanks for being here to celebrate Bryan's House with us," Jericho said. "Meet us for drinks and hors d'oeuvres in the dining hall."

Hawk, Cooper, and Stryker made their way to the front of the room. "Can we interrupt?" Cooper asked.

Jericho and Liv stepped away from the mic.

"I'm Cooper Grant, that's Stryker Truman, and that's Nicholas Hawk—

"I love you, Hawk," a woman hollered from the back of the room.

With a grin, Hawk tossed out a casual two-fingered salute.

After the laughter died down, Cooper continued. "Congrats on baby Savage." Then, he faced the audience. "We've known Jericho and his family for years and love them as much as we love our own families. We, and our close friend, Prescott Armstrong, wanted to make sure Bryan's House is sufficiently funded so Jericho and Liv can focus on helping the residents."

Hawk handed Jericho a folded check. "We pooled our pennies."

Jericho opened it and showed Liv. It was for four million dollars. Jericho stepped up to the mic. "That's a *lot* of pennies. Thank you, my brothers. We'll do you proud."

"You always do," Stryker replied.

Liv stepped up to the podium. "Thank you so much for being here with us today. Join us in the dining room."

Jericho flipped off the mic as their close friends and family gathered around to congratulate them on their baby news.

So many things had changed since Livy had come back into his life.

He'd married the woman of his dreams and, now, their first child was due in August. Together, they'd found a way to honor Bryan so that he would never be forgotten.

He loved his career as an ALPHA Op, he had a family he adored, and a wife who was his life partner in every way imaginable. Liv loved being a watcher and consulting with area PDs.

Life was good, and he was grateful.

When Liv threaded her fingers through his, he gave her a tender squeeze. After the guests made their way out, he turned to his wife, slid his arms around her, and dropped a soft kiss on her lips.

"Our life, our rules," he murmured.

Gazing into his eyes, she ran her fingers through his long hair. "Always," she replied with a smile.

Another Happily Ever After by Stoni Alexander

A Note from Stoni

Thanks so much for reading SAVAGE.

Jericho leapt into my imagination while writing BEAUTIFUL DISASTER, a standalone contemporary romance from my Beautiful Men Collection. He's all alpha with an intensity and an edge that kept me fully engaged. Then, as I wrote VENGEANCE, The Vigilantes, Book 2, he became Cooper's second. It was in this story where Jericho's loyalty to his family emerged. I imagined him as a savage beast, yet filled with tenderness and love for those close to him. He was a phenomenal character to create and so much fun to write!

For every hero, I need an equally strong heroine. Enter Livingston—Liv—his perfect life partner. I'd known for some time that I wanted a character who would keep a watchful eye on ALPHA, but it wasn't until Jericho's story that Liv rose to the forefront. She wasn't a risk taker, like Jericho, but she stepped up to the challenges I threw her way. And there were so many of them! Those are always a thrill for me to write. As much as I love my protagonists, I love hating my villains.

If this is the first book of mine that you've read, thanks very much for diving into my world! My stories are action-packed, filled with spicy times and insane bad guys, yet themes of family, great friendships, and true love prevail in all of them. If you've read <u>all</u> my novels, thank you so, so much. I am immensely grateful that you're willing to continue along this journey with me.

I hear from readers all the time, and appreciate when they drop me a note. On more than one occasion, readers have shared something that sparks my imagination. That's always a great treat and something I love sharing with them because they're just as surprised as I am!

If you want to find out when my next book is coming out, sign up for my occasional newsletter, Stoni's Inner Circle. I'll send over METRO MAN, a short story about a man, a woman, and a steamy train ride. Sign up on my website, StoniAlexander.com.

All my books are available exclusively on Amazon, and you can read them free with a Kindle Unlimited subscription.

I hope you loved the story of Jericho and Liv, and that the escape was a fun one.

Cheers to Romance,
Stoni Alexander

COMING SPRING 2023
THE VIGILANTES, BOOK FOUR

ROMANTIC SUSPENSE
THE TOUCH SERIES

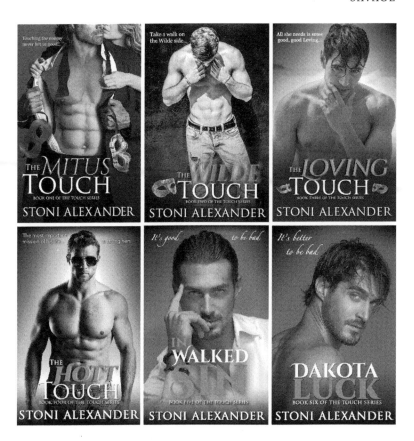

ROMANTIC SUSPENSE
The Vigilantes Series

LOOKING FOR A SEXY STANDALONE?

CONTEMPORARY ROMANCE
BEAUTIFUL MEN COLLECTION

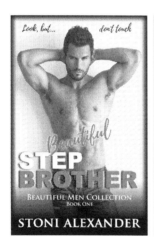

Buy them on Amazon or Read FREE with Kindle Unlimited!

ACKNOWLEDGMENTS

Each writing project is filled with loving and supportive people who root for me, help bring my characters to life, and give me so much joy. These are *my* superheroes who deserve all my gratitude.

Johnny, indestructible, forever and ever. ∞

Son, Dad and I are so, so proud of you. You've chosen an incredibly hard and demanding career, for which we are in amazement. We hope you can enjoy the journey, even the bumpy terrain and winding roads. Marathon, not a sprint. Thank you for being the biggest blessing in our lives. My book heroes aren't real, but you are.

Elayne, thank you for reaching out and for helping design an absolutely fabulous book cover! You are an incredibly talented graphic designer in your own right, so thank you, thank you for turning our SAVAGE cover into WOW! Like I've said many times, your attention to detail blew me away and you totally rocked out the tats! I appreciate your efforts so much and I've loved getting to know you. Despite our distance, I see a long lunch—that rolls into dinner—in our future, our amazing hubs in tow, of course! I'm so lucky to call you my friend! From one proud Navy mom to another… 🖤🖤🖤

Dear friends and fam, thank you for the love, the laughter, the insanity, and for being there. Always.

A special shout-out to my Amazing ARC Team! Thank you for your enthusiasm. Your kind words and love of my novels makes me smile.

Readers, thank you for spending time in my imagination. I'm so grateful you choose my novels. Thank you to those readers who've become fans. It's great hearing from you! Your words of encouragement are deeply appreciated.

Muse, Hawk and Addison are so ready for their story to be told. It's time for our smokin' hot ALPHA to get his adventure, and our beautiful, badass heroine to kick it into high gear. I'm going to need a lot of help writing this one, but don't I always? Let's go a little crazy this time…I think these characters are strong enough to handle it.

ABOUT THE AUTHOR

Stoni Alexander writes sexy romantic suspense and contemporary romance about tortured alpha males and independent, strong-willed females. Her passion is creating love stories where the hero and heroine help each other through a crisis so that, in the end, they're equal partners in more ways than love alone. The heat level is high, the romance is forever, and the suspense keeps readers guessing until the very end.

Visit Stoni's website:
StoniAlexander.com

Sign up for Stoni's newsletter on her website and she'll gift you a free steamy short story, only available to her Inner Circle.

Here's where you can follow Stoni online. She looks forward to connecting with you!

- amazon.com/author/stonialexander
- bookbub.com/authors/stoni-alexander
- facebook.com/StoniBooks
- goodreads.com/stonialexander
- instagram.com/stonialexander

Made in the USA
Monee, IL
29 October 2022